NADIA LEE

PART I

O love, as long as love you can,
O love, as long as love you may,
The time will come, the time will come
When you will stand at the grave and mourn!

—From *O lieb, so lang du lieben kannst* by Ferdinand Freiligrath (S.H. transl.)

1

—nine years ago

Anthony

When I was in Europe, going to boarding school in Valencia, half the people attending the small Catholic church nearby didn't dress with any particular care to go to confession. Nor did they wonder if their God would absolve them. In the face of true penance, they were certain He would.

But my mother, the person *I'm* seeking forgiveness from, is harder to appease.

So here I am, back in Louisiana, in a jacket, dress shirt and slacks. Except everything I put on to make a good impression on my mother—whom I haven't seen or spoken with in nearly a decade—turns out to be a terrible idea. The second I step out of the blue Mercedes Father sent to fetch me from the airport, I begin to feel like chocolate left out in the sun. I'd forgotten how vicious the heat and humidity can be in Tempérane, but then, I haven't been back to my hometown for the last nine years, not since I was exiled.

The huge two-story mansion sprawls before me. The white summer sun reflects off smooth, pale marble and stained-glass windows, making the structure shimmer and glow like a mirage. It was an old plantation house until my grandmother decided she hated it. So my grandfather had it torn down and rebuilt, despite the neighbors' feeble protests. It's hard to complain with much feeling when my family provides jobs to over thirty percent of the population around here.

The happiest and the darkest times of my life were spent here—in this house. The weight of all that was lost bears down on me.

Come on. Time to see if you can get some of it back.

Resolute, I mount the steps to the main entrance. Jonas is standing by the door. Despite the humidity and heat, the family butler manages to look fresh, as though he's just stepped out of the shower and put on a newly starched suit.

He isn't making a move to throw me out. That's another good sign. Father apparently hasn't changed his mind about my being here since I left the airport.

"Welcome back, Master Tony." Jonas's voice is as smooth and even as always.

"It's good to be back. Is my mother home?" It's the question I've been avoiding since I left New Jersey. My palms grow slick with sweat as the surging dread of receiving another cold rejection almost overwhelms the tiny hope of seeing her smile again. What if she's still angry? What if she still can't forgive me after all this time?

Mother didn't object to Father wanting me home, I remind myself. If she had, I wouldn't be here. To my father, Mother's emotional well-being trumps all.

"No, sir," Jonas answers.

"Oh. Do you know when she's coming back?"

His pale blue eyes soften a bit. "I'm sorry, I don't."

"Did she take a suitcase?" A small pang reverberates in my chest as I wait for his response.

"Not to my knowledge, sir."

The tension in my gut loosens. Maybe she isn't trying to avoid me. Maybe Father wasn't lying about her being too sick to travel to Princeton to attend my graduation.

Maybe—just maybe—her hatred has lessened, like an iceberg slowly thawing in more temperate waters.

"It's hot, sir. Shall I take your jacket?"

I hand it over.

"I'll have your bags brought to your old room."

I nod my thanks and proceed into my childhood home, turning up my sleeves. The steps across the portico and in to the foyer quickly take on a significance that becomes almost reverential.

Banished since I was twelve, I've only been allowed to return because I finished my education...and because my father thought it prudent to have me back. The local Chamber of Commerce is giving him an award—Entrepreneur of the Year—and a local TV station is doing a feature on him. Apparently it would look bad if I wasn't around, even if I'm not in the program.

"You're a son any man would be proud to have," he said in a tone that made it clear he wasn't *any man*.

And I wish with everything I have that my father *were* any man and my mother any woman. Then everything I've done to make them proud might mean something. I graduated, top three in my class, from the fancy European boarding schools, the sort of places you can't go unless your parents have the right connections and money to burn. Then summa cum laude from Princeton with a degree in economics. I'm popular among my peers and can play a mean piano, along with soccer and polo. The only thing I can't do is draw, but then, I never devoted much time to art.

None of your accomplishments will be enough to make Mother forgive you.

I steel my spine. I know—even *understand*—that I deserve every bit of her hate. But I also crave her forgiveness. It's the only thing that can lighten the impossible weight on my heart and soul. I can't continue living without the ability to feel true joy or satisfaction. Dating, while superficially fun, leaves me cold. Even the endless job offers—the kind my friends would exclaim over—have left me hollow and apathetic.

I walk into the air-conditioned interior of the mansion. The foyer is huge, with a vaulted ceiling and fans creating cooling breezes. The place is exactly as I remember...except for some puzzling vases with fresh tiger lilies sitting in wall nooks. They aren't Mother's favorite.

"Who's visiting?" I ask Jonas. Mother always fills vases with flowers her guests will enjoy. I'm certain the lilies aren't for me.

"No one, sir." He notes the direction of my gaze. "Those are Miss Ivy's doing."

"Ivy...?"

"Ivy Smith. Your cousin."

The name is familiar. Harry mentioned her in the hundreds of texts he dashed off to me between classes and chasing girls.

She's Uncle Perry's adopted daughter. When he and his wife died in a car crash about a year after my banishment to Europe, Mother took her in. Unlike me, she wasn't shipped off to Europe. Instead, she was raised with my brothers, Edgar and Harry, here in Tempérane. From what Harry wrote, it's obvious Mother treats Ivy like her own flesh and blood...the daughter she so desperately wanted and lost.

"She's home. So is Master Harry," Jonas adds diplomatically. "I believe he is in the sitting room in the east wing."

"Thank you," I say with a nod, dismissing him. Running the family business keeps Father and Edgar ridiculously busy, but not Harry.

I head toward the east wing, walking along the long corridor. Since Mother loves fresh flowers, every vase has tiger lilies. Not a pink rose in sight. I let myself breathe a bit. The hall hasn't changed a bit—freshly waxed hardwood floor and ornately framed paintings. Edgar, Harry and I used to run like little demons along here even though Mother told us to behave, saying we set a bad example for Katherine.

"Good girls are overrated," I told Mother with a cheeky grin.

"Is that so?" She pinched my cheek gently, laughter in her bright gaze.

"A girl's gotta know what she wants and go for it. Daddy said so."

"I want to ride a sleigh!" Katherine yelled, clapping and hopping. She looked like a princess in a lavender dress made with silk and lace.

"Then ride a sleigh you will!" Edgar declared. He, Harry and I pulled the pink wagon Katherine dubbed a "sleigh" up and down the hall. Mother put her hand against her mouth to hide a wide grin, then asked Jonas to prepare a pitcher of iced tea.

When we were too tired to pull the wagon anymore, we clamored for the cold drink. Mother pressed a kiss on my slightly sweaty forehead. "You're a good brother, Tony. Mama's so proud of you."

When I saw her smile, my world couldn't have been brighter or more radiant. My chest puffed out, my heart ready to burst with joy.

Sweet, beautiful memories. I turn them over in my mind

from time to time, knowing the warmth and happiness I felt isn't to be mine again. Not yet. I can only long for them like a child who didn't get an invitation to a popular classmate's birthday party. Only Mother's forgiveness can bring me back into the fold of my family—what it used to be like.

The sound of a piano coming from the sitting room breaks my reverie. There didn't used to be a piano in there, but...

I quietly open the white double doors. Wide-paned windows look out into the immaculate garden where I used to play tag with my brothers and sister. Next to them, facing a mirror, a white baby grand takes up a corner of the room. Both the mirror and the piano are new.

Two people sit on the extra-long bench, playing Schubert's Fantasie in F minor. Engrossed in the music, they don't notice me coming in.

The sight of Harry brings a smile to my lips. My brothers and I got together in Europe when they were on vacation. Edgar even took an overseas semester while at Harvard to study in Paris, and made clandestine efforts to see me as often as he could during those months. During those years, I never thought I'd see Harry in this house again.

He has the dark hair all three of us have, but with a frame slightly smaller than mine or Edgar's, which younger brother Harry tries to hide by wearing shirts that are a size too large. Even if I were blind, I'd know it was him because he can only half-ass the music. Too lazy to practice.

And his partner... The strawberry blonde to his right is pretty. Her gray eyes are large and brimming with intelligence, her nose cute and pert. She looks like a sweet girl next door, except for her mouth. Soft, lush and inviting, it's the kind of mouth that belongs to temptresses and sirens.

Her azure dress is much like her—modest and sexy at the same time. It fits snugly around her breasts and tight waist, then cascades around her hips and legs in a loose skirt. I have a feeling she also has an amazing ass, one that would fit perfectly in my hands.

A sudden urge to kick my younger brother off the bench and carry her away seizes me. *What an impression that would make.*

The girl is playing an incredible *primo* that belongs someplace like Carnegie Hall. Unfortunately, Harry's *secondo* is holding her back, since he's stumbling every other measure.

He isn't worthy of being her partner.

I wince with exasperation when he hits a flat note. Can't he read the music?

"Harry, I thought you said you practiced your butt off," the blonde says, her voice bristling with annoyance.

Normally, I wouldn't like someone talking to Harry that way, but in this case, he deserves it. I also like the sisterly undertone to her irritation. She's definitely not his girlfriend, and the realization makes the room seem a little brighter.

Harry throws his hands up in the air. "What can I say? I haven't studied at Curtis for three years like a certain someone." His voice is entirely too loud, his gestures too exaggerated. He's lying through his teeth.

And the girl sees through him, much to my satisfaction.

She snorts. "Well, if you *practiced*, maybe they'd let you in. Let's try again."

I shake my head. It's a lost cause. Harry will only butcher one of most hauntingly beautiful piano pieces ever composed.

At the same time, she can't play it solo. Fantasie needs a *secondo* to be complete, and Harry's not the man for that. So I tap his shoulder, an eyebrow raised.

He swivels around and stares, his mouth open. "Whoa! Holy shit! Dad said you were coming this week, but...!"

He jumps off the bench and hugs me. I hug him back.

"Shoulda texted me!" he says. "I would've gone to the airport to pick you up."

"It's all right. Father sent a car."

He looks at the piano, then back at me. "You're going to show off, aren't you?"

"Like she said, if you practiced..." I stretch my fingers as I approach the piano. "Now watch and learn."

Rolling his eyes, he gestures at the now-empty spot on the bench. I take his place.

Her curious gaze bores into my cheek, but before she can ask any questions, I start. I don't want her to have any weird preconceptions about me because of who I am, or what people whisper about me behind my family's back. Although I know from Edgar and Harry that my parents have done a lot to ensure the general public doesn't know the real reason I was banished, people aren't stupid. They can put two and two together. They just don't say anything openly because of the power and influence we have in the area.

The girl smells subtly of tiger lilies, but warmer and more alluring. Even though I'm the one who has to start the piece, she's the one who sets the pace, and I let her, looking at her long, elegant fingers.

She's a superb pianist. We're in perfect sync as we play. She doesn't miss a beat or a note, and neither do I. I can feel her soft breathing, the heat of her skin. My breathing alters to match hers, and my body shifts a tad closer to her, as though it can't bear to be away from her warmth. It feels like even my heart is beating to the pace she sets...as though we're one through the music.

I almost falter at the thought, the back of my neck prickling.

She stops when the first movement is finished. Harry claps. "You haven't lost your touch, Tony."

"And you haven't improved." My riposte is almost perfunctory, mainly because I'm still digesting the earlier sensation of being keenly linked to her. During that time, the weight in my heart grew lighter. Made me feel like I could breathe again.

He spreads his arms. "What can I say? I don't have the ambition or drive."

True enough. Harry never cared much for the piano. He only took lessons to please Mother. He whined endlessly in texts, which made me wistful for the luxury of not being the best at everything I do. I have to be so good Mother will have no choice but to forgive me.

The girl's gray eyes are focused on me, her cheeks rosy now. I can't tell if that's from the performance or something else, but I want to stroke them with my fingers and find out if she's as affected as I am. She purses her mouth, and I note a tiny mole below the exact center point of her bottom lip. It seems to beg me to flick my tongue across it while I kiss her. *Yup. A temptress's mouth.* A hint of cherry and caramel tickles my nose as she breathes out softly, and the warmth from her bare arm against mine leaves a shivery tingle.

"You're pretty good," she says finally.

"Not too shabby yourself."

She clears her throat. "I'm Ivy."

The name is like a bat to the back of my skull. Uncle Perry's adopted daughter, Ivy. The one Mother apparently dotes on, if even half the stuff Edgar and Harry said is true.

By the time I recover, bitter disappointment is flooding through me like acid. Thank God for the gentlemanly decorum my European teachers hammered into me. I manage a polite smile. "I'm Tony," I say, then immediately want to kick myself. Anthony is the better choice—the default name I give to people I have no intention of becoming close to. I can't believe I screwed up, but too late now to take it back.

"Tony?"

"Anthony Blackwood, but Tony to friends and family."

She tilts her head as she smiles. "Am I your friend?"

An honest answer won't do. Mother wouldn't approve. "Well, we're related."

"Not by blood," she says hurriedly. A flush deepens her cheeks as she clears her throat. "I have to practice some more."

"I'll do it with you." The offer slips out before I can catch myself. *Shit.*

She looks at me from under her lashes. "Can you do it ten times?"

"Sure. Ten more times."

2

Ivy

It's a good thing I can play Schubert in my sleep because otherwise I would've made an idiot of myself.

Why did I tell Tony I had to practice it? Or say I had to do it ten times? The plan was to work on Liszt's *Liebestraum* No. 3, so I can record it and send it to Yuna. It's a pact my best friend and I made before the summer break started to make sure we continue to challenge each other and improve. We were supposed to practice a few select pieces Tatiana asked us to work on, record them and issue a challenge with "Beat this!" I only spared a few minutes to play Schubert to humor Harry, who insisted he could pull off the *secondo* well enough to accompany me.

The entire Fantasie is a little over eighteen minutes long. At least I recovered enough to say I only needed to practice the first movement, but that's still almost an hour of playing next to Tony, sitting entirely too close to him, our arms and hands brushing each other.

I've played Schubert with other pianists before, but no one quite like Tony. He has excellent control of those strong fingers, effortlessly going from exquisite and soft to passionate and powerful. The heat radiating from his body is too warm—almost searing—but I don't mind. He's like a quietly brewing storm, and I'm aware of his presence like a little bird in a forest, my skin prickling and the fine hair on the back of my neck standing up. Despite my best effort at staying calm, my heart is racing, and it's all I can do to keep my fingers from matching my rushing pulse. I let my hand graze his from time to time just to see if he's as affected as I am, but he's totally focused on his part of the music.

To him, you're probably just a kid.

He just graduated from Princeton, and in only three years. Uncle Lane announced that at dinner a few weeks ago, one of his quarterly, businesslike mentions of how his second son is doing. As usual, Aunt Margot showed no reaction, not even a smile, while Edgar and Harry let out a few excited interjections to express their admiration for Tony's accomplishment. Despite Aunt Margot's lackluster response and Uncle Lane's flat and prideless voice every time he speaks of Tony, I've long been impressed with and wondered about my mysterious cousin.

Well, he's much more impressive in person. And more intriguing.

Maybe Uncle Lane and Aunt Margot didn't look that pleased over all that he's done because they expected more. I've heard whispers from the townspeople about Anthony Blackwood, my aunt and uncle's favored second son. They sent him to Europe to study at the best boarding schools on the continent. Their oldest, Edgar, who graduated from Harvard, didn't merit such special treatment.

Instead of taking off, Harry takes a seat and listens. Tony leaves without a word when we hit the final note for the tenth time. The moment the door closes behind him, the pressure in the room drops. I draw in air as the prickling sensation eases.

"Damn," Harry says. "Sorry he's being rude."

"What?"

"Well, you know. He just...left." Harry frowns.

"It's fine." I didn't even notice because I was wound so tight from the playing. If he hadn't left, I might've, just to breathe a bit and recover. *Did he feel the same way I did?* Hot goosebumps break out over my skin at the possibility.

"On the other hand," Harry says, stretching his arms over the back of his seat, "I didn't think he'd actually play it all ten times. Isn't really like him."

My heart thumps. "How do you know?" I say, keeping my voice as nonchalant as possible.

Harry shrugs. "He doesn't usually have the patience for all the repetition. He's naturally gifted, so..."

"You mean you can't do what he can even with practice, so you're going to attribute it to talent." Gifted or not, nobody gets that good without practice.

Harry's eyes are worried. "Probably be best if you don't get too close."

"What do you mean?" It isn't like him to tell me who I can or can't hang out with, and I don't like the way he's warning me away like...somehow Tony and I are totally incompatible.

He sighs. "Getting too close would mean getting on Mom's shi—uh, *persona non grata* list."

My face heats. He probably noticed my attraction to Tony. "Who said anything about getting close? It was nothing but some piano practice. I just met the guy. Besides, he's your brother, which makes him my cousin. Sort of ick, if you ask me."

"But like you said, not by blood."

"Still ick." I scowl to hide my embarrassment, then gather

my music and leave. I can never tell if Harry is being perceptive or just saying whatever pops into his head.

But one thing's for sure—insightful or not, I don't have to listen to what he says.

My eyes on the ground, I trot down the hall and almost run into Aunt Margot at the bottom of the main staircase.

She's so delicately elegant, it seems like she exists on nothing but air and water. Her eyes are unusual—one green and one blue. She always has her golden hair pulled up into a French twist, and the makeup on her stunning face is subtle and flawless, highlighting her eyes and high cheekbones. Despite her age, she hardly has any wrinkles. Her skin is actually better than some of my friends' at Curtis.

A lavender silk dress hugs Aunt Margot's slender figure, her small, narrow feet in purple Jimmy Choos with skyscraper heels. I've never seen her less than perfectly dressed and coiffed, and it sometimes makes me wonder if she's truly an angel who can do no wrong. I know my life would've fallen apart without her, because my innocent child's world ended the moment my parents died.

When the police told me my parents weren't coming back from the car crash, I was so stunned I couldn't cry for a few moments while my child's mind processed it. They asked me about relatives, and I told them Dad had a sister in Louisiana. We never visited her for some reason. I don't recall any Christmas cards or birthday calls, either. To be honest, I wasn't even sure if I really had an aunt in Louisiana, except for hearing my dad talk about her a few times. But Aunt Margot came for me.

I still remember the first time I saw her. Elegant in a classy black dress, she was breathtakingly beautiful, and I thought maybe she was an angel who had come to put the pieces of my broken world back together.

She took one long look at me, then knelt, hugging me

tightly and whispering into my hair, "It's okay, Ivy. I'll make everything okay. I promise."

She kept her word over the last eight years, and I've done everything in my power to make sure she'll never regret making the vow.

"Hey, Aunt Margot," I say cheerily.

"What's the hurry?"

"Nothing. Just got done with practice."

"Any improvement on *Liebestraum*?" She's always expressed a great deal of interest in what I'm working on, and I give her daily updates.

"Um. Not really."

"Don't tell me you're mentally blocked by what Tatiana said." Tatiana is my teacher at Curtis. Unlike most professors and teachers, she hates being called Ms. Seger. She says it makes her feel old, like her mom.

"I'm not. I ended up working on Schubert instead."

"Oh. You were going to play with Harry." She sighs, vaguely irritated. Although she pays for his lessons, she doesn't think much of his musical talent or discipline. "Don't waste your time and effort on him. He's too lazy to be any good."

"Actually, it wasn't Harry I was practicing with. He couldn't manage the *secondo*, so I ended up playing with Tony."

The pleasant mask slips a fraction. "You met him already? When did he arrive?"

"At least an hour ago." Why doesn't she know the son she hasn't seen in nine years is back? Didn't Tony text or call her when he landed? If not, shouldn't Uncle Lane have done that?

Then I notice she looks anything but thrilled, even though she's still smiling. "I see." She turns toward the stairs, then stops. "I'm thinking about driving down to New Orleans tonight, and would like some companionship. Want to come along?"

"I'd love to, but I'm going to a party with Sue Ellen." She's my best friend and the first girl to befriend me when I came to Tempérane. When we realized we both played the piano, we grew close—almost inseparable, really—until I went off to study three years ago.

Aunt Margot makes a vaguely disapproving noise. "Are you sure that's a good idea? She hasn't been the same since you left for Curtis."

"She was probably just disappointed, that's all," I say loyally. We auditioned at the same conservatories. Unfortunately, she got rejected, while I was accepted at all of them. She tried again year after year with the same result. "It's her dream to be a concert pianist, and it's got to be frustrating." I sometimes feel terrible I'm living my dream while she struggles. I haven't mentioned the competitions I've won out of respect for her feelings.

Aunt Margot places a gentle hand on my shoulder. "Ivy. You are the average of the company you keep. Sue Ellen will never amount to anything, and she's in your past. You're a smart girl. Don't let her drag you down." Then she turns and goes up the stairs.

I sigh. Aunt Margot is never overtly rude to Sue Ellen, but she's never cared for her, either. Aunt Margot considers Sue Ellen lazy and undisciplined, much like Harry. "If she practiced like her life depended on it, maybe she would've gotten in," she said after one of Sue Ellen's failed auditions.

That may be true, but I'm not ditching one of my closest friends whose only sin is she doesn't play well enough to get into a music program. Friendship should be more lasting than that.

I walk up to my room, put the music back on the bookshelf and go to my walk-in closet to pull out the black and white dress I wore on stage at a competition last year. It's sophisticated, with an off-shoulder asymmetrical neckline. It isn't too long, either, ending two inches above my knees. Aunt Margot bought it for me, calling it classy and fashionable. Although it's not as risqué as Sue Ellen would like, it's a bit tight around my breasts, since I've filled out more in the last two years, and combined with a push-up bra, it shows some pretty spectacular cleavage. It should be okay for the "awesome, hot" party Sue Ellen swears is going to blow my mind. She explained breathlessly it isn't an event with "idiots," a.k.a. high school boys, but "college men," and I need to look my age. It's like she's forgotten I'm eighteen because I left high school three years ago.

I hold the dress in front of me and study my reflection in the full-length mirror. *Is Tony going to be there?*

I shake my head. He's in Tempérane only because he finished college and the local TV station might require a shot of the entire family for its feature on Uncle Lane. Tony's been gone long enough that probably nobody knew when he'd be town to invite him. Even Harry and Aunt Margot didn't know exactly when he'd be back, since Uncle Lane just said Tony was returning—without any specifics—at our last Sunday dinner.

Harry, on the other hand, will definitely show. He's good-looking, fun-loving and popular, just the kind of guy you want at a party.

Maybe he can bring Tony. That'd be nice. I'd love to get to know him better, in some place more neutral.

Getting too close to him would mean...

I purse my lips. Why does Harry think his mom's going to be upset if Tony and I get close? She encouraged Edgar and Harry to befriend me as quickly as possible after bringing me to Tempérane. The only reason I never met Tony was because he was away, but if he'd been home, I'm sure we'd be close the way his brothers and I are.

Maybe she has some kind of grand plan for Tony. After all,

he's good-looking, smart and magnetic. And Edgar mentioned once that Tony speaks five languages fluently. So Aunt Margot might have somebody else in mind.

Oh my God. I pat my cheeks a few times. What the hell am I thinking? I'm mulling over this whole thing like Tony and I are Romeo and Juliet. We just met.

Focus, Ivy. You have more important things to worry about than Tony.

Like the party and having fun. After all, Tatiana always says one of the best ways to improve at music, other than practicing, is to *live*. Experience life at its best and worst.

And this party is going to be me living.

3

Anthony

I UNDO MY TOP TWO BUTTONS AND TRY TO TAKE IN SOME air as I reach my old childhood room. I don't remember this house feeling so suffocating, but it does, despite the high ceilings and windows everywhere. It's far worse than that day nine years ago.

What the hell was I thinking, agreeing to play Fantasie ten times, seated so close to Ivy that I could feel her breathing? Schubert wrote the piece out of love for a woman he could never have. The music gave him a reason to be as close to her as possible, feel her arm graze his as they performed together. I should've told Ivy to play with Harry when she asked...

Except the idea of him sitting that close to her and being affected by her presence bothered me. But the connection I felt for her for almost an hour built such a restlessness, I had to leave as soon as I hit that last note.

After gulping a few lungfuls of air, I blink and look at my

old room. It's a suite with a balcony, almost at the end of the hall, and little has changed. It's spotless, the sage bedsheets perfectly spread, not a wrinkle to be seen. My Princeton diploma is already framed and hung—probably Father's doing, since he took it with him after the graduation ceremony—but everything else on the pale mint walls, shelves and desk is gone except for a picture of Katherine on my nightstand.

She's smiling in it, a dimple in one plump, rosy cheek and Mother's golden curls around her heart-shaped face. Fringed with long, curly, dark eyelashes, her blue eyes are wide and bright, the rosebud mouth cherubic and red. And she had the cutest nose. I could never resist pushing it like a button every time I saw her. The dress she's in is frothy pink, with more lace and satin than a fairytale princess costume. Mother designed and made it just for Katherine, spending hours on her sewing machine.

I run my fingers over Katherine's young face, sorrow and the old grief clenching their cold, bitter hands around my heart. She was the best of the four of us—all that innocence, all that vitality. She read better than some of the older kids in the area, much to Edgar's astonishment, and played better piano than Harry, much to his indignation. She sang better than me.

It should've been you. Mother's rage rings in my head, as fresh as though it were yesterday.

Suddenly feeling dirty and unworthy, I yank my hand away from the picture.

"Is everything to your liking?" Jonas says, standing in the doorway.

How long has he been there? Jonas is paid to be discreet, but I hate the idea of people watching me. "Don't you ever knock?"

"The door was open, sir."

I run my fingers roughly through my hair. *Was it?* I can't remember.

"I've had your things unpacked and put away—in the places you preferred before," Jonas continues. "Except for the condoms," he adds, shifting a bit. "The small drawer under the right bedside stand."

So there is something that can ruffle his unfailingly calm demeanor. The idea is amusing for some reason. "Thanks," I say, looking at the dressers and the open door to the huge walk-in closet.

It used to hold my old toys and memorabilia—collectable comic books, autographed baseballs and tickets...all gone now.

"What happened to Bolt's things?" I ask. Bolt is my golden retriever puppy. Well. He must be a big dog by now. Then I realize his photos are gone too. "And his pictures?"

"Your mother had them...removed."

"All of them?"

"Yes."

I pause and draw in a shaky breath. She was furious when the little dog tried to comfort me that day, but I didn't realize her anger went this deep. I swallow an ugly lump stuck in my throat. "He's not here, is he?"

"No."

"Did he at least go to a good family?"

"He did, sir." Jonas's voice is gentle. "I made sure of it."

"Thank you. That's all. I'll let you know if I need anything."

He nods and leaves, closing the door behind him.

I sit heavily on the bed, elbows on knees and head cradled in my palms. Bolt's only crime was being too loyal. If he hadn't sat next to me, whining softly and licking my cheeks in tender canine solace and love, Mother wouldn't have sent him away.

"Get that dog away from him, and out of my home! I don't want to see it ever again," she screamed like a wounded animal, tears streaming down her pale face, while Father held her tightly. If he hadn't, she might've strangled Bolt, a puppy she'd

selected herself for my eleventh birthday and lavished with care and love, calling him clever and beautiful.

Numb and cold, I watched the entire scene unfold. It felt like something out of a psychedelic movie, not something that was actually happening. I couldn't muster an ounce of emotion, although I shivered continuously. It was too cold in the house, and I couldn't warm myself up.

Her hand on my shoulder, the cook's assistant said some compassionate words, although I barely registered them, my entire focus on my mother. But the tone of her voice was low, soothing...

"How dare you! You're fired! Get out!" Mother screamed, pointing at the door.

"Margot," Father said. "Don't do this."

"She doesn't get to make living off us if she's going to side with Tony."

"Mom, please," Edgar said. "None of this is Tony's fault, and—"

He never got to finish. She slapped him so hard, his head swiveled.

"Get out, you heartless bastard," she railed, while Father held her to make sure she didn't strike Edgar again. "Go to your room and stay there!"

I'd never seen her act so crazed, lashing out at people with such violence. But grief has the power to twist and change people. And Father did everything Mother wanted, and more, in a desperate attempt to calm her.

I hoped she'd bring Bolt and the cook's assistant back after I left. But her anger and pain must've run too deep, and I feel the possibility of forgiveness slipping further from my grasp.

A couple of quick knocks and Harry sticks his head in.

I put on an empty smile. I wouldn't want him to notice anything's wrong or try to run interference between me and Mother. That wouldn't end well.

"Hey, Tony. Caleb's having a party. His parents are out of town." He grins. "Lot of hot girls are gonna be there. Booze, too."

I give him a look. "Booze is not a plus."

He groans. "Yeah, yeah. Mister Continental Attitude." He's seen how blasé Europeans are about alcohol, instead of looking at it as a source of never-ending fun like people do in the South.

"I think I'll wait for Mother to get back. I want to say hello," I say, doing my best to ignore the roiling in my gut. Just the idea of facing her makes my mouth go dry.

"Oh, she's here. I saw her go into her room."

"Really?" My gut shifts into overdrive. "Okay, thanks."

"If you change your mind, lemme know. I'll text you the directions. Sayonara!"

I almost laugh at his horrible singsong pronunciation. He's determined to spend at least a semester in Tokyo while in college, and he's been studying Japanese for the last three years. Harry being Harry, he hasn't made much progress.

I inhale deeply and stand up. I have to see her...know if there's any chance of earning her forgiveness. Delaying will only make me sicker to my stomach.

Just think of it as pulling off a Band-Aid.

I check my appearance in the mirror, finger-combing my hair and adjusting my clothes, picking off near-invisible flecks of dust, until I'm satisfied I look perfect.

A perfect son to earn precious forgiveness.

I walk slowly down the hall, mentally reciting all the things I want to say. I've written them out in notebooks over the years, and have them memorized.

I knock softly on the door to the master bedroom.

"Come in."

Mother's voice. I straighten my spine and walk inside. The room's airy and sumptuously decorated with a thick Persian rug, a plush armchair and a loveseat. There's a bench at the foot of the California king bed, the bed itself covered in pearlescent gray sheets that look almost silvery under the chandelier. The furniture, ornately carved out of cherry, is elegant and old-world. A few nicks and scars mar the hardwood gleam of the floor. Mother is in the armchair, and I recognize a long scratch by her feet. I made it when I fell with a pair of scissors, while running around the house with my brothers and sister.

Mother pulled me up, checking for injuries, then hugged me tightly. "Don't ever do that again. You could've hurt yourself!" she said against the crown of my head, punctuating the words with kisses.

The memory suddenly gives me courage. Surely that kind of love can't just die, can it?

"Tony," Mother says, her expression stony.

"I'm home." I swallow. "Mom."

Her chin lifts half an inch higher and she slowly shakes her head. "You don't get to *mom* me."

If my hopes were lit candles, her cool words just doused all but a couple.

She continues, "I heard you met Ivy."

"Yes."

Mother looks away for a moment, then swings her gaze back. "She reminds me of Katherine...my baby...the daughter you stole from me." Her voice is thick with unshed tears and old wounds. "Are you going to do the same with her?"

"No!" Is this some kind of test to see if I'm worthy of her forgiveness? "I'll keep her safe. I swear."

"I trusted you back then, but you betrayed me. I'm not giving you another chance."

"Mother—"

"I wanted to take her to New Orleans, but I can't. She doesn't want to leave town, and your father's reputation is important. We don't want anybody to see our...dirty linen." Her bitter words dig into me like daggers.

The pain is staggering, so much more than I ever imagined.

"You stay away from her. I can't lose her, too."

I see it now: Ivy is what's been holding her together. She'll never recover if anything happens to Ivy.

And I realize Mother is looking at me like a monster who lures children away from their homes and devours them. My heart is so heavy I can barely move. The hollowness in my gut spreads until I feel like a husk—joyless, grotesque and pathetic.

"I'm tired," Mother says finally, her voice thin. "If you don't have anything else to say, you can go." Placing her forehead in one palm, she waves me away with her free hand.

So I leave, my legs like lead. Mindlessly, I go down the winding staircase and out of the house, away from all the painful memories and unhealed wounds.

I breathe roughly, bent over with my hands on my knees. The heat and humidity out here, as afternoon edges into evening, feel so much better than the cool, sterile air inside. Once I regain a modicum of control, I lean against one of the columns at the edge of the veranda and look out over the grounds.

I didn't get to make any of my speeches. I didn't get to tell her how much I miss her, how hard I've worked to make her proud. While my best friend was plowing through all the eligible women in Europe, I stayed the course, making sure I became as accomplished as possible—to be the kind of man people could admire.

A car engine's roar interrupts my dark thoughts. I glare as an obnoxious roadster emerges from the live oaks and pulls up in front of the house. The driver is a young girl—probably still in high school—although she's dressed like she's looking to pick up a john for the evening. If she bends ten degrees forward, her tits are going to spill out of that ridiculous top, and the silly girl isn't even wearing a bra. It's a pathetic attempt to gain male attention.

I start to turn away, but the house door opens and Ivy rushes out. Her eyes on the girl in the car, she doesn't notice me.

Ivy's hair is twisted up into a messy bun, and she's wearing a black and white dress that fits like a glove and emphasizes the high, lush curves of her breasts.

Where the hell is she going dressed like that?

Before I can say anything, Ivy hops into the car, and it takes off.

Damn it.

I glare at the roadster, feeling conflicted. I really shouldn't give a shit. Mother specifically told me to stay away from Ivy. The girl in the car didn't get that warning.

But it's a better than even bet that she doesn't plan on taking Ivy somewhere safe and wholesome. Nobody dresses like that for a study date.

I can't lose her, too.

My jaw tightens. Mother wants me to keep my distance, but...

I go to the garage. My family keeps the car keys neatly organized over the light switches. I grab the closest fob and climb inside a silver Mercedes.

By the time I catch up to the roadster, my temper's simmering. I know I'm being a hypocrite. Normally I don't give a damn what a girl is wearing. So why do I care if the dress Ivy's wearing shows off her breasts a bit too well, or if other guys are going to ogle and drool over them?

Because Ivy's different. She's...

Well. She's my cousin.

Not by blood.

Shut up, shut up!

The roadster stops in front of a huge house I recognize. It belongs to the Wentworths. Joel Wentworth is a good friend of Father's and has been Tempérane's sheriff since before I was shipped off to Europe. But I doubt he's at home just now. This must be the party Harry told me about, the one his son Caleb, who's two years older than me, is throwing. The street is littered with cars.

I shut off the engine and stare at the crowd that's spilled out onto the front lawn. Things will probably be fine. After all, Harry's coming to this party, too.

But my hands clench around the steering wheel at the way the boys leer at Ivy as she walks inside with her friend. I remember the scent of tiger lilies clinging to her, the cherry and caramel on her breath.

I should go. Mother will burst a vein if she finds out I'm here. Where Ivy is.

But instead of driving away, I tap my thumb against the steering wheel, my shoulders tight. The clock on the dash tells me I've been sitting in the car, debating, for over ten minutes already.

I'm blowing everything out of proportion, I tell myself. I've never, ever responded like this to another girl in a similar situation. It's none of my business what anyone decides to wear, who she decides to hang out with, what party she decides to attend.

I'm probably projecting what I would've felt if Katherine were still alive and boys were staring at her like that.

Except...what I feel for Ivy isn't entirely brotherly.

But only because she isn't my sister. She's my cousin.

For fuck's sake. I'm being stupid. There are only two options—go inside or go home. I reach for the ignition, then stop. I should go inside. Just to check on Ivy, make sure she's all right. Let the guys there know they'll answer to me if anything happens to her, then leave ASAP. I tell myself it's the least I can do to prove I'm not beyond redemption, and it has nothing to do with my concern for Ivy herself.

My mind made up, I climb out of the car and walk toward the house.

4

Anthony

Music comes thumping out of the house. Even the lawn under my shoes seems to vibrate. Caleb is lucky his neighbors aren't pulling guns on him for the noise. The good people of Tempérane believe in firm and clear communication.

A rotund idiot with a huge zit on his nose blocks my way at the door. "You got an invite?" His words come out loud and slurred, his breath stinking of cheap beer.

I cock an eyebrow. "Do I need one?"

He sways back and forth. "Everyone does."

"Not Anthony Blackwood," I say coldly.

"What?" He blinks, then peers at me. "No way. Tony?"

"Don't be presumptuous. Only my family and friends can call me Tony."

He flushes. "Right. Anthony." He shoves a hand in my direction. "I'm Bobby. Bobby Darton. We went to Southdowns Elementary together."

His name isn't familiar, but I recognize his family. His father works for mine. I don't take his hand.

Clearing his throat, he drops it. "I thought you were in Europe. Or up at Princeton."

"You thought wrong." I slide by him and walk inside.

The party is already ripe with one too many drunks. People who can't hold their liquor really shouldn't indulge. Disgusted, I scan the crowd.

Some girls stumble toward me with loopy grins. They're uniformly tall, leggy, with big tits and bottle-blond hair. They flutter mascara-caked eyelashes, drawing my attention to their alcohol-hazed eyes, then lean forward to show me cleavages encased in dresses that are too tight.

"Hey, handsome," one says, her voice too loud and brassy. "Wanna join us? We're gonna have *fu-unnn.*" They lift their drinks and grin.

One of them hops a bit, making her tits bounce. "What do you say?"

Attractive, if you like plastic and no depth. I turn away, uninterested.

"Oh, come on!" another one says, slurring her words. "Don't be lame!"

Morons.

I march forward. Too many people are barely standing upright. More than half are underage, and most likely treating this as a God-given opportunity to overindulge. It's the last place someone like Ivy should be with that scantily dressed girl. Drunk boys do stupid shit.

I move around purposefully, looking for her. When people don't get out of my way fast enough, I just shove through. But I don't see her.

Damn it. Ivy isn't anywhere on the first floor or the yard or the pool. Did she go upstairs?

Fuck.

"Hey, Tony! You decided to come," Harry calls out to me, raising two plastic cups. "I was getting this for Danny, but you can have it instead."

He pushes one of the cups at me, and I take it out of reflex.

"Can't party sober," he says, like he's telling me the greatest secret of the universe.

I stare at the dark liquid dubiously. "What's in it?"

"Cranberry and vodka. It's fantastic."

I take a sip, then make a face. "I can't believe you drink this." The vodka tastes cheap—no smoothness at all.

"Caleb can't buy the best liquor." Harry gestures at the crowd. "Look at all these people."

"Have you seen Ivy?" I ask.

"No. Why? Is she here?" He cranes his neck.

"She came here with a girl. Terrible dresser. Fire-engine red lipstick. Curly brown hair."

"That'd be Sue Ellen. They're best friends."

That makes me feel marginally better. Best friends watch out for each other in places like this.

"Come on. Let me introduce you around." Harry puts a hand on my shoulder and pulls me toward a small group of guys by the pool.

I start to follow, then stop. I'm not here to socialize or have fun. I'm here to find Ivy and make sure she's okay.

"Let me check upstairs first, then I'll join you," I say.

"Caleb's not letting anybody go upstairs. Said his dad's going to whip his ass if he lets anybody up there."

"Still..." There are so many people the house feels like a sardine can. Caleb can't monitor all of them. "Just let me check." I start to hand the drink back to Harry until I remember I took a sip. I place it on a table awash with cups, paper plates and junk food wrappers. "I'll catch up in a few minutes."

"Okay." Taking a quick swallow from his cup, Harry ambles toward his friends.

I do another quick sweep of the first floor, checking every room, including the bathrooms. Then I hurry upstairs, a nasty knot forming in my gut as nobody comes out to stop me.

Upstairs means bedrooms. The idea that Ivy might be getting naked with one of these cretins puts a red film over my vision.

The Wentworths' home doesn't have as many rooms as my family's, but there are still a lot of doors on the second floor. I barge into them one by one—guest bedrooms, bathrooms, a home office, some boy's room with posters of pinup girls—but don't see Ivy.

Only one room left.

I twist the knob, but it doesn't turn. I shove my ear against the door and listen. There's definitely some sound coming from inside. I knock. Nothing.

Fuck it. There's more than one way to get inside. I kick the door in. It opens with a deafening crash.

The first person I see is the girl who drove the roadster. She's standing close to the door, looking at whatever's going on in the room with a loose fist over her chest, her eyes wide and bright. I walk past her and see five guys, all of them sizeable, in a loose semicircle around Ivy. Her back is pressed against a wall.

One of them has her wrist and is pulling her forward. "Don't be shy, babe. If you don't want to play the strip drinking game, we can do something else."

"Let *go*, Caleb," she says, trying to jerk her wrist out of his grip, but she's no match for the big bastard's football player body.

He grabs the back of her neck and forces a kiss, while his asshole buddies go "whoop, whoop, whoop" and pump their fists in the air. His other hand pulls the fabric on her shoulder and rips it, then moves down to grab at her breast.

Feral rage burns through me. "Let her go, shitface."

All four of the friends turn to face me. "Hey, what the fuck?" Caleb says over his shoulder, his mud-brown eyes squinting.

"Who let this asshole in?" One of the bigger boys turns to the roadster girl. *Sue Ellen.* "We told you to watch the door."

What the hell? Is she part of this? What the fuck kind of a best friend is she? If she weren't a girl, I'd knock her teeth out.

"Get rid of him," Caleb says, holding on to Ivy.

The four of them approach. They're depending on size and numbers to intimidate me. What they don't know is that I've spent years training in kickboxing in my quest to be the perfect son. My vision suddenly hyper-clear, I duck, punch, kick and circle, making it impossible for more than one of them to come at me at a time. In the confines of the room they get in each other's way, then meet a kick to the head, an elbow in the solar plexus or a knee slamming into the gut.

In moments, two of them are out cold, and the other two are doubled over, wheezing and groaning. Pathetic. I kick them until they collapse in unconscious heaps.

Turning my attention to Caleb, I shove a hand into his hair and yank him back. He yelps, and I get a whiff of alcohol and breath mints. One punch would be enough to knock him out, but I don't want that. Hot blood roars in my head as the monstrous fury inside me expands until all I feel is a raging desire to make Caleb bleed. He needs to feel every bit of pain I'm about to deliver and be beaten until he can't even crawl. Never lift a finger against Ivy or any other helpless girl again.

My foot connects with his belly, then ribs, then his head. He goes down, and I stomp on his hands and fingers until I hear them crunch. He raises his arms to try to block my attacks, but I sneer at his pitiful attempts.

Tears and snot cover his face as he cries and mewls with every blow to his face, chest, belly and back. I even break the man code and lodge the tip of my shoe in his testicles.

"Stop it, you're going to kill him!" comes a thin cry. "Do you want to go to jail for murder?"

Murder. The word is like a bucket of ice water. I stop abruptly. Caleb's blood covers the carpet and my shoes. I lift my head. Sue Ellen is directly in my line of sight. She's staring, both of her hands over her mouth, her eyes wide and fearful. Of me.

She didn't look at the boys on the floor like that. No, she watched them corner Ivy like she was about to witness something grotesque but fascinating.

Dismissing her, I turn to Ivy. She's pulled her dress up to cover herself. I go to the walk-in closet and find a long silk robe in black, probably Mrs. Wentworth's. I take it and drape it over Ivy's shoulders. She's trembling.

"Can you walk?" I ask.

She nods jerkily, her eyes a little glassy. I can smell beer and some kind of hard liquor on her.

I start to escort her out. As we walk past Sue Ellen, I stop and say in a soft voice, "I don't generally hurt girls. But what I just did to that guy is going to look merciful compared to what I'll do to you if I see you around the Blackwood property or anywhere near Ivy again."

She pulls back and swallows.

The crowd on the first floor parts in front of us like the sea before Moses, apparently sensing my murderous mood, even if they don't know the reason. My rage hasn't fully dissipated, and it's all I can do to not run back upstairs and deliver more punishment.

I take Ivy to the Mercedes and help settle her in the passenger seat. I get behind the wheel and start driving. After a few minutes, her teeth start to chatter.

"You okay?"

"F-f-fine," she manages.

"You don't sound okay."

Her fingers tighten around the robe. "Are you going to t-t-tell Aunt Margot?"

What Caleb and his buddies did would upset Mother. On the other hand, maybe rescuing Ivy put me that much closer to earning forgiveness. That'd be nice.

But I can't claim I beat up Caleb and his friends purely to protect Ivy. I did it because they deserved it and because I wanted to hurt them for hurting her. I don't care to delve deeper than that right now. It's too messy, and I don't need messy at the moment.

"Do you want me to?" I ask.

She shakes her head.

"Then I won't."

We come to where the road forks. Turning right would take us home. I go left.

"What are you d-doing?" Her voice is shaky. "I...I want to go home. You can drop me off here and I can walk."

"In a robe and a torn dress?"

She bites her lip, her gaze wary.

The hole in my gut burns hotter, bitterer. What the hell does she think I'm going to do to her? Does she think I saved her from those guys just to take her to someplace desolate and rape her? Maybe she does think that badly of me. Mother obviously thinks I'm capable of just about anything.

Bitter anger pounds in my head until my scalp throbs. "If I wanted to hurt you, I would've done it back at the house."

She gives a small, inarticulate cry and pulls back.

Damn it. My teeth grind together. Frustration and self-recrimination hammer at me. She's traumatized, maybe even in shock, and probably didn't realize she was insulting me. Besides, I didn't make the best impression today. I was rude to her in the sitting room, and I unleashed enough violence to scare any girl whose greatest physical exertion in life is playing Liszt's études.

I shouldn't be so hard on her.

Suddenly, the interior of the car feels suffocating. I lower the windows and let some air in. Although the sun's down, the humid breeze is sweltering as the car skims along the blacktop. But at least it no longer feels like a jail cell.

I drive to a small mound—too low to be called a hill—north of my parents' house. It overlooks a swampy bayou. Not the best view, especially at night, but it's quiet without prying eyes. A good place to regroup.

I park the car. Ivy pulls the robe tighter around herself.

Ugh. I should've dropped her off at the house to cower alone in her room. For some stupid reason, I thought she'd appreciate some time to pull herself together before going home. But for her, of course, home is a place of solace and comfort, not one where she has to be perfect in a quest to earn back the love she lost.

I get out and stand by the car. The air is hot and heavy under the moss-laden trees. Did I make a mistake in coming back to Tempérane? My parents are perfectly capable of coming up with a reason why I couldn't be in town for the TV special. My best friend Ryder's invitation to hang out together in L.A. feels very, very tempting at the moment.

"Open-ended, man," he said. "Any time you want to come out, feel free."

With Ryder, I don't have to be perfect and in control all the time. Although I never told him why I was banished, he understands me better than anyone because he too was exiled. Unlike me, though, he wasn't sent away because he did anything wrong. His parents didn't like that he and his siblings were in the way of the carefree lifestyle they wanted for themselves. So Ryder spent most of his time in Europe screwing girls and doing everything in his power to show his parents he didn't give a fuck. I sometimes can't decide which of us is worse off.

I hear the car door open and shut. "I'm sorry," Ivy says, coming around.

I tense, forty percent relieved that she seems okay and sixty percent unhappy I have to face her. She bothers me. Mother wants me to treat her like Katherine—and stay the hell away from her—but my body doesn't want to. There's a part of me that likes her, and not just because she's beautiful. She's smart and disciplined. Nobody gets into Curtis without talent and a lot of hard work. She's spirited and doesn't like to lose. Contrary to the stereotypical image of a sweet, dignified classical pianist, sipping champagne and waxing poetic about the genius of Mozart and Beethoven, elite pianists are freakishly competitive. They have to be for all those auditions and competitions.

"About what?" I say without looking at her.

"Getting involved in all that." She hesitates. "I shouldn't have gone to the party or gone up to the room with the boys and...you know."

My head hurts. "You have it all wrong."

"Oh." Her voice is tiny, like a mosquito flying over my ear.

"Parties are fine," I clarify.

She nods. "Right. It's just that they...the boys... Sue Ellen said they invited us, and it was going to be fun... I just..."

My head throbs as the murderous urge swells in my chest again. I inhale deeply, then turn and hold her eyes. "Listen, Ivy." I wait until her focus is one hundred percent on me. "They can look, but they can't touch. Understand?"

"Sure." She says it half a beat too fast, like she's uncomfortable.

"What happened wasn't your fault. Not even a little." I don't care if her skin's crawling. She's going to get it through her head one way or another. "Say it. Slowly. Like you mean it."

"It wasn't my fault. I get it, Tony."

"Good." I look away and lean my hip on the hood of the car.

She lets out a soft gasp. "Your hands."

I look down, flexing my fingers. My knuckles are bruised and bloodied, slightly swollen. The damage is mostly from the beating I gave Caleb, but it's not bad, considering how many times I hit him. Besides, the blood isn't mine. "That's what happens when you punch a few thickheaded idiots."

"But...you're hurt."

"What would you have me do about it? Go to an ER for blood that isn't mine?"

"Are you sure? Shouldn't you get checked out or something anyway?"

Ivy is an impossibly young girl, who probably hasn't seen anything rough or ugly in the world. "How old are you?"

"Eighteen."

Okay. Maybe not *impossibly* young. Just three years younger than I am. Still, she seems very unworldly. Innocent. Just being around me is soiling her. She's freaked out about a little blood, but she doesn't see the real blood on my hands. The blood that can never be cleansed, not without Mother's forgiveness.

"I can't believe I have to point this out," I say. *You may be eighteen, but you're ridiculously naïve.* "But my knuckles are nothing compared to what happened to you back there. Nothing's broken, and the skin will heal in a few days. You, on the other hand..."

"I'll be more careful. You saved me, Tony." Her gray eyes shine.

Oh, no. No, no, no...

I don't want that or need that. I'm nobody's hero. I make

my voice colder and crueler than I should. "I did it because my family doesn't need the scandal or ugly whispers, and I couldn't let anything happen to my mother's pride and joy. Otherwise, I wouldn't have bothered." The look in her eyes doesn't change. "You have no idea what kind of monster I am."

I open the car door.

"I'm going home. Get in unless you want to spend the night out here."

5

Ivy

Tony leads me into the house through the back door, ensuring that nobody gets a look at my rather shameful state. Although he didn't say anything else after we talked on the bank of the bayou, just him being there was enough to help me calm down. He might not have been the epitome of tenderness, but he protected me like a medieval knight. Nobody else did that, not even Sue Ellen. He makes me feel safe just by being close.

I don't understand why he called himself a monster. Was it because of what I said back at the party?

You're going to kill him. Do you want to go to jail for murder?

Tony's expression was terrifying when he heard me, but I only said it because I was scared for him. I've never seen rage like that before. I didn't want him to cross a line he shouldn't, especially not over me.

Soberer and calmer now, I can see how stupid it was for

me to go up to the second floor like that. Sue Ellen said—cajoled and wheedled—that we should accept Caleb's invitation for special drinks, but I should've known better than to go up or try that crazy mix of beer and soju. I'd never even heard of soju before, but Caleb said it was a Korean liquor he got on a trip to New York.

I don't know if there was anything else in it, but it got me tipsy so fast, the room was spinning after a few swallows. Thankfully, the spinning effect didn't last long, and I placed the half-full glass on a table even though the boys were insisting I finish it.

As for Sue Ellen, she had one, then stood by and watched when Caleb made his move, instead of calling for help or trying to stop him. She's been increasingly hung up on being part of the cool crowd. It's like she's decided that's what she should aim for, since getting into a conservatory isn't happening.

It makes me angry. Resentful. And stupid that I ever felt the slightest bit of guilt that she didn't get into any of the elite music programs when I did. And that I let that teeny sense of regret make me do things I wouldn't normally do to accommodate her.

But most of all, I'm sad that my friendship with the first girl to be nice to me in Tempérane had to end this way.

"You should put on something else," Tony says, taking a quick look around my frilly room.

"Okay." My voice is still a little quaky. I clench my jaw. "Thank you." Still quaky, but not too terrible. At least, I don't think so.

He nods once.

I go into the bathroom with a long nightshirt. I wipe the makeup—which is smeared and gross—off my face and splash it with cold water. I take off the robe that smells like unfamiliar laundry soap and perfume, brush my teeth and gargle three times with extra-strong mouthwash to get rid of the taste of Caleb's forceful kiss. Then I shower with hot water, scrubbing until my skin's almost raw, to erase his touch.

Bastard. Fucking asshole.

I look down at my hands. People call them gifted. Dexterous. I clench them hard.

It's too bad they only know how to play perfect arpeggios, but not how to throw a killer punch like Tony. It would've been so satisfying to break Caleb's nose.

I finally turn the water off, dry myself and put on the nightshirt. It has a perky Tweety Bird on the front. Tweety was Mom's favorite animation character, and I always feel like I'm close to her every time I wear this thing. Even though my nerves are still frayed, it helps.

"Come on," I whisper. I brace my palms on the edge of the double vanity. "You can get through this. It... The worst didn't happen."

The worst didn't happen. Could have, but didn't. Ever since my parents died in the car crash, that's been my motto. I can carry on as long as the worst doesn't happen. Although I lost my parents, I have Aunt Margot and Uncle Lane, who provide for me in ways most would envy. Although I almost ran into a tree when I first started driving, I didn't...and the car and tree were both fine.

But I can't stop shaking, and tears begin to flow. There have been other boys who tried to steal a kiss or cop a feel. I was always able to deflect them. What Caleb did was far worse —far more violating. The loud party. The closed room. The alcohol. The other boys egging him on. Sue Ellen watching.

It was such a trap. Such a *betrayal.*

I wipe at my wet cheeks. It's stupid to cry *now*, when I'm safe. I couldn't muster a single tear when that asshole grabbed me.

Leaning against the sink, I cover my mouth with a palm. Hearing the sobs out loud would make me feel worse.

I can't tell Aunt Margot what happened because she'd be upset over the attack, but also disappointed that I didn't follow her advice and put some distance between me and Sue Ellen. She'd give me the same speech she did when I was fourteen and starting to make more friends in town.

Be careful who you let into your inner circle, Ivy. People are presumptuous and try to force their "friendship" on us, all the while feigning altruistic motives. What they really want is the things we can do for them using our money and influence. You need to figure out who is and isn't worth your time...and distance yourself accordingly.

When I'm finally out of tears, I stand, blow my nose and wash my face with cold water again. My eyes are swollen, my complexion blotchy, but hopefully I'll look okay tomorrow morning. If not, I'll just hide in my room until I can sneak down to the piano to practice. I hate to miss even a single session, because I can tell the difference.

When I come out, Tony's settled on the chair in front of my vanity, every light out except for the one by my bed. I falter. He doesn't give me more than a cursory glance, but it sears me like a hot iron.

"Feeling better?" he asks.

"Yes. Thank you," I say, my voice still hoarse. "Aren't you leaving?"

"Do you want to me to?"

My room's too dark...too quiet. And suddenly I hate the idea of being alone. "Not really."

"Okay." Tony doesn't move from his seat.

I climb into the huge four-poster bed and pull the sheets all the way to my chin. "Aren't you tired?" I ask, my voice small. After all, he traveled from Princeton today.

"No. Go to sleep."

"You can't just *order* someone to go to sleep," I mutter, inexplicably peeved and grateful at the same time. It's vaguely irritating that he seems to know what I need better than me, while I know almost nothing about him. Certainly not enough to know what he needs.

He doesn't watch me like I thought he might. His face impassive, he's looking at his phone, probably checking some email or text.

Having him here in the room helps. He's like a shield, making me feel safe. And his not staring at me is even better because I don't have to put on a brave face or pretend to be what people expect of me.

~

Anthony

Soon, Ivy's chest is rising and falling slowly and regularly. I quietly put a bottle of aspirin on the bathroom vanity next to her toothbrush, where she can't miss it, along with a sticky note on the mirror, *Take two with a glass of water,* with an arrow pointing down.

I start to exit her room, then stop to look at her. Her features are obscure in the dark, but she seems calm enough. Hopefully she won't have nightmares about Caleb. I wish I could go back and resume kicking his ass. He deserves it so bad, it's almost painful to exercise restraint.

Come on. You need sleep.

I leave, closing the door quietly after me, then walk down the hall until I bump into Father coming up from downstairs. He's an imposing grizzly bear of a man. There's a rough, almost crude quality to the way his facial features are cut, but that doesn't diminish his presence. His shirt strains to fit his broad shoulders and thickly muscled torso. His legs are long and powerful, and he moves like a man who knows exactly what he wants in life.

He pins me with bright green eyes. "Were you just in Ivy's room?"

"Yeah. Her ride ditched her, so I brought her home." That's the closest to the truth I can reveal. A promise not to tell Mother means not telling Father, either.

"And she"—he searches for a word—"required you to show her to her room?"

"No. I just thought it was the right thing to do."

He regards me. I do my best not to squirm under the paternal scrutiny.

"Son, if you care about your mother at all, you'll stay away from Ivy. She's incredibly attached to the girl. Kind of a substitute." Disapproval carves deep lines around Father's forehead and mouth. "And Ivy tries too hard to please Margot. She won't even do the silly things girls her age should be doing."

I think back to the party. "That might not be a bad thing."

"It cements Margot's attachment. It isn't healthy. When Ivy came here, your mother finally stopped crying, stopped mourning. I thought perhaps you'd be able to come back."

Father grows quiet, the silence louder than the words he won't say. But I don't need to hear them to know. Ivy might've stopped Mother from grieving, but Mother hasn't let go of her anger over losing Katherine.

Actually, it's far more disturbing than that. I saw a nature documentary once that featured a mother bird that lost its chick. She soon adopted another and treated it like her own, feeding it, teaching it how to fly, protecting it from predators. Ivy is like that—a substitute for Katherine, but not enough to help Mother make peace and move on.

"The TV feature was an excuse. They're just interviewing me," Father murmurs. "I want Margot to forgive you and welcome you back into the family. If she can do that, she can truly heal. So don't screw up, Tony."

I nod, my heart twisting painfully as I realize he hasn't said a warm word for me. It's all been about Mother.

But I have no right to object to the pangs I'm feeling. It's my fault she's the way she is.

6

Ivy

When I wake up, Tony is gone, the chair placed back neatly by the vanity. It's as though he was never in my room. My mouth feels like it's stuffed with cotton. I have a headache, but it isn't too bad, considering.

In the bathroom, there's a note pointing to a bottle of aspirin. *Tony*.

His thoughtfulness touches me. Although he can be a little abrupt and moody, he's a sweetheart underneath, trying to take care of people and do the right thing.

Grateful, I shake out two of the white pills and wash them down with a glass of water.

That done, I look at my reflection. My face isn't too terrible. A little puffy, but okay. I shower and carefully put on makeup to make myself look as normal as possible before going down to the dining room. The aspirin starts kicking in, making me feel like I didn't have that awful drink yesterday.

Tony is nowhere to be seen at breakfast. Only Harry's at

the table, his lean body clad in a gray T-shirt and cargo shorts. He yawns, then takes a huge swallow of his coffee. "Morning."

"Hi."

"How'd you like the party?"

I flinch as I take my seat, surprised he knows about the party. What else does he know? "Who told you I went?"

He gives me an odd look. "Uh, I asked if you wanted to go with me? Before practice yesterday? But you said you were going with Sue Ellen."

Oh, right. I totally forgot. "It was okay." I clear my throat, then grab a cup of coffee to give myself time. "A typical party." I concentrate on sipping the dark, fresh brew, hoping Harry will get the hint.

But his clue radar must be malfunctioning this morning. "It was, wasn't it? I thought Caleb would do better, but it sort of fizzled, especially toward the end... So blah..." He heaves a huge sigh. "By the way, did you see Tony there? He was looking for you."

I almost spit the coffee all over the table. I swallow, then cough a couple of times to clear my throat. "Yeah... We, uh, ran into each other."

"Oh, good. I was surprised to see him there. He said he wasn't interested when I asked."

"Where is he now?" Then I remember he must've stayed up pretty late. "Still sleeping?"

"Don't think so. I heard him moving around in his room on my way down. Why?"

I want to see him. I want to thank him for yesterday, and for the aspirin, and get to know him better. Of my three Blackwood cousins, he's the only one I don't know, and the one people avoid discussing. He's a fascinating mystery I want to solve to see what lies underneath. I can't forget the way he played Schubert so perfectly, then used those same hands to unleash such violence at the party. Which is the real Tony?

"Just wondering if he wants to practice Schubert with me," I lie. "He's going to be down soon, right?"

"Doubt it. He probably already ate. He's one of those early risers." Harry scrunches his face in distaste.

Well, maybe he did and maybe he didn't. Not everyone eats the second they get up. I linger over my French toast, drinking two glasses of grapefruit juice, until it becomes ridiculous. I go upstairs, then turn the opposite way at the top of the stairs to go to his room and knock loudly so Tony can't fail to hear me, no matter how huge his room is. I count to five. No answer.

Where did he go?

After grabbing my music and phone, I run into Jonas on the way down. "Have you seen Tony?"

"Not recently," he says.

"Did he have breakfast?"

"Yes."

I look up at Jonas, hoping he'll say more.

"Do you need something, Miss Ivy?"

I start to say no, but change my mind. "Is Tony home?"

Half a beat later, he says, "I'm not certain."

Jonas is lying through his teeth, even though his expression is placid and pleasant. He knows everything that happens under this roof.

I know it's no use calling him on it. Time for a different tactic.

I start to play Schubert extra loud. When only one part is being played, I always find it a bit disturbing—like looking at an unglazed donut. If Tony's in the house, he's going to hear it and come down to perform the *secondo*.

After only a couple of minutes, Jonas appears and stops me, saying that Aunt Margot has a headache. Foiled, I go to the digital piano in the other room, put on a headset and practice Liszt's *Liebestraum* instead.

Morning is normally my best time to work, but it's hard to focus today. I keep thinking about what Tatiana said about the music—the poem that inspired one of the sweetest and most poignant compositions ever.

O love, as long as love you can,
O love, as long as love you may,
The time will come, the time will come
When you will stand at the grave and mourn!

I CAN RECITE THE REST, BOTH IN ENGLISH AND THE original German. Tatiana says the poem is about mature, unconditional love, but it makes me think of my parents from time to time, and today is just that kind of day.

I hug myself. I'll never get to feel their arms around me or hear their voices again. And they were so young...

My parents' untimely death taught me that counting on tomorrow for something you want to do today is a terrible idea. But at the same time... I cast a brief glance at the ceiling. It's almost like Tony doesn't want to see me. And it's upsetting and puzzling.

I give up after a couple of hours. I'm not getting anything done when my head's not in the right space. I go to the kitchen for an early lunch of a turkey sandwich and a glass of pink lemonade, which I devour methodically one bite at a time, sitting at the marble counter.

Studying music taught me that any problem can be solved, any skill acquired, as long as you break it down into manageable chunks. Nobody masters Chopin overnight. You do it one note, one chord at a time, until you have your phrasing down, your interpretation down, your tempo perfect. And the mystery of Tony is no different. I'm probably just fascinated by him because he's tough to fathom—a challenge.

Yeah, right. It has absolutely nothing to do with how warm you were or how fast your heart was beating yesterday playing Schubert with him.

My phone buzzes on the countertop. It's a text from Yuna, who wants to Skype. I move to one of the reading rooms on the first floor and close the door behind me.

Yuna's small face fills the screen. Although we're the same age, she doesn't look a day over fifteen—large, wide-set eyes and a small, pert nose with a thin bridge. Her Cupid's bow mouth is naturally red, arresting against her pale skin and jet-black hair. Her long mane was dyed auburn when she first came to Curtis, but she got tired of dealing with dark roots and let it return to its natural black. She refuses to expose her skin to the sun, so she's always wearing long-sleeve tops, long pants and wide-brimmed hats together with vampire-level sunblock.

She and I are studying together with Tatiana, and there's nothing we haven't done in our attempt to "live" like Tatiana suggests, liberally interpreted to include sampling different types of scotch and watching porn in our two-bedroom apartment with a huge bowl of popcorn.

"You look great," I say.

"You look free," she says glumly. "My mom's trying to fatten me up, but also telling me I gained weight in the States! You should come join me so I have someone to talk to and hide behind!"

I smother a laugh. The nonsensical ways Yuna and her mom argue and show love to each other never fail to make me warm inside, even though a small part is envious of their close relationship. What would it be like to have my mom alive? She'd probably text me at random times reminding me to eat, shower, sleep, don't hang out with the wrong boys and so on. Like Yuna's mom does.

"You know you like it when she fusses," I say.

"It isn't just fussing. It's the whole showing off 'my sweet little daughter who's studying in America' that's driving me nuts. She took me to a party tonight, right? I was the only person there under forty. It was unbelievably dull, and I hated the way people asked me to play stuff they wanted to hear. I'm not a jukebox!"

I can't blame her mom for being proud, but I'm Yuna's best friend, so I owe her my support. "Shoulda asked them to feed you quarters."

"We don't use quarters in Korea, although asking for payment isn't a bad idea. So how's Louisiana? What are you working on?"

"Liszt's *Liebestraum* at the moment. You?"

"Nothing! Haven't touched a piano in two days, and I sound like dead dog poop." She seethes visibly. "I wanted to work on 'Mazeppa,' but when can I find the time? Mom's doing everything to show me on the social circuit. And Dad thinks if I get a boyfriend here, I won't go back to Curtis."

"Seriously? Who gives up Curtis for a boy?"

"I know, right?" Her face tightens with outrage. "But he never wanted me to go in the first place. He just got me the best teachers money could buy to humor me. He only let me audition at Curtis because he was sure I wouldn't get in. And it was the only conservatory I could apply to, because my parents weren't going to pay the tuition, not even a penny, and Curtis is the only place that teaches for free."

"Wow." I had no idea Yuna's family felt that way about her musical talent. She's one of the most gifted pianists I've ever met. My respect for her jumps a notch because she's succeeding in spite of unsupportive parents. I don't have to fight anyone to pursue music. As a matter of fact, Aunt Margot has been endlessly encouraging.

"Yeah. He wants to marry me off in a kind of corporate merger."

"What?" I couldn't have heard that right. A *merger?*

"Yeah. To cement a deal. You know, hook up with some heir to a suitable fortune."

"Do people still do that? Isn't that kind of...medieval?"

"Not in *chaebol* circles."

I know the word. It means a Korean conglomerate. Still, I can't decide if she's kidding. As far as I know, her family's filthy rich, and there's no reason for them to marry her off in some financial transaction. She should marry for nothing less than true love.

"Please tell me you're going to get Harry to visit you at Curtis," Yuna says.

"Huh? Why?"

"So I can marry *him*."

If I were drinking, I'd be spewing. Or choking. "You've never even met my cousin!"

She shrugs. "He's cute, so he'll do. Once I'm married, my parents will give up."

"That's crazy. Besides, there's always divorce or annulment."

"Ah, but divorcées aren't as desirable as unmarried young women."

Whoa. I stare at her, feeling like I've just traveled back in time. Like several centuries back.

"It has to be Harry. Middle sons are usually better than the youngest, but the youngest is still better than the oldest," Yuna adds, oblivious to my shock.

"I'm sorry, what?" She's speaking English, but I don't understand a word she's saying.

"I thought you knew this. Pay attention, because I'm about to tell you something every girl needs to know to find the perfect boyfriend and husband. The oldest in the family tends to be boring and serious. Oldest sons also marry to make the family happy, rather than doing what they want."

"Edgar is a little dry, but I don't think he's going to let his parents marry him off in a merger," I say, but Yuna isn't listening.

"The youngest ones have very little sense of responsibility, unless they're jealous of their older brothers." She pauses. "Harry isn't like that, is he?"

"Jealous of Edgar? Ha! No, nothing like that."

"Good. Then he won't try to outdo his older brother. The middles ones are the best—responsible, but also fun. Kind of a compromise."

"I don't know if Tony's a compro—"

"Who?"

"Tony. The middle cousin. Or brother."

Yuna gives an outraged cry. "You've been holding out on me! You never said there was a third one. The most perfect middle one."

I puff out a breath, torn between wanting to shake her and wanting to hug her. She gets like this only when she's frustrated, angry or just a tad panicked. "Tony is only twenty-one. He's not marrying anybody. And he might have a girlfriend." The second the words slip out, my mood plummets. I never considered the possibility he could be dating someone. But why not? He's handsome, accomplished and smart. Girls must flock to him.

"Send me some pics anyway," Yuna says decisively.

"Can't."

"Don't be stingy."

"It's not that. I don't have any."

Yuna pauses for a second. "Seriously? Not even a snapshot from a vacation or something?"

I shake my head.

"That's weird. You have lots of photos of Harry and Edgar. Why not Tony?"

"He doesn't live here." But it occurs to me that I've never seen a picture of Tony anywhere in the house, not even one from his childhood, when he *was* still living in Tempérane. He's been such a mystery, I didn't even know what he looked like until yesterday.

Or maybe Aunt Margot and Uncle Lane did what they could to erase Tony's presence in the house...and family. Harry made it clear after our Schubert practice that Tony and Margot have some issues.

Oh no. Tony. Please let my assumption be wrong. Maybe all his photos burned in a fire or got lost in a flood or something. Maybe his parents just missed him too much to talk about him.

"Well, if you don't have a picture, tell me about him. What's he like?" Yuna sounds more rational now, rather than in "I gotta marry somebody to get my dad off my back" mode.

"He's kind of contradictory. Can be rude...but also nice and protective." I tell her about what happened in the piano room and at the party.

She gasps when I get to the drinking part. "What kind of jerk is that Caleb? Oh my God, don't ever drink *poktahnju*!"

"What?"

"The thing he gave you—the mix of beer and soju. That'll take out even the strongest drinker. Like my cousin. She can handle bottles and bottles of soju, straight, no problem. Her liver is indestructible. But three *poktahnju*, she's out like a boxer who got punched in the face. Doesn't remember anything that happened later, either."

What a dick. Caleb made the drink sound harmless. But he must've known what would happen when he offered it to me. I doubt anything he did yesterday was innocent or without an ulterior motive. *Asshole.* Knowing what that particular mixture can do adds an extra-sinister layer to him. Now I wish I'd waited until Tony kicked him a couple more times before stopping him.

"Tell me Tony beat the crap out of that guy," Yuna demands.

"He did." I give her the rest of the story.

"Good!" We keep chatting, but after a while, Yuna starts yawning.

"What time is it there?" I ask.

"Almost two. In the morning."

"You need to get some sleep!" She usually doesn't stay up past midnight.

"I know." She yawns again, her mouth so wide I think I hear her jaw creak. "Still, it's good to talk to you, Ivy. Nobody gets me the way you do." She smiles. "I'm feeling much better."

"That's what best friends are for. Glad I could cheer you up."

"Next time, you're coming with me to Seoul. Promise me."

"I promise."

"Okay." She nods once regally. "Good night. Or, uh, afternoon."

"Sweet dreams."

I hang up and leave the room, thinking about things. What if Tony's been disowned?

But if he were, he wouldn't have been able to come home...right?

On the way back to my room, I walk past the small meeting den. It's a cozy space with four chairs and a round table in the middle. It doesn't have a door, and Aunt Margot and Uncle Lane usually use it for casual, non-business conversations.

I hear voices, and stop when I realize it's *Caleb's mother* in there with Aunt Margot. Hiding behind a wall, I sneak a peek at their *tête-à-tête*.

Mrs. Wentworth's features remind me of a rodent: small eyes set closely together, nose pointy and a tight mouth with two remarkably large front teeth. The short brown hair on her head is coarse and dull, and no amount of foundation can hide the florid undertone of her skin. The neon lime green of her sleeveless dress doesn't do a thing to flatter her complexion.

"Sorry I'm late," she's saying. "I spent most of the morning trying to convince Caleb to go to the hospital, but that boy is just as stubborn as a mule with arthritis."

I almost sneer. Of course he doesn't want to go. How's he going to explain his injuries to a doctor? *I sexually assaulted a girl and got my ass kicked by her cousin?*

"Is he all right?" Aunt Margot asks. "What happened?"

"Oh, he got into a fight over some girl. Silly." Mrs. Wentworth sighs, half embarrassed and half annoyed. "But what can you do? Boys will be boys."

My lips press together. That dismissive "boys will be boys" attitude is why guys like Caleb exist.

"A fight? She must really be something," Aunt Margot says in a gracious, indulgent tone.

"I don't know. I tell him to be careful, getting involved with girls who don't deserve him, but you know Caleb. Always thinking with that big, soft heart of his."

Indignation and outrage burst in my chest, especially after Yuna told me what Caleb really meant to do with the drink. Before I can stop myself, I jump into the den. "There's nothing soft about Caleb's heart," I say, bristling. "If he even has one."

Shock erupts on Mrs. Wentworth's face. Aunt Margot turns to me, her jaw slack. "Ivy, what on earth...?"

"I don't know what he's telling everyone, but it's all lies." I go over what happened, including how he deliberately tried to get me to have a drink known to knock people out fast, how he forced a kiss and groped me. "If it weren't for Tony, believe me, Caleb wouldn't have stopped there."

Mrs. Wentworth turns bright red. "That's a lie! Caleb isn't like that!"

"Really? Why don't you ask him? He ripped the black and white dress Aunt Margot bought for my competition last year."

She's visibly shaking. Aunt Margot's eyes flash with fury and something else I can't quite put my finger on. She turns to Mrs. Wentworth. "Belinda, I think you should leave," she says, her voice unnaturally calm.

"Margot! You don't really believe this? Whenever a girl feels bad about what she did at a party, she claims she was 'forced' to make herself feel better!"

I take a step toward her, furious. No wonder Caleb is such an asshole.

Aunt Margot's terrible voice stops me. "What I don't believe is that insinuations about my niece are the way to go here."

Mrs. Wentworth pulls her lips in, but her face is red and her cheeks are puffy, like she's barely restraining herself.

"I also don't believe we can continue discussing the fundraiser right now, do you?" Aunt Margot says, her voice as smooth as ice.

After shooting me a death glare, Mrs. Wentworth gathers some brochures from the table and storms out. As she passes by, she mutters, "Little bitch. That sister killer didn't do it for *you*."

I inhale sharply, wondering if I misheard. But there's no doubt about the vicious glitter in her eyes. She didn't speak loud enough for her words to reach Aunt Margot. Not many people in this town want to make an enemy of my aunt. And Joel Wentworth in particular needs the Blackwood family's support if he wants to remain sheriff of Tempérane.

Jonas materializes and escorts Mrs. Wentworth out. I

clench my hands around my sheet music, loathing all the things she said.

Finally, Aunt Margot says, "Ivy," and gestures for me to sit down, her face unreadable.

I take a seat and wait, biting my lower lip. Being under her unblinking gaze is almost worse than being told I was lazy by my first piano teacher because I half-assed my practice sessions. It takes an effort not to squirm.

"Why didn't you say something?" Aunt Margot asks quietly, her tone devoid of accusation or anger.

"I did. Just now." I clear my throat. "The earliest chance I got."

She says nothing, but stares like she's seeing through me.

"I just want you to know Tony's a hero. He saved me," I say, trying to deflect her a little and also wanting her to know how awesome Tony was.

Instead of looking proud, she looks conflicted. "Did he?"

"Yes. It would've been terrible without him."

She looks away briefly, seeing something beyond the wall. "Wasn't Harry there?"

"Yes," I say, hoping I'm not getting him into trouble by admitting that.

"He should've looked after you."

"But he didn't know I went," I fib, suddenly worried she might be angry with Harry. It isn't his job to be my chaperone. Since I want Aunt Margot to focus on how Tony protected me, I add, "Besides, Tony—"

She raises an elegant hand, then stands. "I'm very happy you're okay, Ivy. I don't know what I would've done if..." She pauses to inhale shakily. "I'm tired. I think I'll go rest. Excuse me."

Then she walks briskly away. If I didn't know better, I'd think she was fleeing...from the fact that her son Tony did something heroic and good.

7

Anthony

I spend the entire morning at the gym and grab a sandwich before going home. I'd like to stay out longer, but there are only so many weights you can lift, and only so many things to do in a town as small as Tempérane. The movie theater shut down a couple years ago, and the few coffee shops seem uninspired after Europe. I'm too old to hang out at the mall.

Not to mention the attention I draw just by being who I am. People's curious gazes weigh me down the entire time I'm out. None of them approach, of course. After a while, I feel like yelling, "What? Just say what you want to say!"

But I don't. It would embarrass Mother, and people would make sure she heard. So I go home.

As I walk out of the garage, gym bag slung over one shoulder, I come close to running smack into Mrs. Wentworth. She's leaving the house, her strides short and tense. There is a palpable indignation around her, like a cat popped on its nose with a rolled-up newspaper.

She stops just short of a collision, then pulls her shoulders back, chin jutting forward aggressively. Her squinty eyes glare into mine as she spits, "*Animal.*"

My gut tightens. I deserve the epithet...but not from her. Then I remember Caleb.

"So, did the little weasel go crying to his mama? I hit him a lot less than I should have."

Her cheeks turn bright red, and she straightens her spine further, her mouth tight. I wait, wondering what she'll say to defend her wannabe rapist son.

"*Murderer.*"

The word spears my heart, and I can't draw in air for the searing pain. She smirks and strides off.

I can't move. It's all I can do to stand there, shaking with shame, anger and grief. Mrs. Wentworth is one of the few people who know the real reason my parents sent me away.

It was a mistake—an accident! I'm not a murderer!

The protest sticks in my throat like it always does as my mind conjures up all the ways I could've prevented it. Guilt and shame over my failure keep me rooted to the spot, unmoving, until one of our gardeners walks by and says hello.

I manage a thick-voiced greeting, then hurry inside, my eyes unseeing. The air-conditioned coolness gives me goosebumps.

"Tony?"

I blink, focus, and see Ivy peering at me. Her eyes are clear, no hint of yesterday's drinking, and she looks as fresh as a hothouse rosebud. Her aquamarine dress is modest, but shows hints of the soft curves and swells underneath.

"Ivy."

As I say her name, Father's warning reverberates through my head. I can't stay too close to her. Everything should be about making Mother happy. Giving her a reason to forgive me. Making what's left of my family whole again.

"Excuse me," I say in a cold but civil tone, and go to my room, my strides long and rapid.

"Tony!" Ivy calls out.

I don't look back. I can't.

The second I'm in my room, I dump the gym bag and go to the en suite bathroom to splash cold water on my face. My hands clench the edge of the vanity, and my shoulders tighten, making the muscles bunch around my neck. I stare at myself in the mirror, water dripping from my face.

You're a hero. You saved me.

Animal. Murderer.

Are you here to take her away the way you did Katherine?

Cold dread threads its way through my gut and into my heavy heart. I can't remember the last time someone looked at me like I was worth something—a hero. But the only reason Ivy thinks that is because she doesn't know.

The damnedest thing is that I never want her to. I want her to stay unaware of the awful past so I'll always have at least one person who thinks I'm okay.

I can hear Schubert's Fantasie. Only the *primo*, though. It's way louder than it should be. Doesn't Ivy know what "piano" and "pianissimo" mean?

I run a towel over my face, waiting for Harry to join her.

But he doesn't. Maybe he feels embarrassed after yesterday. If so, it's a damn inconvenient time for my brash brother to finally learn some humility.

Ivy finishes the entire first movement. I let out a breath. My teeth grind together when she starts in again.

I know what she's up to. This is her revenge because I ignored her downstairs. It certainly isn't practice. She's playing the part perfectly, albeit too loudly. She's doing this to get me to come down to play the *secondo* because the piece isn't complete without it, and it grates like karaoke with no singer. Even now, despite my best intentions, my fingers are twitching, mimicking playing the *secondo.*

She's been at Curtis for three years. She can play Schubert all afternoon long, no problem. It isn't uncommon for students at famous conservatories to practice for hours a day.

Fine. I'll go and play the damned *secondo.* But only because I hate the incompleteness of the piece, not because I want to sit next to her on the bench and have our limbs brushing and fingers touching.

By the time I reach the piano room, she's almost done with her first repeat. I open the door and admire her for a moment, my heart beating faster. The light pouring in from outside creates a strawberry-blond halo out of her unbound hair, and she shines like the sun—her skin glowing, eyes shimmering and rosy lips in a soft line.

Patient. Confident. Alluring. She's a force of nature, drawing me as irresistibly as a planet's gravity. And I can't lie about how I feel. I want her. Like she's a last sip of water before I'm banished into a desert. Even though I know how impossible it will be to have her. The situation we're in—that she's related to my family, however distantly, that we didn't meet under different circumstances (in Europe, perhaps) where nobody would care if I wanted her, where she could stay ignorant of my past forever—slides into my gut like a shiv.

Inhaling deeply to calm my roiling emotions, I take the empty space on the bench next to her and start the *secondo* without asking her to start over. Ivy doesn't look at me, but I can sense her smile. And she finally starts hitting her notes without trying to deafen everyone in the house.

"I knew you'd help me practice," she says.

"I don't care for the incompleteness. Or the entire piece played in fortissimo."

"I know." Her voice is quiet over a pianissimo passage. "Thanks for the aspirin."

"You're welcome."

"I ended up telling Aunt Margot what you did yesterday."

Tension grips my neck and shoulders, and I almost mess up a chord. "I thought you wanted to keep the whole thing quiet."

"I did, but Mrs. Wentworth showed up. I couldn't help myself."

I think two things simultaneously: *So that explains it* and *Shit.* "What did Mother say?"

"She asked Mrs. Wentworth to leave. I let Aunt Margot know you saved me. And what you saved me *from.* I didn't want her to think you got into a fight with Caleb over nothing."

"Ivy, no." Mother isn't angry with me for not saving girls. She's angry because I didn't save one particular girl. "It doesn't matter what Mrs. Wentworth said or made Mother think. You weren't going to tell Mother, so you shouldn't have done it, not for me."

"Why not? Don't you want your mom to know you're not a troublemaker?"

I almost laugh at the word. If I were only a *troublemaker*, Mother would've forgiven me years ago. "How do you know I'm not a troublemaker? Or an asshole?"

"Because, um, you aren't? I mean, the way you treated me..." She clears her throat. "You can be abrupt, even rude, but you saved me and took care of me. So, I think you're a good guy, even though you obviously hate being seen that way. It's like you're clinging to a bad-boy rep or something."

This time, I laugh. What gave her this crazy idea? "Bad-boy rep?"

She nods. "But you're not. It's like, you could be kissing me, but if I asked you to stop, you would. Because you're that kind of guy."

She's so earnest, so convinced. I stare at her face—the gentle profile and the clear eyes that seem to be deeper and more beautiful than an alpine lake in winter. And she's making me want things I shouldn't...making me want to believe I'm worthy.

I have to put a stop to this before I get stupid. I have to show her she's being a fool.

Putting on a cocky smirk, I tilt my head. "Want to put that to the test?" Most people say things easily enough, but back off when they have to put their money where their mouth is. I'm betting Ivy will do the same. She's a smart girl.

"Okay." She blinks once, slowly. "Go for it." The angle of her chin is a dare.

Damn. Now the ball's in my court, and I can't avoid or ignore it. I stare at her siren's mouth. A rough, punishing kiss would be fitting, make her regret challenging me. Except I can't bring myself to do it. I want her to like the feel of my lips on hers. I want her to enjoy the kiss, find such pleasure in it that it'll kill her to ask me to stop. And whatever she asks, I'm going to do the exact opposite, just to make my point.

That's the price she should pay for saying I'm a good guy.

Wrapping a hand around her long, silken hair, I brush my lips against hers.

She goes still as a statue, her breath tickling my face. My tongue flicks across her mouth. I tug gently at her lower lip, seeking entry.

A small shudder runs through her. She parts her mouth, and the flavor and feel of her flood my senses—so sweet, lush and soft. I swear she tastes like cherries and caramel. No, better. More addictive and sweeter, disarming me, making me forget what the hell I was trying to do with the kiss in the first place.

Her delicate response reins me in. My lips, tongue and

teeth move over hers with a tenderness I've never shown anybody, but I'm helpless to do anything else.

She tilts her head so we can fit better. Her tongue strokes across my mouth teasingly, stoking my desire until my whole body feels tight and hard. I deepen our kiss, devouring her. She's everything I want. Moaning softly in her throat, she arches until her breasts press against my chest.

"Tony..."

I know exactly what she wants. Our mouths still fused, I move my hand to cup her breast.

She murmurs, "Don't stop..." against my lips. The two words penetrate my lusty haze, hit me like a bucket of ice-water, and everything inside me stills.

This isn't what I was expecting. She was supposed to tell me to stop, then call me a bastard when I didn't. She was supposed to stay away from me afterward, and never say anything in my defense.

I tear away, since I promised myself I would do the exact opposite of what she asked. But even without the promise, I would've done it. My reaction stuns me. I've never given myself so completely over to a kiss. Ever.

Her cherry and caramel taste lingers on my lips, making me want more. I'm already swaying toward her, craving her with an intensity that leaves me breathless.

Hell.

I run the back of my hand over my mouth to erase her taste. If I don't, I'm going to do something I'll really regret. Like continuing the way she asked me to.

Her gray eyes wide pools, she watches me wipe my mouth. Her chin begins to tremble.

I won't be able to stand it if she cries. So I exhale and say, "Did that prove your point?" in a tone designed to annoy her.

She doesn't answer, but thankfully, the trembling stops and her eyes flash with a hint of temper.

I stand up, my motions measured, then walk away, my skin hot and prickling. I need to get away from her. *Now.*

Restless lust churns inside me. I move toward the front entrance. I need to go see if Dalton still owns his boxing gym so I can work off some energy.

Jonas is standing in front of the entrance and—amazingly—doesn't move when I approach.

"What is it?" I ask, my tone curt. Normally, I would never talk to him that way, but I need to get the hell out of here.

"Dinner will be served at six sharp," he says. "Formal attire."

A formal dinner means a six-course meal. "Any guests?"

"Just family. In honor of your return."

My mouth dries. This is a big fucking deal. Maybe the break I've been looking for. I glance at my watch. It's a quarter to four. "Got it."

"Your mother... She's grown very fond of white orchids," Jonas adds quietly.

"Thanks."

Without his advice, I would've gotten her magenta carnations, which she loved when I was a little boy. Guess a lot of things have changed in the last nine years, not that I would know. I sent her so many letters. All of them were returned, unread.

The heaviness in my heart eases a bit. Perhaps Mother's finally decided to absolve me, if she's willing to host a formal dinner. I need to know if I'm forgiven for what I've done.

Without her forgiveness, I'll never be able to forgive myself.

8

Ivy

I RETURN TO MY BEDROOM, MY CONCENTRATION SHOT. The only thing I can think of is that kiss.

He devoured my mouth like it was the most delicious morsel, his tongue stroking mine. I get why he pushed me back when I asked him not to stop. He's trying to make a point because, for some bizarre reason, he has this warped idea he's a bad guy.

But then he *wiped his mouth,* like I was something gross. The whole time, his gaze never wavered. It's like he wants me to feel undesirable and unwanted.

Bastard. My hands clench tightly, and for the first time, I actually feel an urge to punch something. I loved what he did, the heat he made me feel, making me forget all the fumbling kisses I've had before. I thought he felt the same way. Or at least he liked it from the way he ravished my mouth.

Why is he being so mean? Did I do something to upset him? Is it because I defended him to Mrs. Wentworth? Or because I did it front of his mom? Or that I teased him about hanging on to his bad-boy rep? I only wanted to make him smile and realize how silly he was being, trying to make me think he's so much worse than he is.

Throwing myself on the bed, I think back over what happened. He was okay when I thanked him for the aspirin. He only tensed up when I said I told that horrible woman what really happened at Caleb's party, and his mother heard it.

That's it! He was upset his mom knew...

Suddenly I realize he always calls his parents "Mother" and "Father," while his brothers don't. Why so formal? Why the distance?

It's like pieces of a puzzle are missing. I gaze at the ceiling, letting my mind relax, and two words float up...

Sister killer.

Mrs. Wentworth didn't say it loud enough for Aunt Margot to hear, but she definitely wanted me to. Is Tony worried she might announce it publicly and upset his mom? Katherine is a delicate topic in this household. When I first arrived, Jonas warned me not to mention Katherine, ever, lest it upset my aunt. And it's true. Nobody talks about her in Aunt Margot's presence.

But over the years, I've pieced together some facts. Katherine died in a hunting accident when she was six. She wandered off into the woods, and a hunter shot her by accident. She was in a fawn-colored top and brown pants. The deputy sheriff decided it was an unfortunate mistake, but not a crime.

But somehow Mrs. Wentworth thought she could call Tony a sister killer. And her husband has been the sheriff of Tempérane since forever.

What does she know?

I pull out my phone and start typing. I spend the next hour

lying on my bed and poring over Google results for articles or mentions of the death of Katherine Blackwood. If it later came out that Tony was the one who really killed Katherine, there should be some coverage...some mention somewhere.

But no. Nothing.

So why did Mrs. Wentworth say that? He was only twelve at the time. The man who shot her was twenty-six and from Birmingham, Alabama. It's clear Tony didn't pull the trigger.

What could it have been? He wouldn't have dressed his sister in the outfit; it isn't the kind of a thing a boy his age would've done. Was he somehow was responsible for her going along on the hunting trip?

I wish I could ask someone who was here when it happened, but I can't just walk up and say, "Hey, how did Katherine really die?" Jonas probably knows—the man knows everything about my aunt's family—but he's so tight-lipped that it'd be easier to chip an answer out of a statue. Harry was too young to know, and I don't feel comfortable approaching Uncle Lane or Edgar. It might still be too painful for them to talk about.

My phone buzzes, pulling me out of my thoughts.

So. Are you okay? Mom caught me sneaking in and got all pissed off. Like having a few drinks is a big deal.

I stare at the text. *Sue Ellen.* What makes her think we're still okay? She stood by while Caleb attacked me. Apparently helping a friend ranks lower than whatever she thought she'd get waiting by the door like Caleb and his buddies wanted. And this tone-deaf text isn't going to help me forgive her.

I start to type, ready to give her a piece of my mind, but end up deleting the text. No response could be sufficient. Calling her a bitch would be anemic, but text-ranting until my fingers fall off isn't the way to go either.

Honestly, I can't even. If she's expecting sympathy over

her mom getting mad at her... I hope she's not holding her breath. Asphyxiation is a crappy way to go.

The clock says it's already five thirty. I need to change if I want to be presentable for dinner.

Tossing the phone on the bed, I walk into the closet and pull out my lucky dress. It's ivory, sleeveless, with a modest square neckline, and ends two inches above my knees. It's made of two layers; the bottom one is almost sheer, while the top one is all intricate lace. Aunt Margot bought it for me when I started auditioning. Every time I wore it, I killed. She told me it wasn't the dress, but the confidence a good outfit inspired. She was so proud of me, her entire face glowing. It's one of many, many times I felt unconditionally loved by her.

I need that confidence now. Realizing that someone's not really your friend, and that the guy who rocked your world with a kiss wasn't all that into it, can really mess with your mind. It makes you wonder about your judgment and desirability.

9

Anthony

There are two good ways to go when I want to stop thinking. One: drink until I pass out. Two: exert myself until I'm too tired to think.

Option One is out of the question. It makes me lose control, and the hangovers aren't pleasant. Besides, I'm here to see if I can mend my fences with Mom, not to embarrass her by getting roaring drunk before six p.m.

So it's option two, another round of physical exertion. Thankfully, there's a perfect place for that—a boxing gym over in the next parish. It's a utilitarian space with harsh fluorescent lighting, punching bags, a couple of rings and a locker room that smells faintly of old sweat and liniment. There are only three concrete slab showers, but they're clean. Dalton, the owner, might not spend money on frills, but he takes pride in his business. And he was nice as hell to me—patient, too—when I first came here as a wide-eyed ten-year-old, trying to learn how to throw a decent punch.

After taping up my hands and donning some gloves, I work a heavy bag until my shoulders burn and air is sawing in and out of my lungs. Despite the cold air blasting, sweat is pouring down my body in rivulets. When I can't lift my arms anymore, I let myself collapse, legs stretched out on the cool concrete floor.

But no matter how exhausted my body is, my mind keeps bringing Ivy up. *Troublemaker. Bad-boy rep.* She's acting as though I'm some misguided idiot, trying too hard to look cool.

Although I hate that she's so deluded, I'm glad she doesn't know the truth. That way, she won't recoil in horror every time she sees me. She seems too honest and guileless to hide her true reaction if she knew.

"Need some help getting up?" Dalton has a permanent squint, like Dirty Harry eyeing a scumbag.

"No, I'm fine."

"Glad to hear it. I had that extra-soft cement laid in there just for you."

Good old Dalton. I heave myself up and trudge over to the shower. The workout took the sharpest edge off my sexual frustration and restlessness. Now I need to stop thinking about Ivy and focus on the dinner to come. There's a chance it might result in Mother softening toward me, realizing maybe I should be forgiven after all these years. Katherine's death hurt her to the point that Father had to send me away, hoping my absence could help her recover. I guess it did...somewhat. It's a special kind of hell, trying to go on while knowing you're the reason your perfect family fell apart.

On my way home, I pick up a large bouquet of pristine white orchids. Then I change into a black suit with a tie and a crisp white dress shirt—*de rigueur* for one of Mother's formal dinners. My hands shake a little as I knot the tie. She taught me how when I was eight.

"Every little gentleman should know how to tie a perfect

Windsor knot," she said, her voice warm, her smile so radiant it felt like the whole world was awash with love. "Let me help you." Her slim fingers moved, showing me how to loop, pull and tug until the knot was done perfectly.

"Like this?" I said, showing her.

"Yes! My, what a smart, clever boy you are!" She cradled my face in her palms, kissed my forehead and rubbed her nose against mine, making me laugh.

Her cheeks used to glow with health and joy. Now, having seen her, it strikes me that she's pale, rarely smiles, and even when she does, the smiles never reach her eyes. Father said Mother needs to forgive me in order to heal, and I suspect he's correct. He usually is about Mother. And I want her to be able to feel the joy and happiness she used to. I want both of us to be light and happy and free from the painful past.

I time things so I arrive exactly two minutes before six. My parents enter the formal dining room together at precisely six. Father's in a suit, and Mother is in a sleeveless floor-length wrap dress in deep royal blue. Her hand rests in the crook of his elbow, sapphires and pearls around her neck and wrist.

"Mother," I say, my mouth dry. I search her face for any sign of the panicked anger and accusation from yesterday.

"Tony," she says, looking at me. Her expression is blank.

Well, blank is better than yesterday—a vast improvement, I tell myself. Hopefully by the end of the dinner, she'll warm up to me a bit more. Even hold my face between her hands and forgive me.

"For you." I hand her the flowers, praying they help bridge the distance between us.

A faint smile ghosts her lips. "Thank you."

The fist around my heart eases a little. This has to be a good sign.

I start to step forward to give her a kiss on cheek, but Harry and Ivy's arrival distracts Mother, who turns away to greet them. Father gives me a fractional nod over her shoulder, and I nod back, my belly full of nervous hope.

Dinner starts as soon as we're seated. I'm sitting on my father's right, while the seat next to Mother stays empty.

Harry taps an index finger on the table. "Is Edgar coming?"

"He called. Going to be a few minutes late," Father says.

"Must be busy at work," Ivy says.

She looks so innocent and beautiful in her lace dress, not to mention entirely too composed as she glances in my direction. It's as though the kiss never happened...and she never moaned my name with a voice thick with need.

It pisses me off for some reason.

Keeping my face calm, I merely drink iced tea so sugary, it feels like my teeth are rotting. This dinner isn't about Ivy. It's about Mother.

There aren't any mushrooms on the menu...which is odd, since Mother's very fond of them. I comment on it, hoping she'll notice I still remember the small details.

"We don't eat them anymore," Mother says. "Ivy's allergic."

So Mother just gave them up altogether? I glance at Ivy, who squirms. Father wasn't exaggerating when he told me how much she means to Mother. Hell, he might've understated things.

"Nothing life-threatening," Ivy explains. "Just some itchiness."

"It's always important to be careful," Mother says smoothly. "You never know when some mild allergy could turn deadly. After all, seemingly harmless things can be more fatal than overtly dangerous ones."

I suck in a breath. Suddenly the small hopes I've had look smaller...even pitiable. My hands clench and unclench around utensils as I try to calm the self-loathing swelling in my chest.

Harry glances at me, concerned. Ivy is studying me as well. Father is pretending he heard nothing. So long as Mother doesn't become physically violent, he won't object or interfere.

On cue, the amuse-bouche and soup are served. The dining room descends into silence except for the sound of silverware and china clinking. Edgar finally arrives to take his seat. Unlike me and Harry, Edgar takes after Father one hundred percent, face and body. Since graduating from Harvard, he's been working in the family business.

He smiles. "Great to have you home, Tony. Does this mean you'll be joining me in the salt mines?" He winks good-naturedly, trying a little too hard to act like everything's normal.

If it were under any other circumstances... If Mother forgives me, then it's only logical I join the business. Blackwood Energy is privately held, and the family has always run it, ever since its founding.

My gaze slides to Mother briefly, searching for a sign that she won't mind me joining the company, but all I find is blankness. "Well, I—"

"Such a dry topic for dinner," Mother chides, her tone mild.

"Of course," I say. "What would you like to talk about?"

She regards me for a moment, then smiles vaguely. "You've been away for so long you probably haven't heard what's going on in the family. Did you know Ivy is studying at Curtis? It's one of the best conservatories in the world. Harder to gain admission there than to an Ivy League school. Not even five percent of the students who apply can get in, and those who do receive full scholarships. And Ivy got accepted when she was only fifteen." She beams at Ivy. "I couldn't be prouder." She turns to Father. "Don't you agree, dear?"

"Of course. A remarkable achievement." Father smiles, but I have a feeling he doesn't care one way or the other about

Ivy's "achievement." As long as she's doing something to put a smile on Mother's face—even if it doesn't quite reach her eyes—he's satisfied.

Her lips pulled in, Ivy looks down at her plate.

"What are your plans, Tony?" Father asks me after a few moments of silence.

"You must've studied hard to graduate from Princeton in three years," Edgar adds, doing his part to highlight my accomplishments, although I don't think he's picked the right one. Still, I'm grateful. One of the first to defend me nine years ago, he's been trying his best to reconcile me with Mother. Harry's too young to remember everything clearly, but as the eldest, Edgar knows the toll the painful past has exacted from all of us.

"I only wanted to make you proud," I say, my eyes on Mother, praying for some kind of reaction from her, hopefully something positive and warm.

She sips her wine, then studies her salad fork. "I am proud. I didn't expect you to come back after you left for Europe."

A hard lump sticks in my throat at her choice of words. I never wanted to leave. I wanted to stay and earn her forgiveness. But when Father told me it would be best for everyone if I left...

It upsets your mother too much every time she sees you. I can't hold this family together as long as you're around.

Acid floods my belly. Mother is like a field of landmines. One wrong step, and everything I've done will go up in flames.

Harry starts telling a funny story I can't process through the fucked-up concoction of desperation, remorse, anguish and frustration I'm feeling. It makes me wish I were anywhere but here...or better yet, had taken Katherine's place nine years ago. I don't register the rest of the dinner—what we eat, drink or talk about. I laugh when everyone laughs, shut up when everyone grows quiet. Only when dessert is served do I notice that Ivy's watching me, her eyes worried.

Fuck. I don't need her pity.

I shoot her a sharp look, then polish off the chocolate mousse on my plate.

"Tony, why don't you sing one for us?" Edgar says.

It's like the proverbial bolt from the blue. "What?"

"We were talking about a performance we saw on a skiing trip to Switzerland two years ago," Harry mutters. "You nodded when Ivy said she'd love to hear it and if anybody knew the songs."

"Ah. Sure," I say, pasting on a smile, chagrined that I completely lost track of the conversation. What an impression I must be making.

"We only want you to sing if you still have the voice," Harry adds jokingly.

"I enjoyed the folk songs in Switzerland," Mother says, a hint of life in her tone. "It'd be silly to go back just for the songs, though."

"I'd be happy to sing one for you," I say. She loves music. Maybe my performance will remind her how she used to enjoy listening to me play the piano and sing. Maybe giving her some musical pleasure will make her realize I'm not such a terrible monster.

We move to the room with the baby grand. I wait until everyone sits down. Only then do I flex my fingers and play a sweet folk song I learned in Switzerland, singing the words in German. I hit all the notes perfectly, my baritone voice soaring effortlessly. I pour all my longing and love into the music, hoping Mother will notice and finally give me the absolution she hasn't deemed me worthy of for the past nine years.

I want to be home. I want all of us to be happy...as much as we can without Katherine. I want to be able to live without the crippling weight of guilt.

When I'm done, I stand and take a tentative bow. Everyone claps except for Mother.

She lets out a soft sigh. "That's excellent, son."

Son. Hope and yearning twine around my heart. My pulse accelerates. Am I forgiven?

She stands. "I'm exhausted. I think I'll go to bed early."

I reach over and start to lean closer to give her a goodnight kiss.

Before my lips can touch her cheek, she takes a small step back and places a hand on my jaw. "Good night," she murmurs, not meeting my eyes.

She and Father walk out together. I stand there, my hands clenched tight. It's all I can do not to smash the fucking piano.

Edgar pats my shoulder. "Mom's trying," he says quietly. "Give her time."

I've taken something from her that can never be replaced—and left a hole in her heart that can never be filled. So perhaps I deserve to lose her love and suffer, but that doesn't make my disappointment any less bitter.

10

Ivy

The bedside clock reads one twenty-six. Sighing, I stare up into the dark.

I'm really tired, but Tony's face at the dinner haunts me. He was trying so hard to appear stoic and strong, but I saw the tiny tremor in his mouth and chin before he clenched his jaw.

I wanted to reach out to him, but I held back, afraid he wouldn't react well. People as proud as Tony hate to show vulnerability, preferring to lick their wounds in private. I know because I'm like that, too. But now I wish I'd given him a hug. Or maybe a quick squeeze of his hand before I left. No matter how proud or strong, everyone needs comfort when they're hurting.

It's obvious he adores Aunt Margot and wants nothing more than her acceptance and love. But she ignored him more or less all evening long without being overtly rude, only because that's beneath her. It's like...she isn't even proud of him. Like she wishes he were anywhere but here, under the same roof.

If I thought she was incapable of being loving or sweet, I'd just feel bad for Tony, but that isn't the case. The harder I work, the more I accomplish, the prouder and happier she is with me. She's never been stingy with praise, and she shows a lot of physical affection, too. The only thing Tony wanted was a kiss on her cheek after he sang for us so brilliantly, but she wouldn't even give him that.

I've always admired Aunt Margot and thought she could do no wrong. But today... I almost hate her for being so cruel to her own son and wish she'd given him even a quarter of the love she's lavished on me. She has to know what he wants and is purposely withholding it to torment him. I saw the cruel light in her gaze when she thought nobody was looking. She was feeding off his misery.

But why? Any mother would be proud of a son like Tony—tall, handsome, intelligent, educated, polite...

I turn and settle on my side, then give up and climb out of bed. I'm not getting any sleep at this rate.

I pad downstairs to the small room in the back. Aunt Margot bought a digital piano for me when I was in middle school, so I could practice with the headphones on and not bother anybody. Some finger exercises by Hanon should help. Hanon is always meditative.

I push the door open. It moves soundlessly on well-oiled hinges. I start to go inside, the room lit only by tonight's half-moon. His back to the door, Tony is at the piano, playing a hauntingly melancholy melody. The volume is set so low, it's barely audible. An open bottle of hard liquor sits on the piano, more than half empty, and he swigs it before continuing.

I bite my lip. The moment is too private for me to intrude, but I can't help but worry about him. There's nothing capable or controlled about the way he's sitting at the piano. Not even a hint of the cocky guy he was before kissing me. He looks so... desolate. Broken. If I were just a little braver, I'd reach out and touch him.

He's upset enough to be drinking. Let him be.

I bite my lip, but finally decide to retreat. However, to my embarrassment, my slippers squeak a little on the floor as I start to turn back.

"You can laugh. It's fine." Tony's words are slightly slurred. "I was pathetic...*am* pathetic."

"No, you aren't."

"Should've never come back to Tempérane," he continues. "Should've known better." He stands up, his fist tight around the neck of the bottle, and takes another long swallow. "Should've known I'll never be able to make up for what I took from her." He sways. "Should've been the one who died."

"*Tony*."

"Why should I be the one to live? She hates me. She'll always hate me."

Suddenly he folds like an abandoned accordion, his elbow resting on his knees and his face buried in a hand.

Sympathy stirs. He looks so, so lonely, and I can't leave him like this, not after such bitter, self-loathing honesty. I want him to know he's worthy of living.

I sit next to him and put an arm around his shoulders. "Don't think like that."

Tension has turned his muscles into rigid knots, but he shakes anyway, trying to hold on to some vestige of control.

Whatever happened between Aunt Margot and Tony... It's in the past...happened before I arrived in Tempérane. He was a just kid back then, and he doesn't deserve this kind of torment from a mother he obviously loves. Nobody does. "I know you're a good person, Tony," I whisper. "Don't let anybody tell you different."

And I continue holding him in the dark, to let him know he isn't alone.

Anthony

About an hour later, I carry Ivy through the dark and silent house to her bedroom and tuck her in. She fell asleep, her arm around my shoulders.

It probably makes me contemptible that I took comfort in her embrace. But I did...because I was feeling weak and overly self-indulgent.

I shouldn't, though. It's only going to end up hurting me. And her.

I stroke her warm cheek—a barely-there grazing of my fingers over her skin—then hold Ivy's hand. I can't remember the last time someone offered me quiet comfort the way she did...held me like I deserved unconditional acceptance.

Does Ivy know I resent her from time to time? How can I not, when she has Mother's love and I don't? Would she still have comforted me if she knew?

The innocent sweetness in her eyes tells me she would have. She would have considered it a simple human gesture. And as much as I feel humbled and touched by that, a small part of me is alarmed.

Ivy deserves Mother's love. She's obviously been filling the gaping hole in Mother's heart that I created. I can never forget the devastation on her face when she realized what I'd done.

There was so much warm, sticky blood all over my hands and clothes. It was so hot, spilling out of Katherine's little body.

I pressed my hands over the wound as hard as I could, praying that if I did a good job, maybe she wouldn't lose so much blood and die. But I wasn't good enough. Katherine panted softly, each breath laced with the chocolate-minty smell of the sweets she loved. The blood poured through my fingers. I started to feel sick, the sound of my heart like thunder in my ears.

Katherine, no! Don't die! Please don't die!

I felt dizzy from shaking my head so hard. My chest was so tight, I couldn't breathe. The hair on my neck bristled, making the area prickly and cold. It felt like a gentle farewell touch from Katherine's spirit as she was leaving...forever.

Jonas had to pull me away from Mother as she fainted, so I didn't taint her with the blood on my hands.

Now, sitting on the edge of Ivy's bed, I look down upon her sleeping face. I don't know what Mother will do if I taint her with my presence.

"Don't waste yourself on someone like me," I whisper, an ache forming in my chest. "I'll only bring you down."

It's very possible that Mother might end up hating Ivy for being nice to me, just like she instantly reviled Bolt and the poor assistant...and like she slapped Edgar for daring to speak up on my behalf. I wouldn't want that for Ivy, who doesn't have parents to turn to. Father would never side with her, not if it meant upsetting Mother.

Slowly, gently, I disengage my hand from Ivy's. Once our fingers no longer touch, cold rushes through me until I'm shivering, bereft and alone.

11

Anthony

When I hear knocking at my door the next morning, I glance at the clock beside my bed. Not even six. My eyes feel like they're full of sand, but it's too late to sleep now. I roll out of bed and open the door. It's Father. In a suit.

"Morning."

He frowns. "You look terrible."

"You look good." And I'm not just saying it to be a smartass. He looks imposing, sharp, his eyes focused and observant. Every bit the CEO of Blackwood Energy.

"Thanks. Listen, your mother doesn't have anything in particular to do today. On days like this, she usually relaxes and reads. Stick by her, humor her and spend some time with her. Let her see the good in you. You were her favorite son," he adds in a quiet voice.

"Are you sure that's a good idea?" The last thing I want to do is upset her with my presence.

"I want my wife back," he says tautly, a hint of anger and

grief flashing in his eyes. "I've done everything, Tony. This is the least you can do, even if it hurts. You *will* make her forgive you."

Seeing the pain on my father's strong face is all it takes for me to acquiesce. After all, I'm the one who caused it. "I understand."

"Good."

So I make myself presentable and join her. I don't try to engage much. Just stay in the same room, reading my books while she's reading hers.

At the same time, I do my best to avoid Ivy. I don't want her, in her innocence, to do anything to upset Mother. She might inadvertently say or do something to defend me or hint that Mother should forgive me, but that would only result in hardening Mother's heart and earning Ivy the Bolt treatment.

And over the next four days, I do successfully spend quite a bit of time with Mother without running into Ivy even once. Even Harry stays away, as though he knows what I'm trying to do. It wouldn't surprise me if Father also spoke with him.

But Mother doesn't soften, not even a little. She ignores me completely, absorbed in her books and some charity work she's doing for the town. At times I feel like a piece of furniture.

By the fifth morning, I'm skimming the pages without absorbing a word. Am I wasting everyone's time? Should I be more forceful? Maybe even ask Mother point-blank what I need to do to make her not hate me?

She clucks her tongue, making me raise my head. "What is it?" I ask softly, bracing myself to be ignored.

She tenses, then says, "A minor complication."

"Can I help?" *Please say yes. Give me an inch. A small opening. Anything. Please, please, please.*

She scrutinizes me, her gaze roaming every square inch of my face. Then she drops her eyes, her mouth flattening.

"Mother? I'm sure I can help."

"No."

Suddenly I can't stand it anymore. Nine fucking years of wishing, hoping, praying—all so she would look at me without hate or blankness. I know we can never go back to way things were before. Katherine will never come back. All I want is absolution and a few crumbs of warmth from my mother. I want my family to be happy. I want to be able to breathe without feeling like there's a huge, immovable weight pressing on my chest.

"What will it take?" I nearly croak.

"Excuse me?"

"What do I need to do for you to forgive me?"

She regards me. "If I tell you, will you do it? Even if it's something you wouldn't do otherwise?"

"Yes. Anything. I'll swallow broken glass if that's what's going to take." I mean every syllable of what I'm saying.

She looks at me long and hard. I wait, suspended, torn between hope and dread.

Finally, she shakes her head. "No. I won't. I can't tell you."

I burst out of my chair, my entire body clenched and burning with anger and frustration. *"Why not?"*

She doesn't flinch. "To earn forgiveness, remorse should come from the heart. Without any ulterior motive."

"Mother—" My voice breaks.

"You don't deserve to be forgiven, Anthony."

Pain lances through me. The weight on my chest triples, breathing becomes hard, and I feel like my knees are about to fold.

Even as I struggle with my anguish, I see the grief on every line of her face—the deathly pallor on her skin. I did that to her nine years ago. I...I screwed up everything.

"Then hate me, but don't torment yourself," I beg her. I just want her to be happy. Not suffering because of me.

"I do hate you," she says, her voice hoarse and thick with

emotion. "I hate myself, too, for ever thinking a monster like you was pure or perfect."

She couldn't have delivered a more devastating blow. My whole body starts to shake.

"Would it make you feel better if I died?" The painful words tear from my throat. I dread the answer, but I almost wish she'd just tell me to go slit my wrists. My life is pure agony, and now that I know she'll never forgive me, death seems like a better, simpler option.

"Oh no," she says. "I don't want you anywhere near my Katherine. Even in the afterlife."

Anger, frustration, self-loathing and despair flow through me, each a deadly and acidic poison to my soul. Darkness swallows me, leeching all the warmth from my life. My teeth chatter, shivers running through me.

I realize then...I may never be in light or warmth again.

12

Ivy

Since the dinner that night, I don't see Tony anywhere. Not at any of the family meals, not around the house. It's as though he's hiding from me. Is he upset I saw him when he was vulnerable? Or something else?

I want to know if he's all right, if there's anything I can do to make him feel better. Staying home makes me restless, but a couple of days ago when I went to a music store, people stared and whispered. I caught a few "Anthony"s, and it was all I could do not to tell them if they had something to say, they should just say it to his face. The only thing that kept me in check was the knowledge that Tony would be furious if I did that. He totally hates it when I tell him he's not so bad, even though there are warm, delighted glimpses tinged with gratitude in his eyes whenever I call him a good guy. It's weird.

Uncle Lane is busy at work, and he leaves early and comes home late. Edgar, too, so he's hardly ever over. And Harry behaves like nothing's wrong. But that's Harry. He could put someone in a burning building at ease with a smile and a few calm words.

After six days, I can't stand it. I don't know exactly what caused Tony to pull his vanishing act, but I know it has something to do with what happened at that dinner and Aunt Margot's behavior. The tension in the household is awful, and I want Aunt Margot to forgive him for whatever he did wrong and just...chill. No one should have to suffer through a night like that, especially not someone who's obviously worked really hard to make his family proud.

I'm sitting at the piano, my pink dress demurely arranged around my legs...but I'm half-assing Chopin's "Torrent" étude. Tatiana would literally wail, with the back of her hand thrown to her forehead, if she heard me play like this. But it's impossible to focus when I'm trying to figure out what's making Tony stay away.

Sister killer...

My fingers hit all the wrong notes, and I stop. *Oh my God.* There's no way that hateful Mrs. Wentworth could be right. But if Aunt Margot thinks Tony had something to do with his sister's death, that would explain why she treats him so coldly. But the news didn't have anything about him being connected to the tragedy. And nobody in the house has ever hinted Tony had anything to do with what happened to Katherine.

On the other hand...

Maybe there's more to the story.

Who can I ask? I run through the possibilities and end up with Harry. I'll just have to weasel it out of him somehow.

I check the clock on the wall. Almost lunchtime. He'll come down from his room soon, if he hasn't already. Although he's skinny, he eats like a horse with a stomach worm.

I hurry toward the dining room. Sure enough, he's already seated and munching on some chips. I sit next to him, trying for an innocent smile.

"Oh no." He blinks twice. "You've got that look. Don't ask me to play Schubert with you. Not with Tony around."

Perfect. "Is Tony joining us for lunch?"

"Doubt it." He sniffs. "He's probably packing to fly to L.A."

"*What?*" I put a hand over my mouth. God, I didn't mean to be so...*loud.* But it never occurred to me that Tony would just pack up and leave, especially when things aren't resolved with his mom.

The idea of not ever seeing him again slices me like a razor. His faint, self-deprecating smiles, the way he hates for people to think he's good, even though he tries so hard, the way he craves certain acknowledgment and affection but is too vulnerable to actually just reach for them—they all touch the side of me that was forever changed when my parents died. Because eight years ago, I was also too scared to make a fuss or demand anything, lest my new family decide they didn't want me after all. I did my best to make them happy, make them proud...and unlike Tony, I got the love and acceptance I wanted. It's terrible that he doesn't have that from his parents, the two people who should love him more than anyone.

"Does Aunt Margot know?" I ask, unable to stop myself. "What about Uncle Lane?"

"Dunno. But Tony said Ryder asked him to join him there, and I'm sure he'll go. It's going to be awesome."

"Oh really? How? And who is this Ryder person?"

"Ryder's a model and actor. Tony's best friend. And apparently he's getting projects that are going to make him a star. I met the guy once. Unbelievably good-looking. It's going to be wild—parties, girls...you name it." Harry sighs longingly.

I want to throw up at the whole idea. Especially the "girls" part. Reminds me of the dickface CT, my first boyfriend at Curtis. He never failed to flirt and hang out with all the girls who shot him smiles and kisses...while ignoring me the entire time.

I don't think Tony is as shallow as CT, but that doesn't mean I'm still okay with him surrounded by older, worldly models and starlets, who undoubtedly hang out with his model-slash-actor friend. "When did Tony tell you about this... invitation to L.A.?"

"A couple days ago."

My fingers shake. I can't believe Tony didn't say anything.

I can barely eat lunch, my gut churning. I want to find Tony and confront him...to see if he's really going and—if so—when. And if he's okay with the way things are between him and Aunt Margot. I need to know if he hasn't felt any of the connection I felt with him—the kiss, the private moments we've shared, the Schubert we played together. But most importantly, I want to see him because I know I'm going to miss him, and I have a feeling if he leaves, I may never see him again. His complexity fascinates me. It's like looking at a hard piece of music for the first time and trying to figure out how to play it so you can understand every nuance, every emotion.

I dump the unfinished lunch, go to his room and knock. No response.

Oh, come on. You can't ignore me like this!

I raise my fist to bang on the door again.

"Miss Ivy, Master Tony has gone out," Jonas says, emerging from Aunt Margot's study.

"Where?" I ask.

"He didn't say."

Like you'd tell me if he did. But then I feel catty and rude. Jonas protects everyone's privacy, not just Tony's.

I go to my room and flop down on my bed. Los Angeles. Parties. *Models.*

Thankfully, I don't get to stew in my frustration for long. A text from Yuna comes in. It has a video of her playing "La Campanella."

Grab a Kleenex cuz it's gonna make you weep with envy!

Yuna kills it in the video. My God. I stare at the fluid way her hands move, her entire body utterly relaxed and comfortable. She's always been fabulous with Liszt, but this is the kind of performance that can make a career.

Beat this! Send me yours before the day's over.

Okay, now I owe her a video of "La Campanella." And there's no way I'm sending her a less-than-stellar performance. I have my pride.

I work on "La Campanella." I have the fingering, phrasing and interpretation down. But the speed is something else. I need to shave at least ten seconds from my playing time. Otherwise the piece won't have the necessary energy and vibrancy.

After a couple hours of concentrated practice, I finally record myself playing it cleanly at tempo. I smile with satisfaction.

Someone behind me starts clapping. I turn and have to stop myself from groaning with annoyance. It's Marty Peacher.

With slicked-back hair and hooded blue eyes, Marty could be considered classically handsome, except for two things. The bridge of his nose, which is uneven from having been broken and not set correctly. And those eyes. They always seem sullen and vaguely dissatisfied with the world. Twenty-two years old, he always acts like he's so much more mature than me or Harry. But compared to Tony, Marty reminds me of an adolescent—too raw, always trying a little too hard.

He isn't my favorite person. And for some reason, he's decided I need his opinion on music, no matter how ignorant and condescending.

"Bravo," he says.

"Thanks. I guess you're visiting with Sam?"

"Yeah. Dad thought it'd be good to have some face time with Margot. He has some great business plans."

Sam always has these great business plans. He insists on carrying a Dictaphone around, so he can record every brilliant idea that pops into his head. Then he puts it down on a piece of paper and comes over to get Aunt Margot to invest. Apparently it's never crossed his mind that maybe she has no intention of ever giving him money. Or that she doesn't respect him or his family.

"That was pretty good," Marty says, his tone haughty and know-it-all. "But I think it'd be better if you didn't rush through it like you're desperate to go to the bathroom. It should feel like a...a waltz."

Where did he get that inane idea? "There's absolutely nothing waltz-y about this piece, and Liszt never meant anyone to dance to his work...unless your idea of waltzing is to move so fast you pass out from dizziness."

"Still."

"If you're so sure of your interpretation, you're welcome to show me." I gesture at the piano. Marty can manage some simple jazz pieces, which he's studied only because he thinks it looks cool to play them in front of girls. But he isn't nearly good enough for Liszt. He doesn't practice consistently, and his arms and fingers are stiff. He's more interested in how people view his performance than the music itself.

He flushes. "You can be such a bitch. I don't have to know how to play it to have an opinion."

"Sure. But you know what they say about opinions. Some smell better than others." It isn't worth getting upset over the "bitch." It'd be like getting mad at a three-legged dog that can't win a race.

He walks closer, purposely invading my personal space. I tilt my head and look up at him, refusing to retreat.

"One day, you're going to be sorry you're so rude to me."

His voice is low, his mouth twisted into something between a smirk and sneer.

Ooh. I'm shaking in my shoes. "Right. Well, until then, I'll just try to enjoy my life. And I think there's something hanging out of your nose."

After a moment of indecision, he turns and leaves. One hand surreptitiously goes to his nose as he passes through the door.

I gather my music and go upstairs. Once on the second floor, I stare at the door to Tony's room.

I realize I never got to ask Harry about Mrs. Wentworth's comment. Whether it's true or not. My money's on *not*, since Mrs. Wentworth was just pissed off that I outed her son as a would-be rapist in front of Aunt Margot.

But whatever. I don't care. You can't blame someone for a mistake they made when they were a twelve, no matter what it is. And especially not when it's obvious they're still remorseful about it nine years later.

13

Ivy

After putting away my music, I send my awesome video to Yuna with a short message: *Watch it and weep!* It'll be a great surprise when she wakes up in Seoul.

Then I spend the rest of the day in a sitting room, where I can watch the foyer through the doorway and the driveway through the huge bay windows. I need to see when Tony gets back so I can talk to him. I want him to know he isn't alone, like Yuna did for me when I arrived at Curtis with butterflies in my belly. I want him to know I'm hopelessly fascinated by him...that I find him interesting and amazing.

But Tony doesn't arrive. Instead, Aunt Margot and Uncle Lane leave—with a suitcase, which is interesting. I didn't know Uncle Lane was home early or that they planned to be gone overnight. "New Orleans will be nicer. No roaches," he says as he leads her out.

Soon I understand what made them leave: Sam and Marty.

They walk out of the house, their faces red and tight. I guess they didn't get any money from Aunt Margot.

I shake my head. Sam needs to find another backer. Aunt Margot will never give him a penny. It isn't the first time she's snubbed them. She hates it every time they visit, calling them shameless, classless bloodsuckers. But for some reason, Sam is desperate to have her invest in his ventures. Before I left for Curtis, I overheard him tell Marty that as long as she invests, the venture can succeed, and they'll become like the Blackwoods—rich and important. *Somebody.* I didn't understand Sam's logic then, and I still don't. But then, business and economics aren't my strongest suit.

A little later, Jonas comes into view. "Miss Ivy, dinner is about to be served."

"I'm not leaving until Tony's home."

"He came back three hours ago," he says. "While you were practicing."

"Why didn't you say something?"

"Your specific instructions were not to be bothered unless there's emergency or your aunt or uncle needs you."

Unbelievable. "You knew I wanted to talk to Tony."

"I did. But you didn't indicate the desire was urgent."

"Didn't you see me ready to pound down his door earlier?"

"I saw you knock, yes," he says, unflappable as usual.

I might as well deal with a robot that can't do anything unless it's spelled out explicitly. Anybody with a bit of common sense would've let me know. "Did you tell him about dinner?"

"Yes."

Since his parents are gone, maybe Tony will come down. I head to the dining room. Harry is already seated, tapping away on his phone. "Hey, Ivy," he says absent-mindedly.

"Didn't Aunt Margot say no phones at the table?"

He's still focused on the screen. "Mom's not here. And I need to figure out what I'm going to do tonight. Not wasting a night like this at home." Suddenly, he stops and looks at me. "Wanna come?"

Under different circumstances, I'd probably say yes, but I know in my gut Tony won't be hanging out with Harry tonight. "I'm good, thanks."

Dinner is finally served. Tony doesn't show. I keep looking at his empty seat. Is he packing to go to L.A. right now? Is he even planning to at least say goodbye?

I can't focus on the food, and declare myself full after a few bites of soup and salad. I don't want to sit here and *dine* like I'm okay. I want to see Tony.

Harry stares. "You don't want your blackened redfish?"

"Go ahead and eat it if you like."

I stand up and go to the second floor, hesitating at the top of the stairs. What if Tony's determined to leave? There isn't much reason for him to stay in this house where he's unhappy.

Maybe I should just turn around, walk back downstairs and let him go, I tell myself. It might be good for him to hang out with his best buddy. Everyone needs at least one person who sees the absolute good in them, and I don't think Tony's had much of that in his life. I doubt his brothers or friends tell him he's perfect already—men can be terrible at communication.

I don't want Tony to leave, but at the same time, if he has to go, I want him to hear from at least one person that he's amazing and good and deserves nothing but success and happiness. Sometimes a few sincere, kind words are all it takes to help you keep going when you feel like you're dying inside. My parents' telling me I was awesome, and many great, beautiful things would come my way so long as I tried hard and hung in there... That got me through a lot after their deaths...especially when I felt lost in Tempérane and knew no one.

Tony's room is almost at the end of the hall. I knock on the door and wait.

Nothing.

I press my ear to the door. I swear I can hear something on the other side, but maybe it's just my heartbeat.

"Tony?"

Nothing.

Hmm. Maybe I should make sure. Jonas said he's back. I turn the knob. The door opens soundlessly.

I stick my head in. "Tony?"

The room is dimly lit, the curtain drawn. Heart pounding, I step inside and close the door. I feel like an intruder—well, I *am* an intruder—but I can't stop myself from looking around. I want to know everything there is to know about him before he leaves. Besides, he's been in my room before, while I've never been in his, even when he was living abroad.

It's a feeble attempt at justification.

His room's neat, not a speck of dust anywhere. Unlike mine, it's spartan, with almost no personal effects. There's the framed diploma from Princeton on the wall, but the bookshelves are empty. Only one photo is on the desk—a gorgeous golden-haired child.

Katherine. He must've been very close to her. But there aren't any other photos of the family.

I look around, nibbling the tip of my index finger. How strange. This has been his room all along. So even if he hasn't been here in the last nine years, shouldn't there be something—comic books from way back when, posters of musicians or movie stars, school projects? Edgar's room—which is neatly cleaned and organized now that he's moved out—still has his old things. A guitar, scuffed shoes with cleats, jerseys of his favorite football players, trophies from various events and competitions, boxes of old sketchbooks with their edges curled and discolored, comic books, toys and so much more.

If I didn't know better, I'd think this was a guest room.

Then it suddenly hits me. Tony wasn't sent to Europe because Uncle Lane and Aunt Margot had high hopes for him. He was *exiled*, and all his belongings were either packed into storage or thrown away because there wasn't any expectation that he'd be back.

With the realization, my heart begins to ache. I wipe my eyes, sniffing. *Oh, Tony.* How he must've suffered. I didn't know...never suspected the depth of what he must have lost. When my parents were killed, it was something I couldn't do anything about. I miss them terribly, but I also know they loved me to the very end, and that always gives me comfort. Tony has lost his family because his parents *chose not to want him.* That had to create unbearable emptiness insi—

"What the fuck are you doing here?"

Oh my God. I jump at the hostile voice, a hand over my racing heart. My knees shake, but I manage to turn around. "Tony?"

He stands inside the balcony doors, now slightly ajar.

"Didn't Mother teach you not to go in someone's room without permission? She's pretty strict about etiquette," he says, his words biting. He's carrying a bottle in his hand. I can't tell if it's empty.

"Have you been drinking?" I say, since he's totally right about his mom, and I suddenly feel apprehensive about his mood.

"What if I have? What's it to you?" He smirks, walking toward me. "I'm not giving you any, so don't even think about it."

"I don't want any. I can always ask Uncle Lane if I want some." He's very progressive about alcohol.

"Right," Tony says bitterly.

Then I realize he probably didn't know that about his own dad. He hasn't spent any time in Tempérane since he was twelve. Although Uncle Lane went to Europe a few times, it was always with Aunt Margot. I doubt they went out of their way to see their exiled son.

"You still haven't told me what you're doing here," he says.

I lick my lip. There's such a dark edge to his voice that I can't help but wonder if I made the right choice in entering his room. *Too late now*. He's standing between me and the door. I should just say what I came here to say. Honesty is the best policy in a situation like this...I think. "I just wanted to see you."

"Is that so? Mother didn't send her pet up to pack my shit and tell me to get the fuck out of town?"

I gasp at the hostility and anger. "No!"

"Then what are you *doing* here?" He tilts his head until it's almost horizontal. "People don't want to see me. Not really."

"That isn't true, Tony. I wanted to know if you were okay." I swallow, praying for courage, as realization dawns on me that the hostility and anger aren't directed at me. They're more directed at...*himself?*

He straightens up, the smirk wiped clean. "Did you, really?" Then he laughs humorlessly. "You'll be better off staying away from me." He walks toward me. He isn't moving fast, but he looks purposeful—almost menacing.

My heart jumps to my throat. I start to retreat before I catch myself. Tony would never hurt me. Despite his rudeness at times, there's a core of decency inside him.

He raises his hands in front of my face. "You see these?"

"Your hands?"

"Yeah. There's blood on them. I thought I could wash it away, but I was wrong. I could cut them off at the wrists, but the stain would stay. Everything I touch becomes tainted."

Oh no. *Tony*. Mrs. Wentworth's evil words flash through my mind, and I realize he holds himself responsible for whatever part he might've inadvertently played in Katherine's death. My heart breaks for him. The weight of torment he must've carried in the last nine years would have crushed someone less strong. Tears fill my eyes, but I blink them away, worried he'll consider them a sign of pity. He's too proud for that. He needs sympathy. Understanding. And the realization that he's innocent.

I wrap my hands around his. "There's no stain. What happened was a long time ago. An accident. Nobody could've foreseen or prevented it, Tony. It isn't your fault."

His expression shutters.

I grasp for something positive. "These hands are talented, Tony. If you wanted to, you probably could've studied at a conservatory."

He starts to pull away, and I tighten my grip.

"You used these hands to keep me safe from Caleb and his friends at the party. You're a good person. You stopped them from 'tainting' me with their ugly—"

"Shut *up*."

"No. *You* shut up and listen—"

He uses my grip on his hands to yank me forward. I gasp, stumbling against him.

"Tony—"

His mouth crushes mine.

14

Anthony

I hate her.

I hate her for saying what she's saying.

I hate her for insisting there's something good in me.

I hate her for seeing me as worthy.

I hate her for being in my mind every damn moment.

And most of all, I hate her for making me yearn for things I can't have—love, acceptance, warmth and light. She represents all of that and more, and it slices me to ribbons.

My kiss is brutal, designed to bruise and hurt. Even humiliate.

Because she needs to leave me alone. She needs to get the hell out of my head, my mind, my dreams. She needs to stop making me wish for things I can't aspire to, things I can't reach for anymore, not when my soul is stained pitch-black. How fucked do you have to be when not even your death can fix what's broken?

But her fingers tighten on my shoulders. She parts her lips, and our breath mingles—her caramel and cherry flavor going straight to my cock, making me hard and aching.

I push my dick against her belly, deliberately being as crude as possible. I want her to slap me, tell me I'm a monster and leave before I lose control and try to hold on to her. She deserves better. It'll hurt if Mother shuts her out like she did everyone else for being nice to me.

Ivy gasps against my lips. And instead of pulling away, she flicks her tongue across mine.

It sets my body on fire.

I shove a hand into her hair, holding her tight as I devour her, seeking her sweetness and warmth. She takes all my rough aggression and turns it into an aching desperation pulsing through my veins. If we were in medieval times, I'd be on one knee, pledging my life to her. The thought is shocking, but it doesn't cool my lust. It makes me hold her tighter, praying I can somehow be worthy, that I'm the kind of guy with even a sliver of light in his soul.

Then we're moving, and the backs of her knees hit the mattress. She falls onto the neatly made bed, and I follow her down, my mouth still fused to the softness of her eager lips. Breathing hard, she reaches for my shirt, her hands jerky and impatient. I'm gratified at seeing how clumsy her fingers are. They can fly across the piano with perfect control, speed and mastery, playing some of the most technically challenging pieces. But now, with lust flushing her cheeks, she can barely undo my belt buckle.

And I want her a thousand times more for it.

I shed my clothes and stand before her, so she can drink in her fill...and have a chance to run. Instead, her gray eyes are dark and shining with excitement, and she studies me from head to toe. I've never been gladder that I work out and stay in shape. At least my body is worth something.

"You're...bigger than I expected," she blurts out, her gaze on my cock.

I laugh softly. "Don't give me some clichéd 'is that going to fit' line."

She arches an eyebrow. "Not *that* big."

I can't help it. I laugh with genuine humor and delight. Placing my palms on either side of her head, I lean over and claim her mouth, letting her know I plan to go all the way unless she stops me. She responds eagerly, stoking my desire to a fever pitch.

Without breaking our kiss, I take off her dress. She lifts her body here and there to help. Her underwear is plain—a nude padded bra and cotton bikini in the same shade. Totally demure and PG compared to some of the girls I've known, but Ivy's lingerie is somehow more exciting. There's something innocent and sweet about it.

She nervously wets her lips. I kiss them softly. "You're gorgeous."

She gifts me with a smile so radiant it hurts to look. Ignoring the odd hitch in my chest, I trace every beautiful curve of her body, determined to give her all the pleasure I can for the priceless gift she's bestowing on me. She isn't exactly voluptuous, but everything about her is soft and feminine.

Her breathing shallows, and I tease her, trailing my fingers along the edge of her bra. When I stroke the swell of her breast, I can sense her thundering heartbeat. I unhook the bra and slide it off.

Goosebumps rise on her breasts at the cool air. I shower them with kisses and caresses, avoiding the pointed tips. Her breasts are lovely—plump, soft and responsive, her pink nipples beading. I pull one into my mouth and suck hard, using my tongue and teeth to torment her, and she reacts like she's been touched by a live wire.

"Tony." Her fingers dig into my hair. Her shameless

response is like pouring oil over a fire. I'm so damn hard that I want to shove into her right now.

Easy, easy. I want this to be amazing for her. I *need* this to be amazing for her. Despite knowing how broken I am, she's trusting me with her body. It humbles me—that unconditional trust—and makes me want to pleasure her until she screams herself hoarse.

While sucking on the other nipple, I slip a hand under her panties. She's completely wet, her hot juices drenching my fingers. I circle the opening of her pussy and flick the pad of my thumb over her clit.

Her thighs spread wide. She arches her back, then wraps her legs around my hand and rocks in a wild, abandoned manner.

Where did Jonas put the damn condoms? I remember and reach for the drawer, tear into the package and roll the rubber down my steel-hard cock. Ivy watches me with heated excitement.

I pull the underwear down her legs and position myself between her thighs. God. She's scorching hot. I feel like I'm about to explode.

I push inside slowly, giving her time to adjust. She's incredibly tight. I look at her face. Her breath is coming in short bursts.

I brush away hair on her cheek tenderly. "You okay?"

"I think so."

"That's not encouraging." I stop moving.

She reaches up and kisses me. "It'll get better."

I shake my head. "That's totally not what I want this to be for you. It should be fucking awesome the whole time. Because it is for me."

She squirms. "It doesn't hurt that much..."

"And this isn't a punishment and shouldn't hurt at all." I probably rushed things, damn it. She's wet, but too tight.

I pull out and kiss her again, coaxing and seducing her all over. Then slowly I travel down her body, worshipping her gorgeous tits and taut belly. When I'm finally at the apex of her legs, I put her thighs over my shoulders.

"Tony..." she gasps, her face red. "You, um..."

She's so expressive. I can tell she can't decide between screaming for it or fleeing. I close my mouth over her and run the flat of my tongue over her slick folds. Her sweet taste floods my senses, and I groan. She arches her back, a strangled cry stuck in her throat. Her hips jerk.

"It's too much..."

Too much. If she knew all the things I want to do to her, she'd definitely scream and run the other way. "It isn't enough."

I lick and suck while pushing my fingers inside her one by one to stretch her, then pump into her, rubbing her G-spot. She presses a palm over her mouth to muffle a scream as she rocks hard against my face.

So. Fucking. Hot.

Blood roars in my head. I could almost come from her uninhibited response. It's crazy sexy how she can be such a lady and so demanding at the same time.

Air saws in and out of her lungs. Her pussy clamps around my digits right before she screams her orgasm.

"Tony... Tony..." she whispers my name as though looking for an anchor.

"Right here." I kiss her lushly...adoringly.

My dick is so hard it hurts, but I pace myself, pushing into her slowly, determined to make it mind-blowing for her.

"All the way," she demands into my ear. "I want to feel you all the way in."

The tenuous control I have cracks at her sexy urging. I drive the rest of the way in, tearing past the tiny resistance that, even as I become aware of it, is too late to repair.

"Oh, fuck, *Ivy*..."

She kisses me.

I feel like I should stop, even though that's stupid as hell, because I'm already in and there's no way to undo what just happened. *Damn it, I should've asked if she was a virgin.* Instead of just assuming that someone as beautiful and interesting as Ivy would've done it before.

"I don't think you're just supposed to stay still," she whispers. "Right?"

"Just...do what you feel," I say. "Why?"

"Well...in the porn movies..."

I look at her in mock horror. "You watch *porn*?"

She kisses me. "Don't judge."

"I could never judge you." *I could never be good enough to judge you.*

I move against her gently. "Wrap your legs around me." She does, and I begin to drive into her, reveling in a kind of pleasure I've never known before.

Her breathing roughens, and I can tell she's close. I want her spasming around my cock when she comes. I reach between our bodies and rub her clit.

"Oh my God... Oh my God..." She pants.

I increase the tempo of my thrusts until she suddenly stiffens.

"*Tony—!*"

The rest is swallowed by a hard kiss. Her fingers dig into my back as she convulses, the climax claiming her.

And that's all it takes for me to join her in crazy-hot bliss. I come so hard I think I black out for a moment.

When I can draw in air without sounding like a marathoner after a race, Ivy is cuddling in my arms. I run my fingers through her hair.

I don't regret what happened between us. It's the best damn thing I've ever experienced. But is she going to regret it? I'm not the kind of guy she should've chosen for her first time.

I look down between us, see the blood on the rubber. I go to the bathroom to toss it, a little disturbed by the sight. It isn't as if I murdered her, but...

"Come back," she says from the room.

"In a minute." I wash my hands with scalding water and soap before joining her.

She immediately snuggles into me, looking at my face. "What dark thoughts are filling your head?"

"Dark thoughts?"

"You have that look." She puts an index finger between my eyebrows. "You get lines here and your eyes get real serious."

"I was wondering..." I grasp for smooth words and fail.

"About what?"

I feel ridiculously vulnerable, so I shrug. "I was just wondering why you never did it before. You're eighteen."

She thinks for a minute. "Well. Would you let just anybody play a Bösendorfer Imperial?"

"A what?"

"It's this gorgeous concert grand piano I got to play last winter. Handmade in Austria. Really stunning. The tone's slightly dark, mellow compared to other brands and perfect for classical pieces." She sighs. "One day, I'm going to buy one."

I skim the soft lines on her back with my fingers. "So... You're the Bösendorfer Imperial of women."

"Indeed. And only the worthy can touch me."

I laugh at her mock hauteur. I can't think of the time when somebody made me laugh in bed and feel good and glowing all the way to the center of my being. Until now, fucking was just fucking. Nice. Satisfying. Even helped me forget why I'm such a screw-up, albeit briefly. But with Ivy, it's more.

She links our hands, her eyes on mine. "You're beautiful, Tony. I see the good in you."

I stare at her radiant face. The darkness my mother's cold words brought earlier slides away as more of Ivy's light fills me. She is the sun that rises, the moon that shines and the stars that put sparks of happiness in my heart. It was futile for me to try to resist her all this time. Simply through our being together, she makes me feel pure. Noble. Aspiring to be the man who deserves her.

When she presses a kiss on the back of my hand, I know—my heart forever belongs to her.

15

Ivy

I BLINK A BIT, THEN CATCH MY BREATH AT THE unfamiliar surroundings and the body next to mine, until I remember I'm in Tony's room and he's the one behind me, his arm around my belly and his face buried in my hair.

What we did yesterday flashes through my head. After the first time, we cuddled a bit—I might've even fallen asleep—then Tony fed us in his room, courtesy of Jonas the Discreet, and we did it again, with me on top the second time. He said it'd be easier for me that way, and patiently guided me.

And it was. I had a slight difficulty finding the best way to reach my climax, but he knew exactly what I needed to do, and when I came, I thought I'd die from bliss. No wonder the French call it *la petite mort*.

The memory makes me hot and squirmy. But I don't want to move and wake Tony up. It's too nice, having him wrapped around me.

Besides, I have to figure out what to do now that it's *the morning after*. Nobody ever talks about that part. Not in any books. Not in any of the movies on relationships and sex I watched with Yuna in our attempts to "live" like our teacher insists. Tatiana doesn't think we can play anything from the Romantic Era with an appropriate depth of emotion if we don't know what true love is.

Now I wish I'd done more the past few years than just play the piano. After I came to live with Aunt Margot, I realized she was quite taken with my musical talent. So I devoted practically all my time to it to please her. The better I became, the prouder she was, and nothing was too expensive or troublesome if it could help me improve. She got me the best instructors, and even bought a baby grand once she decided I was too good for a digital piano.

But that meant I missed out a lot of what most girls my age did—sleepovers and late-night chats with girlfriends, dating, all those things. If I hadn't, I might've known the things that most eighteen-year-old girls do. Like...

Is he going to regret it? I mean...he seemed surprised at my lack of experience, but he didn't exactly sound unhappy. And I know he came, so... Guys can't get upset if they come, right?

"What are you thinking?" he whispers into my hair.

"Nothing," I say a little too quickly.

"The gears in your head are moving so hard, I could hear them with my eyes closed."

"Then maybe you could also make out what they're saying."

"I'm not that good." He licks my neck, sending sweet sizzles along my spine.

I shiver with delight. "Hey! No fair."

"I don't fight fair." He kisses the back of my neck, then cups my breast, his thumb over the tip.

Biting my lower lip, I arch my back, pressing into his hand

and rubbing against the thick erection that's suddenly sprung up behind me.

"Come on," he murmurs. "Talk to me."

"I was just thinking..." I clear my throat. "I was wondering what people do the morning after."

"Mmm." He shifts, fitting his body closer and toying with my nipple. "This."

God. I'm going to die if he stops. Although I'm slightly sore, I'm already so wet between my legs. Can he feel it? "No, really."

"I'd say people do whatever they want. And right now, I want to make you come." He nips my shoulder as he tugs on the nipple.

Electric pleasure goes all the way to my clit, and I curl my toes. "I'd love to, but I'm a little sore."

"Don't worry. You can still come," he whispers hotly in my ear, his fingers slipping between my slick folds.

I clench my teeth as his clever hands play me like the Bösendorfer Imperial that I claimed to be. Hot blood roars through me. He shows me how quick and hard I can climax against his hand. It's as though my body and mind have no resistance when it comes to him.

"Oh my God, you're the devil," I say, when I finally can.

He laughs. "Good morning."

"I think it's your turn now." I flip around. "I suppose I can torture you the same way." I wriggle my fingers with an extra-wicked smile and swipe the pad of my thumb over the tip of his rock-hard cock. It's slick, and I lick it curiously and taste salt and Tony.

His eyes darken. "Ivy—"

"Tasty. Now don't move."

I wrap my hand around him, then experiment with how hard to grip, how fast I should move along his shaft and how to touch the cockhead. Every time my fingers bump against the base of the head, his breathing grows rougher. I adore the way he looks now. Pleasure twisting his face, making his features stark and almost feral. There's a desperate edge to his lust that's unbelievably erotic and makes me feel powerful. I'm the one who is giving him this... I'm the one he wants, and I can shatter his control.

I cup his balls, scratching them lightly as I pump him in my hand.

He fists the sheet underneath him. "Ivy, you're killing me."

"Want me to stop?"

"Then I'll die sooner."

"We can't have that. I love you too much for that."

Shock pierces through the bliss in his gorgeous green eyes. He swallows, then he says, "Ivy, you shouldn't—"

"I don't want to hear any *shouldn't*s and *don't*s." Not when I'm holding his cock in my hand and telling him I love him. I tighten my grip and pump harder. His eyes darken until they almost look black. Bracing his feet on the mattress, he drives into my fist. It heats my blood until I feel like it's my pussy he's thrusting into.

He keeps his eyes on mine, and I watch the pleasure build in him. I know the moment he climaxes. It isn't just the semen spurting out and landing on his lean, ridged abs. It's the way his eyes lose focus and become so open and full of light, like the starry sky on a clear night. I feel like I could lose my soul in their depths.

I'll carry how he looks this moment in my heart as long as I live.

16

Anthony

We don't talk about it, but it's like we've come to a silent conclusion since that night. I start to join Ivy and Harry for meals, and I also listen to her practice on the white baby grand.

Father's too busy at work to do more than come home to shower, get a few hours of sleep and return to the office. Mother avoids me like she would some filthy rodent. For once, I'm grateful. It means I can be with Ivy and not worry about Mother shifting her cruelty onto someone who deserves nothing but love and support.

Mother wants me to stay away from Ivy, but the reason was that she didn't want me to cause her harm the way I did Katherine. I'm older and stronger now, trained in kickboxing, so I can protect what's mine. I'm never going to let anything happen to Ivy.

The next three weeks go by with a kind of peace I've never known filling me. I spend as many of my waking hours with

Ivy as possible. Well, I also spend all my non-waking hours with her too, curled up around her in my bed. She starts to put tiger lilies in my room, and I let her because I know it pleases her.

Ivy's routines are simple. A lot of her time is devoted to practice because she's convinced that if she skips even a day, it'll show. The extreme level of paranoia and dedication is what makes her so good. She also says she can't goof around because not only does she have to improve her technique, she occasionally has to send her friend Yuna videos to showcase how awesome she is. It's hilariously adorable when Ivy pumps her fist after making a particularly good recording to taunt her friend with. It's equally adorable when an especially good clip from Yuna puts an unholy fire of competitiveness into Ivy's gray eyes.

Ivy sits next to me on the sofa after a session that she mostly spends muttering to herself. I catch a few words—*argh, no no no, ack, what the hell, crap*...

"Problems?" I say, putting away my laptop.

"Yes! This music! It's so irritating. I can't seem to play it the way I want. I can hear it in my head, exactly how it needs to go, but when I play it, it sounds like...like...*dead dog poop*!"

I bite my lip. She takes her music very seriously. "I thought you sounded pretty good."

"No! 'Pretty good' is fine for people who do this for fun! I'm trying to win competitions and make a grand debut one day!"

I run a soothing hand over her back. "Sorry. I meant amazing."

"You're just humoring me."

She's too cute. "What else am I supposed to do with my girlfriend?" It slips out before I can catch myself.

She turns to me, her eyes on my face, searching. "Your girlfriend? Really?"

I nod, slightly nervous. Maybe it's a bit too early. Maybe she thinks I'm being presumptuous. But the nights and days spent together and my growing feelings for her make me want to label her mine. My light. My joy. My everything.

Mine.

She grins. "Awesome. You're mine, too, then. *My* boyfriend."

I can't help grinning back, happiness floating through me like a gentle cloud. I love it that she thinks of me as hers—like we belong to each other. I kiss her, wanting her to know all the ways she matters to me. What she means to my existence.

"Mmm. Now I'm feeling much better," she says when I pull away. "Something to look forward to tonight." She rests a hand on my chest.

"Let me give you something else to look forward to."

"What?"

"My best friend asked me to join him out in California next week. On a yacht. Some kind of private summer party. Be my plus one."

"A yacht!" she shrieks, then covers her mouth with her hands. Pleasure puts a lovely flush on her face. "Oh my God! I've never been on one! I'd love to!" she says, nearly bouncing. "I have to figure out what I'm going to wear..."

"Wear whatever you want. California is *trés* casual."

"Yeah, but it's your friend! I want to make a good impression."

She's so lovely, I feel like I'm in a dream at times. "He'll love you."

"You think so?"

"Yes." It's endearing how she cares about what Ryder thinks, wanting to fit in with my world. I know he'll adore her because she makes me happy.

She tucks her feet under her legs and turns until she's fully facing me. "You should come to Curtis, too, after Labor Day. I want you to meet Yuna."

"I'd love to," I murmur, emotion clogging my heart as I hold her hand and look into her eyes. My life has never been brighter.

17

Ivy

The next day, Tony works on his laptop, his phone on the coffee table, while I'm at the piano, working on everything: fingering, phrasing, interpretation, precision of technique and speed. As usual, I soon get lost in the music. I love Chopin études. They aren't as showy as Liszt, but there's a sweet loveliness. And it's going to take years to master them all.

After two hours on the "Torrent" étude, I switch gears to something more fun. There's a bright cheeriness to Liszt's *Grand Galop Chromatique* I find irresistible. It sweeps you away to another dimension where life's all fun and games. After all, it was what Liszt played to melt the panties off women in the nineteenth century. But I'm also aware how easily you can botch the music if you don't have the control and mastery of technique. I'm planning to send a "beat that" video of me playing *Grand Galop Chromatique* to Yuna before Tony and I leave for California.

When I'm done, I stretch and sit next to Tony on the long sofa.

"Brilliant. Look at that smoke coming off your fingers." He picks up my hands and blows on my fingertips.

"It's a bravura seduction piece from the nineteenth century. Did it make you want to get naked with me?"

Tony shoots me an exaggerated leer. "You didn't have to bother. I always want to get naked with you."

"Good, but hold that thought. I'm tired. Need to nap or something." I yawn.

"Sleepy already?"

"Four hours of focus really takes it out of you. I have to nap afterward to recharge. Otherwise, I'm worthless." I start to close my eyes. "Besides, a certain somebody's been keeping me up late."

"Terrible, what some people will do." He pulls me down until my head rests on his lap. He's so warm and smells amazing. As I start to fall asleep, I feel him pick up my hand, massaging the fingers gently, one after another, pressing tender kisses on each. I've never felt more cherished than I do now.

"I can't believe you like them," I say, a smile in my voice.

"Your fingers? Why wouldn't I?"

"They're so long. Too long, actually, for my palm. If they were about half an inch shorter, they'd look more proportionate."

"I don't care. I've never seen fingers so beautiful and talented before."

I laugh softly, then doze off, my head on his lap and a smile on my lips.

When I open my eyes, we're still in the same position. Tony is watching me. He's gorgeous in the bright sun, the light casting a hazy glow around him. His gentle green eyes are brilliant, his mouth set in a soft line that's not quite a smile but just as sweet and precious.

"Sleep well?"

"Yeah." I stretch. "How long was I out?"

"Twenty minutes or so." He pushes away a few tendrils on my cheek and forehead. "You looked peaceful."

"You watched me the whole time?"

"More or less."

I flush, absurdly happy.

He runs a finger along the faint scar on my right hand, a straight line that starts from my pinkie almost all the way to the heel of my palm. "How did this happen?"

"With a pair of pruning shears. I was twelve at that time, and I bled so much. Needed stitches." I make a face. Aunt Margot was hysterical over the cut, and I felt terrible for the gardener, who didn't do anything wrong but got yelled at anyway. I just wanted to snip some tiger lilies in the garden because they looked so pretty. Since then, Aunt Margot's had the gardener send some to the house every morning. If the garden's out of lilies, we have a local florist deliver.

"Did it hurt a lot?"

"Not a lot. But the stitches were really annoying. Aunt Margot got so upset, she..." I trail off as I realize what I'm about to say. *Crap.* I shouldn't have brought up how much his mother dotes on me. It's like smearing salt over an open wound. I clear my throat. "Anyway, it's an old story. What did you think about my étude?"

Tony plays along. "Stunning. Maybe you'll be another Pollini."

I'm thrilled he thinks that highly of my rendition, but I have to laugh. "No, I won't. He's totally sublime, and I used to listen to his Chopin recordings all the time, hoping I could play like him. But Pollini is Pollini, and I'm me. I want people to listen to me because I'm awesome in my own way, not because I'm an imitation of Pollini."

The smile Tony gives me is so full of warmth and pride, I

feel like I'm about to burst with happiness. Then his phone pings.

"What is it?"

"Just an email. I'm applying for jobs in New England."

"What?" I could have sworn Edgar said Tony was going to be part of Blackwood Energy. "Aren't you joining the family business?"

The light in his eyes dims. "It...probably isn't a good idea."

Aunt Margot. I haven't seen her be outright rude or hostile toward him, but I think her frigid treatment and avoidance hurt more somehow. I search for a way to change the topic and blurt out, "But why New England?"

"You're going to be in Philadelphia. That's my first choice, but if not, I can expand my search criteria a bit."

"I'm okay with just spending weekends together. I mean, if you find a job in Boston or something." That earns me a baleful look, so I try again. "I don't want you to give up on something that's going to open doors for you. And while I'm at Curtis, we can spend all our weekends and breaks together. It isn't a big deal."

The look only grows more baleful.

Later that night, Tony is driven and persistent...and wickedly skilled. He puts me through an evil and prolonged sexual torture. Only when I clutch him desperately and cry out that I can't live without his cock inside me does he let me climax and comes inside me.

When I regain my breath, I kiss him. "You're so bad," I whisper.

He lifts his head from the crook of my neck and looks at me.

"Still," I say, "I love—"

He kisses me before I can finish. If that's where it ended, I'd be kicking his ass...or trying, anyway. But before I can tell him he's being rude and hurtful by refusing to let me finish, he looks into my eyes and says, "I love you, Ivy."

I stare at him. I had hoped...wished... But I didn't realize he already loves me. Happiness and adoration well up. I take his face between my palms and hold his gaze to tell him how much I love him as well. But before I can say anything, he kisses me again, then takes me until I'm out of my mind with pleasure and love for him.

After that, something shifts between us in a way that's vaguely disturbing. Every time I try to tell him I love him, he kisses me before I can get all the words out. It's as though he can't bear to hear me say it. But he always says he loves me like he needs me to know what I mean to him.

So one evening, when Harry rents a mindless action movie and invites Tony to watch it, I say I'll be there too. I have no intention of paying attention to the flick, but I know if I don't go, Tony's likely to decline so he can spend more time with me.

My plan for the evening? Text Yuna while Tony's occupied. That should give me almost two hours to sort it out—in case it's something super-complicated and takes more time than I expect.

We all sit on the sofa, and Harry brings a huge tub of caramel popcorn to share. It doesn't take long for the hero to start shooting up everything in sight—I'm not sure why, but it isn't important in this kind of movie. So I surreptitiously text Yuna. She should be up by now.

Hey, got a ? for you.

No, I'm not going easy on you. I'm going to kill "Torrent."

I almost laugh. I can imagine her arrogant face. *It isn't about that. It's about my boyfriend.*

There is a pregnant delay in her response. *You have a boyfriend and you didn't tell me? WTH?*

I glance at Tony, but he's captivated by the movie. Even so,

I slide my phone a little further around so he can't see what I'm typing. *I did mention him to you. Tony.*

Your middle cousin?

Yes.

Uh... Is it common for Americans to date their cousins?

No. But I'm adopted.

Still. It does feel really forbidden. So tell me. How serious are you guys?

He's thinking about moving to Philly.

Wow. That's serious-serious! Send me pics. I want to know if he's any hot.

I send her a pic of him and me together. A selfie we took a couple of weeks ago. Yuna's big on eye candy.

A moment later, she responds, *Damn. Totally worth it.*

Right? But... I text rapidly, laying out what the problem is —mainly that he won't let me say I love him, even though he tells me he loves me.

If he didn't say the L-word, I'd say he's using you, but it doesn't sound like it. He's really into you.

That's what I think too. He's making plans to be with me in Philly, rather than going to a more glamorous city like New York or Boston. *So why doesn't he want to hear it? I'm so frustrated.*

It takes a moment before Yuna sends me her response. *Any childhood trauma or abuse?*

What do you mean?

I read this book once. Not psychology, a romance novel. In it, the girl was super abused by her ex, who told her, "I love you," over and over again while beating the crap out of her. She couldn't stand hearing anybody tell her "I love you" after that because it brought back ugly memories.

My jaw slackens as my gaze slides toward Tony. He's scrunching his face at the TV, then laughs as something explodes on screen. Did somebody beat him like in Yuna's romance novel, while telling him, "I love you"?

The only person I can think of who would hurt him like that is Aunt Margot, but I just can't imagine her raising a hand against her son, no matter how furious she was. Her MO is mainly giving him the cold shoulder.

So what happened in the book?

Obviously she got over it with the right man. But this is real life. There are tons of things love can't fix. If you can, get out now. Guys like that are high maintenance. The work may not be worth it.

I read it twice, dry bitterness in my mouth, and look at Tony again. What Yuna's saying is totally logical. I'd probably give her the same advice if our positions were reversed. But the idea of giving Tony up feels like one of those huge Amazonian snakes around my chest.

Too late, I reply. *I'm crazy in love with him.*

Sorry, I'm being negative. Haven't had my coffee yet. Okay, forget what I said. If he has some mental hang-ups about hearing "I love you" then just avoid saying the words. Show him in some symbolic way, so he KNOWS *you love him.*

Like what?

Take inspiration from history? Schubert used to write ridiculously romantic music and dedicated it to whichever married woman he was in love with.

Despite my mood, I almost laugh at the suggestion. *I'm not going to do that.*

Maybe a ring? I watched a drama where this girl got a tattoo for her man. In the story they were meant to be together forever, but maybe that's too permanent. You know love doesn't last. Not like that.

Schubert might've been fickle, but I'm not. *Thanks! You're a genius!*

I know. You owe me. Now I gotta go make myself pretty and join the parents for breakfast. Bye!

XOXO, I type and hit *Send*, ideas swirling in my head. If Tony doesn't want to hear me *say* I love him, he can *see* that I love him by looking at something on me. A ring is a definite possibility. People wear one when they get engaged or married...but it seems too temporary. I can always just take it off.

Or lose it. Oh my God, what kind of message would that send? That my love can vanish down a drain because of carelessness?

No, I need something better. More enduring. And a tattoo sounds like just the ticket. And it's not "too permanent," like Yuna said. What I feel for Tony could never be too permanent.

I steal another glance in his direction and squeeze his hand. *Soon.* He's going to know I love him without my having to say the words.

18

Ivy

Hunger wakes me. I rub my eyes, cover a yawn, then smile when Tony's face fills my vision.

"Hello, sleepyhead," he says, looking down at me.

"Hi. I'm hungry."

He nods. "It's a little after one."

I gasp. I lay down for a short nap at a quarter till noon, and didn't mean to sleep for so long. I was up after he fell asleep last night, thinking about the tattoo and where I should put it.

"Sorry, I had no idea. You should've woken me," I say, flushing with embarrassment at having made him wait for so long.

"Why? You were sleeping so peacefully, and I don't mind. I could watch you forever."

"You always know exactly what to say to make me happy."

His gaze grows tender. "All I have to be is honest with you." He brushes the pad of his thumb over my jaw. "You can't possibly know how liberating it is to know that's all it takes to put a smile on your face."

I hold his hand and kiss the fingertips. "Let's eat lunch."

"Wait," he says, catching my wrist before I hop to my feet. "I have something for you."

I raise an eyebrow. It isn't my birthday, and I don't think there a one-month anniversary or anything special like that.

"Here." Tony pulls out a necklace from a long velvet box. An intricate medallion with the sun, the moon and some stars. The celestial objects are made from yellow, white and rose gold. It's so beautiful I'm struck speechless.

"I designed it myself and had it specially commissioned." He clears his throat. "Seems fitting. A one-of-a-kind necklace for a one-of-a-kind woman."

His sweetness is *killing* me. "It's gorgeous. Perfect. Thank you."

He smiles. "Turn around."

I turn and pull my hair to one side, eager to wear his gift. Pressing a kiss to the base of my neck, he puts it on me.

I look down at the cool disk resting on my chest, a warm lump in my throat. This is such an incredible symbol of his love for me. I lift my gaze to meet his. "I love it." I smile. "I lo—"

He takes my face in his hands and kisses me hard. "Love you," he whispers before claiming my mouth again.

I let my lips grow pliant and wrap my arms around him. Since he won't let me say it, I'll show him instead, hoping that whatever block he has about hearing me say the words isn't stopping him from knowing that I truly love him. *Soon I won't need to say anything*, I remind myself, vowing to get the tattoo done before we leave for the trip to California.

19

Ivy

A few days later, when Tony's off at the boxing gym, I get an email from the tattoo shop I found on the other side of town. I read it while sipping grapefruit juice, leaning against the kitchen counter. The artist has come up with a gorgeous design, one that says exactly what I want. She suggests I put it near the pulse point on my left wrist.

Left is your heart side. When your man kisses you there, he can see the tattoo and feel your pulse. When he holds your hand, he can press his wrist against yours. Or you can do it. Very intimate and special, like secret communication between the two of you, she wrote.

It makes sense. And I like what she said about how it can be a kind of private communication between us. I can already imagine us, our hands linked, and every time I press my wrist against his, he's going to know how much he's loved all the way to the bottom of his soul.

Also, I just had a cancellation, so can fit you in right now if you want.

I text, *I'll be there ASAP*, and start toward the garage.

"Ivy, do you have a moment?"

I turn at Aunt Margot's voice, clasping my hands together out of reflex. She's been avoiding me since the night Tony and I first slept together, which is unusual, since she likes to chat at least once a day. I'd bet my right hand she knows what's going on. Nothing under this roof stays secret from her, not for long, anyway. I hope she isn't stopping me to interfere in my relationship with Tony. She can hate him and avoid him if she really wants, but she can't tell me how to feel or act. I'm not her, and I won't hurt Tony for her, even if it lands me on her "bad list," as Harry likes to put it.

"Sure," I say.

"There's a piano quintet performance this Saturday evening at the St. Agnellus Community Center. I know it's very short notice, but their pianist is sick and won't be able to perform. It would mean a lot to them if you could fill in. They're playing Dvořák's Piano Quintet in A major."

I start to say okay, then remember the trip with Tony. "I'd love to, but I'm afraid I can't help this time. Sorry."

Aunt Margot's face goes still like a marble mask, and somehow it's scarier than overt disappointment or anger.

"Surely you can learn the piece in the next couple of days," she says finally.

"That isn't the problem. I've actually already preformed it. It's just that..." I take a deep breath. She's going to know soon enough, so I might as well tell her. "I'm going to be out of town this weekend."

"You are?" Two delicate eyebrows arch over rapidly cooling eyes. "I had no idea."

"Tony and I are going to visit his friend."

"Tony." She says the name like it's some kind of curse. "Is he the one who gave you that pendant?"

Unconsciously, I run my fingers over the gorgeous medallion. It's warm from my body heat. "Yes. He designed it himself. One of a kind."

Her eyes narrow. "I suppose that explains the smile on his face when he was leaving for the gym." Her voice makes me tense. I don't like the weird, hateful undertone.

"He's happy. Why do you make it sound like that's a bad thing?" I ask, genuinely confused and wanting to get to the bottom of this horrible enmity.

"Because I'd rather have him suffer the way I do."

I inhale sharply. Aunt Margot's voice is so brittle and hateful. "He's your *son*."

"And? I have two other sons, both of whom are perfectly happy."

"How can you say that? Why do you hate Tony so much?"

Her eyes glitter like sapphire and emerald. "He killed my Katherine."

"It wasn't his fault!" I fling an arm out, slashing the space between us. "It was an *accident*. A hunter made a mistake. How can you blame Tony for that?"

"You know nothing, Ivy. You weren't here."

"No, but I read the articles about the accident. None of them even hinted he had anything to do with it. So what if he was there? How does that make it his fault?"

"So you think he's a poor little victim with a mean mommy?" Aunt Margot sneers.

The expression leaves me breathless with shock. Her face is like something out of an exorcism.

"I'm *miserable* because of him. Why should he be happy? Why should he know the joy of being loved?" Her eyes, cold before, are now wild. "I miscarried *three times* before I had Katherine. I almost *died* bringing her into this world, only to have a mere six years with my daughter. He should suffer as long as I do, even if he'll never know the true depth of my grief. Losing a child is..." She swallows, her knuckles white.

Her pain is so stark and raw that it's as though the accident happened yesterday. I ache for Aunt Margot. I've never experienced anything even close to losing a child, and can't even fathom what it's like. But clinging to that old pain is hurting Tony, who doesn't deserve it. "Aunt Margot...you have to let it go. Katherine's gone, and Tony's suffered so much."

She raises her face and gives me a cruel sneer. "You're awfully sure for a girl who wasn't even there."

I hold firm. He was only twelve when it happened. Even if he pulled the trigger himself, it was an accident, not something he should still be paying for now. "You're deliberately being cruel because you can't get over Katherine's death and need to blame someone...even if it's your own son."

Aunt Margot's face is at once pale and terrible, rage erupting in her eyes. If her gaze were tangible, I'd be cut to pieces.

Apprehension dries my mouth. My palms go damp with cold sweat, but I keep my chin up.

"You've never, ever spoken to me this way, young lady. But you did just now...and not for yourself, but for him." Surprise and anger lace her hard tone.

"I've seen how he torments himself."

Abruptly, the fury on her face vanishes. "Does he cry?"

"What?"

"Has he wept for my Katherine? Even once?"

"Not that I've seen." I would've been worried if he had after all this time. "But—"

"*Monster*," she spits. "He didn't cry back then either. Not a single tear."

The fine hair on the back of my neck stands. Suddenly, I'm

cold under Aunt Margot's furious gaze. Tears start to fill her eyes, making them glow like a loss-crazed lioness's.

She touches her chest with a shaking hand. "He killed my baby and didn't even cry. What kind of demon does that? What kind of monster have I raised?" Her hand turns into a white-knuckled fist as she steps closer toward me.

My heart starts racing with fear. I move backward, but it's no use. I soon hit the wall, and she isn't finished.

"I thought he was a perfect child," she rages. "He wasn't like other babies. He never fussed, never cried. Not like his brothers. Always smiling and happy, my perfect little prince. Lane and I thought he was an angel, the kind of child who brings blessings and happiness to a family.

"But we were wrong. He is a monster. He came to me with his sister's blood all over him. *He was wet with her blood, but not with his tears!* He just sat and stared straight ahead. The only thing he didn't do is smile, but only because he could will himself not to smile. He couldn't will himself to cry!"

I can't even move a finger. The picture she's portraying is too horrifying, too tragic—for everyone. "Maybe Tony was in shock?" I whisper. When my parents died, I went into a stupor for a while before I could react properly. And unlike Tony, I wasn't covered in their blood.

"You think you're so clever, don't you, Ivy? You think I don't know you've been sleeping with him?" She points to the second floor. "And after all I've done for you."

"Tony deserves love."

"Is that what you tell yourself while you spread your legs for him? You don't know what love is, Ivy. You think sex is love." She laughs. "Sex is anything but love.

"Katherine loved him with all her innocent heart. It might be an accident he shot her, but it sure as hell was no accident he didn't cry!" Aunt Margot invades my personal space until the tip of her nose is almost touching mine. "*Do you think he'll shed a single tear when you die?*"

Holy shit. Her twisted hatred of Tony makes me feel sick. And sad.

"Do you think you're special enough to make him cry? *Is that why you defend him?*" she demands.

My pulse throbs hard and fast, my scalp tight. I've never faced loathing like this before. It's intense, vile; she wants to lash out because she's hurting and wants to make sure I suffer as much as she does. I can't believe Tony has borne it for so long without becoming twisted and broken himself.

Finally, I manage, "Maybe he will, maybe he won't. But I'm not going to hate him for how he chooses to react."

"You're a fool, then. You mean nothing to him, just like Katherine meant nothing." A chilling mix of disappointment, outrage and pain passes over her face. "By the time you realize how deluded you are, it's going to be too late. You'll have nobody standing beside you to make things right." Her gaze unblinking, her mouth bloodless, she turns and stalks away.

My hands start shaking. I clench them. Hard. I've never stood up to Aunt Margot this way, but it was the right thing to do. Even if I could rewind the last few minutes, I wouldn't change anything.

20

Anthony

When I get out of the gym shower, it's close to dinnertime. And I receive a call from Mother.

I answer uneasily. She's never, ever contacted me first.

"Yes, Mother?" I say, my stomach tight.

"Tony." Her voice cuts like a blade. "Do you mind dining out with Ivy tonight?"

"Is there something wrong?"

"She and I exchanged a few words. I think it's better if she stays away until I can decide how I'm going to process our...conversation."

I'm unsure exactly where this is going. *What did you do, Ivy?* "What do you mean?"

"She spoke to me in a way she never has before. Obviously she's very fond of you."

Fuck. Apprehension settles like a lump of old, congealed fat. I remember the way Mother treated Bolt and Edgar nine years ago. I'm no stranger to being banished from my family home, but Ivy is different.

You should've been more careful. You should've known Ivy might say something to anger Mother over you. "I apologize for anything she said to upset you."

"Why? Didn't you fill her head with rebellious ingratitude?" A short pause. "I *told* you to stay away from her. I *told* you to not take her away from me, but you did. You just can't let me have any happiness, can you?"

"Mother, I never—"

"*You have poisoned her against me, Tony*," Mother continues, her voice low and awful. "You pretended to be here for my sake—to earn my forgiveness—but this is what you really wanted, wasn't it? To destroy what little I've salvaged? To show me what a fool I was, to think ever you were good and wonderful? You want me to send her away, too, don't you?"

Each syllable is an ice pick, stabbing, making me bleed inside. "There's no reason to cut Ivy out of your life. I've *never* meant to hurt you, Mother. I'll speak to her and—"

"Stop pretending, *you monster*!" The word burns like a brand as my face heats with shame, guilt and unworthiness. "I hope you're satisfied. You make me sick. I rue the day I had you." She hangs up. And coming from my socially correct mother, it might as well be a backhand to the face.

My hand clenches around the phone, my breathing rough and uneven. I never wanted Ivy to stand up to Mother on my behalf, never wanted her to cause their relationship to sour over me. I didn't think it would happen, either, because I noticed they were avoiding each other over the last few weeks.

Obviously, I thought wrong.

Mother can be upset with me, but shutting Ivy out is unacceptable. She's been filling the ragged hole I left in Mother's life. I rake my hair. I need to figure out how to impress upon Ivy that she should never, ever say a word to defend me.

Soon after my call with Mother ends, Ivy texts me. *Wanna eat out?*

It's like she and Mother are on the same wavelength. Just how bad was their fight?

A small nerve behind my right eye starts to throb. *Eating out is good.* I'll tell her how to juggle me and Mother over food that she likes. *What are you in the mood for?*

Pizza? I'm near a place right now. Cajun Milan.

Perfect. I remember eating there when I was little and liking it. *Didn't realize you were out and about,* I text.

Just some errands. See you soon?

Leaving the gym right now.

When I arrive at Cajun Milan, Ivy's already ensconced in a booth, her hair unbound and slightly curling around her beautiful face. She gives me a heart-stoppingly beautiful smile, the kind that can make a man's knees weak with need, launch a thousand ships...or start a war.

I slide into the booth seat and kiss her.

"How was the workout?" she asks, a little breathless.

"Not bad. But now I'm starving."

We order pepperoni pizza and a pitcher of pink lemonade. Ivy doesn't look upset like I half expected. Instead, she's bubbling with barely suppressed excitement and anticipation. Did I somehow imagine the call with Mother?

"What?" Ivy asks. "Is there something on my face?"

"No." I take a moment to think about how I'm going to broach the topic. "Ivy—"

Our order arrives, interrupting me.

I place a slice of pizza on Ivy's plate before taking one for myself. Then wait until we've both had a few bites. Maybe some food in our bellies will make what I have to say go over easier. It's harder to be angry on a full stom—

"Guess what?" Ivy says suddenly.

"What?"

She pulls up a picture on her phone and slides it over to me. "My new tattoo." She brings her left arm out from under the table and shows me the bandaged wrist. "What do you think?"

A single tiger lily, and *T* and *I* entwined within. It's small, delicate and beautiful, just like Ivy. Normally I would be pleasantly surprised she got such a pretty tattoo for herself. But the *T* creates an apprehension that settles over me like a dark, heavy cloud. At the same time, I'm overcome with emotion at the gesture. "You shouldn't have." My voice is unusually thick and taut.

"Why not? It's perfect. Exactly what I want." She reaches out and takes my hand in hers. "I know you don't like it when I try to tell you how I feel. But it's not fair for me to have to hold it in, while you're always saying you love me. So I got this to show you that I love you. Every time you see it, you'll know you're in my heart."

Oh no, Ivy. No, no, no. She doesn't understand.

I can bear her looking at me like I'm the most amazing thing in the world. What I can't bear is her telling me she loves me. I'm a fraud. She doesn't know how terrible, how stained I am in my heart. In my soul.

"Tattoos are permanent," I say finally.

"Pretty much."

I exhale roughly, running fingers through my hair with more force than necessary. I should tell her the truth, but I can't. If she knows the truth, she'll never hold me in her arms. Or light my world with her presence. I can't go back to the darkness again. "What if you regret it?"

Her eyebrows pinch together, and she looks at me like I'm crazy. "Why would I do that?"

"It hurts to remove a tattoo."

"I don't plan on removing it. When I give my heart to someone, it's forever."

Her words flow over me like warm honey, even though she's saying them because she doesn't know everything about me. Fear that she will learn and turn away, and guilt that I'm deceiving her by withholding the full truth tear at me. I debate with my better self...and lose. "Things don't always work out."

"Wait. Are you worried about us breaking up?" She stares at me incredulously, a hint of hurt and vulnerability bleeding through those expressive eyes. "Who's the guy telling me he loves me every day? Who's looking for a job specifically in Philadelphia to be with me?"

"That's different."

"Oh, different. How?"

"You deserve to be told you're loved. You deserve the best."

She reaches over and puts a hand over my throbbing heart. "Tony, I love you," she says before I can stop her. "You know that."

"Please. You shouldn't say things like that."

"Why? Because of what your mom thinks about you?"

"*Ivy.*"

"She told me."

Shock almost knocks me out. Mother doesn't speak of Katherine's death unless under the most extreme emotional turmoil. The only reason she mentioned my sister when we met again because she was afraid I'd mess things up in Tempérane.

And it looks like I might have, without meaning to.

Ivy adds, "She needs to see an army of therapists, not hold you responsible for something that couldn't have been helped."

"Don't talk like that," I say, my voice tight with panic. "Is that what you told her? No wonder she was furious. You know nothing about Katherine's death. You weren't even here when it happened."

Ivy flinches as though I spat in her face. "Your mother said the same thing. So why don't you tell me?"

I could. I could tell her everything. But then won't she see the blood on my hands? Recoil in horror? *You make me sick,* Mother said. Ivy will feel the same way if she knows the whole story. I'd rather have her angry and frustrated than experience her condemnation and disgust. But it's like having to choose between a guillotine and a noose. "Because it's none of your business," I say painfully.

"None of my *business*?" She stares at me. "When it's hanging over us? When it's tearing at both of us like this?"

Her distress makes me want to share everything. But I steel myself. "It has nothing to do with you. You chose to tie yourself into a knot over it."

"You're shutting me out, Tony. People who love each other don't do that."

Pain darkens her gaze, pushing me to say it. Just confess it all.

I can't. It'll be better to have her upset for a little while than realize I'm a monster beyond redemption.

After several moments of silence, she takes in a shuddering breath, tears welling in her eyes. "You don't even know what love is if this is how you treat me. I love you, care about you and want you to be happy, but you only feel the same in return as long as you're comfortable."

"You're being dramatic," I say, hating the pain I'm causing her.

"What I'm being is honest. Because unlike you, I know what I want, I know what I feel, and I'm brave enough to admit it out loud." Looking away, she starts blinking rapidly. Then finally, she adds, "You're a fucking coward."

Yes. Yes, I am. But I can't be brave like her because I'm too afraid. I have too much to lose—her. "Ivy, look. You're upset right now, but once you give yourself some time to think it over, you'll realize I'm ri—"

"Don't you *dare* pat me on the head and tell me everything's going to be fine as long as I do everything you want! I'm not 'upset,' Tony. I'm *furious.* Disappointed. I thought what we had was better than this. I thought you'd be happy when you saw my tattoo. I thought you'd fight even harder for us, rather than complain about how permanent a tattoo is! If our relationship is so fragile that a tattoo is enough to make you shut me out, what the hell is the point?"

"Ivy, I *am* flattered. Even honored," I say helplessly, realizing the situation's completely screwed up. This is not at all what I was trying for. I just wanted her not defend me in front of Mother. I only wish she hadn't gotten the tattoo because I don't deserve it.

I seem to have made things worse by saying that, though. Her eyes flash dangerously as she stands up. "I'll do what you want, Tony. I'll stay in Tempérane and give myself some time to think. You go see your friend alone. And you'd better hope I don't follow your advice. Don't come crawling back if I think it over and decide I've made a mistake getting the tattoo. Because it'll mean I don't love you after all...and by then it'll be too late!"

Fear closes around my throat. I jump to my feet. "Ivy, wait." *Don't abandon me.*

"No. You finish the pizza. I'm going home."

She steps away before I can reach for her and dashes out of the restaurant.

My knees slowly fold, and I land back on the seat. I hurt all over, like I've been pummeled by a pro boxer. The restaurant seems to undulate around me. This went so bad, so fast, that I don't know how to fix it. I can't lose her, but if I try to force things, our argument will only become bitterer and more volatile. We might even break up.

Give her time, I tell myself. Maybe going to see Ryder

alone *will* give us a little breathing room. Once she calms down and starts thinking more clearly, she'll realize I wasn't being unreasonable. I'll even offer to go to the tattoo artist she hired and put an identical tattoo on my own wrist, so she knows I consider our relationship anything but temporary.

21

Ivy

When the alarm goes off, I hit it, then huff out a breath. I can't believe Tony didn't come by last night. I was so certain he would...and offer me whatever explanation he could about Katherine's death.

Maybe he honestly can't talk about it. I mean...I don't know how I'd feel if I thought I had a part in my family's death, even if it was an accident.

I shower, put on a T-shirt and shorts and go down for breakfast. I'm not sure what I'm going to do when I see Tony. Obviously, pushing him isn't going to improve the situation, and I hate arguing with him.

Just give him some space to think on it? I'm sure we can have a calmer and more rational conversation before the weekend starts. I wish I hadn't gotten so nasty and told him to go see his friend alone. I was just devastated and upset by his reaction to my tattoo, especially coming so soon after my ugly talk with Aunt Margot. I just wanted him to see the tat for what it is—my love for him—and accept it, rather than acting like love vanishes as easily as, I don't know, the morning dew or something.

"Good morning," Harry says, holding a spoon carelessly over his cereal. Next to it is a plate with a few bits of eggs and bacon.

"Hi," I say. "You look chirpy."

"It's a nice day."

"Have you seen Tony?" He usually gets up earlier than anyone.

"Yeah."

Ugh. Why is he channeling Jonas all of a sudden? "Aaand...?"

"He left."

"Left? For where?" I ask, wondering if Tony's decided to avoid me.

"Dunno. Had a suitcase, though."

Panic leaves me breathless. *Don't come crawling back if I think it over and decide I made a mistake getting the tattoo. Because it'll mean I don't love you after all.*

Oh my God! Is that what made him go? I never meant for him to just give up and leave!

I explode out of my chair and dash back to my room. I have to call him, tell him to come back.

His phone rings and rings. "Come on," I mutter, waiting for him to pick up. When he doesn't, I text, *Where are you?*

The moments I wait for him to respond feel like an eternity in hell. Pacing, I nibble on the tip of my index finger. I sometimes forget he can be exceptionally vulnerable, especially when it comes to his mother's horrible attitude and treatment. What she put him through has to be child abuse, even if she never physically raised a hand against him.

"Tony, you better text me back right now!" I hiss at the phone.

Finally, it pings. *At the airport.*

Oh, good. He hasn't boarded yet. *What are you doing? Come back.*

I thought you wanted me to go see Ryder by myself.

I double-check the calendar. *Why? It's only Thursday.* He wasn't supposed to fly out until tomorrow.

I decided to follow your advice and leave a little early. Give us some time to cool off.

My heartbeat slows, although not much. So he's not *leaving* leaving. Just going to see his friend. I hate it that we're going to be apart, and I wish I hadn't said what I said, because he's doing this thinking it's what I really want.

I hesitate, dying to tell him to come back soon and that I only want to understand him better. But at the same time, I would hate for him to think I'm pressuring him again. He already knows I need to know what happened, and that I don't want to be shut out. If he's leaving earlier than planned, he must really need some space.

In the end, I don't text him back. After tossing the phone back on my desk, I go downstairs again. Harry looks up. "Everything okay?"

"Yeah." I give him a pat smile.

"By the way, are you free this weekend?"

"Yeah. Why?"

"A local quintet needs a pianist. They're playing Dvořák or something this Saturday."

"Aunt Margot mentioned it to me."

"Oh, okay. So are you doing it?"

"I guess." I don't have anything better to do this weekend now...and it'd be a shame to cancel the concert when I can help make it happen. Besides, it'll be something to keep me busy and not obsess about Tony every minute until he returns.

After the breakfast, I go find Aunt Margot. She's in the library, reading, and elegant as usual in a pale pink dress.

"About the quintet you mentioned yesterday," I begin, my voice stiff. "If they haven't found anyone yet, I'll do it."

"You aren't going with Tony out to L.A.?" she asks, her expression unreadable.

"No."

"Did you have a fight?"

Is there a hint of glee in her eyes? I can't tell for sure. Still, the muscles in my jaw and neck tighten. "I decided it'd be better if he sees his friend alone."

Her gaze drops to my pendant, then back to my face. "I see. Well, I hope things work out."

Despite the gracious words, I know she wishes for anything but.

22

Anthony

I wish I'd never left Tempérane. Ryder's yacht party is being hosted by some big-shot Hollywood producer who just inherited a metric ton of money and wants to celebrate. When Ryder heard I was arriving early, he sent a helicopter to pick me up from the airport and bring me to the party, the bird landing neatly on the helipad.

The yacht is enormous, and alive with tanned and oiled bodies. A lot of women haven't bothered with bikini tops, reminding me of Spain. The sound system blares out dance tunes nonstop. Top-shelf booze flows freely, and the intoxicated crowd is hopping and gyrating to the music, raising their drinks in the air. And it isn't even five in the afternoon.

Happy fucking Hollywood life!

"This is the shit!" Ryder says, a fresh glass of scotch in his hand. A huge grin splits his disgustingly handsome face. It's almost scary how good-looking the bastard is, not just facially but physically as well. And the craziest thing is he didn't have any plastic surgery, contrary to what a lot of people think. He's one hundred percent natural, and doesn't have to use anything to look good—clothes, props, anything—because it's *him* who makes *them* look good. I've seen him roll out of bed and still look like he could be on the cover of *GQ*.

But it's impossible to hate the guy. He's too fun, too easygoing. And instead of relying on his looks to cruise through life, he isn't afraid of work.

"It's nice," I say, still nursing my first drink. I can't knock back alcohol the way Ryder does. He's impervious to the stuff.

"Why so glum, dude?" he asks loudly over the music.

"Because." I miss the lovely hours I spent listening to Ivy play Chopin and Liszt. Or the quiet hours when she napped with her head in my lap. Or the sizzling hours we spent in bed, exploring and figuring out each other's bodies.

Ryder gives me a look, then elbows me lightly. "You miss your girl."

I fake laugh, a laugh that says everything's great in my world, really. "Yes. I do."

"I was looking forward to meeting her. Sorry she's sick."

The lie makes me feel bad. But how do I tell him the truth, that Ivy's too angry with me to fly out and meet my best buddy? Or tell him what she said about deciding she made a mistake, the possibility of which is haunting me?

She isn't going to leave you, I tell myself. She wanted to know where you were.

But she never said anything else.

"Got a pic?" Ryder says.

"Ha." I pull out my phone, which I've been carrying around in case she calls or texts. The first thing it shows is her face on my lock screen. I took the shot when she was playing *Grand Galop Chromatique*. I thumb through and show him more shots, most of them of her at the piano or napping. My favorite is one of her in the morning. She looks so tender and vulnerable and sweet...but that's too private, so I skip it.

Ryder gives a low whistle. "She's a *babe*. No wonder you're crazy about her."

"Ivy's perfect," I say, a smile on my lips as love swells in my chest.

"Cute dimple. Gives her face a little extra something."

"That's not a dimple, it's a mole."

He leans close to the phone, squinting a bit. "Oh yeah... Well, whatever. You're done, dude. Totally whipped." Ryder laughs, slapping me on the back. "Look at that shit-eating grin."

Let him tease. I don't give a damn. I do love her, and I don't care if everyone at this party knows. "She's amazing. Plays the meanest piano."

"That's awesome."

"She'll debut at Carnegie Hall one day," I say proudly, because I know she will. She's too talented, too hardworking not to.

"She can still come out, if you want. I could send a private jet over. That chick over there"—Ryder points out a tall redhead with a stunning body—"has one I can borrow." He considers for a moment. "Actually...I'll probably have to pay her."

"How is it borrowing if you have to pay?"

"I mean with sex. But hey, no sacrifice is too great for a friend."

It's tempting, but I'm still not ready to tell Ivy everything... and she'll expect that if I ask her to join me now. "Maybe next time. I don't know how she'd feel about having to travel. Kind of a long flight..."

"Your call," Ryder says, shrugging. "Just take her back something nice. Makes up for not bringing her, plus every girl expects a gift when her guy goes out of town."

Ivy is definitely expecting something, but it isn't a gift. I realize I won't be able to return home without making a decision—either tell her everything and bear her disgust, or stay silent and bear her disappointment and anger.

Scylla and Charybdis. Either way, I'm going to be screwed.

23

Ivy

The quintet concert turns out to be a high school production with a donation box at the entrance to raise money for a local youth music program. We meet on Friday for a couple of hours to rehearse. The juniors and seniors are awestruck after hearing that I've been studying at Curtis for the last three years. It's a little unnerving.

Surprisingly, no one is there to turn my music. It's okay, though, since I have Dvořák's Piano Quintet memorized from having played it before. I make it a habit to memorize the pieces I'm supposed to play. It gives me extra confidence that I'm really ready and prepared.

Saturday starts out ominously. The sky is dark pewter with rain-heavy clouds. The wind picks up, scattering leaves and tugging hard at the moss as it sweeps through the trees in the garden. Having spent five years in Louisiana, plus summer vacations and holidays from Curtis, rain and storms don't freak me out like they do some of my friends who come from states like California. But goosebumps rise on my skin anyway. It stormed the day my parents died.

I wrap my arms around myself for a moment before driving out to the St. Agnellus Community Center. It isn't raining yet, but the wind gets more vicious along the way, trying to push the car off the road. As I get out in the community center parking lot, it pulls at my blue dress—the informal uniform all the girls in the quintet are supposed to wear—and tangles my hair.

I dash into the community center and go to the practice room in the back. It's large enough to accommodate about thirty people. An upright piano that hasn't been tuned in ages stands in the corner, and all the members of the quintet are here—the two violinists, the violist and the cellist tuning their instruments and warming up. A lone strawberry blonde is hanging out in the back, her face stuck in a thick Harry Potter hardback. She's also got the blue dress uniform on, so she must be the one designated to turn my music. The only boy in the group—the cellist—is in a suit with a neatly knotted sleet-gray tie.

"Awesome, you're here now," the violist says.

"I'm not late, am I?"

"You're fine. Ready for the final run-through?"

I nod, and we start getting into position, taking our seats and arranging our music on the stands. The blonde comes over, pulling a chair up next to the piano, so she can flip music for me. Others are expected to deal with their own music, but not pianists.

I adjust the piano bench and toss my hair over my shoulders. Something snags it, and I wince. "Ow." I tug, trying to free my hair. I can't play with my neck bent the entire time.

There's a snap and something metallic glides down my body and falls into my lap.

Crap. The medallion!

I twist around to look down on the floor. There's a glint under the bench, and I grab it. This isn't good.

I don't consider myself especially superstitious, but I'm getting an uneasy feeling. Tony hasn't called or texted even once since he left, and I can't help but wonder if the broken chain is some kind of omen.

Don't be ridiculous. It just got caught in your hair.

I put the medallion and chain in my purse under the piano bench. I'll have them looked at later. I'm probably being oversensitive with Tony gone and the awful weather, and memories of the day when I lost the two people who mattered most to me.

24

Anthony

The sounds of partying outside pound the walls of Ryder's cabin, making them throb, but we're pretty well insulated. It's huge for a yacht cabin, and luxuriously appointed with a king-sized bed, seating area, desk and two huge TVs.

Ryder's looking at me with a slightly loopy and satisfied smile. From the way the sheets on his bed are all twisted and pulled, I can guess what he was up to last night. There are five different pairs of very feminine panties and three bras in various places around the room.

"Five? Really?" I inspect the seat of a leather chair by the desk. It looks to be free of bodily fluids.

"More like ten. I dunno. Kinda lost count." Ryder yawns from the bed. He's just finished doing a series of martial arts stretches and is wearing nothing but black boxers.

"Right."

"Hey, those girls couldn't find their rooms. And naturally, I didn't want them to have to sleep in the passageway. Bad things can happen to pretty girls in passageways."

His dramatic delivery makes me laugh despite my shitty mood. It's only been three days since I got on the yacht, but I'm going stir-crazy. It has everything—two pools, a huge hot tub, a super-luxurious cabin for my use, not mention the spectacular ocean off Catalina Island...even a gym, which Ryder and I have made some use of, sparring a bit—but it doesn't have what I really want.

Ivy.

Every moment since I got here, I've been wondering what she's up to. Did she sleep well? What piece is she practicing now? Has she made a triumphant recording to make her friend Yuna green with envy? Is she still mad at me? Has she decided she doesn't love me? Does she even want me now?

Ryder heaves himself off the bed and comes over. "Want something to drink? I have scotch, whiskey and vodka. The girls killed all the wine."

"I'm okay."

He peers at me. "Jeez. At least look like you mean it when you say that. You look like shit."

"Oh, come on. I'm fine."

"The chicks were eyeing you like mad. You're totally the hot, dark, brooding dude. Like the hero you see in one of those romance books." He frowns impressively and lowers his voice. "*It was a dark and stormy night... Suddenly, bright lightning split the sky, illuminating a dark and brooding man full of sexual menace.*"

"What the hell are you reading these days?" The Ryder I used to know read manly-man books, with pictures. Lots of pictures, usually of naked women.

"Not these days. It was a while back. From Elizabeth's stash."

"Why were you reading your sister's stuff?"

"To see what makes girls tick. It was a long time ago, but that opening stuck." Ryder pours himself a scotch. "I'm just saying you're the dark and brooding dude in that story. And the menace, too."

"*Menace?*" What the fuck? I've been nothing but polite since I arrived. I even rejected the women's advances—politely—although though a couple of them were irritatingly persistent. "I've been completely gracious and sociable here."

"How can you be sociable when you keep saying no? The girls can tell you aren't gay." He downs half the glass in one long swig. "Ergo, you must be this brooding, tortured guy who requires the love of a good woman to bring him out of his downward spiral."

My mouth falls open. "Who the hell are you and what have you done to my best friend?"

"Fuck you. I've been reading a lot of scripts recently. Chick flick stuff. Women usually decide what to watch on dates." Ryder shrugs. *What can a guy do?* "But I overheard some of the girls betting on who could get you to sleep with her first. You're the prize stud."

I grimace. Is that why some of them have been getting ridiculous about it? "Last night, some woman knocked on my door at two a.m., then acted confused that it wasn't her room. She was flashing everything but her crotch at me."

"Cool. So what happened?"

"I told her, 'This is my room,' and shut the door in her face."

"Man." Ryder shakes his head. "You're so fucking whipped. All these hot, willing ladies, and you won't do any of them."

"They aren't Ivy."

He shrugs. "Must be true love. I've *never* not wanted to accommodate a willing woman."

"You're going to die of multiple STDs."

"Nah. I might sleep around, but I'm not stupid. Condoms, my man, condoms. The last thing I want is a virus or a little Ryder Junior."

"Ryder Junior sounds...cute." If the son is half as pretty as his daddy, a whole new generation of women will get their hearts broken.

Ryder shudders. "My mom would kill the girl...if my grandma didn't do it first. My family doesn't mess around with that kind of thing."

Most likely true. His mother's side of the family can be a bit...old-fashioned about certain things. His grandmother in particular sounds like a real piece of work from what I've heard.

Ryder polishes off the rest of his drink and claps me on the shoulder. "You know what? Whatever happened between you and Ivy is going to work itself out. If not, you'll just find somebody else."

"What the hell are you talking about?"

"Oh come on. 'She's sick.' Seriously? We've been friends for how many years now, and you think I'm not going to know if you have a girl problem? If she really was sick, you wouldn't be here. Not when you're so obsessed, you can't even sleep with another girl."

Touché. "Fine. We had an argument." I tell him about the tattoo.

Ryder listens, then shakes his head. "Why get hung up about a tattoo? Let the girl deface her skin if that's what she wants."

"It isn't a defacement, for fuck's sake! The tattoo's really beautiful."

"Okay, okay, fine. But like you said, when it's over, it's over. Then what?"

The idea of Ivy and me not being together dries all the

moisture out of my mouth. If it were anybody but Ryder saying this, I'd break the bastard's face.

"True love doesn't exist, man. It's like...this action movie script I looked at, you know? In it, the hero takes a bullet for the girl. Then he says, 'I'm just glad it wasn't you.'" Ryder laughs. "As if! Who the hell takes a bullet for somebody like that, when it isn't their job? I never will, and I don't know anybody else who would, either. But *that*'s supposed to be true love."

I stare at Ryder. *Of course...* How could I have not seen it, not realized it all this time? Laid out so starkly, it's crystal clear. "You're wrong," I say.

"Huh?" He stops in the middle of pouring himself another glass of scotch. "About what?"

"About true love and taking a bullet for another person. I would. For Ivy. I'd rather die than have anything happen to her."

And I know exactly what I need to do: tell her everything —and pray she won't judge me too harshly. Not being fully honest with her—not "letting her in," as she put it—will only hurt her, and I'd rather skin myself alive than see the light in her eyes grow dim again.

I jump to my feet. "I gotta go."

"What, *now*? Where?"

"Home. I have to see Ivy." I look at Ryder. "You're a genius. And an awesome friend."

He seems confused for a moment, but then slowly grins. "I know I'm awesome," he says. "Whatever I did, you're welcome. Let me see when we can get a helicopter to take you back to LAX."

25

Ivy

The high school kids and I do a quick run-through before the actual concert starts. The girl who's supposed to turn my music keeps losing focus, not flipping pages like she's supposed to. Although it doesn't disrupt the performance, it's a little annoying she can't manage the easiest task in the show. If turning pages is too much, she should've let someone else do it. I glance over to see what her deal is.

Her gaze is glued to the cellist, who's doing his best to avoid eye contact. Does she have a crush on him? And is he uncomfortable about it?

I start to feel bad for her. If I'm right, her situation is a lot like mine—liking a guy who can't let you in. Then I note the violist looking daggers in my direction. What's her deal? I barely even know her...

Wait, she's not mad at me, but at the girl turning my music, who's now bristling like an indignant hedgehog. *Oh boy.*

All this silent drama is too much. Nobody should be doing

this during a run-through, especially not right before the actual concert.

If they screw up because they can't focus, I'm going to be furious, no matter how sorry I feel for the girl next to me. If you're going to stage a public performance, you need to be professional.

Despite my worries, the concert goes well. The quintet plays half a beat too slow for my liking, but I don't think anybody notices or cares. I sigh with relief when the crowd applauds after our piece, and we all rise, bow and curtsy to the warmly appreciative audience. St. Agnellus is a small town without a lot of cultural events. People here value them more than the jaded audiences you get in big cities.

And it was a great excuse to get out of the house. Tony's silence is making me restless and disappointed. There are times I'm tempted to contact him first, but I stop myself. I don't want him to think I'm agreeing to his decision to not let me in... even if I miss him with an almost physical pain.

Also, the Peachers are visiting again, and Aunt Margot made her disdain and displeasure known all day long. Not that I blame her. Sam and Marty are being particularly insufferable on this visit from what little I overheard. Apparently, Sam is determined to get her to invest in one of his real estate development projects, even though she's made it clear she'd rather dump the money into Lake Pontchartrain. And if that intolerable know-it-all Marty comments one more time about my interpretation of "La Campanella," using tidbits he's obviously picked up from Google, I'm going to murder him.

By the time I make it to the big door to the parking lot, it's almost nine. The building is mostly empty now—the audience is gone and just us performers are left.

The rest of the quintet plan to hang around and dissect the concert. But I want to go home, even though I hate driving in these conditions. I crack the door open and look outside. It's storming hard, wind whipping the rain around until it hits like liquid darts sailing through the air. You can't even block it with an umbrella. It wasn't this bad earlier, so at least I was able to perform in dry clothes.

I get ready to dash across the lot, until I hear somebody behind me. I turn and see my page-turner. Despite being distracted throughout the run-through, she did pretty well during the actual concert.

"You were really good," she says.

"Thanks. But everyone was great. And you were really helpful." It's awful I'm blanking on her name, but I'm terrible at remembering them.

"I...um..." She licks her lips, then sniffles. Her face turns blotchy.

I wait, praying she isn't about to ask for some uncomfortable favor. Like that time when a guy begged me to hook him up with a "special" admission to Curtis.

"Could I ask you for a ride?"

"Oh. Um, okay. Are you stuck?"

"My sister... I'm sorry, it's a long, boring story." She tightens her mouth, then forces a smile. "I just need a ride home, and I don't have my phone or anything."

I finally notice she doesn't have a purse. The only thing she's holding is a brown paper bag. Doesn't matter what happened between her and her sister. I don't want her stuck out here or trying to walk home alone at night. "Sure," I say. "Where do you live?"

"Augustine."

That's a little out past Tempérane, but it isn't like I have anything pressing. And I *finally* remember her name. "Sure, Charlene."

"Thanks."

I point at my champagne-colored Lexus coupe, a gift from

Aunt Margot and Uncle Lane when I got accepted to Curtis. "That's my car. Let's go."

I hit the fob to unlock the doors as I dash across as fast as I can, but it's futile. Charlene and I are both drenched within seconds.

"Buckle up," I say when we're finally in the car.

She fumbles around, but nothing clicks. "It doesn't work."

"Huh?" I reach over and try it myself, but she's right. There's no click, and the tongue just slides out. Then I remember one of the guys I gave a ride to at Curtis busted the latch when he dropped a paperclip in it last spring. I meant to have it looked at, but kept forgetting. "Ugh. I hate this."

"It's okay," Charlene says. "It's only, like, fifteen, twenty minutes tops."

I worry my lower lip, but she's probably right. It bothers me that she won't have her seatbelt on, but I hate the idea of leaving her behind alone at night more. If the cops pull me over, I'll just have to explain the situation and hope for a warning. But what are the odds in this weather?

I start the engine and pull out of the lot. When we're finally on the highway, Charlene opens the paper bag and pulls out a bottle of whiskey.

"Seriously?" I say, surprised. "Where did you get that?"

"Filched it from my sister's car earlier."

"Aren't you, you know, underage?"

"Almost eighteen." She blinks away tears, then takes a big swig. "I need this."

"Well." I clear my throat. I'm not at all comfortable with her drinking. I'm pretty sure you can't have an open container in a car, much less drink out of it, even if you aren't the driver. Not to mention she's a minor, and I don't think law enforcement will look at this kind of thing kindly if I get pulled over... "I feel bad for whatever problem you're having, but you need to put that away. I can't drive you home if you don't."

She has another drink, then sniffs and screws the cap back on. "Sorry."

"It's okay." Something major must've happened for her to ditch her sister and cadge a ride with a virtual stranger.

There aren't that many cars on the road. This storm is bad enough that even Louisianians don't want to be out in it. By the time we're getting close to Tempérane, my Lexus is the only car on the road.

Charlene's staring outside, occasionally wiping at her eyes. "Boys can be assholes," she says suddenly.

"Oh my God, definitely," I say, thinking of Tony at Cajun Milan. What the hell kind of love pushes your lover away?

"Adam's fucking Jane."

"Uh..." The names are familiar, but I can't quite place them.

"The cellist and the violist."

"Oh." I clear my throat. "Right."

"I caught them red-handed, and he didn't even say he was sorry."

Oh wow. "You and Adam were dating?"

"Yeah. Went to prom together, the whole thing. We were supposed to be...like this!" She makes some gesture I miss. She sniffles, then wipes at her face.

Poor kid. That totally sucks. "Men are stubborn and can be idiotic. Just look at me."

"What about you?"

Normally I wouldn't be sharing, but somehow, cocooned in the car with this girl who's hurting and the weather raging outside, it seems okay. Feeling a bit reckless, I say, "I got a tattoo to show this guy I love him, and he...he just..."

"Flipped out?"

"Basically." I get my purse, root around in it one-handed while keeping my eyes on the road and take the pendant out.

"Look at this. He gave it to me, but he doesn't love me enough to let me in. It's just...weird."

"Can I see it?" Charlene takes the pendant, turning it this way and that. "It's *gorgeous*. So he gave you this, but he won't say he loves you?"

"*He* says it, but he won't let *me* say it. Just won't accept that I have feelings for him. He doesn't want my love—he won't let me tell him or show him how I feel."

"What a douche. I hope he gets blue balls for life."

I don't want Tony to have blue balls. I just want him to realize he loves and trusts me enough to let me in all the way. "Probably not going to happen," I say. "He's hot."

"How come all the hot ones are so bad?"

"Good question. Figure it out and they'll give you a Nobel Prize."

"For chemistry!" We both laugh.

Through the rain, a pickup truck appears, coming toward us, slewing a bit on the slick highway...and in our lane. No headlights, which is why I didn't see it until now. My heart starts pounding, sweat instantly slickening my hands. I hit the brakes with all my strength and honk. The truck doesn't change course.

"Oh my God!" I scream, jerking the steering wheel to the left. *We're too close!*

The pickup hits the Lexus with an unbelievably loud metallic *crunch*. The impact is a shock wave through my entire body. I'm thrown against the seatbelt strap, arms and head snapping forward. Time starts to slow down. The only sound I hear is my own rough breathing.

My vision's warped—everything feels blurry and weird. Something warm and wet covers my face and chest, and my ears feel muffled.

I look to the right. Charlene is unmoving, her face covered in something red.

The truck moves backward... *Hit and run,* I think vaguely, struggling to pull myself together. *Need to get my phone. Call 911.*

But no. It rushes back at me. My head's so sluggish, I can't figure out why...

Instinctively I try to hit the gas, but I can't. My foot seems disconnected from my brain. Or at least it's not hitting the gas hard enough to make the car move. I can't figure out which.

Everything happens in slow motion. The truck moving toward me. My body not responding like it should. Charlene starting to slump toward me. Is this the end? So damn unfair.

I pray for a miracle, even knowing it won't happen. The Lexus is stuck. Maybe I should've stayed back at the community center with the other members of the quintet. I think about Tony. How brilliant. How handsome. But impossible to reach. He made it so clear. I wish I hadn't met him. No. Not that. What I really wish is that I hadn't fought with him on Wednesday. I just want to see him one more time. Hear his voice one last time, saying, "I love you," even if it isn't enough to let me in all the w—

The truck crashes into us again. Everything goes black.

26

Anthony

I wanted to get back to Tempérane on Sunday, but my flight is delayed due to weather...then canceled.

On Monday, the flight leaves five hours late due to mechanical problems. By the time I make it to Houston, it's too late for my connection. The nine-thirty p.m. commuter plane to Tempérane has already left. Since it's the last one out of the city, I have to spend the night in Houston.

I call Ivy from the hotel. She doesn't answer. I text her, but there's no reply. It's as though she's cut me out of her life.

Who could blame her, though? I was a total dick at the pizza joint.

In-person groveling, I decide. That's what I need to make up for this mess.

What if she really did decide she doesn't love you anymore?

The unwelcome question pops in my head. *No, no, no.* Ivy isn't that fickle. Her love is stronger and purer than mine. I'll see her and do whatever it takes to make her happy. If she wants me to get on my knees, so be it. I'm willing to do anything because I know that as long as I'm sincere, she'll forgive me. For some weird reason, she thinks there's good in me, something worth cherishing. I hold on to that all night long...and through the short hop from Houston.

By the time I finally make it to Tempérane, it's Tuesday. I'm so happy to be back that not even the merciless sun and humidity of August can put a damper on my mood. I stop by a florist to grab a bouquet of tiger lilies on the way. The florist gives me a funny look as she hands me the flowers.

I stare back at her. "What?"

"Nothing." She clears her throat, not meeting my gaze. "Just...got distracted. Sorry." She hands me my credit card back.

Huh.

When I come home, Jonas isn't around. It's Harry who's waiting, his face pale and tight.

"What's wrong?" I look around. "Where's Ivy?"

He runs his fingers through his hair. He bites his lip when he notices the flowers in my hand. "Maybe we should go to the living room and sit down," he says. The words come too quickly, as though he's throwing them out to fill a silence he can't stand.

"Is she upstairs?"

"No. She..." A long sigh. "We should get you something to drink first. You must be tired from the trip. What a bunch of shitty delays."

I narrow my eyes. My brother thinks he's slick, but he's as transparent as water, especially when he's flustered. "Cut the bullshit, Harry. What's wrong?"

He closes his eyes for a moment, then runs a hand over his jaw. "Ivy went to over to St. Agnellus on Saturday. A piano performance. She didn't come back."

"Okay. So where is she?" I ask, my hand around the bouquet tightening.

"Well, that's the thing. We aren't really sure. She's not answering her phone, and, uh..."

"Did she go over to a friend's place?"

He shakes his head. "We checked already. Called all around town."

Shit. This is my fault. Maybe she was too upset to stay here, knowing I'd be back. I should've never gone to California. "Let me go look for her."

"I think it's better if we wai—" His phone rings. Eyebrows pinched, he answers. "Hello? Yeah...?" He pales so fast I'm afraid he's going to pass out. He blindly reaches out and grabs the edge of a heavy marble stand. "Are you sure?"

Suddenly I can't speak. The entire house seems to fill with dread.

Harry looks at me, his eyes haunted. "It's Edgar." He swallows. "They found Ivy in a bayou. A car accident in the storm on Saturday. That's...where... Aw, shit. That's why I thought maybe we should just wait because..." He breathes out roughly, shoving a hand into his hair.

My vision dims. The words get caught in my throat. *No. No.*

"It's her car," Harry adds, his voice shaky. "Her ID."

No! I take two large steps, rip the phone from Harry's hand. "Edgar."

"Tony. I'm so sor—"

"Was there any jewelry? A necklace or anything like that?"

"Tony, the ID was posi—"

"Was there any jewelry?"

"Hold on." There's a pause while Edgar confers with someone. "They found a pendant in the car. Some kind of astrological motif..."

The rest of his words don't register. A light-year away, I feel Harry's hand on my shoulder.

It's all fucking lie. A mistake. *It has to be.* Some messed-up prank. Ivy's still mad, so she's doing this to fuck with me. That's fine. I deserve it.

Right? It's just a prank. Her car in a bayou... It doesn't mean anything...

But I know. Deep in my withered, fucked-up heart...I know the truth.

I should've never been such a coward, too afraid to let her in, to let her see all of me. If not, she wouldn't have been in Tempérane over the weekend and she wouldn't have had the accident. She would've known the depth of my feelings for her, that I love her more than anything in the world—more than my ego, more than my pride...more than *anything*—and how that feeling short-circuited my thoughts, flinging me from absolute bliss into an abject fear that she would know everything and cast me aside the way Mother did.

My knees hit the floor as my stomach heaves. The skin around my eyes grows hot, but no tears stream down my cheeks. They're gathering and swelling in my heart instead, growing heavier and eating away my insides like acid, drop by drop.

This is all a lie. *A lie.* But even as I repeat it to myself ...I know. And despair. And rage. And grieve. And loathe myself.

I never realized how dark and cold a Louisiana summer day could be.

The sun no longer rises, the moon no longer shines and there aren't any stars to put a spark of happiness in my heart.

PART II

–Present Day

The monk I met in Raiding, Austria, was fascinating. I'd never seen a Buddhist monk outside of Japan or Korea, so it was a little startling. He said he liked my Liebestraum (he overheard me practicing) and offered to read my palm and tell me my fortune based on my birth date and time. I only know the date, which seemed to disappoint him. He said I wanted something I lost, which was amusing. Such a generic "observation." But the rest of what he said gave me an ah-ha moment. I have to write it down so I don't forget later.

–What did I lose? (I expected him to say an earring or something.)

–People.

–No. (I lost my parents, but they're dead, so...kind of impossible to find them.)

–No? Then tell me what you lost.

–My memories. (I only say it to see what he'll say. Besides, I'm leaving for Vienna tonight, so I'll never run into this monk again, and he doesn't even know my name. But he just smiles.)

–Memories are people. You don't remember things. You remember people, your feelings for them, how they made you feel in return, because those are the memories worth carrying through life. (I think I looked unconvinced, because he added) Ice cream by itself isn't memorable. But ice cream you had with

your parents on a hot sunny day at a park when you were a child...now that's something.

–So how do I find these people?

–You stay here. They will come.

–Stay? In Austria?

–Yes. Aren't you from here?

–I'm a tourist. I've been traveling the last six years.

–How can your people find you if you keep moving around? Choose a place. Settle. And live your life the way you want to live it. Don't hide. Be seen.

–Seen?

–If nobody sees you, they can't find you.

–What if I attract bad people? (I'm worried about the fake friends who came to take advantage of me when I was confused and distraught after waking up from the coma.)

–So? You can't pick and choose your memories, can you? There are more good people than bad. Haven't you seen that during your travels?

I have. And now I know. I have to return to L.A.

–from Iris's notebook

27

Anthony

The Rolls' A/C does a good job of keeping the Los Angeles heat at bay as we wait in the passenger loading area at LAX. TJ, my bodyguard/chauffeur, is up front behind the wheel. I'm sitting in back, arms folded and not happy.

I glare at Harry as he climbs in. He looks like shit, his eyes bloodshot, and reeks of alcohol. If he throws up in my brand-new Cullinan, I'm going to skin him. Then send him the cleaning bill.

"Running off to Vegas is your idea of showing how responsible you are to everyone?"

"You really want to do this in front of..." He jerks his chin toward TJ.

"Yes."

Harry shrugs, totally unrepentant. "My fortune cookie said I was going to meet my destiny in the west, and Vegas is west. Almost west coast."

Palm, meet face. "That was *my* damn fortune cookie you stole last week, and there's nothing coastal about Vegas."

"Same time zone." He flashes a smile in my direction. He knows he's good-looking and can get away with murder with that bright, innocent smile. Except it's never worked on me, so I don't know why he still bothers.

"And 'Destiny' was a hooker."

"She's not a hooker."

"You were paying her to sleep with you. That makes her a hooker." I let out an impatient breath. I wouldn't be bothering except for Edgar asking me to keep Harry in line. He was quite unhappy to see Instagram photos of the hookers our youngest brother was spending time with, and since he's traveling, I'm it. I might've been publicly disowned seven years ago, but I'm still Harry's older brother, and I take care of my brothers, just like they do me.

"You look upset." He stops, then drops his voice. "Are you thinking about Audrey Duff?"

"Audrey? Why on earth would I be wasting time thinking about her?"

He looks incredulous. "Are you kidding? Don't you read the news?"

"Occasionally. But unlike you, I don't get it from OMG GOSSIP dot com."

"It's everywhere. She tried to commit suicide. Over you!"

"Oh, that. Wei said something about it." Mainly to warn me. My assistant knows I don't enjoy surprises, especially those set up to exploit me for someone else's benefit. I instructed him to make sure she's blocked from contacting me, ever.

Harry is staring at me like we don't even belong to the same species. "That's all you have to say?"

"What else would you *like* me to say?"

"How about 'Wow, that's terrible.' Or 'I'm sorry to hear

that,' or 'I'm deeply saddened by the news.' She said she couldn't live without you when you dumped her."

"Harry. It's one thing to be younger, another to be gullible." I give him a cool, pitying look. "Audrey clawed her way out of inner-city Chicago and found a modicum of success in Hollywood. She didn't do that by being half-assed or weak-willed. If she really were intent on killing herself, she would've done it. What she craves is the attention and money she can get by being with me. But my love? Not on the list."

"She tried to kill herself because you dumped her," Harry tries again, as though insisting will make it real.

"I never promised her anything. If she thought going out a few times would entitle her to my undying devotion, she was wrong. I won't be manipulated." Only Ivy held that special place in my heart. It's been nine years, but the pain of losing her is still crippling. I imagine putting it in a box in my heart and closing the lid—a coping technique I've learned. It lessens the pain until the ache is only a dull throb.

"That's cold, Tony. Like, Antarctic. I can't believe you still have an army of women panting after you."

"Like I said, they want my money." Bitterness courses through me. I have more money than I can ever spend, but the only woman I've ever loved is gone. After my parents tossed me out of the family seven years ago, I worked like a man possessed to build my empire. It was going to fill the void in my heart, give me the power and influence to protect what's mine...

But now that I have a fortune and the leverage that comes with it, the aching emptiness in my heart is simply...bigger. More painful.

What's the point when I don't have her?

I look out the window. Ivy's dead, and I'll never get another chance with her. My brain knows this. But my heart... That's another thing. It whispers that maybe she didn't really die. Maybe they made a mistake. Maybe, just maybe, she jumped out of that car before it plunged into the bayou. Or maybe she swam away, or...something. Anything.

I hate these thoughts and denials. Nine years. If she were alive, she would've found her way back to me long before now. I need to accept the truth—the ashes I helped scatter can't magically come together and become a living woman again—but a small part of me still can't. It thinks she has to be alive somewhere because otherwise I would've shriveled and died as well. It doesn't recognize that the living go on living, even if it's as an empty husk.

Harry hesitates, his face tight with concern. "Did you dump Audrey because she bleached her hair and got colored contacts?"

He saw her at the last public event she and I attended together. Even though he's wasting his life, getting yet another pointless postgraduate liberal arts degree, he's still a Blackwood and gets all the invitations my family receives as a courtesy. Since he likes good booze and dolled-up women, he attends as many as possible.

"She's prettier as a brunette," I say tonelessly.

He grows glum. "Maybe some people know."

"About Lauren?" I say, deliberately misunderstanding him. "So what? She's dead." Lauren was the very public mistake I made within two years of Ivy's death. There's no reason for anybody to know about Ivy. I was too young and unimportant back then, our love too short...with the abrupt end that still leaves me reeling every time I think about it. Recently, the old memories have been coming more frequently. Maybe I'm getting old. Or sentimental.

Harry knows better than to bring up Ivy. Silently, he checks his phone. He's almost never off that damned thing. His phone plays *Grand Galop Chromatique*, and I tense at the cheery music coming through the tinny speakers. I can't stand

Chopin and Liszt. Actually, I can't stand most classical piano pieces now. They hurt too much.

It's a bravura panty-dropper from the nineteenth century. Did it make you want to get naked with me?

"Turn that off."

Harry raises a finger. "Wait a minute."

"*I said turn that shit off!*" *Grand Galop Chromatique* is one of the worst. Every rapid note of the music feels like a blender blade shredding me.

"It's from this video that's going viral, titled *Showing the Jerk How It's Done*. But the pianist..." Harry squints hard. "What the fuck?"

Grinding my teeth, I snatch the phone out of his hand. But just a glimpse of the strawberry blonde in the video stops me cold.

The pianist is young—maybe in her mid- or late twenties—and looks exactly like Ivy, from the hair to the posture to the gray eyes. If that were all, I'd consider it a coincidence. But there's more.

It's the way she plays—the sublime expression, her body utterly relaxed. Her technique and tempo are flawless. She has the same unshakable confidence and wild exuberance Ivy used to play the piece with.

It's already a crazy coincidence that there's a woman who looks just like Ivy. But one who plays like her?

To be able to play Liszt like that not only requires talent, but years of diligent practice.

"What the fuck is this?" I find myself asking in an awful voice I don't recognize as my own.

Harry takes his phone back. "I don't know. But somebody posted this less than an hour ago, and tagged the location as L.A. Hammers and Strings."

She's dead, Tony. You helped scatter her ashes. There's no second chance.

I know that. The pain of losing her is still as sharp and excruciating as having my bones shaved. But I can't ignore the video. As crazy as it sounds, I want to go and see this pianist in person.

"TJ, pull over," I say.

The Cullinan stops.

I turn to Harry. "Get out."

"What? How am I going to get back to campus?"

"Call an Uber." I'm not taking him, hungover with no filter on his mouth or brain. I shove him out when he doesn't move, shut the door and instruct TJ, "To Hammers and Strings."

28

Iris

My phone buzzes again, but I ignore it and continue to sip a cappuccino at the Starbucks two doors away from the piano store.

Byron stirs the ice in his latte, his motion elegant and unhurried. That's his greatest charm—no matter what, nothing fazes him. It also doesn't hurt that he's classically handsome, with a boldly chiseled face, stunning blue eyes and dark brown hair. A white button-down shirt is draped over his lean torso, and the coffee-colored slacks fit his narrow pelvis and long legs perfectly. He radiates an air of entitled affluence without trying, which I guess comes from his background. His family is filthy rich.

The women in the café aren't immune. Many are openly staring, and some are even giving me an envious glare or two. I regard them with mild amusement. Their anger with me is totally misplaced, since I'm not in the picture that way. He isn't mine, not like they think.

As usual, Byron's oblivious. Or maybe just pretending not to notice. I can never tell.

"I should've gotten a macchiato." His baritone voice is as lazy and cultured as the man himself. He sighs, then glances over at my phone, which buzzes...*again*. "Sure you don't want to answer that?"

"I'm sure." I don't want to deal with Sam right now. "And I blame you."

"*Moi?*" He puts a hand to his chest.

"If you hadn't put that recording up on Facebook and YouTube, none of this"—I gesture at the phone—"would've happened. Sam's already upset I'm back in the country, and he hates it when I 'show off.'"

A distant uncle, Sam has become my de facto guardian since the accident that killed my parents and almost ended my life nine years ago. Normally, I wouldn't have needed anybody to act as a guardian. I was already eighteen. But a year-long coma meant somebody had to make decisions on my behalf. If Sam hadn't stepped up, I would've died. The doctors wanted to unplug me after a couple months, saying the situation was hopeless. It was Sam who kept the faith and refused to allow it.

"Nothing pleases that old man, Rizzy," Byron says carelessly, using the nickname he gave me. "Besides, you weren't showing off. You were teaching the idiot how it's done in your own imitable fashion. Why not share with the world?" He looks at his phone. "People are loving it. Over five hundred comments and likes already, and it's been less than an hour."

I take a slow sip of my brew. Byron's right about one thing: I did show that abusive jerk how it's done. I couldn't believe the nerve of the guy, coming into the store, berating his girlfriend and the saleswoman, then sitting down in front of the Bösendorfer I wanted to try and playing Liszt's *Grand Galop Chromatique*. He must've thought the music would showcase his virtuosity. Guess he didn't understand that if he played badly, it would make him look like a toddler trying to compete in the hundred-meter dash in the Olympics.

"If he hadn't called his girlfriend a talentless hack, I wouldn't have done it." I sigh as the thousandth text arrives. "Sam's probably ready to explode now. He never wanted me back in L.A."

"Why not?"

"He said I should go to France—Chopin's birthplace—or Berlin, to see Liszt's childhood home." I roll my eyes. "It would help my musicality, or so he claimed."

"Seriously? All he has to do is Google to know Chopin was from Poland and Liszt came from Hungary."

Sam claims he'd rather have me focus on music because he knows it means a lot to me. He doesn't care that I can't be a concert pianist anymore. He says it doesn't matter that I can't take care of myself financially via music, because he can provide for me. The only thing he's interested in is my happiness...

But every time I try to assert my independence, he subjects me to stories of how he had to take care of me for so long, how he ignored the doctors who thought I should go off life support because he knew what was best for me deep in his heart.

"It hurts me you won't consider my perspective, Iris," he's said more than once. "Remember that old friend of yours? You were happy to see him, but it turned out he just wanted to use you to get to me and my money? What did I say when you saw him? That you should be careful, right?" He sighs. "I'm only doing this for you because it's the least I owe your parents, God rest their souls."

Part of me suspects what he really wants is for me wander the world until the day I die, but another part can't deny all that he's done for me. And for all I know, maybe he truly believes traveling is what makes me happy.

But enough. I can't let his charity or good intentions derail me from what I have to do.

"It took me a week to convince him I'm tired of traveling," I tell Byron. "I'm going to be twenty-eight soon, I haven't lived in one place for longer than a couple of months in the last six years, and I've never held a job. I want to settle down and do what normal people do." It's the same rationale I gave Sam.

More importantly, I want to fully regain my lost memories. But that's something I'm keeping to myself. I don't like to discuss the most significant effect of being comatose for a year —partial amnesia. It feels awkward and embarrassing, like undressing in front of an audience, to admit I don't remember or know things I should know—favorite cartoons, the friends I had in high school, what prom was like and so much more.

Of course, Sam is very much aware of my amnesia, but if he finds out I'm going to try to fix it, he'll make himself sick with worry. I tried before, with therapists and specialists, and it went nowhere, just made me increasingly frustrated and angry. That's one of the major reasons Sam made me travel so much, ensuring I'd have no reason to set foot in the States. He believes being surrounded by new people and new environments is helping me to heal, both mentally and spiritually, because there's no pressure to remember things from my past. New people don't know enough about me to sense that I have partial amnesia.

But I'm not going to see any more specialists. It didn't work back then, and I don't think anything's going to magically change this time. I'm trying something else—something totally new and inspired by my stay in Raiding, Austria.

And the first step is living my life, rather than running away and calling it "travel." Becoming gainfully employed is the perfect start.

"You're going to get a *job*?" Byron says. "Are you sure?"

"Yes. I want to prove to myself I can. I can't rely on my uncle's generosity forever. I need to become self-sufficient and live a normal life like everyone else. Nine to five, you know," I say, giving a convincing partial truth.

Byron leans closer with a half-teasing, half-serious grin. "If Sam gets stingy, don't worry. You have me, Rizzy. I have more than enough money to support you in the style you've become accustomed to."

I laugh, then pat Byron's forearm to show my appreciation for his friendly offer, even if it was a joke. "And what happens when you get tired of me mooching off you?" I tease.

"Won't happen." He puts a hand over mine. "I'll never get tired of you, Rizzy."

I stretch my legs and look at him with affection. He's so adorable and charming. He's been an amazing friend since we met in Hong Kong two years ago when I went there to visit with his younger sister.

And speaking of Julie... "You sure you're going to be okay with me staying at your place until I find an apartment? Julie said I could stay at hers instead. She's out of the country until next month."

He waves it away. "The penthouse is huge. Five freakin' bedrooms and eight baths. Stay as long as you want. Besides, you won't like her place. Not only is it small, but it's messy. Pains me to say it, but the sad fact is my baby sister's a pig."

I search his face. Julie is convinced he only offered out of some misguided sense of politeness. According to her, he's very private and hates to share. He's never let a girlfriend move in, claiming he doesn't want another person's mess in his space. He also spent a lot of money to soundproof his home because he hates other people's noise. But nothing on his face makes me think he's being polite. His blue eyes are too warm to be fake.

"Thank you," I say finally. "I promise to be the neatest and quietest roommate ever."

"No, no. It's a cliché, but *mi casa es tu casa*. For real." He glances to our right. "But...are you sure you don't want anything from the store? That Steinway baby grand sounded great when you were playing it."

It did, but the one I really wanted to try was the Bösendorfer baby grand. Unfortunately, the Butcher of Liszt was sitting at it. "There's no way I'm letting you buy me a Steinway. It's crazy."

"Hey, Julie will play it, too."

Except it feels too much like he's buying it for me, not for his sister. "The Yamaha upright at your place is fine." It's Julie's, who's an accomplished pianist. We actually met at a piano store in Austria five years ago. She was playing the "Black Key" étude by Chopin on a Kawai but kept messing up certain notes. I told her if she tried different fingering, maybe it'd be easier, Her hands are on the small side.

She tried, played it perfectly, and shook her fists at the ceiling of the store. "I've been struggling for so long! My dickhead teacher told me I had to do it that way."

"Eh, 'rules.' You should do whatever's most effective for you."

"You're American too, aren't you? If you don't already have plans, I'd love to get a drink together."

And we discovered over a crisp Blaufränkisch that we had a lot in common—a love of classical music, the cities we'd been to, our favorite performers. We kept in touch, then started to visit cities at the same time to hang out together. She's been such a friendly, lovely constant in my life since I woke up.

Byron scowls. "Julie's piano could use an upgrade."

"A piano is a piano. And the Yamaha sounds great. Better than the digital one I usually practice on." I travel with a digital piano because it's easier to ship than an acoustic. But when I want to feel real hammer action under my fingers, I go to a piano store to play on one of the display units. Most store owners don't mind once they realize I can play well.

Part of my plan is no longer hiding my talent. I know Sam's going to hate it, saying I'm just showing off or drawing unwanted attention (his usual response to my playing where people might hear), but it isn't like that. If I hadn't lost my memory, would I be hiding my talent, mainly using digital pianos with headsets or with the sound set so low I can barely hear what I'm playing? Of course not. So I'm going to live my life like I somehow still have all my memories intact.

And I'm going to pray that eventually a few good people from my past will find me and try to reconnect. Hopefully seeing them will trigger something in my brain. You never know.

I wrap my hands around my cappuccino, now cooled enough that I won't get burned. I look out the window at the people and cars, my eyes slowly defocusing.

As much as I'm blessed to have survived the accident and have a couple of close new friends, there's a hollow spot in my chest I can't ignore. At first I thought it was from the loss of my parents, whose absence I feel keenly at times—on Mother's and Father's Days, on their birthdays and mine, holidays...or just because. Even though I've lost huge chunks of memory, I feel warm acceptance and love every time I think of them. Sometimes I feel like we had some conflicts too—again, over something I no longer remember—but what kid has nothing but rainbows and unicorns with their parents for eighteen years?

But then I slowly realize the hollowness goes deeper than that, because even when I'm not thinking of my parents, my heart throbs with emptiness. It's like I'm missing something so vital, so critical, that I can't feel normal even though I have no idea what it is that's gone from my life. Nobody does, not even Sam.

When I woke up eight years ago, my memory was a chaotic mess. It took a while before I started to recall events and people—not always accurately. It was horrifying when Sam had to set the record straight.

Then one day I discovered I could still play the piano. I remembered wanting to be a concert pianist, but after the coma, I wasn't certain I could manage it. The realization that I could play compositions and advanced techniques was heady. I could swear I'd never, ever practiced them at tempo...but clearly I had.

It made me realize not being able to consciously recall whether I've played something doesn't mean it's gone from my deep, subconscious memory. So I've been practicing relentlessly. Discovering new music or drills I can play effortlessly gives me hope that one day I might find all the missing parts of my other memory too, even though right now it's like a million-piece puzzle with all the bits in the center missing.

"Rizzy?" Byron's hand waving in front of my face pulls me back to the present. He's staring at me, eyes searching. "More deep thoughts?"

"Sorry. Spaced out for a moment." I give him a smile because I've learned that it's the best way to stop people from probing too hard or asking questions I don't have the answers to.

"Want to get going?"

"Sure."

His phone rings. He glances at it, then sighs with mild irritation. "I have to take this."

"Why don't I stretch my legs a little while you do that?" I squeeze his shoulder and step outside.

The sunlight feels nice, warming my skin. I stroll in the direction of Hammers and Strings. The Bösendorfer baby grand I saw there keeps calling my name. I don't know why I have such a weird urge to try out that particular piano...or to own it. Maybe I can find out how much it costs and figure out how I can afford it. A girl can dream, right?

29

Anthony

As the Cullinan speeds toward Hammers and Strings, I rub the spot between my eyebrows—the place where I get furrowed lines when I'm having dark thoughts Ivy used to say—and try to lean back, draw in some air. My right foot keeps tapping the floor of the SUV, and every cell in my body seems to vibrate with restlessness.

It's not her, Tony. She's dead. So why are you going?

But I have to see for myself, in person. Crazy, I know. I'm sure she isn't there anymore, so I'm going to be disappointed. Even if she is still there, I'll be let down because she won't be who I want.

There are plenty of strawberry blondes in the world. A lot of them can play the piano well. Those two things don't make the woman in the video Ivy.

If they did... I run a hand roughly over my face. Jesus, I'd date strawberry blondes exclusively if I thought that would get Ivy back. But I know better. I've purposely avoided them for that reason—to remind myself I shouldn't even think of chasing after a ghost.

I press a fist against my mouth to stop myself from letting out a sound that will be half laugh and half sob. TJ doesn't need to hear that. To him, I'm a cold-hearted bastard who pays him well to do whatever job is required.

The second we pull up in front of Hammers and Strings, I hop out of the car. When I walk into the store, a thirty-something brunette hurries out from behind the counter, laminated employee tag bouncing around her neck.

"Hi. Can I help you?" she asks, tucking a few wayward tendrils of hair behind an ear and smiling a smile that borders on flirting.

The gesture's wasted. "Yes. Earlier today a woman came by and played *Grand Galop Chromatique* in this store, right?"

"Yeah, she did. She was amazing, wasn't she?" She sighs dreamily. "I was surprised she isn't a concert pianist. She plays better than some recordings I've heard. As a matter of fa—"

"Do you know anything about her?" I don't need her critique of the performance. To reassure her I'm not a deranged stalker, I give her my best harmless look, hoping my eyes don't look too remote as they often do these days. "Is she a regular here?"

The saleswoman shakes her head. "I've never seen her before. But she came in with a guy. Probably a boyfriend." She grows starry-eyed.

The unexpected revelation punches me in the gut. "Boyfriend?"

"They seemed very close. He's the one who put the video up. And when the jerk who started the whole thing started to get a little nasty, he stopped him."

Now there's a hole in my chest. *Idiot.* Ivy's dead. The girl who played *Grand Galop Chromatique* with such spark and brilliance isn't her. If Ivy were alive, she would've come back to me. I would've found her somehow. And there wouldn't be a *boyfriend.*

"If you're interested in the piano she played..." The clerk gestures at a glossy white Steinway baby grand, the same as Ivy's practice piano in Tempérane.

The sight of it scrapes an old wound that hasn't quite healed. I blurt out, "You don't have a Bösendorfer Imperial?"

"No. We only have a Bösendorfer baby grand over there. Not a concert grand like the Imperial, but still really nice. But if you're looking for a concert grand, we have a Steinway you can try. Black. Very classic."

"It's all right. I don't want a Steinway." I manage an even tone. What Ivy wanted was a Bösendorfer Imperial. Except there's no reason for me to ask the woman about it, not when Ivy's gone.

"I can give you a catalogue of what we can order for you. Just give me a second."

Before I can tell her it won't be necessary, she vanishes into the back. A tight fist wraps around my neck, and suddenly I can't breathe. I have to get out of here.

I turn around abruptly and bump into a woman coming in —hard. She loses her footing on the steps to the store, her body tilting backward.

I instinctively grab her wrist and wrap an arm around her waist to stop her from falling. Her body's soft and slim, and I tense at the familiar scent of tiger lilies. When she turns her face toward me...

Holy mother of God...

Long strawberry blond hair tumbles around a face that is the exact replica of Ivy's—the same gently arched eyebrows, the clear, intelligent gray eyes, the small nose and the siren's mouth... I blink to clear my vision, convinced I'm seeing a mirage. I've been thinking about Ivy almost nonstop since Harry showed me the video.

But no. Her face is still there. She's thinner now, and it makes her cheekbones more prominent, almost stark. I drop my gaze to the spot below the center of her lower lip, my heart thundering.

Jesus. The mole.

Stop projecting onto a woman you don't know. It could be a food stain. A scab. Anything but a mole. You've made this mistake before, remember?

I have. And God, how bitterly that ended—with me being completely disowned by my parents and Ryder as a sworn enemy for life.

"You have something on your face." I swipe the pad of my shaking thumb over it. Her lips part, and I can smell faint coffee, cherry and caramel. Her soft breath fans my skin, making my entire body prickly and hot.

The mole's still there.

The wrist in my hand is her left one. Wound tight enough to burst, I turn it to see the tattoo. Instead of the small tiger lily and the initials T and I entwined, I see an old, jagged scar.

Of course this woman isn't Ivy. If she were, she'd have the tattoo.

Disappointment and denial seep through my veins. I run my thumb over the scar and feel the taut, uneven skin. Her hand—with exceptionally long fingers—is loosely curled, her fingernails neatly trimmed, just like Ivy's nine years ago. I stare at her face. She looks back at me, her eyes curious, but devoid of recognition.

Still... Those long fingers, that face...the mole...

My head says I'm projecting what I want to see because I miss her so damn much. My heart says, *This is Ivy.*

I'm unwilling to sort them and take a side. I feel like I'm in a dream—a cruel, painful but lovely hallucination. It's all I can do to hold her, scared that if I blink she'll vanish.

A couple of tears fall from the woman's eyes. The sight is

jolting, reminding me of the tears Ivy refused to shed during our last, horrible argument. This can't be Ivy. Ivy didn't cry. She straightened her spine and called me on my bullshit.

Although my mind is still a mess, I move on autopilot.

Wordlessly, I reach into my pocket, pull out a handkerchief and dab at the tears.

She stiffens, finding her balance. "I can do it." Her voice is slightly different from Ivy's. More mature, with a hint of huskiness. She takes the handkerchief from my hand. "Sorry, I wasn't paying attention."

"Rizzy!"

"Thanks for the handkerchief." She tries to give it back, but my attention is elsewhere. I'm looking at the man who called out her name. Byron Pearce. The Five-Year-Long Thorn In My Side, all because of a business partnership I had with his brother once.

I don't think he really sees me, his eyes only on her as though she's the center of his universe.

"I have to go," she says suddenly, shoving the handkerchief into my hand. She runs toward him and the black Maserati he's standing beside.

My jaw tightens until my teeth ache. I hate the warm, overly friendly way he smiles at her. I hate his casual, lazy stance. I hate his face. And most of all, I hate it that he called her Rizzy. It's all the proof I need to know she isn't Ivy.

Come on. You knew *she wasn't Ivy.*

I clench the handkerchief, wet with her tears. The salesclerk returns with the catalogue and says, "Oh, there she is!"

"What?" I say, my eyes on the Maserati.

"The pianist. The one who played *Grand Galop Chromatique*. That's her."

What the fuck...?

My legs move of their own volition toward the car, but it's

already weaving through the traffic. Coming to an abrupt halt, I put a hand over my eyes. What the hell am I thinking?

Don't do it. You're about to go down another self-destructive path...except this time, you have so much more to lose.

Except I don't know what I have left to lose. I don't have a heart...or a soul. Haven't experienced true light or warmth in almost a decade. And all the money and power I have can't bring them back in my life.

30

Iris

As Byron drives, my mind is on the man at Hammers and Strings. My heart is still racing from the encounter. I got so flustered, I forgot to ask about the Bösendorfer baby grand.

I can't decide if I would prefer to have fallen than be caught by him. His arm was wonderfully strong as it wrapped around my waist and pulled me upright. Even now, the area tingles.

And when I lifted my head, I saw the most arresting male specimen ever. Everything else seemed to fade into sepia tones.

Tall, at least six three. An expensive charcoal suit over a broad, hard frame. The only thing soft about him was his glossy black hair. His face was boldly cut, everything proportioned and coolly masculine—cheeks high, a blade of a nose and the kind of mouth that can be both sensual and cruel.

When those green eyes focused on me, there was an

intense fire within the depths of his gaze. My mouth dried, and a piercing ache formed in my chest.

Some men promise a fun romp in bed, while some promise trouble. This man promised glorious sex and a broken heart.

He might have said something, but I couldn't hear it over the roaring of my blood. My vision actually blurred for a moment, like I was about to pass out.

I couldn't imagine the humiliation of fainting dead away in front of a stranger. So I focused on his gaze as an anchor to keep me from floating away.

"You have something on your face." His low, raspy voice slid down my spine, causing goosebumps. Then before I could process, he reached out and brushed his thumb across my lower lip.

The most intense longing pulsed through me. To my shock, my nipples beaded. In any other circumstance, I would have stepped away, but I felt hypnotized. I swallowed, wanting him to remove his hand...but at the same time loathing the notion. It was as though my body craved the physical connection he'd established.

His eyebrows drew together as he turned my left arm, then his face went bloodless as bitter despair fleeted through his eyes.

I felt that gaze like a physical touch. He stared like he was trying to see into my head. The idea gave me shivers. I don't like having people look that closely.

Then I realized I was still on his arm, my back arched, my hips uncomfortably close to his. That was a shock, but nothing compared to the stunning realization that I didn't want to pull away. I don't understand how I could feel this way about a man I just bumped into. Granted, he was mesmerizing. But I've seen handsome, wealthy, worldly men before... None of them ever drew me like that.

Thank God Byron came to get me. Otherwise, who knows what else I might've done to embarrass myself?

What if he's someone you used to know before the accident? Maybe that's the reason you reacted that way. Maybe somehow your subconscious recognized him.

No. If he knew me before, he would've said something—a simple "Hi, Iris, how are you?" or "Whoa, long time no see!" Or maybe just a friendly smile in greeting.

And if—a huge *if*—I'd known him before in such an emotional way, surely I'd still have some sliver of memory of him. Like I have about my parents. I remember some...not all, but some.

"What are you thinking?" Byron asks.

It pulls me out of my reverie. "Nothing."

"You okay?"

"I'm fine." I force a smile. "Just wondering what to have for dinner."

"It's a bit early."

"But I'm hungry." I pat my belly.

Byron gives me a look. "Really?"

I nod, even though I'll have to eat more than I really want if I don't want to be caught in a lie. I should've told him I was thinking about a piece of music.

He grins. "Fine. Your stomach is my command. Want to eat out, or...?"

"How about takeout? Something light. I'm a little tired."

"Jet-lagged?"

"Very." I landed earlier today. Although Sam claimed his assistant "forgot" to remind him, I know he didn't pick me up from LAX as a symbolic protest over my return. Thankfully, Byron was waiting at the airport, having heard from Julie about my flight from Vienna. "But don't let me fall asleep too early. I have to get back into my routine as quickly as I can."

He nods. "Thai and a movie?"

"Fantastic. Tomorrow I'm also going to work on my résumé. Well, once I figure out what to put on it." And see who I can ask to review what I've written.

"I can help you with that."

It's like Byron read my mind. "That'd be great. Thank you. You'll know exactly what to say."

"You sure you want an office position, though? You can always be a concert pianist or something. If you get stage fright, you can do duets with Julie."

My mood deflates. That used to be what I was working toward. Sam confirmed it. But I can't pursue that anymore.

I don't have stage fright. What I have is far worse—terrible panic attacks, which developed since the coma, according to Sam. When I tried to force it at a small recital six years ago, I fainted dead away, my heart beating hard and fast, cold sweat drenching me. It was so awful I thought I was in the middle of a heart attack.

But if you were to play with that guy from Hammers and Strings? Something for four hands, so you could sit side by side, his body close...

The question comes unbidden, and I shake my head. Ridiculous notion.

Except the butterflies in my belly don't think it's that ridiculous.

31

Anthony

The original plan for the day was to get Harry from LAX, then stop by Z, one of my most profitable clubs. It's sentimental because it was my first and I built it myself—selecting everything inside, helping with the design, everything. I understand good taste, excellent liquor and the experience I want to give. I make it my routine to go there a few times every time I'm in L.A. to ensure it's still the best, to learn who works there, get a feel for the crowd that frequents the club.

But at the moment, I can't. I'm not in a very good headspace, and it's impossible to oversee a business when I'm like this, obsessing about that woman.

Her delicate features. Those beautiful gray eyes. The mole underneath her plump mouth. Her scent. The hands.

That untattooed left wrist.

If I had a flower in the car, I'd rip it apart, petal by petal, while muttering, "She's Ivy. She isn't Ivy. She's Ivy. She isn't Ivy..."

So I pick the second best option—Harry. Although he can be incorrigible and irresponsible at times, he is great at auditing clubs. He understands fun and what makes people generous—even reckless—with their money. The best thing is, he's done it before for me and pointed out areas I'd never considered or imagined were problematic. Taking his suggestions made a difference in elevating the clubs in L.A., Chicago, Rome and Paris from luxurious and exclusive to opulent and ultra-fashionable. It's a subtle distinction, but it's the difference between a club people think is great and a club people would give their left kidney to get into.

He answers on the third ring. "Thanks for checking up on me. I managed to get to campus in one piece," he says, half sarcastic, but with enough humor to let me know he isn't really upset. Nothing really upsets my younger brother.

"Uber is a boon to humanity. And especially hungover younger siblings."

A snort, extra loud for my benefit. "So." Harry's voice grows serious. "Did you...uh...see her?"

Maybe it wasn't the best idea to call him. I should've known he would ask. "Yes," I say.

"And?" I can hear the tension and worry in his voice.

"And nothing. She isn't Ivy." Her name is Rizzy. Byron called her that. I wish I'd acted faster and punched the bastard in the mouth because he dashed my hope...a small, pathetic hope, but a hope nonetheless.

Harry sighs. "I'm sorry, Tony. I shouldn't have shown you the video. Edgar got pissed off when I told him about it."

Damn. Now Edgar's going to be on my case, but I can't very well be upset with Harry. My past behavior wasn't exactly sane when it came to Ivy, and my reaction probably freaked him out. "It wasn't your fault. The video went viral.

Somebody would've shown it to me at the office." The last part is a lie. Nobody in my office would bother me with junk like that.

And Harry sees right through me. "Right."

"So. Are you busy tonight?" I ask, not wanting to dwell on the video or the pianist. It's the kind of wound you lick alone, in the privacy of your home.

"Nope. Why?"

"Can you go to Z? See how things look there?"

"Oh, man!" he shouts excitedly. "Free booze, right?"

"No. Put it on your credit card. I don't want everyone there to know you're special enough to warrant free drinks."

"They know I'm special enough to cut the line," Harry protests.

"Keep it up and you won't be able to." He shuts up so fast that I hear his teeth click. "I'll cover your expenses."

His good mood immediately returns. "I can bring girls, right?"

"Within reason." Otherwise he'll invite half the co-eds from UCLA.

"Will do. You know I'm going to give you your liquor's worth."

"I'm counting on it. Thanks, Harry."

"Hey, thank *you*!" He hangs up.

I almost smile at his infectious enthusiasm. It's impossible to stay morose around my younger brother.

TJ takes me to my penthouse. The second I step inside, I spot Edgar, helping himself to my best whiskey.

He hasn't changed much. Still the same old Edgar, except now he looks even more like Father. It's like he was born parthenogenetically, with none of Mother's DNA.

Normally I want to be alone in this kind of mood, but Edgar is okay. Smart and levelheaded, he's the one who pulled me out of the abyss of despair and self-destruction after Ivy's death. He also secretly invested in Z, since our parents disowned me. That's why he has access to all my properties around the world. And gets free booze at my clubs.

He lifts his glass, a warm glint in his eyes not enough to hide his worry. "Tony."

"Edgar, good to see you," I say, doing my best to appear normal. As long as I act like a sane individual, he won't try to stick around to hover over me.

We exchange a quick hug, and I take the empty stool next to him. "What are you doing here?"

"A minor change in plans. I have an overnight layover in L.A. before the first flight out tomorrow, so I figured why not drop by?" He shrugs, his lips twitching with a smile. "*Tu casa es mi casa.*"

I laugh, but I don't buy his overly casual explanation. He made a detour specifically to see me after Harry's call. Feeling grateful and guilty, I pour myself three fingers of whiskey, neat. I've needed it since leaving Hammers and Strings.

Edgar cocks an eyebrow, but doesn't comment. Instead, he says, "Thanks for taking care of Harry."

"Don't mention it. If we don't take care of that kid, who will?"

Edgar sighs. "Who indeed? It's like he doesn't even want to try to be responsible."

"Let him be. It's good to have at least one brother who doesn't care enough to be serious." I down half the whiskey in my glass, the fine liquor creating a smooth burn in my throat and belly.

Edgar finishes his, then taps the rim of his glass. "I saw the video."

"Harry said you yelled at him. You shouldn't have."

"Are you okay?"

I start to say, *Sure*, but stop. Edgar's always been honest with me, and he deserves better than a pat answer. "No."

"Did you see her? Harry said you went to the music store. The woman in the video does look remarkably like Ivy."

"She looks *exactly* like Ivy." I knock back the rest of my drink. "I actually ran into her. Physically. She was this far from me." I put a palm in front of my face.

"Tony... Ivy died nine years ago." Edgar's quiet voice is full of compassion and worry.

"I *know*." So much frustration and conflicting desire bubbles up. "I know she died, but this girl really looks like Ivy. She even has the mole." I put an index finger on the spot right below the center point of my mouth. "The same facial bones. Her hair's the same color. Her eyes—that bright, beautiful gray. She even *plays* like Ivy."

"She plays like a recording. A really good recording, but no more special than a thousand top-level pianists out there."

My hand tightens around the glass. I want to tell Edgar he's wrong, that the girl played *Grand Galop Chromatique* exactly like Ivy, but I can't. No artist can play music exactly the same way every time. Hell, even Ivy herself would sound slightly different if she played the same piece twice during practice.

Edgar continues, "You think this woman at the music store looks like Ivy because you're seeing what you want to see. There are millions of strawberry blondes out there. The same for women with gray eyes. And even the mole. When we desperately want something to be true, we tend to ignore contradictory evidence."

He looks at me like he's bracing for an impending breakdown. And why not? I had one after Ivy died. My heart skipped a beat every time I saw a strawberry blonde with a similar build. I couldn't accept that she was gone because I was still alive. If she'd really died, I would have, too—because my heart belongs irrevocably to her, beating only for her.

Edgar puts a hand on my shoulder, his touch as firm and

solid as a battleship's anchor. "Don't make the same mistake twice, Tony. You don't need a repeat of Lauren Tater."

The old anger and mortification burn another hole in my gut, and I want to throw something. Six months after Ivy's death, Ryder invited me to Los Angeles because he was ostensibly worried about me. It was worse in the city. There were so many damned women who reminded me of Ivy in some way. Jaunty grins. Smiling gray eyes. Hands with long fingers. Pretty tiger lily tattoos—but not on their left wrists.

But none of them had the whole package. None of them were Ivy.

Then, after a year in L.A., I met Lauren. It was striking how similar she was to Ivy—her hair, her bright gaze, her laugh and smile, her beautiful long fingers. She could even manage some serviceable Mozart sonatas. I adored her, lavished her with everything I had to give. A small voice inside said certain things didn't add up about her, but I squashed it. Lauren felt like a chance at redemption—to be the kind of man who could've kept Ivy safe...

...until I discovered she and Ryder were fucking behind my back. Ryder claimed he didn't know she was my girlfriend. Said he never saw the two of us together. He was pretty convincing, too—but then, he *is* a great actor.

"How could you not know?" I raged. "She looks just like Ivy!"

He looked confused for a moment, then gaped at me. "Those photos you showed me? Lauren looks nothing like that girl."

"Fucking liar. One day I'll show you what it's like to be betrayed, you motherfucker. I'm gonna hurt you the same way you hurt me!"

I spiraled out of control afterward. Drank too much. Raged like a lunatic. Screamed. Picked fights. Hated everything and everyone. I wanted the world to fucking burn if Ivy wasn't going to be in it anymore.

A few weeks later, Father showed up, ostensibly to tell me to control myself.

Fuck that shit. If I could just control myself like that, I would have, wouldn't I? He thought he was so much better than me, but what the hell did he know? He was shit. Just like everyone.

I drunkenly told him, jabbing my finger into his chest, "Go fuck yourself, Tulane Charles Blackwood. Fuck you and everyone you cater to." That got me publicly disowned—since Father correctly interpreted "everyone he caters to" to mean Mother. For the first and only time since I was twelve, I couldn't contain the fury inside me—the blame, the hate—that if she'd been a little bit nicer to Ivy, just the tiniest bit merciful to me, I might not have lost Ivy so brutally.

Then I lashed out further, telling him I didn't give a fuck if I got officially disowned, because I'd been dead to them since the day Katherine died, and Mother must've danced a jig when she heard Ivy was dead because she knew how much that would pain me. After all, isn't that what she wants—to squeeze every drop of grief and misery out of me until I'm a broken shell?

It was Edgar who came to Los Angeles and pulled me out of self-destruction. "Can't have revenge on Ryder if you're this pathetic, can you?" he said, using my rage to drag me out of hell. "Can't make your mark if you're weak."

By the time I pulled myself together, Lauren had died in a fire in Mexico—dumped by Ryder. Guess the son of a bitch decided he didn't want her after all. Why the hell did he take her in the first place, then?

I heard from the grapevine almost a year later than she'd been pregnant when she died. I should've felt something, but I didn't. I was numb to her and everything she'd done to me because it was the only way I could function. The only thing I felt was pity for the unborn child. The kid likely wasn't mine. Maybe that was why Ryder dumped her so fast—a pregnant girlfriend would get in the way of his hot-shit Hollywood life-style. I was a fool to think he and I had anything in common. He's a shallow bastard, just like his parents.

To avoid making another monumental mistake like Lauren, I no longer allow myself to date strawberry blondes. Brunettes with dark eyes only. Ideally with zero musical talent. Normally proportioned hands, no long fingers.

"Tony. You have to let it go. This isn't healthy." Edgar's voice jerks me back to the present. "Seven years ago, the draw was your friendship with Ryder Reed. Now the draw is you and your financial empire. This woman could be part of a con—they're more sophisticated now, and you've made enemies. Hell, for all we know, it could be Ryder's doing. There are a lot of actresses who would to do anything to star in a movie with him."

Edgar is aware of how I tried to fuck with Ryder and his wife some months ago. I told him over a drink once. Told him I felt like a fucking idiot because I couldn't even be ruthless enough to hurt a woman who'd never done anything to hurt me. Tried to paint myself as a complete loser, but my brother looked at me with some small relief instead.

Edgar continues, "Don't let some unknown woman use you, no matter how much you wish the cops had made a mistake identifying Ivy's body. It'll be a thousand times worse this time."

"I know. You don't have to worry." Even to my own ears, I sound unconvincing.

And Edgar isn't stupid. "Good. Then let me handle it. I'll look into her for you."

"You don't want her to be Ivy, so..."

"I won't tell my investigator anything except to look into her background. That's it. No bias."

I nod because Edgar won't give up until I do. And he'll keep his word and be scrupulously fair.

He goes to the guest room to get some sleep before his flight. I finish another whiskey, thinking back on the encounter at Hammers and Strings. If there's even the slightest chance Ivy somehow survived...

I pick up my phone and text Wei, sending a link to the video. *Find the pianist.*

You're an idiot, Tony. Chasing a ghost, my head says in a voice full of disgust.

My mouth twists bitterly. It doesn't matter what I agreed to. I can't sit on my ass and do nothing, even though this is probably how men fall and empires crumble.

32

Iris

The next morning, a call wakes me up at seven. I roll onto my stomach and grab my phone. *Sam.* Must've gotten tired of me not answering his texts.

I don't really want to talk to him, but he's probably no longer in a rage about the video or the fact that I came back to L.A. Ideally, he'll have sort of fizzled out to just peeved. "Hello?"

"Iris. You're a difficult child to reach."

"Sorry. The battery died," I lie.

He harrumphs, but doesn't pursue it. "Listen, I need you to play at the Peacher & Son spring reception tomorrow."

"What?" I thought he was calling to give me another around-the-world ticket or complain about the video, not ask me to play. In public. And at an annual business event I've never, ever been invited to before.

"The quartet Marty's assistant hired can't come." Sam's tone makes it clear what he thinks of the poor woman's professional capacity. "And we can't find a replacement. Too last minute."

Wow.

"You can probably swing something. I like this song in particular." He hums the main melody from "Claire de lune." Off-key, of course. "Chopin, if you don't know."

"Mmm." Debussy must be rolling in his grave that one of his most recognizable works is being attributed to Chopin. "Can you just have the venue play recordings? I have some MP3 files that are pretty good."

"*No!* That's what poor people do to cut costs! I've never, *ever* not had live music at a reception. It's simply too important." He takes a breath. "Iris, receptions are where we mingle with our best clients and investors. The music's there to make them feel relaxed, appreciated...and generous with their money."

I bite my lip. I haven't had any coffee yet, but my mind starts whirring slowly. "You know I get panic attacks when I have to perform in front of an audience, right?"

"It isn't like a recital. Nobody's going to be watching you. You'll be more like pleasant background music to elevate the event. Not the focus of attention."

I purse my mouth. Perversely, it actually bugs me that I won't be the center of attention. Maybe it's a remnant of my old ambition to be a concert pianist. No concert pianist would want to perform, only to be more or less ignored by everyone. Still... This is my opportunity to assert two points I want to make. "I thought you hate it when I 'show off.' As a matter of fact, you didn't even want me back in Los Angeles."

"This is business—what feeds our family and provides for us." There's enough emphasis on *provides* and *us* to signal he's really talking about me. Although my parents had a sizable life insurance policy, it wasn't enough to pay for all my medical care while I was in the coma...and subsequent therapy once I woke up. Sam stepped up and took charge, so I didn't have to worry about anything except healing.

"You're right; business is important. But this means I can stay, right? I can help in all kinds of ways. And please don't yell at Byron about the video because he didn't mean to upset you, and I didn't realize he was going to post it. *Pleeeeease?*" I add cajolingly, so it doesn't feel like a negotiation...even though it totally is. He always responds better if his pride isn't too hurt.

"Well... I suppose you can stay in L.A. Although I don't know how you plan to get a job and all that. It's going to be terribly stressful," Sam says, suddenly radiating paternal concern. "The economy is atrocious, and employers are really picky these days." He's phrasing it kindly, but what he really means is that nobody's going to want to hire me.

Thanks for the confidence booster. "I promise I'll let you know if I need anything," I say, although I'd rather eat a cardboard casserole. Sam will always indulge me...so long as I do as I'm told. But I'm doing this one *my* way—to not only live my life but to recover my lost memories.

"As for Byron..." He sighs. "How can I be upset with him? He's like an unleashed wild dog."

Whaaaaaaaaaaaa? I almost sputter at the ludicrous comparison. At least Sam's consistent. He used to call Byron a bumbling bear, and he uses whatever animal that pops into his head to label my other friends as well. He calls Julie "that flighty fox."

"Anyway, I knew you'd come through for me," Sam says, rather pleased with himself. "You should also add some other nice, easy songs by Chopin. Mozart isn't too bad, either."

For someone who knows nothing about music, he tosses out those composers pretty carelessly. "Leave the selection to me, Sam. I know what you want."

"Fantastic. Perfect."

I'm unable to figure out my precise reaction to his exuberance. Annoyance isn't right, but uneasy isn't quite right either. It's a mix of uncomfortable feelings that makes me want to squirm and shower. But I decide not to dwell on it. I got what I wanted—for Sam to back off on my living in L.A. and not comment on the video.

"By the way, where are you staying now?" he asks.

"With a friend."

"Who?" There's an unyielding edge to his tone. He won't give up until he knows.

"Byron."

"Iris, you should be staying with me." There's a deep frown in his voice.

No way. Still, I keep my tone light and even. "I know, but I think it's better if I stay with a friend. I don't want to impose too much, and you've already done so much for me, Sam."

Even if I had zero friends in L.A., I wouldn't go to Sam's mansion. It may be huge and luxurious, but it isn't welcoming or warm the way homes should be...like my parents' cozy house was. His place is more like a museum, full of expensive, meticulously dusted things that discourage you from touching. And every time I'm there, I feel like I'm being closely watched, like some exotic new zoo specimen.

Besides, my blood pressure shoots up whenever I spend more than ten minutes in the same room with his son, Marty, mainly because he delights in mansplaining everything. To him, nothing is too small to leave unexplained. Sometimes I wonder if he's going to start demonstrating how I should hold a fork.

"Byron Pearce isn't the kind of 'friend' you want to live with," Sam says.

Ugh. Could he make it sound any sleazier? "I'm not *living* with him. It's a temporary arrangement until I can afford my own place. He's a great friend."

Skepticism colors Sam's grunt. It's the same sound he made when my "friends from the past" came out of the woodwork to be closer to me once they realized how much money Sam had. I was too naïve to realize what they were up to until Sam got rid of them. I don't understand why he's reacting this way to Byron, though. Byron's family is wealthier than anybody I know, and they're old money.

"Still, I—"

"Hey, listen. I gotta go shopping if I want to look good tomorrow." I have a few dresses I can put on, but I'm going to be busy working on the repertoire for the reception. "Bye, Sam." I hang up, then write down a summary of our call and the fact that I have to be at the party in my notebook. It's a new habit since the coma. This way, I'll never lose anything again.

I add, *Feels good to win what I wanted without having to ugly-fight Sam. Playing at the party is a small price...although I'm worried about having a panic attack. But if I do okay there, can I play at parties from now on? Do I even want to?*

I stop because my pride bristles at the idea that the best I could ever be is someone's background music. I don't know what to think. Wouldn't making a living from music be better than a nine-to-five job? I shut the notebook and put it in my purse. I can't answer that question yet. Not until after the party. For all I know, I'll faint dead away at the piano.

I shower, change into a loose T-shirt and shorts and go downstairs to the huge kitchen. Byron doesn't cook much—his attitude is "why bother when you don't have to"—but the kitchen is simply to die for, with the latest feature-rich stainless-steel appliances, marble countertops and island.

Byron's already there, pouring two mugs of coffee. The plate in front of him is clean except for a few crumbs and a knife with white streaks.

"We have Greek yogurt, chopped fruit, bagels with cream cheese, lox and cereal. Pick your poison," he says with a grin, pushing me a coffee with double cream and sugar, just the way I like it.

"Thanks. Cereal sounds about right." I grab a bowl and fill a third of it with crunchy flakes with nuts and dried fruit chunks.

He hands me a spoon and some milk. "That's all?"

"Uh-huh." Ever since the accident, my appetite hasn't been the same. I enjoy good food, but I don't have any desire to eat more than a few bites. Often, I just forget to eat. My doctors didn't think it was a huge concern and told me to eat at least three small, nutritious meals a day...and that was that. Given the extent of the damage I've suffered—messed-up memories, emotional outbursts, extreme mood swings, loss of muscle tone—a lack of appetite isn't really a priority.

"Guess we can do an early brunch before I have to fly out."

"You're leaving town?"

"Unfortunately. Got a call last night. I need to be in Hawaii for some business stuff over golf, blah blah blah." He puffs out a breath. "Probably take a week or two. No more, I hope."

Tilting my head, I study his lazy, model-like pose, his bare feet hooked to the rungs on the stool, his body lean and beautifully proportioned. "I can't understand how you don't like golf. You seem like you'd love it, leisurely walking around and whacking a small white ball."

"It's boring. And I have to pretend to suck to protect fragile corporate egos."

I pat his shoulder. No matter how much he hates it, he has to go and do a good job. Julie told me their father's decided only the most capable son is going to inherit the family business, and now Byron and his older brother are engaged in a battle to prove who's the best.

"You'll be great," I say soothingly. Although Byron appears

easygoing, he's ultra-competitive. I've seen him play tennis and actually felt sorry for his opponents.

"So what do you say to the early brunch? Maybe we can do something fun afterward."

"Can't. I have to master a few Debussy and Mozart pieces for Sam." There's no way I'm doing Chopin or Liszt.

Byron frowns. "Why?"

"Apparently the quartet hired for the reception tomorrow can't come. So he wants me to play instead. He was so desperate he decided he was okay with me being in the city and he doesn't mind the video from yesterday too much either."

Byron shakes his head. "You don't usually play Debussy or Mozart, do you? You're going to learn them in one day?"

"The fundamentals are the same. It'll take all day, but I can learn enough to manage. It's only the first arabesque and 'Clair de lune,' which he specifically asked for. I can fill up the rest of the time with Mozart sonatas."

Byron's handsome face scrunches. "Can I just say how much I don't like your uncle right now?"

I almost laugh at his petulant tone, wondering what he'd say if he knew Sam called him an "unleashed wild dog" less than an hour ago. Byron prides himself on his urbanity. "Why don't we do something together after you come back from your trip?" I suggest. "By then I'll be over my jet lag, and Julie should be back too."

He gazes off to one side for a few moments, then sighs. "Okay, deal."

33

Anthony

The Peacher & Son reception is a textbook example of too much money and too little taste. But then, taste is one of those things money can't buy. Sam does, however, know how to Google, so he's made sure to have the most expensive wine and liquors and the finest hors d'oeuvres.

I wouldn't have bothered to attend this orgy of excess if Wei hadn't told me the pianist from the video was Iris Smith, distantly related to Sam Peacher. Wei added he heard she'd be at the party, although he wasn't sure in what capacity. He gets all the gossip because he looks sweetly unassuming and is great at making people think he's tight-lipped. Which he is...except when he thinks it's something I should know.

Sipping a flute of Dom, I look around the glittering ballroom. It's filled with people dressed to impress in silk and jewels. I don't understand how Sam managed to get Mother to invest in his first major real estate deal. It wasn't a bad plan, but she never liked him well enough to give him a penny all those years. She'd rather have torched the money. Edgar and Harry told me with disbelief about the series of loans she's made to Sam because they couldn't figure out why she changed her mind so abruptly. It's obvious she despises the Peachers even now.

I can feel myself squinting a bit, trying to make Iris appear. *Where are you?*

I'm only here to check if I'm hallucinating, like Edgar said. I have to be certain, regardless of whatever this woman is calling herself now.

For all I know, she might not have come back to Tempérane because Mother sent her away. Maybe she didn't reach out to me all these years because she didn't know how much I truly love her. Because I left town instead of staying and fixing what I messed up.

Ivy, if you only knew. I would've crawled naked over the Himalayas to have you back in my life.

The famous melody from Debussy starts up from a corner, and I slowly turn around. Ivy is at the glossy black Steinway baby grand, so breathlessly beautiful. I stand there, drinking her in. She's exactly like before—only more mature now. She glows like a dark ruby in a wine-colored cocktail dress. Every cell in my body is vibrating with deep longing. How can she not be Ivy?

You thought Lauren was just like Ivy too, a voice that sounds suspiciously like Edgar reminds me.

Once she's done with "Claire de lune," she goes into Mozart. It's as though she's doing her best to avoid pieces that can show off her technical mastery. Mozart, however, isn't the best choice. It only serves to highlight her musicality.

"Tony! I didn't realize you were coming," Sam says, clapping my shoulder as though we're long-lost friends. His eyes are shrewd and calculating, even as he's smiling in my direction. He's aged well the last few years, with a comfortably round stomach, florid complexion and a few gold rings he didn't used to have.

I step away slightly, neatly shrugging his hand off my shoulder. "Anthony, if you don't mind."

Sam's expression sours for a second before smoothing. "Right. I forgot how particular you are about your name."

Obviously money has affected his memory, since I've never allowed him to address me as Tony. "I don't like people being overfamiliar." I look down at his left hand, which he used to clasp my shoulder just moments ago.

He pastes the smile back on. "I see you have a drink. Very good," he says, his voice annoyingly jovial.

I tilt my flute in Ivy's direction. "She's not bad." What will he say? I don't like it one bit that they're supposedly related. Nor do I believe it's true. It can't be. "Where did you find her?"

Sam's graying eyebrows pinch together with vague dismay. "A distant relative."

"Oh?"

"Not on the same branch as your mother, obviously." Sam shifts his weight. "I've been caring for her since her parents' accident. Nice folks. Truly unfortunate."

"Generous of you." Ivy was taken in by my parents after a car crash killed hers. Isn't it always good to mix lots of truth with your lie so it looks convincing? "When did it happen?"

"Nine years ago."

I almost snap the stem of my flute. *Motherfucker*. How stupid does he think I am?

"She was in the car with them. It put her in coma for a year or so." His voice is theatrically heavy. "Simply wasn't the same after she woke up."

I bet she wasn't. It's all I can do to not beat the truth out of him.

He plucks a glass of white wine from a waiter passing by. I wait until he has a mouthful.

"She looks remarkably like Ivy."

The muscles around his eyes twitch, but he swallows without choking or sputtering. "Ivy? Oh, you mean... Yes. What a loss. What a shame." He takes another drink of wine. "But other than the fact that they share similar coloring..." He shrugs. "I don't really see a resemblance."

That's what Edgar said too—strawberry-blond hair and gray eyes and that's it. So what if they share a similar physical build?

Edgar's right. You're seeing things.

Sam adds, "And Iris is nowhere as good as Ivy on the piano."

He's trying too hard. Harry and Edgar both thought Iris's *Grand Galop Chromatique* was great. "Did you ever hear Ivy play?"

"A few times. Very talented girl. Didn't she go to some fancy music school?"

"Curtis." I tilt my chin toward Iris. "Is she planning to debut as a concert pianist at some point?"

He laughs, looking away as though he's embarrassed. "No. She never went to a conservatory or anything. Probably going to get a nine-to-five somewhere, since she doesn't seem to want to travel anymore." Dismay fleets over his face as quickly as lightening. "By the way, have you seen Margot recently?"

Is this some kind of petty revenge for my probing into Iris's background? I won't give him the satisfaction. "You know I've been disowned," I say lightly, as though I'm discussing the weather. There's no reason for anything except bluntness here.

He blinks, a picture of innocence. "Still haven't reconciled?"

"Wouldn't you know if we had?" He received funds from Mother as late as last month. Harry bitched about it because apparently she was in a horrible mood afterward and called him for some cheering up.

It's laughable how obvious this ploy to distract me is. Seven years ago, Sam might have succeeded. But I'm not a young man floundering in grief anymore. I'm older, more experienced, with a war chest big enough to destroy the petty fortune he's built. And just monstrous enough to do it if he doesn't watch himself.

34

Iris

The reception is much fancier and classier than I thought. Food and wine flow, served on silver trays carried by waiters in crisp livery. The glitzy ballroom is full of people decked out in their best outfits—exquisitely tailored tuxes and dresses, glittering jewels and watches, and fine shoes that cost more than most people make in a year. I almost wish I hadn't returned the ice-blue Ferragamo dress Sam sent yesterday. I'm in a simple merlot-colored cocktail dress with spaghetti straps. I remind myself that the cut of the dress is classic, and no one knows I found it on sale last year in Prague.

More to the point, no one cares. They're here to dine and wine on Sam's tab.

After finishing the Debussy and Mozart I prepared, I step away to take a short break. Sam thinks I should play the entire time, but I'm not a machine.

I take a glass of white wine from a passing tray and move to a corner. Small excitement sparks in my belly as I think back on my performance. My hands shook a little in the beginning, but I was able to maintain my composure. I didn't make any mistakes, and easily played everything at tempo.

And...I actually felt pretty good sitting there.

Does this mean I might not panic if an audience focuses on me? I'll have to find a way to test that theory. Maybe Julie can help. God, I wish she were here with me right now so we could talk about it. She thinks it's a bummer I can't play before a crowd. If my heart will just quit beating like it's about to choke me, I might be able to have a career as a musician. Anxious excitement fills me, and I can't stand still anymore. I start pacing in a small circle, staring at nothing as I try to think.

Have to calm down, though. Who knows when I'll be able to test the theory and see how my nerves hold up at a recital? Until I can, I need to maintain my course: stay in L.A. and get a job.

A guy suddenly appears in front of me. "There you are! Can you help me?"

I look up and see one of the men Sam introduced me to when I arrived. It takes a moment to recall his name... *Jamie Thornton.* A potential investor in Sam's next big development. He shook my hand while politely flattering me about how pretty I looked. Afterward, Sam whispered that Thornton was important and asked me to be extra nice to him. I'm not sure what I can do for him, though. I'm not prepared to take requests.

"What do you need help with, Mr. Thornton?"

"Jamie. I insist." He beams at me, revealing a row of straight white teeth. An attractive man in his mid-thirties. High forehead. Carefully trimmed and shaped brown eyebrows above deep-set brown eyes. His nose is a tad too long, the lips a tad too thin, but they don't detract. Still, I don't care for him. He has a disturbing way of looking at me, letting his gaze linger over my bared shoulders and my breasts, half a beat too long to be polite, but not so long that it veers into creep-tastic territory.

And I hate that he's so...ambiguous on the creep-meter. Guys should be one way or the other.

"I think I lost my phone," he explains finally.

"Did you check with the front desk and concierge?" Why is he talking to *me* about this?

"They didn't have it. They said they'd look, but..." His sigh says he has no confidence in them.

"Where did you lose it?"

"In the courtyard, I think. I was texting out there, and then..." He slaps his pockets, then raises his hands in a helpless gesture. "I have to find it. It has all my data."

"I understand." I'd be beside myself if I'd lost mine. It has all my contacts, texts, emails, photos...everything. But Jamie evidently wants more than just sympathy. He's looking at me way too expectantly. "Would you..."

I didn't want to do anything except just rest a few moments before returning to the piano, but Sam did ask me to be nice. And if he hears that I didn't help, he'll be upset. Last thing I want is to disturb the truce we established yesterday. Although Sam can be autocratic, he has done everything he thought would be best for me since the accident, regardless of the cost. I owe him. "Sure, I'll help you look."

We walk through one of several French doors leading to the dark courtyard. It's lush with a sweet-smelling lawn, every blade cut with military precision, lively shrubs and night-blooming flowers.

Jamie leads me to a spot underneath a tree, far from the ballroom and off the main path.

"So this is where you lost it?" I ask, looking around on the ground.

"Yeah, I think so. This is the last place I used it. I was texting my assistant."

The small faux candles around the area don't provide enough illumination to locate his phone on the ground. I start to reach into my clutch to grab mine.

Suddenly Jamie's arm wraps around my waist, and he pulls me toward him. My clutch falls from my grasp. Before I can recover my balance, his mouth crushes mine.

The whiskey on his breath overwhelms me; his tongue is a slimy slug against my lips. Chills spread through my body. I clench my jaw and jerk my head away. "No!"

"Come on," he says, one hand gliding over my butt, then trying to slip under my skirt. The other is pulling on my shoulder straps. "We both know what you really want."

Oh my God! Terror and outrage roughen my breathing. Shaking, I twist, trying to get away. I have to make this bastard stop. "Cut it out before I—"

I don't get to finish.

35

Anthony

I wrench the son of a bitch off Iris. Thornton hollers, "What the *fu—*"

My fist lands in his face. Blood spurts from his nose and a killing rage roars through me, along with the cold knowledge that I was too late to stop the bastard from hurting her.

Just like I was too late to save Katherine from bleeding out.

Just like I was too late to prevent Caleb from touching Ivy.

Just like I was too late to save Ivy from dying.

I tried to reach Iris when she stepped away from the piano. But a business acquaintance stopped me to chat, and Jamie Thornton led her away.

I only listened halfheartedly, my gaze tracking the two as they headed toward the garden. I had no clue why he led her outside, but if I had, I would've walked away from my acquaintance, manners be damned.

I sweep Jamie's feet out from under him, dropping him to the ground. My foot strikes his soft belly, chest and ribs with cold, ruthless precision. Thornton curls up, moaning pathetically, but it doesn't help. I've had years of kickboxing training, and he doesn't even know how to cover up properly.

"Stop!" he begs, putting a hand out. I break his middle finger with a vicious twist. It's the finger he used to break the strap on her dress. Jamie howls.

"Come on," I say. "We both know what you really want."

"She was just playing hard to get," Jamie whines. "Look at her dress. The bitch was asking for it."

Fucking bastard. Always blaming women. "And look at the way you behaved. *You're* asking for it." I deliver another brutal kick.

Jamie mewls and sobs, tries to crawl away. His face is glistening with tears, snot and blood.

"Oh no, you aren't getting away this easy." I follow him, looming. "A parasite like you doesn't deserve to live. The world will be better without you in it." I pull him up and punch his face a few more times until it's a complete mess. Then I drop him.

He collapses like a rag doll, but I know he hasn't passed out. I've been very careful to keep him conscious. He needs to feel every bit of pain.

"Stop it, you're going to kill him! *Do you want to go to jail for murder?*"

Everything inside me goes still. It's the same thing Ivy said when I beat the shit out of Caleb. The sound of my breathing's too loud as I slowly turn and face her.

She catches her breath. "You... You're the guy from Hammers and Strings."

"What did you say?" I take a step toward her.

She retreats a step, licking her lip nervously. "I said we met at Hammers and Strings."

Another step. "Before that."

"Um. That you were going to kill him?"

"Why?"

She stares at me, half wary, half confused. "You were beating him pretty hard. You know people can die from getting beaten up, right?"

"Is that all?" I say, continuing to approach.

"He's a creep, but not a deserve-to-die creep." The heel of her shoe gets caught in a crack, and she loses her balance.

I jump forward and wrap an arm around her waist before she can fall.

I can feel shivers running through her, smell the scent of tiger lilies. There's still that same mole on her face.

Jesus. I'm either going mad or this really is Ivy.

You have enemies who would love to break you, Tony, Edgar's voice of reason says in my head.

"I'm okay now," she whispers.

"How can you be all right?" I almost snarl, furious she's trying to brush it off like nothing when I'm still burning with rage.

"Let go." This time, she's firmer, her muscles tensing as though she's getting ready to fight.

I pull away, realizing she needs to have some control of the situation, and me snarling at her isn't helping. She's shaking.

Then she finally realizes a third of her bodice is drooping forward from the broken strap. She curses under her breath and holds it up, one arm crossed over her chest like a shield, her gaze alive with an animal wariness.

The look in her eyes puts shards of pain into my heart because it proves Edgar's right. She isn't Ivy, no matter what my heart wants to believe. Ivy wouldn't have stared at me this way. She would've let me hold her, comfort her, take care of her. She would've let me shield her because she knew I'd protect her, no matter how badly I screwed up everything else.

I shrug out of my jacket and put it over her, pulling the lapels together. Then, very deliberately, I imagine myself getting a hold on my emotions, pushing them into a box and putting a lid on it. Because right now, Iris needs to be looked after. I can deal with my own feelings later.

~

Iris

The jacket's warm from his body. His scent envelops me, and the fine hair at the back of my neck rises, my skin prickling. I clutch the lapels tightly, pulling them closer. I'm thankful for the cover the jacket gives me and touched by the protective gesture.

The man is a mystery—a total contradiction. When I ran into him at Hammers and Strings, I thought he was a gentleman—he caught me so I didn't fall, then used a handkerchief to try to dry my tears when I cried. Tonight, he's an absolute savage.

The ruthlessness with which he dealt with Jamie Thornton was terrifying, but I'd be lying if I said some part of me wasn't grateful. He did it for me—to keep me safe.

But don't you think it was too extreme? You ran into each other at the music store, but you're basically strangers...

It *was* extreme...almost personal. Did something like this happen to someone close to him? Or maybe he and Jamie Thornton have a history.

His face is like granite, hard and unyielding. A sliver of apprehension ripples over my mind. Not a fear of him, per se. But of what could happen if I let myself get too close to him. He's the kind of man a woman could easily get attached to... without ever being let into his heart. I'm not in L.A. for that kind of complication and emotional upheaval. I'm here to regain my memory. And to see if I can have a normal, fulfilling life just like everyone else.

Suddenly I feel drained and exhausted.

"Thanks for your help. I should..." Actually, I have no idea what I'm going to do next. There's no way I can play the piano or drive home in this condition. Seeing Sam may not be the best—

"Do you want me to get you someone? A friend, maybe?"

I think for a moment, but can't come up with a single person for him to call. I don't have any family left, and Julie and Byron are both out of town. "It's all right," I say. "Nobody's available."

I suddenly realize even though Sam's right here in this building, he isn't on the list of people I think of when I need unconditional love, acceptance and comfort. That makes me feel infinitely alone and vulnerable. If only my parents were alive...

"I just want to leave now." I meant to say it firmly. Instead, my voice breaks a little. I swallow, then shoot him an "everything's fine" smile. He's done enough. He doesn't need me to break down and unload a bunch of messy emotions on him.

The muscles in his jaw flex as he regards me. Then something inside him shifts, pieces coming together to form a tight, cohesive whole. His eyes gleam with an unshakable resolve, which makes me apprehensive for some reason.

"Tony," he says, his tone decisive. "My name is Tony. And I'm taking you home."

36

Iris

"That won't be necessary," I say.

"Are you able to drive?" Tony asks, looking at my shaking hands.

Although his tone is calm and even, there's a hint of rage seething underneath. I move a little so that his back will be to Jamie Thornton. Keep Tony's eyes off him and there will be less reason to start beating him again.

The thought is strangely comforting. I need every scrap of protection and sense of security I can get. I'm not certain what it means that I'm getting both from this stranger, but I do. He will keep me safe. I know it at the most basic level—the one that lets me play piano pieces I didn't know I'd mastered.

"I'm taking you home. Period." He moves closer, shielding me with his body.

And I appreciate it that he's like a wall around me, keeping me safe. I can sense the curious gazes from people in the lobby, and the last thing I want to do is deal with them.

As he takes me to the main lobby, he texts someone rapidly. I keep my head down and walk as quickly as I can to leave the hotel—and the ugly near-rape experience—behind. Tony matches my pace.

But this evening just isn't going to go my way.

"Iris! Wait!"

I turn and see Marty. He's coming toward us, his step light and fast. Cringing, I pull my hair forward to hide the smeared makeup and look away.

Tony narrows his eyes. He looks like he'd love nothing more than to start hitting someone else. And Marty will do.

"Oh, hi. I didn't know you were coming," he says to Tony, then starts to reach for me. "Where are you going?"

Tony shifts, blocking Marty's hand. "I'm taking her home."

Marty takes in the jacket around me. From the shrewd look on his face, some kind of feverish calculation is going on. "What about the reception? Iris, you're supposed—"

"The guests in there can amuse themselves without live music," Tony says. "It isn't like they're children."

Marty jerks his gaze toward Tony. "Didn't you bring a date?" he says almost too aggressively. "How will she get home if you bail on her?"

I inhale sharply. The idea Tony might have a date never crossed my mind. The notion sets my teeth on edge for some reason.

"I came alone." His expression the very definition of cold apathy and disdain, Tony dismisses Marty with the arch of an eyebrow.

A gleaming silver Cullinan pulls up. The driver emerges—a mountain of a man in a suit, one whose dark eyes miss nothing and has as much hair below his nose as above it. He nods at Tony, then almost falters when he notices me. I sense Tony shake his head, a subtle gesture, and the driver's mouth flattens as he opens the door.

Their silent communication bothers me. I'm certain Tony won't hurt me, but this chauffeur, who looks like he should've been born thousands of years ago as a Visigoth warlord, is another story. He's giving off a vibe like the only reason he's behaving toward me is Tony.

"She owes me a dance," Marty interjects suddenly.

I slowly turn to stare at his face, which rapidly turns red. He and I have never danced, and I have no intention of changing that. Why would he toss out such an unbelievable lie? Because he doesn't want me to leave with Tony? It makes me want to do the exact opposite.

Tony's eyes glint with derision. "You'll just have to find yourself a new dance partner. Surely you're capable of accomplishing that much on your own."

Marty takes a step forward, his hands clenched.

The last thing I need is another fight. "I'm not dancing with anyone tonight," I say, tugging at Tony's sleeve. "Let's go."

Without waiting for an answer, I climb into the car. He follows me in, and the door closes with a solid, comforting *thunk.*

I give the driver instructions to my place. He grunts and maneuvers the car away from the hotel.

Now that I have a moment to gather myself, I take in the opulent luxury and wealth etched in every line of the interior. The engine purrs quietly in the dark, and I can't help but feel a slight tremor inside, like a small aftershock from an earthquake. It's probably an aftereffect of what almost happened in the courtyard. Although Jamie looked at me in that slightly creepy way, he seemed harmless. I'd never, ever have suspected he'd try something like that at a business function. He *knows* I'm Sam's niece. Did he not care what would happen if he got caught? Or does he not care about keeping his business relationship with Sam?

Or maybe he thinks Sam will put business ahead of a personal issue...

That's hard to believe. Sam's focused on his company, but he isn't that callous.

Except for the times he insisted on that you travel even when you said you were getting tired of it. The times he implied —subtly—that you should do what he wants whether you like it or not because he's the one who's been providing for you. Who knows if that wouldn't include giving yourself to an important investor?

What the...? I shiver, unsure where that cynical voice is coming from, and uncomfortable with it. If he were such a morally bankrupt man, he wouldn't have spent his own money to keep me in the hospital, given me the care I needed. He would've listened to the doctors who told him that maybe I should be taken off life support. Or later...the advice that any incremental improvement in my physical and mental health was going to cost too much to make it worthwhile. Not that they put it so bluntly, but that's what they meant.

No, what Jamie Thornton did has nothing to do with Sam. Rapists rape because they're rapists.

"Here. This might help you feel better."

Tony offers a tumbler of...something. My eyes drop to a small bottle of whiskey. It might help, but I'm feeling too nauseated from the attack to risk drinking and making a mess. "I might throw up."

He stares curiously, like what I'm saying doesn't compute.

"In your car. This nice, expensive car."

"Don't let that stop you. The car can be cleaned."

His response surprises me. Most guys think their cars drive on water, especially one as nice and expensive as this. Even Byron, who's pretty laid-back, babies his Maserati and won't let anybody eat or drink in it. So why is Tony so cavalier when he and I are virtually strangers?

"It's just a car," he says. "If it can't be cleaned, I can replace it."

My cheeks grow hot as I realize I said the last part out loud. "Well... If you're sure," I say, a bit more primly than I should to hide my embarrassment, then take the drink and knock it back.

The fiery liquor warms my belly, and the heat starts spreading immediately. Soon my tremor vanishes.

"Thank you," I say. "You were right. It helped."

He starts to say something, then changes his mind and hits a few buttons on the center console. Schubert's Fantasie fills the silence, each note beautifully poignant. As the music goes on, my heart seems to expand with hot, fierce longing. I notice with shock that my eyes are wet.

Why am I reacting like this? I'm pretty sure I've never played it—I don't like duets, especially ones that require you to share a piano, because it feels too intimate—and this piece isn't particularly tragic.

I turn my head away and surreptitiously wipe my face dry. I've met Tony twice so far, and both times I've shed tears. He must think I'm a broken faucet.

I want him to turn the music off, but I don't know how to ask without appearing unreasonable. The music isn't offensive. It isn't loud. There's nothing wrong with it...except somehow it's making me grieve for things I've lost—my earlier memories, my old life, my now-dead ambition to be a concert pianist.

"Are you all right?" Tony asks.

For a moment, I feel like he can sense everything. But it's dim inside the car and he probably can't see much. "I'm fine."

"'Fine' is the last word a woman in your condition should be using."

I squirm, uncomfortable how he isn't letting me get away with the arsenal of empty words I use to disguise how I'm really feeling. I've started doing that because every time I'm a bit too honest, Sam frets, then insists on having me see a specialist, whose prescription for what's ailing me is always something Sam would've suggested I do anyway—like traveling, online (but never on-campus) college, shopping, a nice, long retreat alone in some secluded place to listen to my inner voice...

Then the habit continued because I didn't want to worry Julie or Byron. They aren't close enough to Sam or Marty to gossip about me, but they're in a similar social echelon and do socialize with one another. Julie or Byron might let something slip.

But not Tony, I realize. Tony and Marty obviously don't get along at all, so Tony probably isn't close to Sam, either. Ironically, his disdain and unfriendliness toward the Peachers make him the perfect person for me to be honest with.

"You're right," I say. "I'm not fine. I'm..."

"Yes?"

"Angry. Shocked. Humiliated." I pause for a second, then add, "Frustrated. Scared. But determined to not let it beat me or make me afraid." I look down at my hands. "I wish I knew how to throw a punch like you."

"I hope you never have to."

My stomach flutters at the fiercely protective tone in his voice. Nobody's ever spoken to me like this before. His reaction is thrillingly intense. "Have you done this before? Rescued a damsel in distress?" The words tumble out before I stop them. I can't blame the liquor because I only had one.

Tony turns to me, his face stony. "Once. A guy tried to get an eighteen year-old girl drunk and force a kiss—and much more—at a party. I stopped him, but not before he got to grope her. I should've broken every bone in his hand for that." I have no doubt that if the man were here, Tony would do exactly that.

"I'm sorry to hear that. But you saved her, right?" I say, trying to point out the good he did.

"I was too late. If I had been there earlier, he wouldn't have gotten near her." His voice is quiet.

"You can't protect people twenty-four/seven, Tony. I'm sure she was grateful you helped her, just like I am that you helped me." I reach out and pat his hand, wanting to cheer him up. It's unfair that someone who tries so hard can feel so down about himself, while bad people go on blithely like they did nothing wrong.

He looks at my hand on his, then raises his eyes to meet mine. A current of awareness passes between us. It isn't just attraction. It's more...like we both understand how unjust and cruel the world can be regardless of what we do.

But oddly enough, he looks even more disappointed and sad. "Thank you," he says softly.

"You're welcome."

The car stops in front of Byron's penthouse building. "Thanks for saving me...and for the ride." I open the door and get out of the car.

Tony climbs out as well and looks at me, his gaze expectant.

Oh. The jacket. I begin to shrug out of it, but he puts a hand on my shoulder.

"Don't," he says. "You should keep it."

"But it's your jacket."

"You need it more than I do at the moment." His gaze drops to where my strap broke.

I can feel my face heat, and I look away. I totally forgot.

"I'll walk you to your door," he says.

"You don't have to." It occurs to me he must've been on business at the Peacher & Son event. He sure wasn't there to hang out with Sam or Marty.

"I insist. I'll sleep better knowing you made it home safely."

From the resolute way he speaks, I know he isn't budging. And honestly, I don't want to argue. Maybe something terrible happened later on to that girl he saved, and he's trying to make sure nothing happens to me. It's sweet and considerate.

I let him escort me all the way to my place on the top floor.

"Thank you. As you can see, all safe and sound. You can sleep well tonight," I say brightly, hoping the darkness in his eyes will ease and unsure what else to do. I'm not equipped to deal with this kind of thing. Maybe I was good at comforting people before, but I've forgotten how. The majority of people I've met since waking up from the coma are medical professionals. Sam. Marty. My two closest friends are Julie and Byron, and they're pretty well adjusted. Basically, I'm the biggest mess in the picture.

Tony stares at my mouth, and my lips prickle. His eyes narrow. "You have a cut."

I touch the left corner of my lower lip and wince at the slight sting. I hadn't noticed.

He lifts a hand, and the backs of his long fingers almost brush my cheek. All the air rushes out of me, and I start to bite my lip until I remember the cut.

"It needs to be looked at," he says. His expression is unnaturally calm, but that only tells me how furious he really is. "Can't believe I missed that."

"My hair was covering my face," I say. "And it's not that bad. I didn't notice either."

"Do you have a first-aid kit?"

"Uh... I don't know." I've never asked Byron. "But I can check." I enter the passcode and press my index finger to the biometric reader on the digital lock.

Tony puts a hand at the small of my back and ushers me

inside. He leads me to a couch and exerts a gentle pressure on my shoulder to sit. Then, after rearranging the jacket around my shoulders to keep me completely covered, he goes to the kitchen, rummages around and brings back a small bag of ice wrapped in a clean towel.

"Here. This'll help with the swelling." Instead of handing me the ice, he crouches in front of me and presses it gently against my mouth, his eyebrows pulled together in intense concentration.

I try to take the ice away without touching him. But my hand brushes his, and I feel the connection as intimately as a kiss. I look at him, not understanding why my reaction is so extreme—tears the first time we met, and now this. My brain injury can't be the cause. If it were, I would have responded like this to someone sooner. Not one of the men I've met made me feel the way I do with Tony.

He takes my right hand and gently turns it over. His thumb traces the faint scar that cuts across my palm from pinkie to the base of my thumb. The muscles in his jaw work, and his intense scrutiny leaves me jittery.

"How did you get this?" he asks, his voice taut.

"In a car accident. It was a long time ago."

He lifts his gaze to my face. There are questions in his dark green eyes, and suddenly I'm not ready for them, whatever they may be.

"Do you have any painkillers?"

"Huh?" That's the last thing I expected him to ask.

"Aspirin. Advil. Tylenol."

"I have some Advil in my bedroom."

He nods, then helps me up. "Which way?"

"That way." I gesture, almost in a daze. None of this is what he wanted to ask earlier. What I saw in his eyes wasn't some ordinary inquiry.

He starts to escort me. I want to tell him I’m fine and can manage on my own, but that’d be a terrible lie. My knees are too shaky. Maybe it’s the sudden relief at realizing I’m home and safe that’s making me feel weak.

I wonder vaguely if I should’ve offered him something to drink. After all, he helped me and brought me home. He even gave me that nice whiskey, and I haven’t even asked him if he wants a glass of water. But somehow I don’t.

He takes me to my bedroom. As his gaze sweeps the room, he seems to relax a bit. “Do you want to call someone to stay with you?”

“No. It’s just going to be me.” As I speak, I suddenly realize I don’t want to be alone in the vast place. Not that I think it’ll be unsafe or anything, but... “You have to go soon, right?”

“No. Why?”

“Um. I don’t ” I hesitate as something glimmers in the back of my mind, tickling me like a tiny feather. Somehow this scene, this scenario, doesn’t feel new. It’s similar to the sensation I get when I sit in front of a piano and start playing the first thing that comes to me and end up with a perfect Chopin étude. If I resist or second-guess myself, my fingers freeze and I can’t play at all.

Trust.

If I don’t trust my instincts, I may never recover all my memories. I inhale sharply, then let it all out. “I don’t want to be alone right now. That’s all.”

“If you want me to stay, I will,” he says.

Oh. I didn’t expect him to agree so easily. He should be at least somewhat reluctant, since he has to be a very busy man. Suddenly, I’m flustered, unsure. What if I’m just imposing on him, and he can’t bring himself to say no because he feels bad about what happened?

"You're thinking too much," Tony says. "I don't mind. Really."

"Do you want me to show you to a guest room?" I blurt out. I realize my mistake. Instead of just going with the flow of my instinct, I stopped, questioned and got anxious. Now the sliver of memory that was shimmering at the edge of my mind is gone, leaving me frustrated and annoyed. I feel like I missed a question on a test I should've known the answer to.

"Don't worry about me. Take care of yourself." When I don't respond, Tony peers at me. "Do you want to brush your teeth? Clean up and change?"

"N—" Actually, I do. I want to wash up and wash away everything that happened this evening. "Yes."

"Go ahead. I'll wait."

"Okay."

I grab a change of clothes and go to the bathroom. I lock the door, the latch closing quietly, and run the water. I brush my teeth with extra toothpaste. It stings in the cut, but I don't care. I need to erase the disgusting, slimy feel of Jamie Thornton's tongue. After gargling four times with mouthwash, I strip, dumping everything on the floor, and walk into the glass stall. I adjust the water until it's almost scalding and scrub myself with enough soap to clean an entire high school cheerleading squad. It's too bad there's no bleach in the bathroom.

After I dry myself, I put on a white Tweety Bird night shirt and shorts and come out. The bedroom's dimly lit by the one small lamp on my bedside table. Tony's still there, just like he said he would be. The sight's comforting, like a shield between me and the world. How strange that I'd feel that way about him. But how many guys would come to my rescue the way he did, make sure I got home safely and take care of me?

He's in one of my two chairs, which he's moved closer to the bed. His back is slightly curved, his legs stretched. The pose looks indolent and relaxed—a predator in repose—but there's nothing indolent and relaxed about whatever going through in his head, from the icy intent in his narrowed, faraway eyes.

I check the time. I was in the bathroom for almost forty minutes. He shifts, and the light hits his hand. I notice a rust-red crusting over the knuckles.

"You're hurt," I say.

He looks slightly amused at the idea. "Me?"

"Your hand."

He glances down, flexing his fingers. "It's nothing."

I go to the bathroom and bring back a warm, wet towel, along with his jacket. I give him the jacket, then take his hand and gently wipe away the blood, checking to make sure there aren't any serious injuries. Once I'm done, I eye the other hand. He gives it to me without a word. It's bloody, too. I clean it with care.

"Told you it was nothing." Tony's voice is artificially facile, an attempt at nonchalance that doesn't really come off. "Go to sleep, Iris."

"You're probably busy. I shouldn't have asked you to stay." I shouldn't continue to impose when I've lost what little hold I had over that thread of memory.

A corner of his mouth lifts into a faint smile. "After you go to sleep."

"I can't fall asleep while someone watches," I say, climbing into bed and pulling the sheet all the way to my chin. Part of me thinks what's happening here is surreal, but another part is anxious, full of anticipatory flutter, as the same little feather that tickled my mind earlier returns, this time more persistent.

He leans back in the chair and looks up at the ceiling. "Nobody's watching you now. Sleep."

"You can't just order someone to sleep like that."

Did he flinch? I can't really be sure.

I stay tense under the sheet, waiting for lightning to strike and reveal some piece of memory that's buried in my head, but nothing comes. Disappointment slowly permeates me, and I swallow a sigh. I should've known it wouldn't be that easy. But this is the closest I've ever gotten to sensing memories that have nothing to do with music in the last thirty-odd months.

And I know instinctively that Tony is the key.

37

ANTHONY

EVENTUALLY, IRIS FALLS ASLEEP, THE QUIET SOUND OF her breathing even and slow. I ease the kinks out of my stiff neck and study her in the dim light.

When she asked me to stay, I felt like a man given the key to a treasure chest. Edgar said I was confused, projecting onto her what I want to see.

But looking at her freshly scrubbed face, I can't help but notice the same delicate curves of her cheekbones, the same small nose and full lips. How can I be confused? I worshipped her, have her etched in my heart and soul.

Then what was Lauren?

That was different. I was younger. Still wallowing in grief.

So you don't grieve for Ivy now?

Of course I do. I'll always grieve for her, the way I still grieve for Katherine. But looking at Iris, I have to question if she really is Ivy somehow—

She died, Tony.

I take her long-fingered hand in mine gently. *Just look at it —that's Ivy's hand—*

Lauren had long fingers, too. They don't mean anything.

If Edgar could hear half these thoughts or the debate I'm having with myself right now, he'd worry himself sick.

Maybe I am crazy. How much is sanity worth if clinging to it means walking away from this woman right now and never looking back? Because if I accept that Edgar is right, I need to get the hell out of here and forget I ever met Iris.

I trace the scar on her palm with my forefinger. Isn't it proof that I'm right? But when I asked her about it, she said it came from a car accident. And she wasn't lying. I looked at her carefully for even the slightest hint of deception, but there was nothing.

If Iris is really Ivy, and bent on pretending like she doesn't know me to punish me, then Ivy's become a remarkable actress, one who can stick to her role even through a traumatic attack.

Some things about her add up all too well—her musical ability, her appearance, the scar on her palm. Other things add up to a one-way ticket to an asylum. Her reaction to me, as though I were a complete stranger. The lack of tattoo—if she'd had it lasered off, it wouldn't have left a scar like that. Her ties to Sam, whose sleaziness has grown along with his bank account, and Byron Pearce, who thinks I'm a piece of shit.

Sanity or madness?

What does it say about me that both options look equally attractive? Every time I think I've reached bottom, I find a way to sink lower into the abyss.

I reluctantly release her hand and tuck it under the cover. I remember the cut on her lip, and stand up. I have unfinished business.

38

Iris

I JERK AWAKE WITH A STRANGLED SCREAM AND SEE A man's dress jacket draped over a chair near my bed. I stare, confused, then remember it's Tony's—the one he put around my shoulders last night. The sight gives me an odd sense of comfort and safety.

"Tony?" I call out, then try again louder. I hear nothing except the soft hum of the air conditioner.

Did he leave? Maybe not. He would've taken his jacket, wouldn't he?

He was such a gentleman last night, making me feel safe. I think of the protective way he put the jacket around me, then deflected Marty's attempt to keep me at the reception and brought me home. Such a contrast from the violence he showed when he pummeled Jamie like a punching bag. Normally I'm not a big fan of fighting, but I shudder—half angry, half grateful—thinking of what could've happened if he hadn't been there. Jamie would have...

Nope. Not going there.

Hating the sweat clinging to my skin, I kick the covers off and sit up. The air is chilly, congealing the sweat into a sticky layer. Placing a hand over my chest, I breathe in and out slowly to calm my galloping heart.

The nightmare I just had replayed Jamie Thornton's attack...except it didn't happen in the garden. It happened in a bright bedroom I don't remember. Large, faceless young men surrounded me, while Jamie pushed me against a wall. He forced a kiss, smelling like beer and some kind of hard liquor, while groping my breast. The other men watched and hollered encouragement. Tony rescued me again, but in the dream, he killed Jamie with a single punch to the face. The pieces of shattered skull and brains fell on me, and Jamie's headless body and I plunged into a murky swamp as the floor vanished underneath our feet. I couldn't breathe as water filled my nose, mouth, lungs...

I shiver again. *It's just a dream.* I've had dreams that didn't make any sense before, although nothing this horrible and violating. My doctors said the dreams don't necessarily mean anything. But I can't shake the feeling that it's not something my subconscious conjured up entirely out of thin air. It felt so...real.

I press the heels of my hands against my temples. Of course it felt real. Half of it happened—the attack and the rescue. My mind just embellished some details. It's a normal way for a brain to process traumatic or memorable events.

I need to pull myself together. Dreams can't hurt me. Jamie's probably hiding somewhere, since showing the face that Tony used as a punching bag last night would be embarrassing. Then it strikes me that he's an important investor for Sam. Is he going to try to pull his money?

I shake my head. I have no clue what Jamie Thornton's going to do, but Sam doesn't need money from that kind of scum. If his business ideas are good, surely he can find others who'll be happy to invest.

It's only six thirty in the morning, but I know I won't be able to go back to sleep. I get up, splash some water on my face and brush my teeth. Blue bruises have blossomed over my wrists, forearms, right shoulder—where he broke my dress strap—and thighs. All of them hurt to varying degrees. The cut on my lip throbs when toothpaste gets on it, but I ignore the pain. There isn't much I can do about it, and a couple of Advil should tide me over until my body heals.

I put on black tights and a gray long-sleeve top that reaches almost to mid-thigh, then swipe my mouth with red lipstick. The key to feeling as normal as possible—in my experience—is to try to maintain as normal a routine as possible. And do one thing to make myself feel pretty.

I learned the trick from a sweet, patient nurse who took care of me when I was in the hospital after waking up. She came one day with a pink lipstick from a drugstore and offered it to me. Told me that if I made myself look pretty, I'd feel better. I resisted it at first, since nothing—absolutely nothing!—could make up for what I'd lost. She gently persisted for a week and finally put the lipstick on me, then placed a hand mirror before my face so I could see her handiwork. She was right. I still looked like pale death, but at least my lips had some color. And staring at the improved reflection, I started to feel better. A tiny bit more like my old self than a broken shell.

Since then, lipstick has become my cheer-me-up.

I go to the kitchen and munch on a granola bar, wash it down with a cup of coffee, and walk slowly toward the Yamaha. Finger exercises might help me regain some equilibrium. It's what I do when I need to forget everything and relax.

I begin with Hanon's *Virtuoso Pianist*. The repetitiveness is soothing—almost meditative. After a few arpeggio exercises,

I stop, my hands still resting on the keyboard. Then, almost out of impulse, I start Chopin's "Waterfall" étude.

My fingers play lightly, quickly over the keys. The movements feel effortless. I repeat it ten times—which doesn't take more than twenty minutes, tops—then stop, exhaling softly. The restlessness inside me hasn't subsided with music. It's still there, lingering...making my scalp throb.

The intercom buzzes. I check the time. It's only eight thirty. "This is the concierge. Delivery for you. Special courier."

Must be Byron or Julie. If it's Byron, he's probably sending me a box of dark chocolate because he knows chocolate is the one thing I can't resist. But with Julie, it could be anything from thoughtful to crazy. She once sent me a box of wool winter socks from Switzerland because she said the patterns on them were just too cute...even though I was in Ecuador at the time.

A young man arrives, hands me a small box and a bouquet of tiger lilies—my favorite—then pushes his small tablet in my way. "Sign here."

I scrawl my name with my index finger. Shoving the tablet into his shirt pocket, he vanishes before I can thank him.

I take everything to the kitchen. Who sent them? The box is too small to contain more than a couple of truffles. Not Byron's style. Julie has never sent me flowers before. Besides, if she were behind the delivery, it would've been a bottle of premium vodka, since she's in Russia right now.

I open the box first and see an elegant pink, gold and white jar. I sniff the clear, gel-like substance inside, but there's no scent. There is, however, a note.

Put it on your cut. It'll help with the pain and swelling. You may also want to consider taking something stronger than Advil. You're going to feel worse today.

–Tony

He also put his phone number in a postscript, explaining that if I need anything else, I should call. I stare at the unexpected gifts for a moment, then dab a bit of the ointment over my lip. Within a few seconds, the cut no longer hurts.

Smiling at his thoughtfulness, I put the tiger lilies in a vase. Their vibrant color cheers me up, and I start to feel sunny. It's hard to be depressed in the presence of such gorgeous blossoms. I wonder how he knew what my favorite flower is. Most guys I know—even Byron—would send roses. Not that I'd mind, but tiger lilies... They're special. Bright. Tall. Fragrant. Functional, too, since the bulb and flowers are edible. Everything about them is perfect.

I put the vase on a stand near the piano and start playing again, my mind no longer in turmoil. A call about ninety minutes later interrupts my practice. It's Marty. I don't want to talk to him so early in the morning, but when I ignore it, he texts me.

I know you're there. Pick up the fucking phone.

That is usually a warning that he'll make a scene the next time we meet unless I talk to him. If I were traveling, I'd ignore him, but we're in the same city now, and he knows where I live. Might as well gird my loins and deal with it now in private.

He calls again. I snatch the phone from the top of the piano. "You should say please if you want me to do you a favor."

"*Favor?*" He sounds like he's choking on the word. "Like how you fucked Jamie Thornton up?"

"What are you talking about? Did he say I beat him up?" I ask, incredulous. What kind of guy says he got beaten up by a girl?

"Dad and I had a brunch scheduled with him today. He canceled. Actually, his secretary did."

"And what does that have to do with me?" *It isn't my fault he's a creepy rapist wannabe* is on the tip of my tongue, but I don't say it yet, since I want to know what lies he told Sam and Marty first. "What did he say?"

"He disappeared right after you did last night, and now he's stuck at a hospital for cracked ribs, smashed knees, a broken pelvis and a fractured right wrist!"

What the heck? The rib part makes sense because Tony kicked him pretty hard, but the rest? Jamie crawled away just fine.

Marty continues, "If it has nothing to do with you, I'll eat my shoes."

"Well, I hope you enjoy the taste of leather. Oh, by the way, it'd be better if you and your dad didn't get involved with a creep like that. He tried to rape me last night!"

"Please. You aren't hot enough to rape."

I explode off the piano bench. If I were a volcano, I would be shooting fiery lava a thousand feet into the sky. "What the *hell* is wrong with you?"

"Shut up! There's nothing wrong with me. You're the one messed up in the head."

What a cheap shot. Suddenly my rage quits running hot. It's now icy cold.

"He wouldn't need to force a girl like you," Marty continues. "So what if he touched your shoulder or whatever?"

"You think I left last night because he felt up my shoulder?" I say between clenched teeth. "Or is that what he's claiming?"

"He didn't say shit, but isn't it obvious? His girlfriend is *hot*."

"He has a girlfriend?" I feel sorry for the woman. "Does she know what kind of creep he is?"

"Obviously he's *not* a creep, which is *why* he has a girlfriend!"

If Marty were here now, I'd bash the vase over his head.

"If you had any idea what Dad has done for you, you wouldn't have fucked the deal up! He saved your fucking life, Iris! You didn't have to sic Anthony on one of his investors."

I laugh. "Marty, seriously. Are you trying to show off how little talent you have for fiction? Because what you're suggesting is so idiotic, I have no words. Tony brought me home and spent last night here to make sure I was okay because, unlike you, he's a decent human being who actually gives a damn when a creep assaults a woman. I doubt he had the time to go beat Jamie Thornton up even if he wanted to."

Except he didn't stay the entire night. He could've left any time after I fell asleep. On the other hand, why would he go for Round Two? He did enough damage the first time. And he and I don't know each other well enough for him to react to that extreme a degree. *Right?*

"Oh, so it's *Tony*? And you guys spent the night together last night?"

"Stop making it sound dirty, Marty. It wasn't like that."

He explodes. "You are *such* a moron!"

"*Me?*" What the hell? "You're the moron who can't see beyond money! Listen, a guy who will sexually assault a potential business partner's niece won't think anything of screwing his partner over. Tony is a gentleman, a far better man than Jamie Thornton—or you—for sure."

"Your *Tony* is an asshole and a sociopath. His family disowned him seven years ago after putting up with his shit for so long. His parents won't even acknowledge his existence now. He's dead to them. *Dead.* So do yourself a favor and stay the hell away from him. And stop calling him Tony. It makes you look stupid."

"No and no," I say.

"I mean it, Iris. It's for your own good."

Is there a tinge of panic in his voice? I remember how desperately Marty tried to stop me from leaving with Tony, with his ridiculous claim that I promised him a dance. What's really going on between the two? "If you don't like the guy, why did you invite him?"

"We didn't. He invited himself."

"Can he do that?" Don't Sam and Marty screen the guests to make sure nobody can just waltz in and eat their caviar?

"A long story, but he did. Don't know why because he's never, ever associated with us before."

How strange. It's a coincidence that Tony and I not only ran into each other at Hammers and Strings, but he just happened to be at the garden when Jamie attacked me? That seems more than a coincidence. Was he following me? But why?

Argh. What am I even thinking? I'm not important enough for Tony to attend a party just to meet me. I can't let Marty's paranoia make me crazy.

"Maybe he's going to invest in the venture Jamie Thornton was going to put money in," I say.

"No fucking way. And that's not funny," Marty hisses furiously. I've never heard him speak this tautly or urgently. "Just forget about him before you get your hopes up and get hurt. You aren't his type. He doesn't like blondes. He only likes brunettes with big tits and a tight ass, which is the opposite of you."

Marty's warning stokes my temper. When did he start caring about me being hurt or who I spend time with? "Thanks for the tip, Marty. I was just thinking of changing my hair color, and a chestnut-brown dye job will look great. Don't you?"

He snarls, and I hang up, not interested in his bullshit. He calls again. I ignore him. He can text me or email me. I'm not listening to that whining, grating voice anymore.

And I don't care if he makes a scene next time we run into each other. Let him. I'll make it super embarrassing for him.

I return to the piano to continue practicing, but the intercom stops me. This time it's the front desk reception.

"Ms. Smith, we have a Mr. Anthony Blackwood," the man says after a short greeting. "He says he'd like to see you, but he's not on the guest list."

Anthony Blackwood...? Oh, *Tony*. "He's fine. Let him up, please." I hang up and glance at the clock. Almost eleven.

My nerves are still prickling from my argument with Marty. I take a deep, calming breath, tuck my hair behind my ears and smooth my shirt. I think I look okay. I turn on the front camera on my phone and check just in case. My cheeks are a little flushed, but that's about it. As I adjust my shirt neckline to hide the bruises, I stop for a moment, struck by the fact that I'm fussing over my appearance. The most I ever do is run my fingers through my hair and maybe apply a fresh coat of lipstick. But with Tony, it feels different. More anticipatory. Almost nervous, like his opinion matters so, so much.

I don't want him to notice I'm messed up in the head, like Marty said. I want Tony to think I'm normal. Maybe even pretty.

My God. Am I crushing on him? A guy I've only met twice?

My cheeks heat, but this time not with temper. I tap the floor with my toe, bouncing my foot over and over again. It's such an unfamiliar sensation. A little uncomfortable, too. But it isn't entirely unpleasant. It's more like...the feeling I sometimes get when I sit in front of a piano, about to sight-read music I don't remember having played before, full of excitement and wonder and discovery.

But unlike music, my excitement isn't where this ends. I

want Tony to like me, too. Or at least think I'm not too messed up. Even if I don't have brown hair or huge breasts or whatever, like the women he usually prefers.

A few minutes later, Tony comes up, and I let him in.

Yesterday, Tony had his hair slicked back. Today, it's slightly tousled. Dark stubble covers his strong jaw. He's dressed casually in khaki shorts and a blue T-shirt that turns his eyes forest green. Somehow he makes them look glamorous enough to be on the cover of *GQ*, while I'm fairly ordinary and boring in my gray and black. To top it all off, I'm barefoot.

I gesture at the flowers. "You sent me those—and the cream—earlier, so I didn't realize you were coming by. Thank you, by the way. I love tiger lilies."

"I'm glad. I wanted you to have that cream for your lip right when you woke up, so that's why I had them delivered so early."

"But you didn't want to come by until now?" I'm curious about what he does. He obviously has money and influence if he can just crash a Peacher & Son party with Sam and Marty unable to stop him.

"I had an early meeting."

"Ah." Of course. He's a busy man. I start to tuck my hair behind my ear, then stop as I realize it's already tucked.

"Have you had breakfast?"

"A granola bar and coffee. Why? You want something to eat?" I ask, then wonder if there's anything to offer in the fridge.

"How about brunch? French toast sound good? I know a great diner."

Actually, food is the last thing on my mind, but when he asks with that faint smile on his lips, it does sound a little tempting...mainly for the company. I grab my purse and some slippers and follow him out. I owe him at least a brunch for his help last night.

39

Anthony

TJ doesn't bother to express his disapproval and mild irritation anymore. He made himself clear last night when I came down from the penthouse.

When I hired him, I gave him a few specific instructions. One was never to let me be near a strawberry blonde, no matter what. He followed it to the letter, and no strawberry blonde, regardless of how hot or wily, could get past TJ to reach me.

But last night, I brought Iris with me. Shook my head when TJ wanted to pull her away. It's not a good idea to break rules, make exceptions. Your employees don't like it because it creates confusion and uncertainty. If Iris is okay, then what about other strawberry blondes? Are they okay too now?

If I told TJ why Iris is an exception...

Would he encourage me or drive me straight to his sister, who's a shrink?

He eyes Iris coolly, although he can't quite hide his

surprise. She isn't dolled up like all my previous dates. Her unbound hair frames her face, fresh and without makeup except for lipstick. Her shirt is a bit too large, designed to be comfortable rather than seductive, and the ballet slippers on her feet are plain black, nothing fancy. She isn't wearing a single piece of jewelry.

But she couldn't be more beautiful or radiant. She draws me like sunlight does a plant. Like a fragrant flower lures bees.

She's chosen a long-sleeve shirt to cover the bruises from last night—the weather's too warm for it otherwise—but I can see the edges of a couple at the neckline. I realize I didn't hurt Jamie enough. His left wrist is still unbroken. So is his nose.

Iris doesn't try to talk. She sits and studies me through her lashes from time to time. When I look at her, she quickly looks away.

The drive is quiet except for Schubert's Fantasie. I'm deliberately playing it again to see if Iris will react to it in some way.

I could swear I saw her cry last night, but that was after that subhuman trash attacked her. She might not have noticed the music at all.

But today's different. Although the attack is still traumatic, it isn't so fresh that she can *not* notice the music.

Ivy and I played it ten times the first time we met. Surely it still has some meaning. But this woman isn't reacting to it in any particular way. She's tapping her fingers to the tempo, her eyes slightly narrowed, as though she's appreciating the phrasing of the pianists.

Is Edgar right? Am I chasing a ghost?

Walk away before you lose it all, Tony.

Except what do I have to lose? Money, billions of dollars of it, is nothing if it can't give you what you want.

The car stops at an intersection, and Iris looks out her window. A harried mother is struggling with a stroller and some glossy shopping bags. She's carrying way too many things. But when the baby waves its plump arms, she looks down with a blinding smile as though her battle with the stroller and bags no longer matters.

Some people deserve that kind of love. Some don't. It doesn't matter what kind of public façade a family tries to create out of shame, out of pride. At the end of the day, the truth will come out, and everyone will know who didn't belong.

Mother smiled at me like that once. When I was much, much younger. And until seven years ago, my parents at least pretended like they didn't hate me. In front of other people, anyway. Now, everyone knows I'm a fucked-up child my parents consider a mistake. Edgar and Harry get the respect of our family name. I get the respect my empire commands. But I couldn't be more apathetic about the company I built. These days, the only thing that makes me care enough to get out of bed and make sure we're still profitable is the thousands of people we employ...and their families, whose livelihoods depend on the financial health of Vice Enterprises.

The car starts moving again, and I look away, suddenly feeling dirty and unwanted, yet greedy for unconditional acceptance, and ashamed of that greed.

I steal a quick glance. So let's say I'm crazy and confused and Iris isn't Ivy. Can she be *like* Ivy—be the sun, the moon and the stars of my otherwise dark and barren life? Or am I being selfish for even wishing such a thing?

You have enemies, Tony. You have to be more careful.

Edgar, ever the sensible brother, would say that to me. But he hasn't lived in the darkness like I have. He's heir to the family fortune and loved by all. Deservedly so. Even though I'd be lying if I said I'd never felt a tinge of envy...or guilt and shame for that petty emotion.

TJ pulls over in front of a diner with a hip retro décor. A

bright teal, dark forest green and vivid orange color scheme adds to the cheery atmosphere, and movie posters and LPs from the sixties and seventies cover the walls.

Iris looks surprised. "Here?"

"Yes."

"Oh. It doesn't seem like your kind of place," she says, then flushes like she just realized she said something she shouldn't have.

"What is my kind of place?"

"Really expensive and glitzy," she says, wrinkling her nose. "I'm wrong, aren't I?"

"Expensive and glitzy is fine. If you want, we can head to a place like that."

She shakes her head emphatically. "No!"

"Good, because I like this place more. It isn't fancy, but it's cheerful and bright." Just what I need at regular intervals.

A host seats us at a table for two in the middle of the restaurant and leaves a couple of laminated menus. I don't pick mine up, and neither does she.

"They have great French toast," I say. "And bacon."

"I'm not that hungry, so if they have a half-portion French toast, I'll take it. I'm really here to keep you company and buy you brunch."

"You are?"

"You saved me last night. It's the least I can do."

"I didn't do it for some kind of repayment." Her money is the last thing I want. But her company...that I can't refuse. I just wish I'd known she wasn't hungry. I would've suggested something else.

See? Another bit of proof she isn't Ivy. Ivy enjoyed her food, and she ate more than just granola and coffee in the morning.

"I don't like owing people," she says.

"Accepting kindness isn't owing. Nobody's following you around with a ledger."

"Kindness comes with a price tag," she says softly, the light in her eyes subdued.

"Not this time." Who's tried to manipulate her? Then what Jamie Thornton said last night surfaces back into my mind.

He wouldn't have minded! The fucker said she owes him her life!

Sam is still healthy only because Jamie explained—after a few more broken fingers—that he never received explicit permission from Sam to assault Iris. But I don't like the precise way Jamie put it—that she owes Sam her life. The only thing he did was deal with her medical care while she was in the hospital. Given the kind of shit he is, I doubt he did it out of altruism.

"Did Sam make you do things you didn't want to do?" I ask bluntly.

"You mean like sex?" She looks horrified. "No!"

"Not necessarily sex. Anything."

Lips parted, she stares at me like I've grown two horns. Maybe even hooves. But I also catch a flash of anxiety in her gaze. "What are you talking about?"

"I know Sam took you in nine years ago. He told me," I say, since I can't tell her about my conversation with Jamie.

"He's done a lot to help me." Her voice is almost too quiet, her intonation like a child reading a schoolbook. "Without him, who knows what could've happened?"

Our server comes by, interrupting the conversation. Iris gestures at me to order.

"French toast and bacon. Same for her. Grapefruit juice and coffee," I say.

When the juice arrives, I push it toward Iris. She looks at me, surprised. "For me?"

"Yes."

"How did you know I like grapefruit juice?"

The question is like a jab to my mind.

"Most people would've gotten OJ. Even Byron does when I have him order for me." Then she quickly adds, "Byron's my friend. You might've seen him when I left Hammers and Strings."

I hate it that she's close to Byron because I can't stand the bastard. He's too damn perfect—perfect face, perfect manners, perfect pedigree. His family loves him, his friends think he's a great guy, and women fawn over him until I want to vomit. But it's a small victory that Perfect Byron doesn't know what Iris likes.

"This place has the best grapefruit juice. Freshly squeezed. That's why," I say, since I can't tell her the truth—that it was Ivy's favorite. And because I'm being a crazy fucking bastard, I keep testing to see if there's even the slightest chance she's Ivy.

If Edgar were here, he'd kill me for not letting him handle this like I promised. But it's like a fresh scab over a wound. Impossible not to pick at it, even knowing I'm going to end up making it bleed again.

Our server brings the food. The toast is cut thick and has a generous amount of fresh berries and powdered sugar, maple syrup on the side. The bacon's also thick and perfectly cooked —crispy and not overly greasy. Again, this used to be Ivy's favorite.

I attack the food, monstrously hungry from skipping breakfast. But Iris merely picks at hers, cutting the toast into little pieces and moving them around. She doesn't eat more than a couple of small bites.

"If you don't like it, we can get something else," I say, torn between disappointment and chagrin. Maybe I should've let her choose her own food.

"No. It's fine."

"You barely ate."

"I don't have a lot of appetite."

"How come?"

"I had a car accident nine years ago. Since then, not much appetite. I eat because I have to, but..." She shrugs.

"Sam mentioned the accident. It sounded serious."

A pained shadow crosses her expressive face. "If he told you, then you know about my parents' deaths."

"Vaguely. It came up at the reception yesterday. He and I didn't get to talk long." Partly because I can't stand the old man and his presumptuous ways.

"Hit and run. I was in the car, too. I lived. They didn't." She looks briefly down, then away, her eyes unfocused. Hunching her shoulders, she wraps her arms around herself. "I heard they died instantly. No pain," she says, still not meeting my gaze.

I recognize what she's feeling because I felt it too. When Katherine died. When Ivy died. Survivor's guilt.

I want to say something, do something to make Iris feel better, but I don't know what. I'm not a man who naturally knows how to comfort others. I wish I had even a tenth of Harry's ability to cheer people up.

So I flounder for a moment and say, "I'm sorry for your loss." Then I stop, hating how inadequate those five words are. How I loathed them when I heard people say them to me. "I'm sure they're glad you survived," I add, then wince inwardly at how empty that sounds.

She studies me, but she isn't judging me in the least. Her face isn't showing the contempt and anger that simmer when someone tosses you a bullshit platitude and the only thing stopping you from telling them off is social decorum.

"Thank you," she says. "You're right. They would've wanted me to live. I've been fortunate to have people who were there for me."

"Like Byron?" Most likely Sam was there first. But I want to understand exactly what's going on between her and Byron.

She shakes her head. "No, I didn't meet him until two years ago."

"But you're staying at his place."

"I am, but only until I get a job and can afford an apartment." She stops. "How did you know it was Byron's?"

Because his place is featured in magazines, and I've heard a few of my female employees talking about it breathlessly, discussing the price, location, décor and more. They admire the luxury home and covet the man.

"The front desk person told me when he was checking to see if I was on the guest list for Byron Pearce or you," I say.

"Oh." Iris nods, apparently buying it. "I'm only staying here because it's more...convenient. It's really my uncle, Sam, who took care of me. He still does that...a little."

"So why isn't he paying for an apartment for you?" I ask, starting to get annoyed with Sam for being cheap. She shouldn't have to live with Byron.

"Because I already have a place to crash until I get a job and my own place. I'm going to work on a résumé this week and start applying."

I don't give a shit—Sam still should've gotten her an apartment. "Why a résumé? Aren't you going to be a musician? You're easily good enough to turn professional."

She shakes her head. "No, I can't. It's a long story, but I'm applying for office jobs. It'll be a good first step to become independent and lead my own life, even though Sam doesn't like it."

Good ol' Sam. Trying to exert influence over her life even though he's too cheap to pay for her own place. I don't like it. "What does he want you to do?"

"Continue to travel around the world. Europe, Asia—it doesn't matter where, as long as it's not here in the States. But six years is long enough, don't you agree? I'm tired, and I want to be home."

"Definitely," I say, hiding my outrage at the revelation. *Six years?* That's a damn long time to force someone out of the country. Basically an exile.

And it's worse than what I had. At least I was in one place long enough to make friends. Not her. Sam ensured it'd be nearly impossible for her to create a network of people she could depend on...

He wants her beholden to him forever.

Is this why she hasn't been able to get in touch? Is this why she's pretending she doesn't know who I am? Is this why—

I stop. Why would she ever contact me when I made it clear the last time we spoke that I didn't love her enough to let her in? How could she know that all she has to do is crook her finger and I'll gladly jump into a sea of fire to get to her?

"Iv[illegible] Iris," I say. My voice is too thick. I swallow a quick sip of coffee, which has gone cold during our talk. "If you had someone else you could depend on, other than Sam, would you have reached out?"

"I don't have anybody else. That's why Sam had to come through, even though he wasn't particularly close to my parents."

"How about your...friends?"

"They were young and moved on. We weren't in the same place mentally or physically. Young friendships don't survive everything." She looks almost wistful, but then straightens her spine, pulls her shoulders back. "It's okay, though. I can always make new friends. The flip side of being young, right?"

Suddenly I can't stand that she's talking about her past relationships like that. It's like she's given up on them. On *us*. It's so unfair. I never got a chance to tell her I made the decision to be brave, to let her in. "You should've reached out anyway. Young or not, they would've come back," I say, doing my best to not sound bitter. But from the slightly confused and defensive look on her face, I've failed.

"They wouldn't have. I was in a coma for a year after the accident...and a mess when I woke up. By the time I recovered, it'd been years. It was just too late."

"It's never too late, Iris."

"It was for me. My memory was patchy when I woke up. And what I did remember, I couldn't trust completely. Sam sometimes had to correct me."

"Really?" What did he correct? What the hell did he do when she was so vulnerable?

"Yeah. For example, I thought I'd graduated early, but Sam told me I didn't—even though I could have—because I wanted to graduate with my friends."

"Did he have any evidence for what he was saying? Pictures? A diploma?"

"There was a yearbook. From my class. I was a popular kid. It had lots of messages from friends." Her smile is bittersweet.

Sam's lying. He has to be. People can falsify passports. How hard would it be to fake a yearbook?

He had to have been using his position to manipulate her. How simple would it be to make a confused and grief-stricken young woman depend on you? Look to you for guidance and "truth"? And then feed her lies, knowing she'd accept them without examining them too closely?

"How about now? Are you all right now?" I ask, and hold my breath.

"I remember most of what I need to remember. All the important people in my life. Schools, friends. You know."

What about me? I want to probe her head, see if there's even the slightest hint of me in her past. Or was I so unimportant she forgot me completely? "How can you be sure you haven't forgotten anything...essential?"

"Because of what my doctor told me. I had the same question, but he said all the really relevant stuff should be there... although he couldn't guarantee it, of course. He compared my memory to a glass bowl. The injury that put me into the coma broke it into pieces, but my body didn't want to let it stay broken. So it put the pieces back together."

"Perfectly?"

"Ha. No. There are still holes, and certain events are out of order in my mind. Like the high school graduation thing."

I gesture at her to continue, needing to know exactly what she's suffered, what she's lost, why I went from someone she loved to someone not important enough to remember.

"Anyway, the doctor said my body wasn't able to 'fix the bowl' perfectly, but it re-created the bowl even if some pieces were missing or out of place. But as far as my body's concerned, a misshapen bowl with a few insignificant missing bits is better than nothing. And I have to agree. I mean, I'm alive."

She is. She so is. And I'm nowhere in her mind.

I reach for my coffee and down the rest of the cold, bitter brew. I have to be going insane. I keep reacting like I'm talking to Ivy. But if I give myself a moment to think logically, it's obvious she isn't. Her parents died nine years ago. Ivy's parents died eighteen years ago. It's clear Iris has never been to a conservatory, much less Curtis. If she had, she would've remembered such a milestone.

Still, I keep thinking about those memory gaps like a drowning man grasping for a rope. Sam was there the entire time to "correct" her. Did he correct me out of her mind? Could he even do that?

But *why* would he? There was no reason. Although he and I were never close, I was away for so long that we didn't have any bad blood, either. Certainly nothing so bad that he'd do that to me.

"How are your hands?" she asks suddenly.

"What?"

She gestures at the little cuts that have scabbed over.

"They're fine." Nothing, in fact, compared to the wound bleeding inside me.

She fiddles with her napkin, shredding a corner. Another of Ivy's old habits. I forcibly remind myself a lot of people do that when they're nervous or thinking.

She finally stops and looks at me. "Did you know Jamie Thornton's been seriously injured?" The question is a whisper.

News sure travels fast. "Yes. How did you hear about it?"

"Marty called. He was furious...and accused you."

Well, well. So Marty isn't a complete moron. I was wondering after that idiotic attempt to prevent Iris from leaving with me last night. "A garden at night can be a dangerous place. Who can Jamie blame for his injuries other than himself for being so clumsy?"

She looks skeptical, of course. She's smart. But I can't tell her the truth. Violence upsets her, even when it's directed at scum like Thornton. He deserved every bit of what I did to him. And he will never be able to touch another girl without thinking of my punishment.

"So you had nothing to do with it?"

"If I had things my way, Thornton would be dead." That's honest, although it doesn't really answer her question.

She shifts in her seat. "I don't know how you can talk about death so casually."

"I don't. I take death very seriously." She has no clue how much. "Some men believe they aren't bound by social norms or human decency. If they want to live like animals, they should expect to be treated as such." Then, out of uncharacteristic impulsiveness, I add, "I've always regretted not doing more nine years ago when that guy tried to rape the girl I told you about. I stopped him, but...I didn't do enough to ensure he would never do it again."

There isn't even a glimmer of recollection on her face. "Don't be hard on yourself, Tony. I'm sure she was grateful to you for saving her."

A hint of admiration touches her tone, and suddenly I can't stand it. I didn't save Ivy. I'm the reason she's dead.

I'm the reason so many beautiful things are broken.

40

Iris

I WONDER IF I SAID SOMETHING TO UPSET TONY. HE GOT pretty quiet after I told him the girl he saved must be grateful. Picked at what was left on his plate rather than finishing his meal.

Despite my protests, he paid for brunch. And we're back in his car, moving toward Byron's place. This time, there's no music and we aren't talking. I almost wish TJ would put Schubert back on because this silence is really awkward.

I go back over our conversation at the diner. I probably said more than I normally would. Tony's so easy to talk to. Unlike most people who squirm and look away when they hear bits of what happened to me, he leaned closer, asked questions and showed a genuine interest. Maybe I unloaded a little too much. I told him things that I haven't even told Julie or Byron.

What were you thinking? No wonder he's gone all silent. He was probably being polite. Marty said I wasn't Tony's type because I'm not a buxom brunette, and now my mouth has made sure I never will be.

Finally, the car stops in front of the building. TJ goes around and opens the door for me. Before I climb out, I turn to Tony. "Are you okay?"

"Yes," he says. "Just thinking."

He's too guarded. Unlike me, he isn't going to unload on a virtual stranger, no matter how inviting they might seem. "If I said anything—"

"You didn't, Iris. It isn't you."

"Do you want to come up?" I blurt out. Maybe there's something I can do to lift his brooding mood.

"Can't. I have an appointment." He runs his thumb across my lower lip, making my heart speed up, my skin heat, but stops before touching the cut. "Does it still hurt?"

I shake my head, then have to swallow before I can answer. "It's better now. The ointment helped."

"I'm glad," he says, studying my mouth.

Suddenly, I feel parched. He's going to kiss me. I can tell.

Normally, I wouldn't want a kiss from a virtual stranger, but Tony's an exception. Anticipation spikes. I feel like I've waited my entire life for this.

His head dips, his large, warm hand on my shoulder, a finger under my chin angling my jaw slightly...

I part my lips, almost lightheaded with suspense and excitement. But his lips press against my forehead. They're firm and hot, and his breath tickles my skin. It's such a sweet gesture, full of affection and something else I can't quite identify. I feel the touch all the way to my toes, which curl in my shoes, and my heart hammers.

He pulls back. "I'll call you."

I get out of the car on unsteady legs and watch him go, realizing for the first time in my life that with the right man, a kiss on the forehead can be more intimate and romantic than anything with anyone else.

41

Anthony

On Monday, I arrive at the Pryce Family Foundation, the feel of Iris's skin on my mouth still lingering. I wanted to kiss her for real, but there was that damn cut...

I spent yesterday afternoon and evening thinking about her. I just can't believe Iris isn't Ivy, logic be damned. Even if she is using a different name and has no recollection of our time together.

It hurts that she doesn't remember, when there hasn't been a day or night I haven't thought of her. Is it just the head injury? Is it too emotionally painful to recall? All the silly movies and shows have that kind of nonsense, but this is real life. If you could just erase painful stuff from your head, I wouldn't remember Katherine...or Ivy's death.

It's just possible she's a ringer, a setup by some enemy, like Edgar said. But I can't believe it. If someone was going to dig nine years back, they would do better than amnesia, a different name and no tattoo. And if she weren't Ivy, she wouldn't have said or done the things she has.

What she said when I was kicking Jamie's ass. Piano practice in the morning. How she still loves tiger lilies. Grapefruit juice being her favorite.

Yeah, sure, Edgar's voice says, then ticks off its points. No tattoo on her wrist. Didn't attend a conservatory. Has no ambition to become a concert pianist. Her parents were alive until nine years ago. The scar on her palm is from a car accident, not gardening shears. Didn't care for the French toast and bacon. The yearbook that proves she was just an ordinary high school kid who graduated on time with a bunch of other ordinary high school kids.

Shut up. It's enough to drive a man out of his mind. Mainly because unless I find answers to all those points, there's no way I can really be certain that I'm not repeating the mistake I made with Lauren.

To get some answers, I picked up my phone last night and texted Jill Edelstein. She's a PI that I sometimes use. She's thorough, nasty and loyal, which is exactly how I like the people who work for me to be.

Good to hear from you, but I'm out of the country at the moment. Can't take the job.

Fuck. *When are you coming back?*

Don't know yet. Three weeks? Could be earlier, could be later, depending. If urgent, I can give a referral.

No need. I don't want a referral. I want the best.

So I'll do this circuitously until Jill's back in town.

I walk into the foundation's neat, contemporary and functional office. I spot the Russian—assistant to Elizabeth Pryce-Reed, now Elizabeth King—in the vestibule. His sandy-brown hair short and military, he looks like a cross between a pit bull and a Rottweiler. I'd bet my entire fortune he has the tenacity and aggression to match those breeds as he studies me with pale, emotionless blue eyes. He's in a dress shirt without a tie, a jacket and slacks. Most likely carrying. Since the attack in her home some months ago, Elizabeth is probably being extra careful. And this *assistant*'s prominent presence is obviously part of her plan.

I put on a pleasant expression. The last thing I want is him sniffing out the real reason I'm here, since I plan to use both him and Elizabeth. The Russian's ability to dig up stuff not even the CIA can get is a well-guarded secret, but I've made it my business to know everything related to Ryder Reed, and that includes his sister and the huge charity foundation she runs.

"Got an appointment?" he asks, his voice chilly.

I nod. "Yes. Would you let her know Anthony Blackwood is here?"

He squints like he'd rather kick me out of the office, but hits a button on a tiny Bluetooth earphone. He nods, then tilts his jaw toward Elizabeth's office.

I walk in. The space is large and tastefully decorated, without that self-conscious humblebrag that many charities and foundations have. The walls have pictures of the difference the foundation has made since its inception, and none of them look particularly posed. It used to do mostly international work, but recently it's acquired a more domestic focus, helping the people who are most vulnerable and helpless. Pretty fulfilling work.

"Hello, Anthony," Elizabeth says from her desk. As usual, she's stylish in a pink dress. Her ring finger sports an enormous pink princess-cut diamond.

Since her marriage, Elizabeth has changed. Her eyes seem more gray than brown, and she's less uptight. I met her through Ryder while we were in Europe together. He and his siblings, including Elizabeth, were banished together for being in the way of the lifestyle their parents wanted. Elizabeth was easygoing and spontaneous in Europe, but once she returned to the States, she turned into such a robot of propriety that I couldn't help but wonder if she ever had any fun.

But now she's more relaxed, and her smile's more genuine than camera-ready. It's obvious marriage has been good for her.

"I don't suppose this is a social visit," she says.

I sprawl in a seat opposite her. "Not really."

"Are you here to donate?"

"That depends."

"On?"

"There's a young woman. A high school graduate, I think. No job experience, but she's smart, articulate and very well traveled. Unfortunately, she hasn't been able to land a job. She's staying with a friend now, but is starting to run out of money." It's necessary to lay it on a little thick if I want to sell Elizabeth on the idea. She can't resist helping people down on their luck. More than half the staff here were homeless or pretty close when she hired them. "I want you to give her a job. You have an opening for an admin position. My assistant checked."

She cocks an eyebrow. "Me?" she says. "What about you? Z always needs people, doesn't it?"

"She doesn't know how to bartend." Even if she did, it wouldn't matter. I'm not having a bunch of drunkards come on to her.

"It can't be that hard to learn. Besides, it probably pays better than the foundation. Customers tend to be generous, especially if you know how to flirt."

My teeth clench involuntarily.

"Guess that isn't what you want," Elizabeth says, smiling. "Fine. I'll do it, provided she can handle the office work and is trainable. I need a new assistant anyway. But it's going to cost you."

"Of course." I start to pull out my checkbook.

Leaning across the desk, she puts a hand over mine. "No."

"No?" I don't know what she could want more than a sizable check to fund some new cause.

"I want you to make up with Ryder."

Of all the ludicrous crap... "He has nothing to do with this."

She leans forward and says in a low, steady voice, "Anthony, he would *never* have approached Lauren if he'd known. He isn't that kind of guy. If he were, the two of you would've never been friends."

I'm surprised she knows so much. Did Ryder tell her everything?

"He should've been more careful, but you know deep inside he didn't do it on purpose. If you didn't, you would've done everything in your power to wreck what he had with Paige instead of backing off when you did."

I hate the way she tries so hard to make me into a nice, reasonable man. "I got busy and lost interest," I say coolly. "Otherwise, you don't know what kind of scandal I could've created for him. Or Paige."

"Anthony...just imagine how you would feel if you made a mistake and the other person absolutely refused to forgive you."

Her statement is like a blade digging into an old wound. "I'm not here to discuss Ryder with you, Elizabeth," I say, my voice frigid.

She shakes her head. "You're such a stubborn man."

I give her a bored look, unwilling to negotiate further. I don't care what she calls me as long as I get what I want. A job for Iris, so she can move out of Byron's penthouse. I'd offer her my own place if I thought she'd take it, but that's premature.

There's another reason as well, but I dare not contemplate it, not within this building. That Russian of Elizabeth's can probably read minds.

Elizabeth waves a hand. "Fine. I'll hire her, provided there isn't anything weird in her background. But she has to apply. I can't just offer a job to someone without going through the right procedures."

"Fair enough." I hand her a check. "A small token of my thanks."

"I'm not doing it for money."

"I need a tax deduction this year." And I hate owing people, especially someone related to Ryder. I place it on her desk and stand. Since nothing makes her happier than feeding the poor and hungry, the donation should placate her even if I don't make up with her brother.

Without touching the check, she gives me an even look. "You're an impossible man, Anthony."

"You're a meddlesome woman, Elizabeth." I study her mild irritation with amusement, then, out of impulse, add, "And you really should call me Tony."

42

Iris

Monday morning, Tony sends me an MP3 of György Cziffra playing Liszt's "Mazeppa" étude. I've always wanted to hear this particular performance, but never had a chance. I immediately start listening with a headset pressed tightly against my ears, a half-eaten granola bar and freshly brewed coffee abandoned on the kitchen island. Cziffra's performance is divine. I sigh when the music ends. It's too bad they didn't have better recording technology back then.

I text Tony. *Thanks for the music. I love it.*

It made me think of you.

I pause at his response. Other than *Grand Galop Chromatique*, he only heard me play Debussy's "Claire de lune" and Mozart. There's no reason for Liszt's "Mazeppa" étude to remind him of me.

Have lunch with me, Tony texts.

I tap the side of my phone, dithering. But I want to know

why he kissed me on the forehead that way. And don't I want to find out why it seemed so intimate?

I've dated a few times in the last six years, but none of the guys I spent time with made me feel the way Tony does. Is it because of my strong reaction to him the first time we met and the way he rescued me?

Whenever I'm with him, the hollowness in my heart seems to ease. I'm not sure why. If I knew him before the accident... But no. I couldn't possibly have. Tony has never once indicated he knew me before.

But it's also clear he's been less than fully honest with me. His answer about what happened to Jamie was evasive. And there was Marty's total freak-out. Last night, as I was jotting things down in my notebook, it struck me that Marty never flipped out like that before over someone I met or spent time with.

Whatever Marty knows, Sam does too. Marty's a daddy's boy. I want to discover what really freaked him out. I doubt it's just Tony being disowned by his family.

My mind made up, I call Sam.

"Iris. I heard about Saturday. Are you all right?" he asks.

If he was that worried, he could've called to check up on me. As soon as the thought pops into my head, a tiny bit of guilt wriggles in my conscience, reminding me of everything Sam's done. But more and more over the last two years or so, I can't shake the uneasy feeling he isn't being nice to me entirely out of altruism. I don't know if it's just from resentment that he seems to want to control me forever or the fact that I've never really sensed any genuine warmth from him.

"Didn't Marty tell you?" I ask. I'd be amazed if he didn't run to his daddy to complain.

"Only that Jamie Thornton groped you and you left early. I apologize for that. I didn't realize he was that kind of man."

"Me either," I say, relieved and happy Sam's reacting like a decent human being—unlike his son. I don't know if I would've been able to handle the disappointment and anger otherwise.

"So. What can I do for you?"

He always says "what can I do for you" in that brisk, businesslike tone every time I call him. It's as though he doesn't want me to call him just because. Or maybe it's his way of communicating that I shouldn't be in touch unless I need something. That's why I quit calling to say hello unless I had something else to discuss. Sam has never complained about it, though, so I guess he's okay...even though I think it puts a distance into our relationship. Another reason I don't sense genuine warmth from him and feel like he didn't take care of me purely out of familial concern.

"I was wondering, did I know a man named Tony Blackwood before the accident?"

There's such a long pause that I wonder if we got disconnected. I pull away and check the phone. *Nope, still on the line.*

"Sam?" I say.

He coughs once. "Sorry. Tony Blackwood?"

"I met him at the reception."

"Ah. Right. He did come by."

"So...?"

"You might have. I can't say. He's distantly related to us through marriage, but not to your side of the family. You might've seen him at some point when he came to visit me, but I doubt you were that close to him. Why?" His voice grows incisive. "Did he say something?"

The wait is pregnant with an anticipation I can feel even through the phone. The hair on the back of my neck stands. "No. Nothing like that." I tuck my hair behind my ear. "It's just... I felt like I knew him."

Sam laughs, but there's a brittle undertone. "If you knew him that well, you wouldn't have had to call me to ask. Your mind can be confused on details, Iris, but it still remembers all the important people in your life. As for your...curiosity about how you might've heard about Tony, he's always been bright. His family and everyone around him had high expectations. His parents sent him to Europe for the best education they could afford, and later he graduated from Princeton in three years, top of his class.

"So it's natural maybe you heard one of us—me or your parents—talk about him at some point. But you didn't have any close personal relationship."

"Ah, I see." What Sam's saying is perfectly logical. I remember my parents were big on education, always expecting me to do well in school. They could've talked about Tony in front of me. But my instinct—the same one that tells me when I'm totally off in my interpretation and phrasing for a composition—says Sam isn't leveling with me completely. And the same instinct is saying he's not going to give me any more information.

"Okay, well, thanks," I say. "I was just wondering."

"We should have lunch this week," he says suddenly.

"Actually, I'm busy this week. And also tired. Still a little jet-lagged."

"Still? It wasn't that bad of a flight from Paris, was it?"

"Vienna, actually. And no. Just not used to the time zone here yet."

"Well...if you're tired. I'll have my assistant send you a few possible dates."

"Sure." I hang up, then sigh. I don't know why I turned down his lunch offer. About two to three times a year, when he and I happened to be in the same city—him on business and me on my endless travels—he asked me to lunch or dinner, depending on his schedule. I always said yes because he took the time to tell me tidbits about my past. But this time... somehow I don't want to hear it.

I look at Tony's text. If I ask him if we've known each other before, is he going to give me the same answer Sam just gave me?

Most importantly, can I believe Tony? He was evasive yesterday about Jamie. He could be that way again. Based on Sam's reaction, there's something he doesn't want me know about Tony. Given that Tony didn't bring up anything even though he had opportunities to do so during our conversation when I brought up Sam and Marty, it could very well be something Tony doesn't want to share with me either.

I wish I had someone whose words I could take at face value. It's exhausting to have to second-guess my own memories.

I pull up Tony's text, then type, *Sorry, had a late breakfast.* My finger hovers over the send button. But I can't bring myself to hit it.

I sigh, delete everything, then type, *I had a late breakfast, so I won't be able to eat at the normal time. You have to work today, don't you?*

There. That feels less...rejection-like. I don't really want to say no, even if I'm afraid Tony might not be entirely honest, just like Sam. *Ugh.* I prop my head on my hand. Why am I so contradictory? This isn't productive.

A text arrives. *No problem. I can eat late.*

Hmm. When a guy's persistent, that means he's definitely interested, so I can use that to get what I want. Except I've never been much of a femme fatale or cajoler of men, and I have no idea how to use my "feminine wiles," as Julie put it. Instead of trying to be like her, i.e., great at that sort of thing, I should just be myself. Tell Tony point-blank that I want him to be honest with me, because otherwise there's no point in us spending time together.

My mind made up, I reply, *One thirty.*

I practice the piano, recording myself and then listening to see where I'm not quite on point.

Do you know how important it is to live? *Art is an expression of life! How can one play music about love if one has never loved?*

The words slide into my mind. The voice is accented, gentle but slightly exasperated.

Then another voice...younger, giggly... Something's on TV and I'm watching it with a girl about my age. A pretty Asian.

"No way that's a real penis! It's gotta be a special effect!" she says, throwing popcorn at the screen.

"I'm pretty sure they don't do CGI for porn," I say, unable to tear my eyes from the thing that looks more like an elongated watermelon than anything human.

"Don't they audition to hire more realistic looking actors? What are we going to tell Tatiana? Sorry, the porn we watched had a very unrealistic depiction of sex?"

The Coke I've been sucking down gets caught in my nose, and I cough until I can't breathe. "Holy shit," I wheeze. "Who said we have to tell her anything?"

"I want her to know we're trying really hard to experience life in full! We've already seen sixteen romantic movies and ten action flicks."

"Just switch to a different movie."

Who's Tatiana?

The second the question appears in my mind, the vision vanishes. I close my eyes, willing it to come back. Something about the scene felt so familiar. And it wasn't like remembering a movie. I was definitely a participant. It was my own memory.

"*Oh, come on!*" I jump to my feet and start pacing, pressing the heels of my hands against my temples...but I know it's not going to come back. I didn't even catch the girl's name. So unfair!

The buzzing intercom interrupts me. It's Tony.

It's a little after twelve. What's he doing here? Didn't I say one thirty?

What does it matter? I was on the cusp of discovering something, except I blew it by thinking about Tatiana, whoever she is. Obsessing about it isn't going to make it come back. Better to be grateful for a small breakthrough than angry I didn't get a large one. And maybe more will come later.

I open the door, having taken a calming breath, but I might as well have not bothered. Everything stops for a moment as the impact of Tony's presence hits me fully, and I drink him in.

He's gorgeous, stubble covering the lower half of his face. I curl my hands, wanting to stroke that strong jaw, feel its texture, even knowing I shouldn't. He's in a charcoal gray, custom-tailored suit. The clothes outline the perfectly proportioned lines of his tall, strong body. I've seen a lot of men in suits, but until now, I've never met a guy I wanted to strip out of one.

And the impulse is startling. I appreciate handsome men and nice bodies, but it's never gone beyond that. Never felt any reason to.

So why Tony? Is the inexplicable attraction the same as listening to a performance and either liking it or not within a few seconds? But with concerts, I can critique them, analyze and articulate why I like or dislike them. My gaze sweeps over Tony, head to toe, then back up. How do you critique a man like this? How can I analyze and articulate when I don't fully understand my own attraction to him?

"I thought you were coming at one thirty?" I say, hoping my face isn't flushed from the excitement of glimpsing a sliver of my past...and now being with him.

"That's for lunch."

"Don't you have to work?"

A tiny shrug. "I did."

"You're already finished?"

"Close enough. I'm the boss, so I can leave when I want."

That's nice. "What do you do?"

"I own clubs...some real estate holdings."

"Oh. Maybe I've been to one of them."

"You go clubbing often?"

I shake my head. "Not really. I've been to a few with Julie when we were in the same city, but otherwise... It isn't really something to do alone, you know?"

"If you want, I can take you."

"Yeah?" I say, perking up at the offer and the possibility of seeing a totally different side of Tony. "Are you going to dance and all that too?"

"If you like."

"Okay, it's a date." Hopefully when Julie's back from her trip to Moscow, we can all go together.

He looks at the piano. "Were you practicing?"

"I'm done. I was going to nap for a few minutes." An intense practice session in the morning always leaves me feeling like my brain's fried. And nothing other than a catnap makes me fully recovered afterward. I've tried to slog through, and it's never worked out very well.

Something shifts on his face, but it's gone quickly.

"That's why I asked you to come by after one thirty or so because..." I sigh. "I guess we can eat now, and I can nap later."

"No need to change plans on my account." He pulls me to a sofa and puts gentle pressure on my shoulders. I sit, and he settles next to me. "A focused practice session can be tiring."

"Yes." It's amazing, but he's saying *exactly* what I think. Even Byron laughed when I told him I needed to nap after practice. He told me I just needed more coffee—or ought to sleep more at night—because Julie doesn't nap after practice. He doesn't get that not everyone's the same.

Tony tugs at my wrist and waist. My balance shifts, and my head ends up in his lap. It's a little too intimate, the way I'm lying on him.

I should get up. With any other man, I'd move immediately. But looking up at his handsome face with that small smile on his lips, I just feel like I've come home.

And after a moment, the way I'm lying doesn't feel unfamiliar or awkward. Which is weird. I would definitely feel that way if it were Byron, and he's the closest male friend I have.

"What are you thinking?" Tony asks.

"Oh, nothing. Just about Byron and how—"

His eyebrows snap together. "Byron?"

"Uh-huh."

"What about him?"

Here's a chance to make a point he might not like. "Do you really want to know?"

"Yes."

"Remember yesterday, when you sort of evaded my question about Jamie Thornton?"

His lips thin, but he doesn't deny it.

"I'll be honest if you promise to do the same with me in the future."

He nods once, curtly. Not particularly gracious, but I'll take it. And I feel good about that because that means I can take what he's saying at face value. And that's important.

"I was thinking that lying here like this doesn't feel awkward...even though it would be with Byron."

The tightness in his expression eases.

"See what promising to be honest gets you?" I say sweetly. "If you'd said no, I was going to say Byron was super hot."

Tony smirks. "Were you now?"

"Uh-huh."

"So he *isn't* super hot?"

"He's handsome, but not hot. There's a difference. He's a good friend...but that's it."

"Thank you for your honesty, Iris."

Tony massages my hands, his touch gentle and firm. He knows exactly how much force to exert to make me feel good. Nobody's ever massaged my hands like this before. And it nearly brings tears to my eyes.

"You have beautiful fingers," he murmurs.

"They're like crab legs," I say sleepily. "Too long."

A fraction of a second's pause before he continues to rub my hands. "Talented. Just look at what you practiced."

"It's just some Liszt," I say, closing my eyes.

"Uh-huh. Talented."

His thumb strokes the scar on my right palm. I always feel self-conscious about it, but somehow with Tony, it's okay that he's touching the jagged line.

"How did you get this?" His question is like a small tickle on my half-asleep mind.

Could've sworn I told him... "A car crash nine years ago. Almost lost the use of my pinkie."

His grip tightens, but not enough to hurt. I feel his kisses on my fingers as I finally drift off.

But even as I do so, I can't shake off a sense of déjà vu that makes my heart ache with a yearning I don't understand.

43

Anthony

I run my fingers along her silky hair, watch her chest rise and fall gently as she sleeps, her eyelashes like dark fans above her cheeks. I think back on what she said—almost an exact match of a private conversation I had with Ivy.

If she's a setup, a plant...how could she know those things? Only Ivy and I know them.

At the same time, why did she say—again—that the scar came from the crash? I thought if I asked when she was on the edge of sleep, she might slip and tell me she hurt herself with gardening shears. So either she's mentally much tougher than I thought, or she isn't Ivy and really did hurt her palm in that car crash.

And if she's Ivy, why is she calling herself Iris now? Even people with partial amnesia don't forget their names, do they? Then there's the thing with her musical talent. She was studying at Curtis. She wasn't studying there so she could get a normal nine-to-five job, for fuck's sake. She was studying there to be a concert pianist. Can losing one's memory change both ambition and personality as well?

But most importantly, if this really *is* Ivy, whose body did the cops find in the Lexus? She was wearing Ivy's concert dress. Had the pendant I gave her.

No matter how I turn them, the pieces don't fit. Unless I'm just going insane and imagining the conversation I had with her. But I don't feel crazy.

Crazy people don't know they're crazy, Tony. You didn't think you were out of line when you lashed out at your parents after the whole Lauren fuckup.

Hmm. Well, until Edgar says I'm insane, I'm going to assume I'm not.

The accident that killed Ivy was a hit-and-run. I'm convinced Sam had nothing to do with it. He's a bottom feeder, but he doesn't have the stomach for murder. And he certainly doesn't have the mental fortitude and utter lack of conscience required to look a victim in the eye and lie for years.

At the same time, he knows something about the event. How else would he have ended up with her? But no matter what I say or do, that bastard won't tell me. I wanted to back-hand the oily grin off his face at the reception so bad, I had to excuse myself and step away.

But first things first. I'm going to help Iris with her résumé so she can get that job at the Pryce Family Foundation. Elizabeth runs a thorough background check on everyone. Well, her Russian hound does. If there's even a whiff of something fishy, he'll find it and report to Elizabeth. If it's serious enough that she won't hire Iris, I'll have my answer. Otherwise, I'll casually check in with Elizabeth later and see what she's discovered, if anything. Maybe dangle the possibility of a reconciliation with Ryder to make her spill.

Damn, I wish Jill were back in town. I could have her look

into all this rather than use Elizabeth. But I need someone extraordinary to pick Iris's life apart, and I don't quite trust whoever Edgar plans to hire to be as thorough as Jill.

And there's no way I'm waiting three weeks.

Iris's new job will come with one additional benefit: moving out of this penthouse. The fact that she lives with Byron makes me want to hit something. I don't give a shit whether she's actually sleeping with the bastard; he's definitely planning on sleeping with her.

I start texting. Byron's in Honolulu on business—a contract with some Korean firm. I know the head of the negotiation team well, and he owes me a favor. I'm sure things can be arranged to tie Byron up for a while longer.

44

Iris

When I wake up, Tony's still in the same position, one hand stroking my hair and the other holding his phone.

"You're still here." I can't imagine someone as busy as Tony just...sitting around patiently. Or letting me use him as a pillow the entire time.

"It's only been half an hour. Not even."

I sit up, and he puts an arm around my shoulders as though it's the most natural thing in the world. And I like having it there. I lean against him, my head resting on his shoulder and my eyes half-closed.

"Hungry?" he asks, his breath tickling my forehead.

"Not really. But if you want to eat, we can get something. I'm not picky. Just no mushrooms."

He stiffens. "Why not?"

"I'm allergic. Nothing life-threatening, but I break out in hives and feel really itchy for about a day or so, depending on how bad it is."

"I see." He says it casually, as though a mushroom allergy is something he hears about every day, but his arm muscles are tighter than a piano string. He hits a few keys on his phone. "How about roast beef sandwiches?"

"Sounds great."

We get lunch delivered. It comes with plain baked chips, pink lemonade and Coca-Cola Classic. When Tony hands me the pink lemonade, it surprises me again. How does he know what I like to drink? And my sandwich has nothing except Dijon mustard, tomato and pickles, exactly how I prefer it. His has more—cheese, lettuce and tomato plus horseradish mayonnaise.

Tony seems to know me very well, even though Sam said we most likely didn't know each other. But if Tony and I were close enough that he knows my food preferences, I would've remembered him. I recall the sense of déjà vu I had when he stayed with me after Jamie's attack. Was that because of Tony himself? Or was it just my mind getting ready to let me have more of my memories back…?

"You said something about getting a job," Tony says.

"Yeah. I need to work on my résumé. I listed a few things I could potentially put on it, but… I don't know anything or have any interesting job experiences," I say, embarrassed and discouraged. I skimmed some how-to articles on résumé writing and looked at sample résumés last night, but I don't have anything to make mine sound as good as the samples, especially when the examples featured people with a master's or PhDs with a bazillion skills and experiences that I can't even dream of having.

"Everyone has a few useful skills. It's just you aren't used to thinking about yourself that way. What if I help you with it? There's an opening at a charitable foundation I know. Everyone says it's a great place to work."

"Really?" I lean forward eagerly. "What kind of position?"

"Administrative assistant. The pay's pretty decent, and the woman in charge is a fair boss."

"That sounds great, but won't there be a lot of applicants?" I nibble on my sandwich and wash it down with the lemonade. "I honestly don't have *any* experience. And no college degree." I was nineteen when I woke up. Instead of going to college, I was stuck in hospitals for rehabilitation and counseling for close to two years. A few months after my doctors declared me healthy enough, Sam sent me on a series of trips to help me get over my depression—even though I wasn't exactly depressed—and find some *joie de vivre*.

"I don't think that'll be a problem. And if you don't try, you'll never know. Right?"

"Yeah. Yeah, okay."

"But first, you should finish your sandwich. It's important to eat well," he says, looking at me with concern. "Didn't anybody ever tell you that?"

"Of course, but nobody was this persistent about eating." Except for a doctor two years ago who said I was too thin and encouraged me to find food I enjoy and eat more, no one cared enough to say anything. Most people assumed I was on a diet. Julie even openly admired my self-control. But not Tony.

"If you don't like the sandwich, just toss it and I'll get you something else. It's not a problem."

"No, it's fine." There's absolutely nothing wrong with the food.

As soon as we finish lunch, Tony helps me with the résumé. He sits next to me on the couch, one arm stretched along the back, toying with my hair. Instead of being distracting, it's soothing, like it's exactly what should happen between us. Tony gives me a few pointers. It's magic how he crammed "excellent time management," "ability to calmly deal with chaos and unexpected last-minute changes," "works well with people from many different backgrounds and cultures" and "highly adaptable" into the résumé using my travel experience.

"You're good," I say after we're done.

He smiles lazily. "I impress even myself sometimes. Now send it off."

I email it to the foundation he mentioned, plus a few other openings just in case. Then I turn to him. "How did you know about the job opening at the foundation?"

"My assistant mentioned it."

"She wants to go there?"

Tony laughs. "He. And no, he does not. He's very happy where he is."

When I open my mouth, he lets go of my hair and massages my neck. I sigh with bliss. I didn't know I had so much tension there. Or that he was so talented with his hands.

After a moment, he says, "There's still got an hour or two of daylight left. Let's go out."

"Where?"

"Anywhere we want." His eyes sparkle, making me excited.

I smile. "How about a drive along the coast? I've heard it's beautiful, but I've never had a chance to see it."

"That's a crime, and we'll fix it right now."

No silver Cullinan this time. Instead, we're in an indigo Audi convertible. And no TJ. I can feel myself grinning hugely. This is the first time we've driven without the disapproving Visigoth.

Tony lays his suit jacket in the trunk, and we're off up the coastline. I inhale the Pacific's slightly briny breeze, and all the weight of living with my imperfect memories and the anxiety of trying to settle in one place long-term float away. The wind ruffles Tony's hair and shirt, and his mouth is curved into a faint smile. He looks utterly masculine...and at the same time charming and adorable.

Acting purely on impulse, I press a kiss on his cheek.

I feel his gaze sliding toward me under his dark sunglasses. The smile widens, he links his hand with mine...and I'm more content than I can ever remember. Here's a gorgeous guy who knows about my baggage and issues but isn't running away. He helps me, cares about my well-being, and he doesn't judge me for being damaged. He accepts me the way I am, and I can't believe how liberating it is to just...be *me*. I adore him for the sense of freedom he's given me.

We make our way up PCH, along the winding splendor of the California coastline, hills rising on our right and the ultramarine expanse of the Pacific to our left. I like the drive along the coast, but finally Tony pulls into a lot at a seafood shack by a beach. The exterior's white, with paint peeling around the edges from the wind and sun. The restaurant is cute and rustic, with bright, colorful lights and a gritty, sandy floor made with wide wooden planks that squeak with every step. A cheery waiter in a white shirt, khakis and a red apron around his hips greets us.

The place is pretty busy, but we're seated quickly at a table with a great view of the water. Instead of looking at the menu, I turn to the waiter. "What do you recommend?"

"For a couple like you, definitely our seafood platter for two. Comes with salad and fries. It's got everything—shrimp, clams, crab cakes, fried fish and, um—"

"Sounds great," I say, stopping the waiter from listing "everything." I turn to Tony. "What do you think?"

"Whatever you want," he says, shooting me a smile so easy and carefree that he looks years younger.

My pink lemonade and Tony's tonic water arrive quickly. As I sip my lemonade, I spot some women staring at Tony rather blatantly, taking in his chiseled features, his fine clothes and the light smile on his face.

When they notice me, they look at me up and down, then

dismiss me like I'm no competition. Maybe I'm not, in their minds. They're taller and leggier, with bigger breasts. Not to mention they're tanned and have the gorgeous beach-girl features that say they're probably going to Los Angeles to try their luck with the movie business or modeling. And they're brunettes, just the type Marty said Tony likes.

Their blatant staring, along with the way they dismiss me, starts to get irritating. The feeling is new and surprising. Women do the same thing when Byron and I are out together, and I always just find it...amusing.

"You all right?" Tony says.

I tilt my chin in the women's direction.

He turns his head to look, and I suppress an urge to bare my teeth as they preen and shoot megawatt smiles at him. I shouldn't have pointed them out. Instead, I should've put a big neon sign flashing MINE over him. It's insane how possessive I feel about him. But I feel like I'm with someone so special, I don't want to share him at all.

Oh my God. Am I jealous? Is that what this is about? It's such an unsettling, unpleasant sensation. The weirdest thing is I can't decide if I'm allowed to feel it. It isn't like Tony's mine. We haven't established anything. We haven't spent enough time together to do that, even though I keep feeling like I've known him forever.

I steal a quick peek at Tony. His expression is blank—mildly annoyed, if anything. The women could be plucked chickens for all the interest he's showing.

Tony turns back to me and takes my hand. "Unfortunately for those ladies, I like a beautiful strawberry blonde with long fingers, who can play the piano like a dream, likes to nap after practice and has a cute little mole under her mouth. I even adore the scar on her palm, and I doubt any of those ladies has one."

The quiet intensity of his words makes my chest constrict

while hot longing pulses through me. He and I have met before, I'm sure of it. The kind of connection I feel for him is too extreme. It's as though my mind's decided he's The One.

And there's no going back.

He kisses my fingertips. "What I'm saying is, don't let them upset you. I'm not here with them. I'm here with you."

The ugly, tight knot in my chest eases, and I stare back at him. Oh my God, I'm in *deep*. I should be scared at how fast this is happening, but I'm not.

45

Iris

After dinner, Tony drives us back to my home, then comes with me all the way to the top floor. In front of the penthouse door, I turn and look at him. "That was fun. Thank you."

"My pleasure," he says, his voice warm and velvet soft. He tilts my chin up, and once again his thumb brushes over my lower lip...

...and stops right next to the cut. My whole body stills, anticipation unfurling in my belly.

He lowers his head. I don't want another kiss on the forehead. As surprisingly intimate as that was, it's time for a real one.

I angle my jaw, my hands on his shoulders. His lips graze mine. I stretch, rising on my toes, until our mouths fit tightly. His lips are firmer than I imagined.

He moves his mouth over me, restrained and careful of my injury but also hungry. I follow his lead and memorize the shape and texture of his mouth with my lips, hot excitement sizzling through my veins. The air between us grows thinner and hotter, my breathing shallower. I put a hand over his heart. It's racing hard and fast.

Feeling mischievously bold, I flick my tongue over his mouth. A low groan tears from his throat. He pulls me tighter, one arm wrapped around me and the other hand cradling the back of my head. His tongue glides over my mouth and pushes inside, sliding against mine in a lush, carnal kiss.

His masculine scent and taste saturate my senses. My head spins, and I wrap my arms around his neck, pressing closer until there's no space between us.

A thick erection is pushing against my belly. It sends pure lust pumping through me, and I want him in ways I've never wanted anything before. I fumble with the lock, my mouth wild against his.

Suddenly, Tony's phone rings. He ignores it, continuing to devour me, while his hand travels along my waist and toward my breast. My nipples are aching, the flesh between my legs slick.

The phone rings again. When it goes off a third time, I finally break the kiss. "I think you may have to get that."

He looks at me, his mouth glistening and his eyes burning darkly. The sight of his desire stokes my lust, making my blood hot.

"The faster you take care of it..." I say.

He pulls it out, his heated eyes on mine. "What?" He scowls, then takes a couple of steps backward. As the caller continues, his gaze slowly cools. "Are you sure?" He curses under his breath. "I can't talk now. I'll call you back." He hangs up, exhaling heavily. He stares at me like a puzzle he can't solve. Suddenly, I feel naked under his gaze.

"I have to go," he says finally.

I swallow, confused and acutely aware of the wetness between my thighs. "Um...okay."

He starts to walk away, then stops and comes back. After touching the mole under my lip, he kisses me hard. "I'll see you tomorrow."

Then, before I can say anything, he vanishes into the waiting elevator.

I stand there for a long time, residual lust shivering through me. Then, slowly, I turn and go into the vast, empty penthouse by myself, feeling bereft.

46

ANTHONY

THE SECOND I GET TO MY CAR, I STICK A BLUETOOTH headset into my ear and dial Edgar. He picks up.

"Tell me again," I demand, sitting behind the wheel. I leave the engine off.

"Iris Smith does exist. Used to live in a small town in Northern California called Almond Valley. Distantly related to Sam Peacher."

I hate him for telling me the same thing he told me just moments ago when I was with the woman herself, my mouth full of her taste. He should be telling me he made a mistake... that Iris is Ivy. "There have be thousands of people named Iris Smith," I snarl.

"And how many are related to Sam?" He lets me digest that for a moment. "She's actually related to Mom, too, very distantly, on the Smith side of the family."

"Fuck!"

"I looked into Ivy, too."

"*Ivy?* Why the hell would you do that?"

"Because she was adopted by Uncle Perry. I thought perhaps Iris could be a twin sister, someone we didn't know about."

"And?"

"Nothing. Ivy never had a long-lost twin, or any sibling. Her birth mother died when Ivy was ten in a burglary gone wrong." Edgar's quiet for a moment, letting the news sink in. "Damn it," he says tautly. "You need to get the hell away from that woman if you haven't already. I know you, Tony. Regardless of your promise, you've probably already made a move to get to know her, to see if she's Ivy."

"She is *so* much like Ivy. She has—"

"Argh, I *knew* it!" I can practically hear Edgar pacing. "If she really was Ivy, don't you think Sam would've said something? He met her, and he knew what she meant to Mom. Telling her Ivy was alive would have been the best way to get her to like him enough to want to invest, and you know how much he wanted that."

"Mother started to invest with him anyway, so it doesn't matter."

"It would be the best way to make Dad like him, too," Edgar continues. "Right now, Dad can't stand him, and the only reason he hasn't done anything to Sam is because Sam's been scrupulous in his dealings with Mom. Besides, what about all the people Ivy knew at Curtis? Don't you think someone would've said something by now? They must've seen that video, but nobody's said, 'Hey, that's Ivy Smith, who used to study at Curtis with me!'"

"They might not have seen it. They might not have a younger brother who's glued to junk news sites and social media all day long," I say, bitter and furious because Edgar's right. My rebuttals are about as sturdy as tissue paper. It's all I can do to not smash my phone to pieces so I don't have to hear him anymore.

"Tony," Edgar says kindly, "it's been *nine years.* Let. It. Go. It's destroying you, eating you up inside. I've already lost a sister. I don't want to lose a brother, too."

He's lost more than a sister. He's lost a loving home because of me. Mother was never the same after Katherine died.

I finally understand Mother—why she could never forgive me. Why she hates me to the point she doesn't even want me dead. Why nothing I did to atone was ever good enough.

Nothing can bring Katherine back.

Just like nothing can bring Ivy back.

Did Mother feel like she was going crazy, like I do now? We both had "closure"—the funerals, the eulogies, the flowers—but none of that means anything when you can't accept that the one you love is gone. I used to wake up thinking that God might appear in my bedroom and say, "Just kidding! Ivy isn't really dead." I even prayed that He would do just that—I'd give Him anything He desired. Until I became so furious one rainy day, I broke every piece of glass in my place and raged until my throat was hoarse—fuck all the gods and wishes and prayers because they're stupid torments we inflict upon ourselves for nothing.

I lick my lips. She even *tasted* like Ivy...but is that my imagination too? I press a hand against my eyes. They burn, but shed no tears. Instead, my heart grows heavier. It seems to press against my lungs, making it impossible to breathe.

Can one die from heartache? The pain is so sharp and intense, I feel like I could. Surely there's a point where your body just gives up, preferring the oblivion of death over the agony of living.

"Tony? Are you still there?" Edgar says hesitantly.

I swallow the odd thickness in my throat. "Yeah."

"I'm sorry. I know how much she meant to you."

"Thanks. Um, I have to go." I hang up. The phone slips from my hand and lands on the floorboards.

Then, the back of my head pressed against the headrest and breathing harshly, I pound on my chest with a fist, as though that will fix the broken heart inside.

47

Iris

Six thirty a.m. No contact from Tony after his rather abrupt departure. I want to stay in bed and wait...except that seems entirely too pathetic and needy.

He's probably just busy. Whatever pulled him away last night must've been important. And I know how high-powered business guys can be. Sam and Byron sometimes leave or cancel plans abruptly because of work.

I force myself to get up, shower, have half a bagel and coffee. Afterward I practice, working on the "Mazeppa" étude because Cziffra's performance put some fire in my veins. He didn't even use the pedal and still played at tempo with amazing clarity and precision. I can play the étude pretty well, but suddenly, "pretty well" isn't enough. I want to reach Cziffra's level just to prove to myself that I can—the way an eagle soars just because it can.

But that's not all. There's a small part of me that hopes

snippets of my old memories will surface like they did before. It was such a breakthrough, and I want more.

I stop around noon, mentally and physically exhausted. I've made some progress, so that's a plus, but God, whoever said that the piano is a percussion instrument and requires a lot of strength was right. And "Mazeppa" is notorious for being physically demanding. Maybe I'm just getting old and decrepit. I should start hitting the gym to build up my stamina.

I wipe the sweat off my face and neck, then flop down on the couch, my knees over the armrest. Nothing came to me during practice. Still, it's best not to be too impatient. I've never been able to force myself to remember.

Relax. Let your mind work itself out. It'll come.

I close my eyes and breathe slowly and deeply. The memories feel like they're getting closer to the surface every day. I just need to let them come. Even the most difficult symphonies are played one note at a time.

The intercom buzzes, and I heave myself up off the couch. *Tony.*

As I open the door, pleasure is warring with a tiny bit of exasperation that he didn't call after he left last night. But my irritation doesn't last when I see the haggard lines on his face, the faint circles under his eyes.

He comes in, takes one look at me and frowns. "Are you feeling all right?"

"Just a little tired. How about you? Everything okay from last night?" I say, peering at his troubled bloodshot eyes.

Resignation crosses his face. "Yes."

"If you need more time to take care of—"

"I don't. Not anymore. I just need to see you."

He hugs me tightly, and I hug him back, wishing I could take away the thing that's bothering him. Whatever called him away last night no longer seems like business. He's too tense, too brittle, and he doesn't seem to be the type to get worked up over money. He's spending a lot of time with me—lunch and the rest of the day. He was almost cavalier when he talked about his clubs, as though they aren't the main focus of his life.

Eventually he lets go, and we walk over and sit on the long couch. I peer at him. "Are you really all right?"

"Of course." A faint smile, then very deliberately, his face relaxes. But I know it's not a genuine reaction. There's a tight, slightly discordant undertone in his voice.

"Why are you faking it?" I ask.

"Um... What?"

"Something's bugging you. It's in your voice. We decided to be honest, right?"

He takes my left hand and massages it. "We did. It's just... I can't tell you." He looks at me, a little wary. "Are you upset?"

"N... Okay, yes." It's surprising how many responses are automatic, like my mind just knows what's appropriate to say regardless of what I really think. "A little. I mean, I wish you could tell me, but I understand if you can't."

He looks away, his shoulders collapsing a bit, like a man who's failed.

"Tony, I'm glad you said you can't tell me rather than lying about it. I'd be more upset if you lied and I found out later."

He pulls me closer, placing my head on his shoulder, and kisses my hair.

I close my eyes with contentment and snuggle closer. At least he wanted to tell me and was upset he couldn't. The fact that he doesn't want to keep secrets from me makes me feel better.

I sense the weight of Tony's gaze on me even through sleepiness. I sigh softly, wondering what's going through his head right now. Is he thinking about the kiss from yesterday? Or is he thinking about whatever it was that stopped us?

He can't tell me what it is, but of course I'm still curious.

Whatever killed Tony's lust yesterday evening must be something serious.

What personal news could douse a fire like that in a man so fast? Or put such an oddly haunted look in his eyes?

~

Anthony

Iris has her eyes closed, but the gears in her head are turning. It takes a while before she finally falls asleep. Her beautiful face relaxes, and she lets out deep, even breaths, her hands on her thighs.

I arrange her to be more comfortable, her head resting on my lap. I run a finger lightly over her gently arched eyebrows.

Iris Smith does exist. Used to live in a small town in Northern California called Almond Valley. Distantly related to Sam Peacher.

Edgar's words still ringing in my head, I glance at the music on the piano. "Mazeppa." Nobody attempts that unless they have technical chops of the highest caliber. Decent amateur pianists who can manage a serviceable Mozart or Beethoven usually give up after about three or four seconds of it. I wouldn't try it, and I'm better than decent.

I study the scar on her right palm, the mole right below her mouth and the slightly marred skin where Ivy said she got a tattoo. I run my fingers along hers, the same long, dexterous digits that used to delight me in and out of bed. I recall the taste of her lips—cherry and caramel—the same as Ivy.

All night and morning, I argued with myself. Plastic surgery might be able to change a person's face to match someone else's, but can it change the length of one's fingers?

Or the way a person tastes? Or the way she speaks, plays and lives?

I know Edgar's a second away from catching a flight back to L.A. If I were the smart, self-preserving type, I'd do as he suggests and stay the hell away from Iris. The clubs I own in Paris, Tokyo and Seoul could use some personal attention. The local management teams would love some face time with the boss.

So I fiddled with my phone all last night, picking it up and dropping it, turning it in my hand, studying my contact list—all the people overseas who'd like to talk to me about business opportunities or improvement.

But ultimately, I couldn't make myself text Wei and tell him to ready my plane.

48

Iris

I dream a crazy dream, something so psychedelic I can't forget it. The sky's a deep electric-purple dome, the field mossy and soft. I run barefoot, my arms spread out under a golden sun, silver moon and glinting stars. Somewhere in the distance, somebody's playing Schubert's Fantasie—*secondo* only. My fingers itch, and I start to run toward the music, but the field is endless. The moss starts to grow softer and wetter, and my feet sink deeper with every step.

Suddenly, water reaches my ankle. It isn't cold, but it makes me shiver anyway. I look up at the sky. The sun and the moon are gone. Only pinprick lights from the stars remain.

The music's growing fainter. I resume my run, trying to reach the piano.

The stars grow brighter and bigger. Then they fall, their tails silver needles across the amaranthine sky, and pierce my body from all directions. I gasp, try to evade the bombardment, but now my feet are rooted...

"Wake up. It's just a dream."

Not a dream. I'm submerged in the water, and I can't breathe. I can't swim.

I struggle to rise to the surface, but something tugs me downward. A girl in a blue dress is holding my ankle. Her hair unfurls in the water like reddish-gold ink. Smiling up at me, she waves with her free hand, turning my blood to ice.

"*No!*"

"Ivy!"

I jerk awake, panting, my skin sweat-sticky and uncomfortable. Tony is holding me, stroking my back and offering comfort.

I shiver, unable to forget the mermaid girl. She was terrifying. Her grip felt so real...

"It's okay. It was just a dream," he whispers into my hair.

"Right... Just a dream." Except I've never had a dream like this before. And I almost never remember my dreams, although I have been starting to remember them since returning to the States. I wipe at my cheeks, and my hands come away wet.

Tony pulls out a handkerchief and dabs at my cheeks and hairline. I let him take care of me, trying not to tremble. I've never had a nightmare during a nap. God, it was so vivid, so *horrifying*. I could have sworn I was dying.

He presses a kiss to my temple. "It's okay. You're safe," he whispers. "I won't let anything happen to you."

Gradually, my nerves settle. Then something occurs to me. "Who's Ivy?"

"What?"

I lift my head. "You said Ivy."

"You must've misheard."

"No, I didn't. I know what I heard—"

His stomach growls then, cutting me off. "Let's have lunch," he says, too smoothly.

"Let's wait until you answer my question. I want to know why you said Ivy."

His lips compress until they're white. His whole body coils like he's ready to bolt.

No, no, don't do that. Just tell me. I can handle whatever the truth might be...although the tightening in my gut makes me wonder.

Finally, he exhales. "She was someone I knew. I was thinking about her when you started thrashing around, and the name slipped out. Sorry."

That's it? All the tension drains, leaving me slightly dazed. "Why didn't you just say so?"

He gives me a look. "What woman is going to be okay with being called another woman's name?"

"Well, yeah, okay...nobody. But people can make mistakes. Ivy is sort of close to Iris," I say, trying to sound casual. But *Ivy* knots my gut, and it isn't jealousy. It's something else, almost like fear. Not the kind that makes you flee screaming, but the kind that makes you pick up a knife and edge toward it, while your heart is pounding and cold sweat is breaking out along your spine.

Tony's belly growls again. I let him order us lunch, and we sit down to eat. He's quiet, probably embarrassed about using the wrong name. Since I can't probe Tony about Ivy—he's too chagrined already—I'm mulling over my weird dream. Specifically, the girl in the blue dress. She seemed familiar. Is she a friend? Did she play a prank on me in a pool when I was younger? Somehow, it felt more sinister.

Ugh. I wish everyone in my dreams came with nametags, especially when they feel this real. That way I could figure out who they are. I can't draw well enough to do a sketch like the police.

My phone rings. It's an unknown number. "Hello?"

"Hi. This is Rhonda from the Pryce Family Foundation. Is this Iris Smith?"

Oh my God. I clear my throat. "Yes, this is she."

"We liked your résumé and would like to invite you for an on-site interview. Is this Friday good? Say, ten a.m.?"

"*Yes!* It's fantastic!" I say, then put a hand over my mouth as I realize how ridiculously eager I must sound. But I can't help it. This is a huge milestone. And a vindication, especially after Sam said it'd be hard for me to find a job.

She laughs warmly. "I'm glad you're so excited. We love people with a passion for what we do. Please come to the office by nine fifty-five, then."

"I will! Thank you!"

I wait until she hangs up, then drop my phone on the counter and start hopping like a kid before Christmas, hands clenched and arms bent and pressed tight to my sides. "Oh my God! Oh my God!"

"What is it?" Tony asks, laughing.

"That was the Pryce Family Foundation! They want me! I mean, they want to interview me! I guess they liked my résumé."

"Of course they did. It was as awesome as the woman herself. Congratulations."

"Thanks, but what do I do to get ready? I've never gone to one before." It's embarrassing to admit. "Do I have to prepare something? A short speech on why I want to work there?"

He laughs again. "No. Just put on something nice and neat, then...relax and talk."

"That's it? Just...talk? About what?"

"Whatever they ask. Don't think of it as trying to make them like you. They have to make you like them, too, or you won't be working there, right?"

"Well, yeah, if I had a ton of options. I need the job more than they need me."

"They don't know how many options you have. And you won't tell them."

Right. That's how you negotiate. I know that, but somehow when it's about me, my mind goes blank. "I wish there was a script or something so I could practice."

"How about a mock interview? I've done lots of them. On the both side of the table."

"You sure? Aren't you, you know, busy with your own business or...?"

"I pay my workers a lot of money so I don't have to be there all time."

"Well then, yeah. Yes! Fantastic! Thank you."

We do mock interviews that afternoon and a few times over the next couple of days to help me get ready. We don't talk about the kiss or the nightmare. Or the fact that he called me Ivy.

49

Anthony

I call myself a hundred kinds of idiot all through the week. I can't believe I slipped and called her Ivy. But when she didn't wake up, even after I called out her name repeatedly and shook her, I panicked. And got stupid.

The dismay I felt, however, was nothing compared to the crushing disappointment of realizing the name Ivy meant nothing to her. It didn't trigger anything.

If it were her real name, wouldn't she have said something like "That sounds familiar" or "That's what people used to call me"?

But it still doesn't change the fact that I can't stay away from her. And over the last few days, I've come to a decision.

I don't care what her name is. I don't care if she remembers me or not. I don't care what her past is or who she's related to. Whether she's in my life by accident or sent by my enemies.

The only thing that matters is she's alive. And that's enough.

I know Edgar's going to freak if he finds out. He's going to say I'm irrational, making the same mistake I made with Lauren...and that I couldn't possibly have learned enough about Iris to come to such a decision after only a week together. But I'm tired of fighting my feelings. After a certain point, logic means nothing if your heart is screaming something else.

A crazy-happy life with the woman I want is better than a sane, miserable life in darkness without her. If the only way I can have the light in my life is through madness, I'll embrace it with open arms, consequences be damned.

I look at the clock in my office. It's ten. She's doing the interview right now. Unless something goes horribly wrong, Elizabeth is going to hire her.

A call to my cell phone jerks my gaze away from the clock. It's Harry.

"Yes?"

"Hey, Tony. What do you think about letting me use your jet to fly home?"

"Commercial beneath you?" Ever since we flew on my jet together once, he's been trying to get back on it, using whatever flimsy excuse he can come up with.

"I need to see Mom."

I sit up straight. "Why? What happened?" Must be bad if it requires Harry's presence.

"I just heard from Edgar, so I don't know the details. But it sounds like Sam Peacher asked her to put in more money into that new luxury condo he's building."

"Okay. So?"

"She doesn't want to. Like, *really* doesn't want to."

"So what's the issue? She should just turn him down."

"That's the thing. She's apparently going to invest anyway."

What the hell? From what Edgar says, Mother hasn't lost

any money with Sam's ventures. But that doesn't explain why she would feel compelled to invest with him if she doesn't want to. Father makes plenty, and our family's old money anyway, with a few billion in the war chest.

"Anyway, she's seriously upset, and Edgar thinks it'd be a good idea for me to spend a few days with her. So...what do you say?"

There aren't many people Harry can't cheer up, and it makes sense Edgar wants him to come home if Mother's that agitated. But it still doesn't answer my question. "If she hates dealing with Sam that much, why is she doing it? What's really going on, Harry?"

He lets out a frustrated sound. "I don't know. Edgar doesn't, either. He actually tried to stop Sam from visiting, and Mom told him to butt out. So who the hell knows what's going on, but I don't like it any more than you do."

I run a hand over my face. I probably shouldn't give a fuck. I mean, I've been disowned. But I still owe a debt to Mother I can never repay. "Fine. I'll have Wei take care of the flight."

"You're the best."

Leaning back in my seat, I steeple my hands. Mother could never be described as sentimental or forgiving. She didn't think anything of banishing me to Europe for my role in Katherine's death. And she's always kept Sam Peacher at arm's length, like a somewhat dirty rag she needs to throw out. What's changed?

Normally I would suspect blackmail. But Edgar said Sam has been aboveboard with Mother, and I trust my brother's judgment.

Still...the whole situation stinks worse than a dead fish left out in the sun.

50

Iris

My feet feel light as I return home from the interview. Elizabeth King is one of the nicest people I've ever met. Sincere and gracious, she didn't say a word that wasn't kind or encouraging or inspiring during the hour we were talking. I was in awe the entire time, thinking that I want to be just like her.

She also said she liked me and offered me the job on the spot.

And I stared like an idiot for a moment before my brain kicked in. I managed to squeak a *yes*, then grinned like I just won the lottery.

Hell, this is better than the lottery! The lottery is pure chance. I got the job because she liked me! *Me!*

I text Tony, *I got the job!*

Congratulations, he responds. *Celebratory dinner?*

Of course! What time?

I'll pick you up at seven.

Perfect, I type, and hit send.

When I enter the penthouse with a pirouette of victory, I see four pink suitcases with red heart stickers all over them in the foyer. "*Julie!*" I call out, dashing inside.

She pokes her head out of the kitchen. "Hey, girlfriend!"

She comes out, and we hug like it's been centuries rather than three weeks. She looks a lot like Byron—the same soft brown hair, brilliant blue eyes and finely carved facial bones—except she's super feminine. And unlike me, she has the most beautifully proportioned hands.

Right now, she's in travel clothes—a pink hoodie and soft cotton pants, cropped at the shin.

"When did you arrive?"

"Like an hour ago."

"What are you doing here? Don't you have your own apartment?"

"Ah, thought I'd drop by to see you before going home. And I might even stay a night or two, since Byron isn't here to kick me out." She grins cheekily, then glances at the piano. "I see you're working on 'Mazzepa' again."

"It's coming along," I say, leading her to the couch. "Now tell me all about your trip to Moscow." We sit side by side, my feet tucked under, her legs stretched out.

"Oh my God, Moscow was amazing!" Julie gushes in that speedy breathless way she speaks when she's overly excited. "I wish you'd come. You would've loved it! All that history and culture and those hot men! And they're *nice,* too! I couldn't believe it."

I laugh. "Of course they're nice to you. Everyone likes you." Julie's bright and funny, and guys flock to her.

She snickers. "They plied me with vodka. Good stuff, but you know I don't drink more than three."

That's Julie's hard limit. She says every time she has more, the next morning she feels like a zombie that's been hit by a semi.

"But what about you? You okay? Byron, of course, just *had* to go to Hawaii." She pouts. "So unfair. I told him to help you get settled in and show you around."

"It's fine. He had a business thing. You told me he's in an all-out war against Milton for the family business."

She heaves a huge sigh, rolling her eyes. "*Game of Thrones* without the dragons or hot Dothraki or body count. Brother pitted against brother."

"So he had to go. The last thing I want is for him to lose because of me." I smile and prop an elbow on the back of the sofa. "Hey, I have good news. I found a job!"

"Ooh, something to do with music because of that video Byron posted? It went viral in Europe. I told everyone I met the pianist was you."

I flush. "Oh my gosh." But it's so like Julie. I swear she's prouder of my musical ability than I am.

"Some of them didn't believe me. Jerks. Like, why would I lie about that? Anyway, forget the idiots and tell me about your job!"

"It has nothing to do with music. I'm an assistant at the Pryce Family Foundation."

"You mean...the Pryce Family, like you'll be working for Elizabeth King?"

I nod.

Julie's eyes grow wide. "Holy *shit*. That's a big deal."

"It is?"

"If you end up working for her long-term, you're going to go places. She knows everyone in the world—all the politicians and ambassadors and stuff—and everyone loves her. I think even Byron had a bit of crush on her way back when. She has everything a man could want—looks, pedigree, money, connections, personality... Her marriage broke a million male hearts,"

Julie says, putting a hand over her own heart dramatically. "But you couldn't have been spending all your time job hunting. This is *L.A.*! Have you met anybody hot? Maybe even considered doing him?" She waggles her eyebrows suggestively.

My mind drifts to Tony. The most arresting, magnetic and confusing man I've ever met. I don't know if he really feels any kind of sexual attraction for me, since he hasn't made a move after the kiss. Can a single phone call kill lust for days? Or is he still embarrassed about calling me Ivy by mistake? Regardless, he's been super helpful and friendly, and he touches me constantly, every chance he gets—massages, little squeezing of the shoulders and arms and hands—but is that really *attraction?*

Julie snaps her fingers. "I know that look! Tell me! Who is he? Anybody I know?"

"Well... This, uh, guy..."

"Oh, come on! Name? What does he look like? Pictures? Is he rich? Young? Hot? Good in bed?"

I raise a palm to stop the flood of questions. "Tony. That's his name. I ran into him at Hammers and Strings, then at a reception Sam threw, and, you know..."

"Keep going. Give me all the deets. Tony *who*? Anybody famous?" She leans closer. "A movie star?"

"Blackwood. I don't know if he's famous, but he's definitely not a movie star."

Suddenly, all the humor vanishes from Julie's face. "Tony *Blackwood*? You mean Anthony Blackwood?"

"Yeah, I think that's his real na—"

"Oh, *shit*. Does Byron know?"

Why is she being so weird? "No. I haven't had a chance to talk to him." Even if I did, why would I tell him about Tony? Why does Julie think I should?

She leans forward. "Are you guys sleeping together?"

"What? *No!*" Am I protesting too much? We didn't sleep together, but we might have if not for that call.

"But you said 'Tony.' He only lets his family and closest friends call him that. I read on a gossip site that not even his exes are allowed to call him Tony. If they do, he corrects them, saying his name is Anthony. A little odd, right?"

From the very beginning, he asked me to call him Tony. In light of what Julie's saying, it *is* odd. He and I were strangers then...

"Anyway, I guess if you really want to date him, it's okay, but..." She looks at me like she can't decide if she should say more.

"What? Spit it out." The suspense is killing me.

"He and Byron, like, *hate* each other. And he has certain rep. Like, he's cold and probably, uh, a little deviant."

"*Deviant?*" My stomach is fluttering as I wait for the other shoe to drop. "In what way?"

"He never, ever dates blondes. It's always some brunette with dark eyes."

Marty said the same thing. I dismissed it, assuming he was being his usual asshole self, but having Julie say it is different. "That's just a preference. I thought you meant in bed or something."

"There's more. His latest girlfriend—well, *ex*-girlfriend—tried to kill herself over him. It was all over the gossip rags."

No way. I haven't heard that, but then, I don't read tabloids the way Julie does.

"He was dating Audrey Duff, who you have to admit is stunning."

Audrey Duff is a rising star, and is known for her sultry, voluptuous look. And now I hate her.

"He dumped her after a month. The rumor is he did it because she bleached her hair."

"That's ridiculous. Nobody dumps someone over their hair color!"

"The timing works out."

"So if I belch after listening to Chopin, Chopin's the reason I belched?"

"Oh, fine! But you know it's weird anyway. That poor woman. She must love him to attempt to kill herself over him."

"More like *she* needs some serious therapy. It isn't normal." Poor Tony, having to put up with this kind of nonsense. Is this what that call was about? If so, no wonder he was weird and closed off afterward.

"True love. But that's not all to this drama. He totally ignored the entire incident. No statement, not even a basket of flowers to wish her a speedy recovery. It's like he just...doesn't care."

I doubt that. Just because you don't publicly react to something doesn't mean you don't have any feelings about it. "So what happened to her?"

"Nothing. She survived, and I heard she's going to costar in a new movie with Ryder Reed."

Maybe she got the help she needed. Or... "I wouldn't put too much stock in that kind of stuff. You know how the tabloids are."

"But—"

I wave a hand, not interested in any more pointless gossip about Tony and his mentally unstable ex. "If it makes you feel better, Tony's been nothing but a gentleman."

"I just don't want you to get hurt."

I manage a smile. If it was someone other than Julie, I might doubt their sincerity. But Julie's an amazing friend, the kind who is happier than you for your good fortune and who sheds more tears than you over your setbacks. "Thanks. But so far, he's been great, and you know how cautious I am."

She sighs. "I know. That's why I'm worried. Careful

people tend to fall harder. And you've been so picky about who you date."

Maybe she's right, but I don't want to dwell on it because—short of her telling me he's a murderer—how I feel about Tony isn't going to change. "What pieces were you working on in Moscow? You did more than just hanging out with hot Russian men, right?"

Julie perks up and launches into a long, involved explanation of how she reinterpreted Tchaikovsky's concerto. I listen and nod. But her comment that careful people tend to fall harder circles faster and faster in my head until I barely register a word she's saying.

51

Anthony

I pick a fancy steakhouse for the celebratory dinner, the kind of place you see in noir films where men dine, drink and smoke a cigar or two afterward. There's even a baby grand piano.

The dress code is formal, so I'm in a crisp suit and freshly laundered white shirt. I didn't bother with a tie, opting to leave the first two buttons undone.

Iris is gorgeous, absolutely breathtaking in a pale cream cocktail dress and silver heels that flatter her figure and accentuate her beautiful curves. I'm not the only guy who thinks so. Several men turn their heads to check her out.

She sidles closer, and I pull her tighter to me. They can look until their eyeballs freeze. She's mine and I'm never letting her go, not this time.

"I feel like I should puff a stogie or something," she says as we're seated at a table set away from the rest of diners, but with a direct view of the piano.

I laugh. "Unfortunately, no smoking inside."

"This place is so glamorous. It makes me *feel* glamorous."

I smile, half indulgent, half tender. Her good mood is infectious. "I'm glad. I thought this would be the place for the celebration."

"Do you come here often?"

"When I want to have a nice steak, relax and think, yes."

"Think? You don't come here with company?"

I shake my head. "You're the first."

Pleasure shines in her eyes, and the flush colors her cheeks like blooming flowers. I wish I could capture this moment forever because she's achingly beautiful.

"Anything in particular you recommend from the menu?" she asks.

"Everything's great as long as it's steak."

She looks at the menu. "Everything's huge, too."

"Order what you want. You don't have to finish it. But we're definitely having cheesecake, so save some room. This place has the best I've ever tasted."

"Deal!" She orders the smallest filet mignon. I get a porterhouse and ask her preference in wine.

"Anything's great as long as it's red," she says. After a quick perusal, I select a burgundy from France I had earlier this year. The vintage is great—berries and oak and nuts with a hint of rose at the end. Iris should enjoy it.

Our waiter brings out a bottle quickly. I approve it after a taste.

Iris lets out a soft *mmm* after a sip. "This is amazing."

"I thought you'd like it."

"Tony...thank you," she says after finishing the first glass.

"What for?"

"If it weren't for your help, I'd still be staring at a blank Word doc, wondering what I'm supposed to put on a résumé."

Her gratitude makes me squirm, since I didn't do it

entirely for her. But I can't tell her that. "My pleasure. If I had a suitable opening at my company, I would've given it to you without bothering with a résumé, but...the one I have isn't really for you."

"I wouldn't take a pity job, so I'm glad you didn't. When I told Sam I was going to get a job, I didn't mean a job I don't qualify for through some connection."

She's going to be pissed when she finds out you talked with Elizabeth.

Obviously, I'm not going to tell her. Besides, Elizabeth said she wouldn't hire Iris if she wasn't qualified.

"What opening do you have at your company, anyway?"

"Bartender."

"Oh! You should've said something. I'm actually pretty decent at it. When I was in Germany, I met this girl who was a bartender, and she taught me a few things."

"Iris. If you were the Goddess of Bartending, I wouldn't have given you that job."

A couple of blinks, then she pulls back, her spine straightening. "Why not?"

"You know what makes a great bartender?"

She thinks for a moment. "Making a tasty drink fast? Getting the order right?"

"Any competent bartender does that. A great bartender is a great conversationalist. They get people to talk and flirt."

"And?"

"And...I don't want anybody flirting with you."

Surprise flickers over her lovely face. "Really?"

"Do you have any idea what bastards some of the men who come to my clubs are?"

She shakes her head.

"They're terrible players. Unfit to be in your company." It's not quite true. Almost all the people who come to my clubs behave. And they aren't dicks. But they do get flirty and a little too touchy-feely when they have too much alcohol. Many bartenders don't mind too much as long as they don't cross the line because they tend to tip outrageously. But I'll be damned if anyone's going to touch Iris.

"What kind of clubs do you run again?" she asks, amused.

"The absolute best."

"Is that so? You have yet to take me to any of them."

"Just say the word." Now that I've decided to accept my feelings for her rather than fight or doubt them, I want to show her everything I have. I want to prove to her I'm a man who's worth her time and more.

"I'm going to have to check with Julie and see when she can find time to come with us. Is that okay?" she asks.

"Sure." She can bring an entire entourage if that's what she wants.

After we're served our steaks, a pianist sits at the baby grand. I've just cut a bite when the man starts *Grand Galop Chromatique*.

Iris winces a little.

"What's wrong? The food not to your liking?" I ask.

"No, it's fine. Probably the best steak I can remember having."

"Then…?"

She hesitates, then says, "It's the music." She glances toward the piano, then starts coughing.

I pat her on the back. "Are you all right?"

"Fine," she says hoarsely, then takes a quick sip of wine. "That's him."

"Who?"

"The guy at Hammers and Strings. The real reason Byron's video is out there. Byron took me to the store, saying maybe I wanted something other than the Yamaha upright he has at his place."

That asshole. Trying to worm his way into her bed with a

piano! It's so fucking obvious. "Don't tell me you let him buy one for you."

She shakes her head. "Of course not. I wouldn't take something that expensive from anybody. Anyway, he"—she tilts her head in the pianist's direction— "was there, and being really rude. He was criticizing his girlfriend and the store clerk, going on and on about how stupid and ignorant they were. And get this. In order to show off? He started *Grand Galop Chromatique*."

I laugh, knowing the technical difficulty of the piece.

"Normally I wouldn't care if he was abusing the damper pedal and banging on the keys like a donkey on crack. But since he was so horrible and condescending, I was annoyed enough to demonstrate how it *should* sound." She rolls her eyes. "It's supposed to be a bravura panty-dropper, not a bravura migraine-inducer."

Everything inside me freezes, and the laughter dies an abrupt death. "Bravura panty-dropper" are the exact words Ivy used to describe *Grand Galop Chromati—*

Suddenly, Iris's wine glass is snatched off the table, and the burgundy tossed in her face. The red vintage drenches her, plastering her hair to her skull and forehead, then dripping down her cheeks and chin to fall on her white dress.

What the *fuck...?*

"You bitch!" Audrey is towering over Iris in a skintight scarlet dress, her brown eyes flashing murder. "I knew it!" She lunges forward, her long, manicured nails ready to claw the skin off Iris's face.

I explode out of my seat and grab Audrey's wrists, flinging her away before she can do any real damage. She stumbles and falls against a man behind her; he backs up out of reflex, and she lands awkwardly on her butt on the floor.

I turn with a snarl, then stop at the sight of Ryder. *Him, too?*

But he's not looking at me. He's staring at Iris with a weird combination of shock and recognition etched on every line of his disgustingly pretty face.

Audrey scrambles to her feet. "You can't do this to me! Not over her!" She points at Iris.

A large florid man standing behind Ryder steps forward. I recognize him. Some big-shot agent. "Audrey, honey, stop it."

So that's what this is. Ryder having dinner with Audrey. Just my luck the son of a bitch had to choose this steakhouse out of all the restaurants in L.A.

"The latest candidate for your humped and dumped club?" I bite the words out.

Finally, Ryder turns to me. "For God's sake, Anthony, I'm married," he says, his voice bristling with frustration and angry humiliation. "Audrey's a costar."

I can feel Ivy's gaze on me and Ryder. I hate it that she met him. I hate it that he met her. Was studying her like he knows her.

The infuriating memory of what he did to Lauren swirls in my head like a hurricane. Never again will I allow him near anything of mine.

"Why are you doing this? You're the only one I love! You know that!" Audrey says in a theatrically tragic voice. "I almost *died* for you!"

Ryder glares at her. "Shut up, Audrey."

"You can't talk to me that wa—"

"I can talk to you anyway I like. Ralph?" The agent takes Audrey's elbow in a meaty hand and pulls her back.

Ryder turns to Iris, searching her face. "Are you all right? I'm so sorry." He takes a clean napkin from an empty table and starts to approach.

Over my dead body. I block him, putting an aggressive hand on his chest. "Stay the fuck away from her." The only thing holding me back from turning his face into bloody meat is that he hasn't thrown the first punch.

He's looking like he can't decide between an apology or defending himself. I almost wish he'd just punch me. Spit in my face. Anything so I'd have an excuse.

"Anthony, come on." He doesn't call me Tony anymore because he knows he's no longer in that special circle of people.

"You don't get to touch her. Don't even *think* about her. If you're dying to *help*"—I sneer the word—"control your fucking date." I pull a handkerchief out and start drying the wine on Iris's face. "I'm sorry," I say. *Next time I'm renting the entire restaurant.*

"It's not your fault, Tony. I can do it."

I let her take the cloth, violent rage boiling inside my chest.

Iris adds, "I'm fine," in an attempt to defuse things.

"Yeah, well, I'm not," I say, even though I know my temper isn't helping.

"Call me and I'll have the dress replaced," Ryder says, offering Iris a card.

I knock it away. "*Fuck off.*"

"Anthony—"

"You're so transparent, it's sick." Unbelievable that he thinks I'm going to let him near Iris after what he did to Lauren. Does he think I'm still that gullible and stupid? Does he think I give a damn that he's married now? Loyalty and friendship mean nothing to a man like him.

Audrey reaches out a beseeching hand. "Tony, stop! You're making a mistake!" Overacting as usual.

"You don't get to *Tony* me. You were dead to me the moment you pulled that 'attempted suicide' stunt. Maybe it's some kind of Hollywood disease that makes you people think anyone gives a damn about your theatric bullshit. But no one does." I look her dead in the eye. "Stick to your fake life in front of the cameras. You do it better than the real version."

Audrey goes pale.

Iris puts a hand on my sleeve. "Can we go? I...kind of need to shower and change."

She does need to be looked after. I pull myself together. "Of course," I say gently. I put an arm around her shoulders and turn to the maître d', who has appeared and is hovering nervously. "Our check."

"I'll take care of it," Ryder says.

Asshole. "I'm not taking anything from you."

"Payment won't be necessary," maître d' says, a small tremor in his voice. "Your meals tonight are on the house, Mr. Blackwood."

I escort Iris out. Tension is thick inside the Cullinan as it moves through the heavy L.A. traffic. TJ notices Ivy's appearance, but wisely says nothing.

I can't believe I didn't rent out the entire restaurant. That would've prevented the travesty. Show Iris what I have to give, huh? And what the hell did she see? A screw-loose ex and a former best friend who had no problem fucking one of my girlfriends.

Welcome to the shit-show that is my life, Iris. If you want to leave...

But I can't continue the thought. Selfishly enough, I don't want her to leave.

"It's ruined," Iris says, gesturing at her dress and my handkerchief. "Even if you don't like Ryder, you could've at least demanded Audrey replace it," she says in a feeble attempt at levity.

I don't deserve her. "Sorry your celebratory dinner got ruined."

She squeezes my hand. "It wasn't your fault."

"Yes, it is. Audrey is my problem."

"She's a person, Tony. You couldn't have known. You can't control her."

Iris has no idea how much her words mean right now. I pull her close.

"You're going to get stains on your clothes."

"I don't care. I just want to feel you." I exert gentle pressure around her shoulder until she's pressed tightly against me. She rests her head on my chest. The weight is comforting. It tells me she's *here*. With *me*.

The Cullinan pulls up in front of my building. "Where are we?" she asks.

"My place." I kiss her forehead. "It's closer, but if you want to go to your place, that's fine."

She pulls back and peers at the tall, gleaming structure. I wait, agonizing over which she'll choose. If the dinner had gone as I'd hoped, I might not have brought her here because it might feel like too much, too fast. But with the botched evening, I want to show her I'm not totally messed up.

She has an odd look in her eyes. "I've been to other guys' homes before, but this feels like more," she says softly. "Like some new...hierarchy of intimacy."

"It is. I've never brought a woman here before."

Her gaze turns tender as her hand wraps around mine. Then, tugging at me, she climbs out of the car.

52

Anthony

Iris steps into my home. Her eyes take in everything, inch by inch, from the gleaming foyer to the living and dining rooms and the huge kitchen. The city glitters on the other side of the gigantic sliding glass doors leading to the deck and an infinity pool.

I want her to love the place, and now I wish I'd spent more time looking around. I had a real estate agent bring a few suitable listings, and Wei made the purchase based on my list of priorities after seeing what was available. Back then, this was a place for me to rest and sleep. Now, it's more. Iris makes it more.

Her gaze finally lands on the Steinway. It's a practice piano, a white baby grand from Tempérane. Mother was going to throw it away, but Edgar saved it for me. It was in storage until last week, when I had it brought over, cleaned and tuned.

I watch Iris carefully, looking for signs of recognition. She used to practice on it for hours and hours. Surely she remembers something.

But she doesn't seem to recall anything. There's nothing but surprise and admiration as she looks at the piano.

"You play?" she asks.

"Used to." I quit when Ivy died. It hurt too much. But now... Somehow it's okay to see the instrument. I run a hand over it and realize with a shock that I'm slightly shaky.

Thankfully, Iris doesn't seem to notice. "A lot of people give it up when they get a job or something." She looks around. "Is there a place I can change?"

I lead her to my bedroom. "Take anything you want from the closet. Unfortunately, I don't have the guest bathrooms ready to use, so you'll have to make do with mine. The housekeeper should've laid out fresh towels. If not, let me know."

"Thanks."

I close the door behind her and exhale heavily, as though doing so will expel the bitter self-reproach inside my chest. *I'm such a liar*. After telling myself I don't give a shit who she is, my belly flutters every time I see a sign that she's Ivy.

It hits me all of a sudden that it might be safer for her if she's Iris, a girl who plays the piano really well and has partial amnesia. The only problems Iris has are an imperfect memory and scummy relatives. *But if she's Ivy...*

That's much scarier. Terrifying, really, because somebody purposely set things up to make it appear as though she died. Killed another girl who was very much like her to accomplish the task. Did unspeakable things to Iris to make her lose her memory. Then somehow Sam ended up with her, whether he was an accomplice to the crime or got forced into it later.

If whoever responsible thinks that I know she's Ivy, what will they do next? Come after me? I'm a hard target, and in any case would actually enjoy facing those fuckers. But they might just kill her, for real this time. I don't know who *they* are, what their motivations might be, no way of predicting their next move. And the idea that I might lose her...again...

If you quit digging... If you quit probing...

I bury my face in my palms, trying to think through the options. I can take her away. Anywhere she wants to go. We can be together in Paris. Rio. Tokyo. The choices are endless.

But she came back to the States because she hated being away, forever on the road and unable to form a lasting friendship or have her own social network of people to count on. She has a job here now and has already made friends. I don't have the heart to uproot her unless I absolutely have to. And until I know who's responsible for the hit-and-run accident, I'm never going to be certain of Iris's safety. Even living abroad, we might have to move around.

I look at the Steinway. I haven't played in years, but muscle memory doesn't vanish overnight. I go to the piano and touch the cool key in the center above the keyhole, pressing it softly until the perfectly tuned middle C sounds.

When she's out of the shower, I'm going to test her.

I have to know who she is, *for certain.* I need to understand what happened to her. Or I'm going to lose her. Again.

53

Iris

The door closes, leaving me alone in Tony's room. It's overwhelmingly masculine, not even a hint of a feminine touch. Lots of blue and green with pale earth-tone accents. A huge contemporary bed and dark wood furniture dominate the area. The floor is bare except for a thick rug at the foot of the bed.

I go to the enormous walk-in closet. He has rows of crisply ironed dress shirts, suits, belts and cuff links under glass covers. I start to reach for the drawers, then stop. *Why am I so curious about what he has in there?* I've never nosed around in another person's private space before. But with Tony, I want to know everything about him.

Still. It's rude to snoop. I drop my hands, feeling like a naughty kid trying to filch a cookie.

I pull a large shirt off its hanger and hold it in front of me, making sure it doesn't touch my soiled dress. It's long enough to serve as a micro-dress.

Shirt in hand, I cross over to the bathroom. It's huge and ultramodern, with clean, minimalist lines. A little *too* modern for my taste, but it has a towel warmer, where a thick, fresh blue towel is resting, and heated flooring that feels divine on the soles of my feet. There's a separate multi-headed shower and sunken tub with Jacuzzi spouts.

As immaculate as it is, there isn't much of a personal touch. The cabinets only contain aftershave and a bottle of aspirin. There's one toothbrush and a half-used tube of toothpaste on the vanity. It reminds me of a nice hotel suite—well appointed and clean, but utterly impersonal.

As I turn, my reflection in the mirror catches my eyes, and I gape. *Oh no...* A drowned rat probably looks better than I do at the moment. My hair's flat and stringy from the wine, and my face has a reddish tint. My mascara and eyeliner are smeared, and the dress has red stains all over. Basically, I could star in a horror movie.

Suddenly, I feel like screaming. The date was going *so well.* Tony was charming. The food was great, the wine perfect. Okay, the music was sort of crappy, but whatever. The mood was sweet and romantic. I was relaxed and happy. Tony even laughed, which was thrilling because he so rarely laughs like that. But then that crazy actress had to show up!

I almost didn't recognize her. I thought Audrey Duff would be more...delicate. I mean, she ostensibly tried to kill herself over love. But the woman in person isn't as pretty as in her pictures and movies. There's a taut, rusted-sheet-metal quality to her. And she directed all her misguided anger at me, throwing the wine and making a scene so awful, I felt utterly paralyzed. It was like it wasn't even happening to me, more like I was watching the whole drama play out.

If she hadn't interrupted, who knows how the date might've ended? Tony and I could be kissing again by now.

Maybe even taking it a step further, into the bedroom. Because I really wanted him to kiss me again at the end of the date. And then go from there.

I wish I could have a do-over, but what's done is done. Happy and relaxed Tony is gone. He was tense the entire ride home. He was tense when he brought me to the bathroom. He's probably still tense right now.

Frustrated and exasperated, I strip out of my ruined dress. The stains will never come out. I step into the shower, which instantly spews hot water. I wash myself thoroughly, making sure the wine's completely gone from my hair.

Once done, I dry myself with the warm towel and put on the shirt. After rummaging around, I realize Tony doesn't have a dryer. Guess it makes sense, since his hair is short, but...

Ah, who cares? It isn't like we're going back out. I towel-dry my hair as much as possible, then go down to the living room. Tony's at his Steinway, a crystal tumbler half-full of amber liquid in his hand. His head swivels in my direction. As he takes me in, his green eyes darken with a need and yearning so stark it leaves an aching hitch in my heart. I feel pulled closer, as though we're connected with unbreakable chains.

"Are you feeling better?" he asks.

Better isn't how I'd put it. I want to reach out and brush my fingertips over his cheek, but there's a touch of bleakness to him that makes me hesitate. So I keep my hands by my sides and say, "Yes. Thank you."

He finishes his drink in one swallow, his eyes still on me. Thoughts cross them like quick-moving clouds, and finally something that looks suspiciously like grim determination settles over his face.

I start to step forward, reaching for him. I don't want him feeling guilty over what happened at the restaurant. I'm grateful for everything he's done for me—saving me from

Jamie, helping me look for a job, showing me the beautiful coastline, comforting me when I had a nightmare...basically, treating me like I'm a normal person rather than some damaged girl.

Suddenly, he turns to the piano and starts playing *secondo* from Schubert's Fantasie. *What the...?* I drop my hand, feeling slightly rejected by his abrupt shift in mood and action. And why is he playing this? It isn't complete without someone to play *primo*.

He keeps playing. The incompleteness of the piece disturbs me. Although I've played a few trio or duet pieces, I don't remember playing anything that requires partners to share a piano. But my fingers twitch as though they know exactly what keys to strike.

Finally, unable to bear it, I sit next to him on the long bench and let my hands do what they will. At least I've listened to the music before, so I'm aware of what it should sound like.

My fingers move on their own, striking the chords and notes perfectly. Tony alters his pace to match mine. We're in perfect sync, and his body heat warms me until I'm feeling almost too hot.

Da-dum, da-dum, da-dum. My heart beats to the music, and I can sense Tony's does, too. My mouth dries. Fantasie doesn't require the technical dexterity of Liszt's études, but it isn't a simple composition. Haunting, with a hint of hesitation and reluctance, but delicately graceful and flowing. Just hitting the right notes at tempo will turn the lyrical piece flatter than two-week-old Coke, without the careful building of tension to the climax toward the end. The only reason I can play it so well must be because I've practiced it to the point of mastery. My hands are relying on muscle memory, even though I have no recollection of ever performing this.

By the time I hit the last note, my breathing is uneven and

shallow. I stare at Tony. He said he didn't really play the piano, but he was virtually perfect, as though he knew exactly how I needed him to perform his part. Like we've played this together many, many times before.

His Adam's apple moves once. Then he leans forward and presses his mouth to mine.

54

Iris

The contact makes my soul sigh. I love the way Tony takes charge, the way he leads me into a pleasurable state where nothing matters but us.

He tastes like a man in need, his breathing rough and fast. It's thrilling, sending a hot pulse of desire that ends between my legs. I wind my arms around his neck, my fingers toying with his hair. I press my body against his, letting him know I don't have a bra on underneath the shirt I filched from his closet.

A rough growl reverberates deeply in his throat and chest. My nipples grow hard, and I arch into him. One of his hands is against my back and the other is cupping a breast, the thumb moving over my pointed nipple through the shirt. Electric pleasure shoots through me, and I moan against his mouth.

Impatient, I bite his lower lip. "I'm making a mess," I whisper.

"Are you?" He tugs at the nipple.

I cry out, shuddering with pleasure and a crazy, mounting need for more. "You're making me wet. And I'm not wearing any underwear."

He curses. I laugh under my breath. It's hot I'm making him curse—I'm driving him crazy with lust, the same way he's doing with me.

Holding me, he stands up. I wrap my legs around him. His hot, large hands cup my bare ass as he carries me to the bedroom, where he deposits me on the bed, his teeth, lips and tongue devouring my mouth like he could never get enough.

We feed off each other's hunger. He dumps his clothes and shoes, flinging them on the floor. His fingers are slightly shaky by the time he reaches for the shirt I'm wearing. He fumbles with the first few buttons, then growls and rips the starched fabric apart. I thrill at his uncharacteristic impatience, my eyes riveted on his beautifully sculpted body with lean, strong muscles. His cock is rigid, long, thick. The tip brushes his glorious abs, leaving a glistening spot.

I laugh, then pull him down for another kiss, loving the solid weight of his gorgeous, masculine physique on me. Tony's large, greedy hands move over my bare skin, feeling and learning the texture and the shape of my body as they trace every line and squeeze softness of my curves. Desperate for more, I rock against him.

He toys with my nipples, his lips and tongue wicked and talented, while his hand dips between my thighs, his fingers gliding smoothly along my slick flesh.

I arch my back, a breathless cry caught in my throat. He pulls a nipple into his mouth and sucks hard as his thumb rubs against my clit and a long finger drives into me.

My hands fist the sheet. It's as though he knows exactly what I want, how I need to be touched.

He pulls the other nipple into his mouth, and I'm going

crazy with desire. He drives another finger into me, thrusting lazily, bumping the sweet spot in my pussy.

When he moves downward, leaving a hot trail of kisses on my belly, the cool air makes my wet nipples bead. I clench my inner muscles, and he grunts.

"You're really tight." He pulls his glistening fingers out and licks them clean, his smile devilish. "Mmm."

The unabashed way he enjoys himself is too damn hot. "I want you," I demand in a thick, unsteady voice. "*Now*."

He looks into my eyes.

"Don't tell me you want to make it last. We can do that later," I say.

"Later, huh?"

"If you don't take me now, I'm going to die of frustration and there won't *be* a next time."

"Well, we can't have that." He grabs a condom from a drawer near the bed. As soon as he's sheathed, he positions his cock, then slowly pushes forward, stretching and filling me.

I gasp. He feels unbelievably good inside, fitting like a missing piece I've been looking for all my life.

He kisses me, tasting like him and me—as though I'm the woman he's been seeking for all eternity. As he moves in and out, the friction blissful, a small part of me thinks it feels familiar somehow. But the unfurling pleasure pushes everything out of my head except for the toe-curling sensations running through me.

I clutch him to me, my fingers digging into his shoulders, tension winding tighter in my belly. An orgasm finally breaks, as powerful as a hurricane sweeping through. Tony pulls his mouth away, letting me scream, the ragged sound bouncing off the walls. He drives into me twice more and shudders, the tendons in his throat standing starkly.

Wrapping his arms around me, he rolls over until we're lying on our sides. I lay a hand over his thundering heart and wait until my breathing settles. *Amazing, amazing, amazing...* Not just the actual orgasm; I've never felt so deeply connected to a person before. It wasn't just our bodies merging—it was like our souls came together, our hearts beating as one. He completed me like no one ever has.

He disposes of the used rubber, and we spoon.

"That was awesome," I say softly.

He kisses the back of my neck. "It was."

I trace patterns on the back of his hand with a finger, writing "T" and "I" in different ways, waiting for him to say more. When he stays quiet, I suddenly feel vulnerable, wondering if I'm the only one who experienced that amazing connection. Tony's older and worldlier. It might've been good for him, but not divine like it was for me. I stop tracing the patterns.

"I knew you'd be worth it," I say, trying to regain some equilibrium by acting like I didn't feel naked all the way to the deepest core of my soul.

"Did you?"

"Uh-huh. I'm very particular. Would you let just anybody play a Bösendorfer Imperial?" I say cheekily.

Tony tenses up.

I blink, then turn in his arms. "What's wrong?"

His gaze searches my face. "Sometimes...I wonder..."

I wait, holding my breath. Something's off. He was supposed to laugh at my cocky impudence, and I was supposed to laugh in response. I want to find out what went wrong so I can fix it and we can go back to feeling sated. "What?" I whisper.

He shakes his head. "Nothing. You're so damn hot, you make me forget what I was about to say." Then he kisses me like I'm the missing half of his heart.

I kiss him back, even as my mind tells me I said something

to disturb him. Should I not have said anything about being picky? I didn't think he would care.

But soon I'm lost in the sweet need building between us. The only thing that matters is Tony, holding me, held in my arms.

55

Anthony

A few hours later, I lie beside a sleeping Iris and stroke her back. I should have guarded my reaction better, but when she mentioned the Bösendorfer Imperial, I couldn't control myself.

I tenderly push a few strands of hair away from her face. She smells like a well-satisfied woman, plus my soap and shampoo—a combination that's insanely hot and gratifying. I wanted to kiss her the moment she stepped into the living room, and ravish her until she turned to a happy, boneless puddle. But I had to play Schubert. I have to truly know who I'm with so I can figure out how to proceed and protect her.

Eventually, I slip out of bed and shower. I don't need much more than a few hours of sleep at night, but Iris is different. She doesn't stir even after I get dressed and press a kiss to her temple.

I listen to her soft, even breathing for a while, gratitude swelling until I feel like I'm about to burst. I can never forget how cold and still the world went when Harry told me Ivy was gone forever. My own world going blacker than ink. And most of all, how much I hated myself for being a fucking coward. Not being strong enough to keep her with me. Keep her safe. I deserved to lose her back then, but not through death. She deserved to live, to shine like the brightest of stars. So I could at least gaze upon her from afar, like a sailor lost at sea.

Quietly, I go to the kitchen to get some coffee. I have so many questions about the accident and what happened, but I can't get immediate answers to any of them. I need Jill back in town.

I check my phone on the counter. I forgot to charge it last night, but there's still some juice left.

One text from Wei, informing me Audrey called him twenty-eight times and sent seventy-four texts. She wanted him to know (and tell me) she was in love with me, hated Iris and couldn't understand what Iris has that she doesn't. Her seventy-fourth text finally contained an apology for being a bitch because she didn't mean to embarrass everyone. I don't have to read Audrey's own words to know by "everyone" she means Ryder and me. She is so self-absorbed, with the media fawning over her fleeting beauty, that she can't accept that there are men who don't put her on a pedestal and worship her.

Like me.

As for Ryder, I have two missed calls and one text from him.

I'm sorry about what happened. I didn't know you were going to be there, and I certainly had no idea Audrey would do that. I meant what I said. I'll have her dress replaced and give her whatever compensation she wants.

I smile thinly. *Sorry, Ryder, no,* I think. *You already screwed up once, and in this case, one strike means you're out.*

The coffeemaker is done, and I take a slow sip of the fresh brew, then call Ryder. He picks up after the second ring.

"Anthony?"

"Control your women, Ryder. I know you thrive on scandals and publicity, but I don't, and neither does my date."

"I swear to you, I didn't arrange that on purpose. Audrey is just a costar—*was*. She won't be working with me anymore. Don't like getting involved with people who can't control themselves."

I cock an eyebrow. That must be incredibly upsetting for Audrey. "She didn't pitch a hissy fit?"

He snorts. "Of course she did. But my agent and manager will handle it. There are hundreds of young starlets starving for opportunities. She isn't that special."

I laugh dryly. I wish I were recording this conversation, so I could send it to Audrey.

"But Anthony..." He clears his throat. "Your date... She looks like that girl from Louisi—"

"Don't even say it," I warn him, my voice hard. I don't need him talking. People lap up every syllable out of his mouth like he's Buddha incarnate. I don't want anybody to know that Ryder and I are aware of a possible connection between Iris and Ivy.

"But—"

"You lost the right to comment on my life when you betrayed me. I haven't forgotten a thing, Ryder. Just because I sent your wife a gift for the baby doesn't mean we're good again." I hang up before he can respond.

I know what he wants to say. He's going to try to appeal to our time together in Europe. Like somehow we should go back to being best buds again.

Just like I can't undo my fuckups, Ryder can't undo his. He and his circle of toxicity aren't getting anywhere near Iris.

56

Iris

When I open my eyes, it's pitch-black in Tony's bedroom. The bedside clock says it's after ten. I don't usually sleep this late. I stretch, then wince at the small aches all over my body.

Tony was insatiable last night. Julie told me once that men can't go all night long, no matter how young and fit, but he did. If I hadn't practically passed out, there's no telling how long...

Not that I'm complaining. I stretch like a cat. He has the most magical ability to make me forget everything and just *feel*. Other than music, nothing does that.

After a quick shower, I discover an extra toothbrush on the vanity. I pick it up and brush my teeth, then put on a new dress shirt from his closet and go downstairs. It smells like fresh java.

"Please tell me you have some coffee for me," I say as I step into the kitchen.

With a small smile, Tony pushes a large, plain white mug

with two creams and a sugar in my direction. I sigh happily, dump them into the dark brew and stir.

Tony looks well rested and sharp, even though it's obvious he got up hours ago. His blue T-shirt and shorts are casual and ordinary, but settled over the lean, strong lines of his body, they look like high-fashion items.

He's looking at me with a particularly satisfied smile.

"Reliving your glory last night?" I say.

"Among other things. You want some breakfast?"

"Isn't it a little late?"

He shrugs. "So?"

"I don't eat breakfast this late."

"You didn't have a decent dinner last night. We didn't even get to have that specialty cheesecake. You must be hungry." His lips press tightly together. "And you're so thin."

I am? "You weren't complaining last night."

He gives me a look. "Don't be obtuse. I have granola bars, Greek yogurt and fresh berries. Bagels, too. What sounds good?"

"Yogurt and fruit. How did you know?" Pretty sure that's not what *he* eats for breakfast. Men as big and muscled as Tony need more.

"I noticed them in your kitchen." He serves the yogurt and berries in two azure glass bowls.

I pick up a few berries with my fingers and toss them into the yogurt, which turns out to be much richer in consistency than what I normally eat. I make a mental note to see which brand Tony got.

As I eat, Tony comes around the island and stands behind me. Then, very gently, he massages my neck and shoulders.

"Mmm, that feels so nice."

"Keep eating."

His fingers are firm and knowledgeable, finding all the tight spots and working on the knots underneath my skin.

"Don't you have to work?" I ask. Men who are well off seem to be working all the time, even on weekends. Sam once told me he worked virtually nonstop back when he was building his company. Julie complains Byron is actually a little boring because he works so much, even on weekends and holidays. And Tony's at least as successful as those two.

"Why should I? It's Saturday." He buries his nose in my slightly damp hair. "I like the way you smell. My shampoo and soap on you."

"You mean I smell like a guy?" I joke, over the last spoonful of the yogurt.

"No. You smell like you're with me." He kisses the back of my neck.

The spot tingles, and my breath catches, desire heating my blood as though he and I didn't spend most of last night pleasuring each other.

"Stay," he whispers against my skin.

I shiver. "Okay."

57

Iris

I stop, the final note of "La Campanella" fading into the air. I turn to Tony, who's been listening from an armchair he moved closer to the Steinway.

"Well?" I say. I'm dying to know what he thinks, because his opinion matters. *He* matters.

"You've gotten much better," he says.

"That's a funny thing to say. You've never heard me play 'La Campanella' before.

He closes his eyes briefly. "I meant compared to the video."

Does he think I'm *that* scatterbrained? "That was *Grand Galop Chromatique*. And silly, empty flattery will get you nowhere." A mock pout on my lips, I stand.

He takes my wrist and pulls me onto his lap. "You sure? I'll be happy to prove you wrong."

I laugh, then try to tickle him. During our weekend

together, I discovered one small spot on his side where he's particularly sensitive. I love it because it's unexpectedly vulnerable and sweet that a man as sophisticated and hard as Tony can be ticklish.

"Don't even think about it," he warns me, but there's a smile in his voice.

"Oh, come on. One last time before I have to go home."

He sobers. "Go home?"

I nod.

"Why? You can leave from here tomorrow."

"I can't go like this." I hold out his dress shirt.

"I'll have a new set of clothes brought for Monday."

It's really tempting, but... I shake my head. "I want to get a few things and get some decent sleep. It won't be possible with you next to me, so...home."

His eyebrows pinch together, his mouth set in a mulish line. I rub his lower lip until he no longer looks vaguely dissatisfied. "I still don't like it," he says.

"Why?" I think of a compromise. "How about if we spend the evening together at my place untiiil...let's say ten?"

"I hate that you think of it as your home. It's Byron's place."

Oh my. "Are you jealous?"

"Yes." He gives me an "and I'm not ashamed to admit it" look. "Why should you spend another night under his roof? The very idea is offensive."

Tony has a point. If I were him, I'd be annoyed, too, but only because I didn't understand the real situation. Time to clear things up once and for all. "Byron's just a friend, Tony. You wouldn't object if I stayed with Julie."

"Because she's a girl, and you don't play for the other team."

"I don't play for Team Byron either."

"Maybe. But he's definitely playing on Team Iris."

Huh? "What makes you think that?"

"I saw you and him outside Hammers and Strings."

"And you got 'Byron's trying to sleep with Iris' out of that interaction?" And I thought *my* imagination could go a little wild from time to time. "He gave me a ride. That's all."

He gives me a look reserved for the hopelessly naïve. "Iris, no heterosexual guy becomes a hot woman's friend without wanting to worm his way into her bed. It's a universal truth."

"That's preposterous! He's Julie's brother."

"Exactly the point. He's not *your* brother."

I give up. "You're insane. Completely, totally bonkers."

Suddenly, he grows serious. "I am when it comes to you. I can't think straight because my head is filled with questions—how do I not screw this up? How do I make you happy? How do I keep you safe?"

Oh, Tony. The glimpse of his vulnerability makes whatever we were bickering about seem inconsequential and silly. I reach out and hold his face. "You aren't screwing up. You've already made me happy and kept me safe." I kiss his forehead and eyes. "You're perfect the way you are."

"Iris..."

The rawness lingers in his gaze. I wonder what happened to put this kind of pain in a man so strong and powerful, and I wish I could erase it. "I swear you are, but if it'll make you feel better, I promise to tell you if you do anything to 'screw up.' Okay?"

"Okay."

"As for my going back, it's a temporary home, Tony. I'm not going to stay there forever. I never intended to. Byron's not even there right now. Julie's returned from her trip to Moscow, and she's staying with me. And it doesn't matter who's playing for Team Iris because the only team I'm playing is Team Tony."

He nods. "Okay. Can I ask you to do a couple of things?"

"What?"

"First, take the spare keys to my place."

Wow. "Are you sure?"

"You're welcome to come over anytime, even when I'm not home."

I nod, realizing that Tony's signaling he's ready to take our relationship further than just fun sex on weekends, and glad—turned on, in fact—that he's taking charge and letting me know what he wants because this is exactly what I want, too. "Anything else?"

"Take my number. And TJ's."

"Your number's fine. Who's TJ?"

"My bodyguard and chauffeur."

"Ah. The Visigoth."

Tony laughs. "TJ would like that."

"But why would I need his number?"

"If you can't reach me, contact him." Tony takes my hand, running his thumb over my fingers. "Call either of us for anything, no matter how small or insignificant. We'll be there for you."

"Are you sure? What if I call you to get me ice cream?"

"Then I'll get you ice cream." He kisses my fingers, his eyes on mine.

He's dead serious. I don't know what I did to deserve someone like Tony. After my parents' deaths, I felt like I'd never have anyone who would love and care for me unconditionally. Waking up a year later and not being able to connect with any of my old friends only fed the fear, which I've tried so, so hard to ignore. "What if I want to couch-surf here?" I toss it out, swinging to a more demanding request. I'm aware I'm testing Tony, but I need to know.

His expression softens as though he knows what I'm doing. "Fabulous. But we can do better than a couch for a woman of such excellent taste and exacting standards. After all, you seem to find my lovemaking marvelous...and I have the better piano."

Laughing, I wrap my arms around his neck and kiss him, showing him what I can't quite put into words.

58

Iris

When I return, Julie's at home, barefoot in a pink T-shirt and gym shorts. She jumps off the couch the moment I step inside. *The Sound of Music* is playing on the TV. "Holy shit, tell me you didn't spend the entire weekend with Anthony Blackwood!"

Since I can't tell her that, I say nothing. She's so biased against him, and I need to find a way to fix it. Maybe a dinner together and hanging out at his club afterward. Julie's the only really close girlfriend I have. I want her to like Tony.

She looks at me. "Oh my fucking God. Is that one of his *shirts*?"

I nod. At least I have my underwear, so I'm not totally indecent. But the way Julie's reacting, I might as well be buck-naked.

"Damn," she says, her gaze sweeping me up and down as though she's seeing me for the first time.

Which is irritating. In the background, Maria is teaching

the kids how to sing "Do-Re-Mi." Does Julie think I should be virginal like that? "What is it?"

"Haven't you seen that video? It went viral."

"What, Byron's video?"

She shakes her head. "You and Audrey Duff." She gasps as though she just remembered something. "Ryder Reed was there, too, wasn't he? Is he as hot in real life as in the movies?"

"Hotter," I say automatically, since that's the easiest part to answer, and I'm not following her very well at the moment. "What happened?"

"I tried calling you, but everything went to voice mail."

"Sorry. I forgot to charge my phone." I was too busy, immersed in those lovely private hours with Tony.

"Okay." Julie rakes her hair. "Well, somebody at the restaurant filmed it. Actually, more than one person. And they uploaded the videos on Facebook and YouTube."

I run a hand across my forehead. "Great," I mutter. "Just what I need right before I'm about to start my first job. A viral fight video." *And with someone like Elizabeth as my boss.* She seemed so elegant and saintly in our interview. I bet *she* doesn't have a scandalous video.

"Don't worry. Your boss won't blame you for it. Did you forget her brother is Ryder Reed?"

"I don't know if that's going to make it better. There's a difference between your brother and your brand-new employee starring in a fight video."

Julie rolls her eyes. "Oh, please. It wasn't like you threw that wine. But seriously, what the hell was Audrey Duff thinking?"

"She just...lost it when she saw me with Tony." I tell Julie what happened, blow by blow, since she won't shut up about it until I do.

"Hey, karma's a bitch." Julie lifts her arm straight up in the air in a victory pose. "So Audrey was trying to push you two apart, and it only made you screw like minks over the weekend."

"Well, I wouldn't say *minks*..."

She leans forward. "Was he good?"

My cheeks heat. "Very."

"Are you going to do it again?"

"Uh-huh." I sigh. "I really like him, Julie. I've never felt this way about a guy before."

"Hey, if he makes you happy, I'm totally on your side here. But it's probably better if you don't let Byron know."

"I wasn't planning on advertising how I feel about Tony, but I'm not going to hide it either." And frankly, I don't see why Byron would care, even if Tony is convinced Byron wants to sleep with me. There's never been any spark between us.

"I'm not saying you should hide it. I'm saying you shouldn't let Byron know. See the difference?"

"Uh...not really."

She squints at me long and hard. "I swear to God! For a woman who plays the piano with such sensitivity, you can be so obtuse. Byron hates Tony, and he's going to be resentful you're doing him. Get it?"

"Noooooo... I can see him getting upset if *you* slept with Tony. I mean, you're his sister. But me? Why would he care?"

Julie sighs, giving me a look that's a cross between pity and exasperation. "Fine, have it your way. But don't say I didn't warn you if Byron gets pissy."

"Yeah, yeah, Miss Overactive Imagination! I'm going to go get ready for work tomorrow." Shaking my head and laughing, I go to my room and plug my phone into the charger. It starts up and begins notifying me of a bunch of texts and missed calls. I cringe at the ones from Sam. He's pissed off about the videos Julie mentioned, although his texts are so typo-laden that it's impossible to figure out exactly what the problem is.

There are also some from Byron. He's more coherent than

Sam, but most of his texts are about how vile Tony is and how I need to be careful and stay away from him.

My phone rings, and...speak of the devil.

I debate briefly, then answer it. "Byron! Hey, how are—"

"My God, that video! What were you thinking, Rizzy?"

Sigh. "That the wine was colder than expected?"

It only seems to upset him more. "No! Anthony Blackwood. He uses people, and the only thing he cares about is money. Don't think it'll be different with you."

I need to cut this off, because the more he says, the less I like him. "Okay, stop. You don't know anything about—"

"Oh come on, Rizzy, you have no idea—"

"Yes, I do. He isn't using me for anything. I don't have money or fame. In fact, I have so little that I'm crashing at your place at the moment. If what you're saying is right, then he's made a pretty big mistake. But he doesn't strike me as the type to screw up like that."

"Rizzy, I'm trying to protect you. He isn't someone you can rely on."

"I don't need your protection, Byron. And since you didn't know, he's the one who helped me write a résumé and land a job."

"He did that to fool you."

"Look, the only thing I want to hear from you right now is *congratulations*. If you can't bring yourself to say that, then just hang up."

I can hear him breathing, but that's all. It hurts that he can't bring himself to say congrats. He sat in that café and heard me talk about wanting a job. Or is he just upset that *he* wasn't the one to help me with the résumé, emotionally stuck in some weird competition with Tony?

"Goodbye, Byron." I hang up.

I resist the urge to throw the phone down. Byron's never reacted this way to anyone I've associated with, and I don't understand what his deal is. Julie said he and Tony don't get along due to their business rivalry, but does he have to be so condescending about it, pulling that "I'm doing this to protect you" crap? He sounded *exactly* like Sam at his worst!

He's just trying to look out for you, my mind whispers.

Well, I don't need him to do that. I'm almost twenty-eight, not eighteen, and I don't need him hovering and trying to tell me who to get involved with.

59

Iris

The morning is bright and sunny, the temperature perfect. The second I walk into the marbled vestibule of the Pryce Family Foundation, I spot a very large man with eyes like a Siberian winter. He's in a suit with no tie, and he looks at me like some bug he's trying to decide is harmless enough to let in.

"Hi. I'm Iris Smith. I'm new." I extend a hand with a smile.

He engulfs it in a huge paw and pumps once before letting go. "Tolyan." His voice is rusty and harsh, but somehow not unpleasant. "Lizochka told me about you."

Lizoch—? Oh... Elizabeth.

"Your employee badge," he says, handing me a lanyard that has a laminated photo ID with my name and the foundation's logo. "She's waiting for you."

Already? I made sure to arrive ten minutes early. I overheard Sam say once that workers who show up after their boss were worthless leeches. But clearly, I need to do better tomorrow.

I walk to her office. The door is open and Elizabeth is at her desk. Her unbound hair hangs loose in golden curls around her stunning face, and a classy blue dress fits her model-like body like it was made just for her. I'm in awe of her beauty and poise...again.

She looks up and smiles. "Great. You're here." She beckons me closer. "I was just going over these numbers and thought you could help." She turns a huge external monitor my way. "It looks complicated, but isn't, really. It's for our main projects for the rest of the year."

She explains what she wants me to do, the reports I need to generate for her on a regular basis and where to find all the people I should contact to organize funding and sourcing of the material we need. "Let me know if you need any help."

"Okay. Thanks."

"And Tolyan should have a laptop for you."

For the rest of the morning, I sit at a desk outside her office and work on the numbers she gave me. The projects I'm dealing with are all domestic. Most are for Thanksgiving and Christmas. The foundation is partnering with religious and secular organizations in various communities to supply meals and gifts for people who have no place to go and children whose parents can't afford anything. Only three projects are about delivering school supplies to needy families for back-to-school activities, although those are in some of the poorest and most underserved districts in the country. When I see the total amount the foundation's raised, I have to double-check the report. Holy mother of God, that's a lot of zeros!

During lunch, Elizabeth leaves, saying she has an appointment. "We should have lunch this week, though," she says. "To welcome you to the foundation."

"I'd love that. Thanks."

I grab a sandwich from a deli, then bring it back to my desk and fiddle with my phone. There's a text from Tony.

Hope your day's going well.

I smile. *Fabulously. Elizabeth is amazing.*

You having lunch?

Yes. A sandwich. You?

I miss sharing lunch with you and holding you while you nap.

Maybe this weekend?

Too far away.

If you can't wait until the weekend, I'm probably going to practice after work. Although I'm not working in the music field, I want to keep it up. Maybe more memories will come. Some clue about who Tatiana is...or the name of the girl who threw popcorn at that ridiculously proportioned porn star. I already looked through my high school yearbook, but didn't see her photo.

My place?

That works, but I need to pick up a few things first.

Deal.

My phone rings. "Hi, Sam," I say.

"What the *hell* is the meaning of this, Iris! The first one was bad enough, but now videos with you and Anthony?"

"It was just dinner," I say, swallowing a sigh. What is up with everyone around me reacting so weirdly? It's not like I asked to have wine thrown in my face.

"But with Anthony! In videos!"

"It's not a crime to have dinner with Tony. He was a perfect gentleman at the restaurant." In bed was another matter, but Sam doesn't need to know that.

"But the *videos*...! *Every*where...!" He's so furious, he can't even finish.

"If you're that upset, talk to whoever uploaded them," I say, deliberately misunderstanding him. I don't want to fight about Tony over the phone with Sam on my first day at work. "There's not really anything I can do."

"You need to stay away from him. I'm getting you a ticket to Tokyo right now."

My jaw slackens. "What? You can't do that!"

"You need to leave the country. Immediately."

"Why?"

"Because I said so. Don't forget about your brain damage, Iris. I can have you declared incompetent or worse!"

I pull the phone away from my ear and stare at it, incredulous. *Just who the hell does he think he is?* Just because he helped me when I was in a bad spot doesn't mean he gets to bully me like this.

I put the phone back to my ear. "Are you out of your mind? Do you think anybody's going to believe I'm incapable of making my own decisions because I had brain injuries nine years ago?"

"Don't think I can't. I *will* find a judge who agrees with me."

Sudden panic flutters in my belly. He's entirely too serious. And I have a feeling he might be able to find somebody who'll do just that. "*Sam—*"

"Tonight. That's the earliest one out. So pack your fucking bags."

"I'm not going anywhere. I just started a job."

"*What?* You never said anything about a job."

Because every time I told him about my plans, he ignored me. It isn't my fault he didn't know. But bringing that up is going to be like pouring gasoline on a fire. "I told you I wanted to settle down."

"Settle down in Tokyo, then."

What the hell is wrong with him? There's nothing for me in Tokyo. I don't even speak Japanese! "Look, I'm not quitting."

"Whoever you're working for can't be paying you enough to give you the lifestyle you've accustomed to."

"It's meaningful work."

"Cubicle slavery is the same whether you do it in L.A. or Tokyo. Tell me where you are. I'm sending a car."

"You can't make me go, Sam. I mean it."

"You *will* go. I'll make sure of it." He hangs up.

I stare at the phone. What's this *really* about? Why is he so freaked about the videos and my date with Tony? So what if they went viral? Byron's video did the same, and Sam didn't flip out and try to ship me off to another continent.

Five minutes later, my email pings. I check it and see a one-way ticket to Tokyo in business class, departing from LAX around midnight. Guess he didn't hear a word I said. *So typical,* I think bitterly. Well, good luck trying to drag me to the airport, kicking and screaming. No airline is going to board me against my will.

But from the urgency and panic in his voice, I can't help but wonder if he might try to do just that.

60

Iris

Other than the call from Sam, my day goes well. After lunch, Elizabeth reviews the reports I created. "These are great. But I also need a breakdown by community and the number of households that require assistance. The goal is to help every child in need, so we have to understand exactly how much additional money we need to raise to make that happen."

"Got it."

"And can you go through the feedback and letters over there and organize them by our past projects? Make notes about anything that stands out as being an area of improvement or something inspiring that we can feature in our next campaign. We always need fresh stories to get donors to open their wallets." She smiles ruefully.

It takes an hour to modify the reports like Elizabeth suggested and email them to her. That done, I go over the huge bundle of letters and surveys. Most are glowing with happy anecdotes, only a few pointing out minor things that could've been done better. I jot them down as I go for easy reference.

Then I get to the last envelope. The brown paper feels cheap and rough, like it was cut from a grocery bag. I open it. A couple of photos and a letter in loopy handwriting fall out. It's from a mother, thanking the foundation and Elizabeth. Without a medical intervention the foundation arranged, her daughter would've lost an arm. The photos feature the little girl—before and after the procedure. In the before shot, her eyes are downcast with her shoulders drooping. After, she's smiling shyly at the camera, a cute little dimple in her cheek.

Thank you for all that you do and God bless you. You're an angel the Good Lord sent to answer my prayers, the mother wrote at the end of the letter. The sincerity and gratitude in every line stagger me.

I start sniffling. The world needs more happy endings for everyone. I'm so lucky to be working at a place that's making a real difference and impact. Rhonda looks up from her desk and silently hands me a Kleenex, and I dab at my eyes.

"Sorry. I don't normally cry," I say.

"It's okay. You never get used to reading those letters."

"I don't see how you could. *Look* at them. Look at what Elizabeth has done."

"She helps everyone she can. Like a lot of us here. Like me."

How? In her mid- or late thirties, Rhonda is incredibly capable and smart. I don't know how someone so competent and intelligent could ever need help.

Apparently, my thoughts are transparent.

Rhonda adds, "Everyone needs help, Iris. Even me, because I wasn't this together three years ago. I was living in shelters with my kid when I heard about the opening here. I was desperate but felt like it was hopeless. I had experience, but I'd been struggling to find work after I was let go. It was terrifying to realize I was competing with candidates who were younger—and not homeless—and could afford nice interview clothes. I had to borrow some from a local charity. When Elizabeth asked me why I wanted to work here, I told her I wanted to help give people a future because everyone needs a helping hand at least once in their life. I bawled like a baby when she said I was hired." Her eyes grow misty, and she reaches for a Kleenex. "I couldn't have been the best candidate based on what I saw of other people interviewing for the same position, and if it had been anyone but Elizabeth, I wouldn't have gotten the job. But she decided to give me a chance, knowing I was a homeless single mom with a young kid. It wasn't just a job she gave me. She gave me my dignity back...and a future for my daughter. Now I can raise her in a stable home, give her the growing-up experience all kids should have." Rhonda dabs at her eyes, then sniffs. "She always says it's all of us who make the foundation work, but she's the heart."

I'm speechless, experiencing the same sort of reverent awe as when I first saw the Sistine Chapel. I crane my neck and look at Elizabeth at her desk through the open door. What would it be like to make a difference in people's lives? To be so certain of her place, to be loved and admired for the amazing work she does?

One step at a time, Iris. You can do it too. You're doing it right now, helping her make a difference.

Five o'clock comes and Elizabeth bids us all farewell, even though she's staying behind. "Are you sure?" I ask. "I can stay and help."

"I'm fine. One of my brothers is coming to pick me up in half an hour for dinner." She smiles. "You did very well today, Iris. I'm thrilled you're here."

"Thank you. *I'm* thrilled I'm here." I can feel myself grinning.

"See you tomorrow."

"Bright and early."

I drive home, nearly vibrating with happiness. It's so empowering to be acknowledged for good work. And the fact that I'm helping people. Even if I don't find all my memories or meet the significant people from my past like the monk in Austria said, this job confirms that my decision to come home was the right one. I need to anchor myself and discover a purpose in life. I lived aimlessly for too long.

When I'm about to step inside the elevator in the penthouse building, Julie texts me. *Your uncle is here to pack your bags. I let him in, but... You're going to Tokyo?*

My teeth grind together. Is Sam kidding? I put the phone back in my purse as the elevator doors close. Impatience and anger simmer in my gut as the car moves upward. Who the hell gave Sam the right to disrupt my life this way?

I march inside the penthouse, my spine stiff and shoulders pulled back. Biting her lip, Julie points at the stairs. "He's up there. I've never seen him so upset," she whispers. "If I'd known he was going to be so weird, I wouldn't have let him in."

"This is bullshit," I say between my teeth.

She stares at me. She's probably never heard me talk this way about Sam. "Are you all right?"

"I'm going to murder someone."

"As long as there's no blood to clean up," Julie says weakly.

"Don't worry. You stay here. I'll handle this myself."

I trot upstairs and into my bedroom. Three suitcases are laid open—one on the bed and two on the floor. Sam's dumping my clothes and shoes into one of them.

"What do you think you're doing? Don't touch my stuff!" I say, my voice loud and sharp.

I start to move toward the bag to take my stuff out. Sam puts a hard hand on my arm and jerks me back. "Don't even think about it."

"You can't make me board that plane."

"Oh, yes, I can, Iris. And I will."

This is too much. Sam has never physically forced me to do anything. His method is subtler, usually involving trying to guilt me into doing things his way. I want to know what's got him acting like this. "Why are you doing this to me? I like it here, Sam!"

His jaw works like he's rolling words in his mouth and debating which to spit at me. Finally, he says, "L.A. isn't safe. You're better off elsewhere."

"That's the silliest thing I've ever heard. No big city is safe."

"You shouldn't have let those videos get online. Or be seen with Anthony Blackwood of all people!"

So we're back to that again? "Sam, be reasonable. I'm not going to flee the city like some criminal. And over some videos or a date with a perfectly respectable man? I have friends here. A job! Am I supposed to tell Elizabeth, 'Great working with you for a day but adios' because you're freaked out about the videos—which, by the way, happen to have her brother in them?"

Sam blinks once, frenetic calculations running over his face. "You're working for *Elizabeth King*?"

"Yes."

"How do you even know her?"

"I don't, really. I interviewed for an open position."

"And she hired you. Like that." He snorts, then mutters something that sounds like *fucking bullshit*. "It doesn't matter. Tell her you got a better offer. The end. She can't make you work for her."

"No!"

"There are other jobs in the world!"

"Yes, but I want this one."

"What's so different about this one? You think you can be like Elizabeth if you work for her?"

"I'm not trying to be her. I'm trying to *live my life*. You say you want the best for me, but you won't let me make any decisions about my life. Every time I do, you find a reason to overrule it or undermine me somehow. Like now. When you needed me to play at the reception, you pretended like you were fine with me deciding to settle down here, but now look at you! Trying to force me to go to a country halfway around the planet!"

"I'm doing this *for* you!"

"I'm twenty-seven years old!"

"You're a child! You don't know everything! You remember only what I told you." He karate-chops his open palm after each sentence. "Your head is blank! An empty canvas." Sam is practically screaming now.

I'm shaking so hard I'm afraid I'm going to fall. I had no idea he felt this way about me. I thought he wanted to help me recover and lead a productive life. I thought he was overprotective and worried too much about my "fragile mental state" because he saw me break down like my world was ending after waking up from the coma and learning that my parents were gone. Or that time when I tried to perform and panicked so much that I thought I was having a heart attack.

"Sorry to be such a heavy burden, Sam," I say stiffly.

"That's not what I mea—"

"What the hell is going on here?"

Sam swivels his head at the cold voice from Tony.

Tony takes one look at my face, comes over and puts an arm around my shoulders. "Are you all right?"

I start to nod, then change my mind and shake my head instead.

He takes in the suitcases and glares at Sam. "What's the meaning of this?"

"She can't stay in Los Angeles."

"Why the hell not?"

"It's all your fault, you son of a bitch," Sam hisses.

"That's where you have it wrong. I definitely want her to stay here, and I'm not letting you abuse her this way."

Sam regards Tony, then laughs dryly. "Have you ever considered what Margot would think if she saw that video of you two together?"

The name Margot creates a tiny ripple on my mind, like a snake under a sheet.

Tony's voice grows colder. "Leave my mother out of this. You'd do well to remember I don't take kindly to people trying to use her."

"Why the hell do you care? She disowned your ass."

"She's still my mother."

Sam sneers. "You wouldn't be saying that if you know what she really is—what she did."

"There's nothing she could've done that'd change how I feel about her."

"Even ruining your life?" Sam's gaze darts toward me so fast that I almost miss it, then swings back to Tony.

"Even that."

"Well. I still can't have you making decisions for my darling niece."

"If she doesn't want to go, you can't make her. Don't push me, Sam. I can destroy what you've built."

"At what cost to yourself?"

"Unlike you, I don't give a damn about the cost. But you..." Tony sneers. "You're different. You couldn't bear to be a nobody again. You need your money like a baby needs its mother's tit."

An ugly shade of red blooms on Sam's face. "You fucking bastard."

Tony smiles, a mere baring of teeth. "Get out before I throw you out."

Sam shoots me a "this isn't finished" look, then storms out.

The tension in the room drops, and my legs turn to jelly. I sit heavily on the edge of the bed, my hands an inch above my knees.

Tony pulls me into his arms. "Hey, it's okay." He cradles my head, stroking me, offering solid comfort and warmth as I shiver.

"How did you get here? I thought we were meeting at your place."

He shrugs. "I couldn't wait any longer."

That's really sweet, but... "I'm sorry you had to see that," I say, humiliated. How many of Sam's horrible, ugly words did Tony hear?

"I'm glad I was here to put a stop to it. He won't do anything like this to you again."

I rest my head on his chest. "Is he going to have an unfortunate series of falls in a dark garden, too?" I ask, half-serious.

He laughs softly. "No. I'll just leave him penniless. That'll be the cruelest fate of all for someone like Sam."

I shake my head, remembering what Sam said about how it would cost Tony. "Don't. He's not worth it."

"There's nothing I won't do to keep you safe." He places a tender kiss on my forehead, then starts putting my things away.

"Hold on," I say from the bed, my legs still feeling like noodles. Shivers are still running through me. "I don't want to stay here tonight."

I get up unsteadily and make a concerted effort to regain control of my body. Then I grab my toiletries from the bathroom and add them to one of the suitcases. Tony takes it, and I hold his hand as we go downstairs.

Julie clears her throat. "Is everything okay? I'm sorry. About Sam."

"It's okay. You didn't know." Besides, I've always told her

he took care of me, so she had no reason to believe he would be such a jerk. "But if he comes back again, don't let him in."

"Definitely. You need anything?"

I shake my head. "I think I'll stay with Tony tonight."

She gives Tony a small nod. "Take care of her."

"I will," he replies.

She hugs me. "Sorry again. Be safe."

I hug her back, squeezing hard, so she knows we're good. Then Tony and I leave, climb into the back of the waiting Cullinan and pull away.

After a few minutes, he asks, "Does Sam always become that agitated over videos?"

"'Always'? It's not like I'm a big YouTube star or anything." I shrug. "He was unhappy about Byron's video, but didn't yell about it too much because he wanted me to play at that reception. This time, though… I mean, he's never tried to forcibly ship me off to Asia before. He's usually more on the persuasive side."

Tony's eyes narrow into two brilliant green slits. "What's his deal this time, then?"

"I think he was more upset we were together, but…" I pause. Sam seems to know this Margot, and maybe, just maybe, he's worried about how Tony's mother will feel. Will she disapprove of me? "Do you think your mother's going to be upset?"

Tension starts radiating from Tony. "I don't know." He hesitates, then adds, "I haven't seen her in the best part of a decade."

Oh, crap. If I were alone, I would literally be kicking myself. Marty and Sam both said Tony was disowned. Of course he hasn't seen his mother, or knows what she might think about who he dates. But he obviously still loves and cares about her deeply. Ugh, I'm *such* an idiot, picking at his painful past. I should just stop talking before I do any more damage.

Tony's quiet for a moment. "If Sam weren't trying to force you, would you want to go to Tokyo?"

"No! Do you know why I came to L.A.? To settle down. I'm tired of traveling around the world."

"Okay. It's just, most people would love the opportunity."

"Believe me, I've had the opportunity. It's fun your first year. After that, not so much. It's like..." Suddenly, the way I felt traveling in Europe and Asia finally clicks.

"What?" Tony asks.

"Like being exiled," I whisper.

Oh my God. *How come I never thought of that until now?* It was a punishment...never allowed to return...forever forced to wander the globe, like some medieval curse. It didn't matter what I wanted. Except I don't know what I've done to deserve it. Or why Sam always presented it as a treat for me. Or as a way to recover and be happy. Maybe that's why it took me this long to put it together—because deep inside, I needed to believe he truly wanted me to be happy. But now, I see how foolish I was to cling to that belief, putting an optimistic gloss on his motivation because he was the only person by my side when I was at my weakest and most vulnerable.

"I know it sounds melodramatic, but seriously, that's how it was. The trips were always luxurious and nice, but it was clear I wasn't supposed to come home." I lean closer to Tony. "Do you understand what I'm saying?"

"Yes," he says, his eyes sympathetic. "I know *exactly* what you mean."

"So you don't think I'm weird for feeling this way, right?"

"No." He looks at me, thoughts I can't fathom crossing his face. "I've had the same thing happen to me."

Oh, Tony. I lay a hand over his and squeeze. "I'm sorry to hear that."

"It was a long time ago," he says in a low voice. "Doesn't

matter now." He lays the other hand over mine and squeezes gently.

"Do you still want to hear me play?" I tilt my head. "We can do something else if you want."

He leans closer until his lips are almost brushing my ear. "You know what I want—to be inside you, feeling your pussy spasming around my cock all night long."

White-hot heat sizzles in my gut, slickening the flesh between my legs. I let out a slow breath and squeeze them together.

"But we can do what you want tonight," he adds.

"How about both?" I say, my voice slightly thick.

He laughs wickedly, the sound rippling over me like a physical touch. And when he kisses me, every thought vanishes from my head except for how much I adore him.

61

Iris

The next morning, I look through my suitcase and blink when I see at least six office-appropriate dresses and shoes. "Wow. I expected something I could wear, but didn't realize Sam packed it for office work."

"That was me. I put those in while you were in the bathroom grabbing stuff."

"But *six*? You know I'm not that picky," I say as I slink into a mocha- and cream-colored dress, my hair dry. Tony bought a dryer.

"I know," he says, handing me coffee. He's already showered and in a crisp white dress shirt and dark slacks, ready to conquer the world.

While I sip the fresh, bittersweet brew, he zips my dress in the back and presses a kiss to the nape of my neck.

"Then why did you bring so many outfits?" I smile slyly. "You couldn't figure out what I'd be in the mood for, could you?"

He chuckles. "I know exactly what looks good on you, but no. I brought them all just in case you want to spend the week here."

He says it so casually, it takes me a second to process. *Oh my.* I thought I was falling too fast, but here he is, practically asking me to move in. My head says it's way, way too soon, but my heart says it's not.

"You have keys, so..." He shrugs.

A hint of vulnerability, and my heart wins. "Of course. Besides, it'll be easier anyway. The commute yesterday was horrible."

"We can leave together, and I can pick you up after work."

"Do you know Elizabeth shows up early? I feel like I should too."

"She's a workaholic, but her husband's out of town this week. Some big deal in China happening for his company."

"Someone else said something similar. What does her husband have to do with her coming to work early?"

"When he's in town, she's usually on time...or a little bit late."

Aww. "That's really cute."

"Match made in heaven. Unexpected, too—they're from *very* different backgrounds." He reaches into a drawer in the island in the walk-in closet. "You need a necklace to go with that dress."

Hmm. The scoop neckline could use a little something, but...

Tony pulls out something shiny and puts it around my throat, then looks at my reflection, his hand resting on the slope between my shoulder and neck. A gorgeous, round disk with the sun, moon and stars rests a few inches below the hollow point on my throat. Made with yellow, white and rose gold, the pendant hangs from a simple white gold chain.

"It's beautiful," I say in awe, running my fingers over the

cool, uneven surface. A faint sense of familiarity tickles me... Maybe I saw it in some European jewelry store?

"A fitting necklace for the beautiful woman in my life," he whispers against the side of my neck. His lips are so close that each syllable brushes my skin.

Delicious shivers run through me. "Where did you get it?"

"It's custom-designed. One of a kind." He lifts his head and studies me. "Why?"

I stare at the pendant, and the oddest sense of déjà vu passes over me once more. But...I'm probably confused. I wish I hadn't said anything, but Tony's waiting for a response. "It just feels like I've seen it somewhere."

His hand flexes slightly against my shoulder. "Really?"

"But that can't be right. Sometimes my mind plays tricks on me, making me think I've seen or heard something I haven't, or vice versa. Like Schubert."

"What about it?"

"I don't remember ever having practiced it, but I was able to play it with you."

Tony looks down briefly, hiding his gaze from mine. "I remember. Does that happen a lot?"

"With piano pieces, yeah. That's why I started to practice so much, just to see what I could do. Sometimes I wonder what else I can play. It's weird, isn't it?"

"I think it makes you especially wonderful." He inhales softly, then smiles. "Let's get ourselves fed or we're going to be late. Nobody cares if I'm late, but I'm sure you're going to care if you are."

I link my hand with his and we walk to the kitchen together. Something is a bit different about Tony this morning, more resolute and sweeter somehow. The latter I don't mind, but the former? It leaves another ripple on my mind, just like the name Margot did.

62

Anthony

You don't know everything! You remember only what I told you.

Sam's raging words replayed in my head last night and all through the morning and afternoon. Just what the hell did he do? What did he tell her?

Your head is blank! An empty canvas.

Iris said she was in a coma for a year. Can you actually erase somebody's memory? Or was he exaggerating? It would be like him. He likes to talk big and spend bigger than he can really back up. Still...

I swivel in my office chair and look out onto the bustling city at my feet. He doesn't want me near her. He even brought up Mother in an attempt to manipulate me.

Edgar's findings float up in my mind. Iris is a real person. She checked out. So she can't possibly be my Ivy...at least, according to my brother.

But...

My phone pings with a text. It's from Harry.

FYI I'm still in Tempérane. Mom fainted dead away at dinner yesterday.

My gut tightens, a sour tang flooding my mouth. *Is she okay?*

She's okay now.

What did the doctor say?

Nothing. She didn't see one.

Shouldn't she, though? Mother's so frail, so delicate, like a hothouse orchid that's never faced even the gentlest of breezes.

She says she's fine.

I grit my teeth. *Didn't anybody tell you when a woman says she's fine, she's lying?*

You think I can make her do what she doesn't want to?

I start to type *no*, then stop. Why...yes. *Sam.* A sudden chill sweeps through me, especially after the confrontation last night. There was such a superior look in his eyes, and it wasn't from money. It was from having something on someone. But first things first. I reply, *You used my jet to fly there because you're the only one who can cajole her into doing something. So fire up your magic. Get her checked out. If anything happens to her, I'm going to have my pilot run you over with the plane you love so much.*

Then I call Jill.

"Yes, Blackwood," she says briskly. She's never touched a cigarette in her life, but she has a smoker's voice, low and raspy.

"I don't care what you're doing out of the country. If you come back now, I'll double—no, triple your fee."

She clicks her tongue. "Lucky for you, things wrapped up early, and I just landed in LAX."

"I want to know exactly where and how Sam Peacher got his initial investment to start Peacher & Son and made his fortune."

"Read articles about him and his company. There should be plenty," she says.

"I thought you liked money."

"I like giving my clients value."

"I don't want some junk a journalist on a tight deadline dug up."

She sighs. "All right. How deep?"

"All the way till you hit the bottom. Then bring out another shovel."

"I see." I can almost hear her mind whirring. "It won't be fast."

"Just don't take too long. Report back every week."

"Will do." She hangs up.

I lay the phone down carefully on my desk and consider. One way or the other, I'm going to break whatever hold Sam has over Iris...and find out exactly what "memories" he's filled her head with.

63

Iris

The rest of the week passes in lovely routine. Get up and get dressed for work, share a quick breakfast with Tony, ride to the foundation in the Cullinan with our hands linked, then nine to five and back home in his car to the penthouse, where we have dinner. I practice the piano for about an hour, and then we go to bed, where we drive each other crazy with lust.

I enjoy my new life much more than I expected. Having structure to my days makes things easier, somehow. I tried to maintain as much as possible during my travels, doing my best to stay in the same city for at least a month so I could set up some kind of routine. It's nice to know what's happening each day, so I don't feel like I'm spending time wondering what I should be doing and frittering my life away.

Then there's Tony. He makes my week brighter, more fun. Every time I'm around him, I feel protected and cherished.

Sometimes I wonder if it's love. Neither of us has said the word, of course. It seems a bit premature, but...

"We should celebrate your first week at work," Tony says on our way to the foundation on Friday.

"Oh? What do you have in mind?" I lean closer so TJ won't overhear. "Other than nocturnal activities."

Tony laughs. "How about a weekend trip to Napa?"

"*Really?*"

He nods.

"I'd love to! I've never been."

"We can leave after work."

"That's perfect." I lift our linked hand and kiss his. "You're perfect."

I've been on more trips in the last six years than most people take in a lifetime, but this one feels special because it's my first with Tony.

"I'll pick you up at five," he says as the Cullinan stops in front of my office.

Impulsively, I kiss him, blurt out, "Love you," and jump out of the car before he can respond. I run toward the lobby.

My face is hot and my heart is racing like crazy, but my reaction has nothing to do with my little sprint in low heels. It's got everything to do with the fact that I said the L-word.

Maybe you shouldn't have run off right after like he's Typhoid Tony, part of me chides.

Yeah, it's immature, but I'm inexplicably feeling shy. I've never said that to a man before. And even though it seems early, I wanted Tony to know.

I'm reaching into my purse for my employee badge when a large hand takes my arm and spins me around. I blink up at Tony, who's looking at me with an emotion so intense, it's positively riveting.

"You can't just leave like that," he says, his voice thick.

I'm searching for something to say when he says, "I love you too," and kisses me, just a soft brush of his lips over mine.

My heart swells, knocks against my chest with such force, I can't speak...or breathe.

"Now. Have a good day at work," he says, squeezing my hand like he can't bear to let go.

"You too." I smile, then watch him walk backward toward the Cullinan.

When he finally slips inside the car and vanishes, I go to the office, my step so light that I feel like I'm floating.

Tolyan gives me a coolly appraising glance. "You seem happy."

"Yes. Isn't today beautiful?" I look out the windows. "Sunny, too."

"It's always sunny in Los Angeles."

"I know, but today's *extra-special* sunny."

His eyes stay on me for a few more seconds, then he grunts and goes back to his paperwork. I start checking the final list of organizations Elizabeth wants to partner with this year to deliver holiday meals and presents. Then I hit the phone.

Just as I finish the final call, Audrey Duff walks in, her narrowed eyes on me. Her bleached hair is curled and swept to one side, tumbling over a shoulder. A skintight dress in the same shade of red as her lips is molded to her slim body, and she strides across the vestibule in stilettos with needle-thin heels.

Crap. Is she here for an encore? I quickly check my desk. Nothing she can throw in my face. And she isn't holding a Starbucks cup, so I'm probably safe.

She stops in front of me.

"Elizabeth isn't available today," I say with a fake smile.

"I'm not here to see her. I'm here to see you," Audrey says, in a voice so creamy and dulcet that it feels like melted butter in my ear.

I suppress a shudder. "I don't believe we have an appointment."

"I don't believe I *need* an appointment to see an *assistant*."

Condescending much? Would it kill her to be nice, since she obviously wants something from me? "Is there something you want to discuss?"

"I wanted to apologize for my behavior on Friday if it, you know, upset you. That wasn't my intention."

"*If* it upset me? Wasn't that exactly what you wanted when you threw the wine in my face?"

"Honestly? No. I was doing it to upset Tony."

Can she hear herself? Must be the acting experience to spew non-logic with a straight face. "Then you should've thrown it in his face."

"But as you saw, I didn't. So I'm apologizing," she says like she's talking to an imbecile.

"You don't even know why you're sorry, do you?"

"Just accept the gesture. I'm not going to grovel."

Wow. What the hell kind of an apology is that? I cross my arms. "I wasn't expecting an apology, so I'm not sure what you're trying to do here."

"All you have to do is sign this." She slaps a sheet of paper on my desk.

Since I'm not dumb enough to put my name on something without reading it first, I lean forward and skim it. It basically states Audrey apologized and I am satisfied and bear her no ill will whatsoever. In addition, I want nothing but the best for her.

I look up. "Why would I do that?"

She sighs impatiently. "Does it matter?"

"Are you afraid I'm going to sue?"

Blinking, she pulls back, then titters. "Oh my God, no, I'd never." She fans her face with a hand. "That's the silliest thing I've ever heard! No, it's for Ryder, sweetie. Ryder Reed. He got upset about the whole restaurant thing and won't make the movie with me. I need this. It's going to be my breakout. So this will show Ryder we're all good now."

Even a month ago, I might've signed it, not wanting to ruin a woman's dream. But not now.

"No."

"What?"

"Your apology was half-assed, and grudgingly given. I couldn't care less what happens to your career."

"*What?*"

I wince. Is she trying to make me deaf now? "You heard me."

"You mousy little bitch! You think you won?" She reaches across the desk, trying to grab my wrist.

But a bigger, meaner hand takes her forearm. "You don't abuse the foundation's employees, especially not in the office," Tolyan says, inexorably pulling her back.

"How dare you!" She struggles, but she might as well be struggling against a silverback. "Do you know who I am?"

His cool, disinterested gaze sweeps over her. "Of course. Everybody knows all the third-rate actresses who desperately need to ride Ryder Reed's coattails to fame."

Audrey turns redder than her dress. "You...you..." Suddenly she puts on a seductive smile. "You wouldn't abuse a woman, would you?"

"I see no woman. Just someone who's overstayed her welcome." He swings her around and propels her with enough force to make her take a couple of quick tottering steps toward the lobby. "Now leave."

She glares at me, one hand rubbing her arm. "You're going to regret this. Do you think Tony's with you because he cares about you? He's—"

"Enough." The word sounds like a knife. "If you don't shut

up and get out now, you won't be able to take any more roles that require a pretty face."

She pales under the artful makeup. "Bastard." She storms away, those heels hitting the floor with more force than necessary.

"Thank you," I say.

Tolyan merely stares at me. The frigid look in his pale blue eyes makes me shiver. He isn't looking at me like a coworker. He is looking at me like a bug he can't decide whether to squash or not. "Your uncle is sending a car for you in half an hour," he finally says.

"Um… What?"

"He decided to make a donation and requested that you go pick up the check in person. And have lunch with him as well."

You gotta be kidding. I thought he'd given up, but I guess not. He was just looking for another way to bend me to his will. "No," I say.

"Pardon?" The two quiet syllables from Tolyan's lips sound more threatening than "I'll kill you." How does he *do* that?

"He can mail it, or his driver can bring it in."

"Those were not the terms Lizochka agreed to."

I lick my dry lips. "But…"

"It's your uncle, Iris. Is there a problem?"

Tolyan has no idea.

"He said if you don't come, no donation. Lizochka has already earmarked the money for the children's medical fund. He was very specific."

I close my eyes. Sam has totally outmaneuvered me. The last thing I want to do is air my dirty laundry to Elizabeth. Or fail her in this. I remember the letter from the mother of the girl who had her arm saved because of the foundation. I can't not do this.

“Okay,” I say. “I’ll go. But if I’m not back by two...” I hesitate, unsure how to phrase the next part.

“Yes?”

“Send someone to get me,” I say, trying to hide my nerves. “Please.”

64

Anthony

I walk inside La Mer for lunch. It's one of the most fashionable restaurants in the city, but I've never been here because it's owned by one of Ryder's cousins. As far as I know, they're pretty tight, and I can't be certain of my welcome.

But Elizabeth wants to eat here. Her cousins all think she walks on water, and apparently she can get a table any time she wants, bypassing the three-month-long waiting list.

The restaurant's interior is exactly like what the glossy lifestyle magazines and TV features have shown. The walls are constructed of aquaria filled with tropical fish. The deep, soothing blue makes you feel like you're surrounded by sea. Combined with the lazy motions of the fish, the interior has a calming, almost meditative effect. I can understand why people come here for the ambiance alone.

The hostess takes me to a private room all the way in the back. Elizabeth's already seated there with a glass of white wine. She's dressed in a magenta Chanel—classy and expensive, just like the woman herself. Surprisingly, her Russian guard dog is absent.

"Tony, thanks for seeing me on such short notice," she says pleasantly.

"No problem," I say, sitting opposite her.

"Lunch?"

"Sure."

A sharply dressed waitress materializes, takes our order and vanishes. We sip our drinks and exchange pleasantries while I wonder what this meeting is about. We don't have the kind of relationship that includes leisurely lunches. I don't have much to say to her, but she'll start when she's ready to broach the reason for this meeting.

Unless... Did her Russian dig up something about Iris? But if there was anything really irregular, Elizabeth could've just called. I can't think of anything that would require a face-to-face chat.

When our lunch is served, she takes a bite of her salmon. My ahi tuna is perfectly seared and sliced. I start eating, projecting a man who has nothing better to do than waste time with her.

After a few more bites and finishing her wine, Elizabeth leans back in her seat. "Tony, what are you planning?"

"Excuse me?"

"I know you don't like Ryder, but the foundation has nothing to do with him."

"And...?"

"And he's married, too. He's very much in love with his wife."

I stare at Elizabeth, completely confused. "I'm not sure why he's relevant."

"You and I both know you don't like him."

"I'm not currently doing anything to sabotage his life. Didn't he tell you I sent his wife a gift? Well, it was for the baby, really, but..." I shrug.

Elizabeth's gray eyes narrow. "You sent me a dead woman."

I sit up straight. My brain's refusing to process what I just heard. *A dead woman*. "What did you just say?"

"Iris Smith died nine years ago. Her parents were driving drunk after a piano recital in early fall, and she was in the back seat."

Apprehension scuttles along my spine like a scorpion. Of all the things I thought her Russian might dig up, this never, ever crossed my mind.

"You've...lost me completely," I manage, my voice hoarse.

Elizabeth's gaze turns hard. "We run background checks on everyone. She looked clean initially, but Tolyan found some minor inconsistencies. Digging deeper, he discovered Iris Smith from Almond Valley is dead." Her voice loses all of its warmth. "Now tell me what game you're playing."

"I'm not playing a game." Someone else is. And I have no idea who. Or what the final goal is.

"Then what's going on?"

"I need to go to the foundation and see Iris." I start to stand.

Elizabeth gestures at me to sit down. "You can't. She went to see her uncle to pick up his donation check. I told him it was fine for them to have a long lunch together if he wants."

My heart thundering in my chest, I explode to my feet. *Fucking Sam Peacher!* Should've ripped him apart when I had the chance.

"Damn you, Elizabeth!" I snarl. "You shouldn't have done that!"

Eyes wide, she jumps to her feet as well. She reaches out, her fingers brushing my arm. "Tony, you're scaring me."

"You think *you're* scared?" Shaking her off, I run out. I have to reach Iris. *Now*.

65

Iris

The car Sam sent stops in front of his mansion. Damn it. I thought he'd take me to his office or a restaurant. There aren't any witnesses or people to make Sam behave himself. I haven't forgotten the way he tried to forcibly pack me off to Tokyo.

Apprehension creeps over me like a mist. At least I had the foresight to ask Tolyan to come get me if I didn't return by two. But I can't decide if he'll actually do it or not. He's so difficult to read. I still don't know if he even likes me.

"Miss Iris." Sam's butler greets me, spine straight and chin held high. He's quite tall, and if I tilt my head just a bit, I can look up into his huge nostrils.

"Hi, Max. Is Sam here?"

"Yes. He's expecting you. Right this way."

He turns smartly and leads me through the glittering halls with high ceilings covered with Cubist murals. At the end, Max steps through the French doors to the huge pool. Sam's seated at a table near the water at the opposite end of the pool, cutting into a pork chop on his plate. He's dressed like a British country gentleman—a starched shirt, dark brown slacks and a vest with a bow tie. A monocle and pocket watch chain hanging out of his vest would complete the look.

Max and I walk along the pool until we reach Sam's table. "Miss Iris is here," Max announces.

"Thank you," Sam says pleasantly, then gestures at an empty seat opposite him. "Have a seat, Iris."

"Sorry, but I'm only here for the check. Busy with work."

A glimmer of smug triumph shines in his eyes. "Not according to your boss. Elizabeth said you could take as much time as you want."

Ah, crap. I didn't think he'd check with her. "I'm really not hungry," I say, refusing to take the seat.

Sam purses his mouth. "You practically quit eating after the accident. It's changed you."

I look away. This is such a waste of time, but he's not going to hand over the check until he's satisfied. "Why are you doing this?" I ask, still standing.

"I should've never let you come back to L.A. Look, if you don't like Tokyo, go to Madrid. It's beautiful. Healing."

I face him again. "I don't need Madrid. I've already made progress since coming back, and it hasn't even been three weeks."

"Progress? How?"

"I've regained some more memories, which is more than I can say about the last thirty-six-plus months on the road, when I didn't remember anything new."

Sam squints. "Which memories, exactly?"

"Someone named Tatiana." I throw that in his face with satisfaction. "Some girl I used to go to school with. An Asian girl."

"Name?"

"I don't know."

Sam considers. "That's it?"

"Yes."

Leaning back in his seat, he gives me a pitying smile. "For all we know, you could be remembering them because of your trips. Besides, *Tatiana*? Who is she? And the girl? You don't even know her name. Do you know how many Asians there are in the country?"

I bite my lower lip, hating that he's making my progress sound small and insignificant. Like I'm stupid for ever having been excited about it.

Sam sobers. "Iris, listen. I'm asking you to leave for your safety. Anthony has enemies. You'll become a target if you stay with him."

Where the heck is this coming from? "Like more Audrey Duffs and wine tossed in my face?" I have no idea what's making him say this nonsense, and the only thing that could've triggered it is that date gone bad. "I think I can han—"

"No! Nothing that juvenile. They will want you *gone*."

"Gone? As in *dead*? You're crazy," I say. "Out of your mind."

"It's true. You don't know what kind of enemies Anthony has. How vicious they can be."

"So because somebody hates Anthony, they're going to try to kill *me*? How does that make any sense? Nobody tried to kill his exes." Julie would have said something about it when she told me about Tony and his exes.

He slaps the table with his palm. "You're different!"

"How?"

"I can't tell you."

Suddenly, I'm tired and disappointed. What did I expect? Some illuminating revelation? "Sorry, Sam. This blank canvas isn't so blank anymore. You know what? Just send the check to the foundation. I'm done here."

I spin around to leave.

"You can't go!"

Sam jumps out of his chair and grabs me. His thick fingers wrap around my arm tightly, and I yank back hard.

"Let go!"

"Shut up and listen!" He pulls me toward him. "Do you think Anthony Blackwood or your snotty boss is going to give a damn about you once I tell them what a mess you are?"

The words hit hard. I shake with panic and anger...tinged with fear. It always comes back to this—my amnesia.

"I wasn't joking when I said I'd have you declared mentally incompetent!" he hisses.

"*No!*" I jerk back with all my might and manage to free myself from his grasp. But it comes at a cost. I lose my balance, and my feet slip.

I cry out right before I hit the cool water. I sink down...

It's so *blue* under the water. Not like...

Darkness surrounds me. The water's rough, torrential rain creating pockmarks on the surface that vanish almost as quickly as they appear. My body sinks...sinks...along with everything else around me.

I look across, see a girl in a blue dress... The same one from my nightmare. She's not waving, though. She's trapped in the car and unmoving. Red spreads around her. Her unbound hair... No. Blood. It's almost beautiful in a terrifying way.

Similar tendrils are unfurling around my own head. And my mind is so foggy... So tired. I'm halfway out the side window, but no air left. I can't swim. I never learned how. Why? I don't know.

I sense somebody diving. Strong, rough hands grab me under the armpits and pull me up and up and up... I turn my head slowly toward my rescuer and see...

Sam drags me out of the water and dumps me on the side of the pool. The California sun is momentarily blinding.

Wheezing and gasping for air, I shade my eyes with a hand and look at him. He's drenched, his hair plastered to his skull. Water drips from his eyelashes and tip of his nose and chin.

Just like...

He looks at me. "Are you all right?"

Are you all right? a voice that sounds exactly like Sam's asks me in my mind.

And I *know*.

"Oh my God," I whisper in horror. "You've pulled me out of the water before!"

ABOUT NADIA LEE

New York Times and *USA Today* bestselling author Nadia Lee writes sexy contemporary romance. Born with a love for excellent food, travel and adventure, she has lived in four different countries, kissed stingrays, been bitten by a shark, ridden an elephant and petted tigers.

Currently, she shares a condo overlooking a small river and sakura trees in Japan with her husband and son. When she's not writing, she can be found reading books by her favorite authors or planning another trip.

To learn more about Nadia and her projects, please visit http://www.nadialee.net. To receive updates about upcoming works, sneak peeks and bonus epilogues featuring some of your favorite couples from Nadia, please visit http://www.nadialee.net/vip to join her VIP List.

Printed in Great
Britain
by Amazon

31494390R00241